In the Light of the Moon
Book One of The God's Wife Trilogy
JW Kingsley

Vellichor Ink

Important Note

Everyone has limits on things that trigger them. While my goal is to write empowered, strong main characters, they sometimes get there via trauma.

This story has the following:

-Religious Trauma

-Sexual Assault (not graphic or gratuitous, but there all the same)

-Violence and torture of animals (again, not graphic)

-Violence and torture of humans

This story also contains:

-Love

-Found family

-Magic

-Resilience

-Friendship and sisterhood

If any of the warnings make you pause, I totally understand—not every book is for every reader. I wish you peace and that you find the right stories for you!

To everyone who gives it a shot, I hope you enjoy this story and love it like I do!

This first one's for me...
For the girl full of stories and dreams that longed to hold her
own book in her hands.

Prologue

*H*atshepsut, the fifth Pharaoh of the Eighteenth Dynasty, ruler of Upper and Lower Egypt, the God's Wife, and the Great Goddess Maatkare bore the pain imposed upon her with grace. She had been beautiful once—beauty that angered the advisors to the throne so much she'd worn a false beard and bound her breasts to grant them an erroneous sense of peace. But her beauty had wasted away, leeched out of her skin by poison and power. As she lay dying, her thoughts weren't of power, prestige, or even the bittersweet memories of youth. Her only thoughts were of the dangers her death would bring.

The moon and its god hung full and unwavering above her. The doors to her balcony were thrown open to let in the night air, and she longed to get up and bathe in the light of the moon. She could feel its pulsing power calling to her, but she was too weak to move. Sending a final prayer to the god of the moon, she closed her eyes, a single tear slipping down her ruined cheek.

A breeze fluttered the curtains framing her doors, and her fevered body shivered.

"Daughter, it is time," the breeze whispered.

Her breath caught, and she felt her heart slowing. The tears flowed freely down her cheeks now—the hot salt stinging her raw skin. The gentle caress of a hand on her face erased the pain.

It reminded her of her lover's touch, and she spared a heartbeat for him, longing to hold him one last time.

"You have served me admirably, daughter," the breeze said. Hatshepsut could no longer open her eyes, and the moments between heartbeats were growing. "Your devotion gives me life, Shesout. Let me ease your final breaths, and I will carry you to Duat*."*

Relief poured over the pharaoh's body like the warm water from her ritual pool. It washed away every open sore, every twinge of pain, every fearful thought. In her last earthly moments, Hatshepsut knew peace.

In a liminal space between life and death, Hatshepsut opened her eyes. The goddess to whom she had promised her life stood before her in all her glory. Isis shimmered with power—larger than life with magic and beauty so perfect it almost hurt to look at her. Hatshepsut dropped to her knees, supplicant and overwhelmed with divine love and an absence of pain.

"Arise, great Goddess Maatkare, and greet me as an equal in this plane." Her voice was rich like honey, resonating within Hatshepsut's chest. Her voice was love and magic, infinite possibility and divinity, and the most beautiful sound she'd ever heard.

Hatshepsut bowed her head, touching it to the floor before her goddess.

"Blessed mother, there is none equal to you," she said, weeping. The goddess stooped down beside her and gathered her into her arms. She rocked Hatshepsut gently as a mother to a child, stroking her hair and soothing her soul.

"Know that I am your divine mother, your goddess, your sister, your friend," she began.

Hatshepsut clung to her every word.

"Now, the world delights in magic. It rules the empire and holds up the throne. It heals broken hearts and mends bones. It is a gift. It is a calling. But there is a growing unrest among men who wish to tamp it down and drive it out. They desire it secreted away, forgotten, stolen from the wombs that carry it within them.

"The son of your heart leads the charge in darkness. He is cloaked in dark magic and hatred and calls many to his side. They will drive witches out of their homes to burn them at the stake in spectacle and warning. But he will not hold his empire forever.

"I have blessed my priestesses and your temple, dear daughter. I have wrapped my protection around their power and will breathe life and magic into the worthy to carry on in your name. You will not be forgotten, and your death will not be in vain."

Hatshepsut shook with emotion—pain, and relief in equal measure flooded through her like the blood that once rushed through her veins.

"Come, let us journey now to Duat. *The fields of* Aaru *await you."*

Hatshepsut took her goddess's hand and let her lead the way in death as she had in life.

1

Float

I n that held-breath moment between night and day, I floated
above the earth. A dizzying array of fabric bubbled around
me—hot air balloons in varying stages of flight created a surreal
landscape of color and desert starkness.

"Everyone look to *za* river!" the pilot shouted, his deep voice
husky and accent thick. "There's your sunrise! What did I
say? *Mashallah!*"

We turned toward the growing light behind us, and a col-
lective gasp murmured through the balloon basket. Rising over
the Nile River was the hot orange ball of the sun. There was just
enough dust in the air to filter the light to be able to look at it
without going blind—and it was stunning.

The chatter and noise faded away. I couldn't hear anything
but the rush of blood through my veins and my heart pounding
in my chest. Tears sprang to my eyes, and a lump formed in my
throat. I was filled with overwhelming joy and, simultaneously,
a longing for my grandparents to have shared this experience
with us—the grief of missing them was almost equal to my
elation. After all those summers spent with them going to the
balloon festival in their hometown and wishing I could be one
of the lucky ones on a hot air balloon—I was finally living out

that childhood dream. I couldn't wait to call my Grams and tell her. I hoped my Gramps, wherever he was, could see us now.

"Well? Is it everything you hoped it would be, Jules?" My husband Andrew's lilting whisper tickled my ear, and his arms wrapped around me, resting his chin on my shoulder as he leaned down to hear my answer.

I nodded, throat holding my words hostage. He kissed the back of my neck and laughed gently, giving me another squeeze. Time stood still around us, and the moment painted itself onto my soul.

We floated through the valley, occasionally dipping low enough to get close to the famous temples and burial sites. The effortlessness of the balloon felt like some sort of sorcery as it drifted through the sky. It was like nothing I had ever experienced before. Egypt had been on my bucket list since I first learned about mummies in middle school. I'd never dreamed I'd actually get to make the journey and see it all firsthand. My pre-teen self was giddy in the balloon basket.

After an hour of floating through the air, the pilot announced it was time to land. The basket didn't lurch, but prickling adrenaline rushed down my spine, leaving a trail of sweat in its wake. Nervous energy coursed underneath my skin, begging to escape, making my body stretched and taut. I let out a strangled noise, grabbing Andrew's attention. It was as if I was moving through molasses as I turned towards him to reach out and steady myself.

"Hey—you okay?" he asked, his concern evident. I shook my head, unable to speak. My throat constricted, tightening against my plea for help. Andrew knowingly wrapped his arms around me, trying to cover as much of my body as he could—touch points to anchor me. I pressed against the comfort of his body and forced deep breaths into my lungs.

All I could hear through the ringing in my ears was a buzz of voices around me muddled together— the mix of languages nothing more than a noise against my panic. The weight of the altitude pressed against me. The prickling heat of the burning fuel from the balloon set my skin on fire, and the fug of bodies pressed close overwhelmed my senses. I lost the feel of Andrew's arms around me and the cadence of calming words he was murmuring.

The blood pounded even louder in my ears, and the edges of my vision swam before giving way to complete darkness.

———✦———

An abrupt jolt pulled me back into consciousness. I heard the muffled shouts of direction from our pilot to the ground crew, who must have been tying us down, and the hushed murmurs of the fellow passengers around us. I opened my eyes to find myself staring up at a pale-faced Andrew with beads of sweat forming along his hairline and damp curls at his temples. He had braced himself and my limp form together against the side of the basket for the impact of our landing. I tried to sit up, but Andrew held me firm against him.

"Just wait a second. Take a few breaths first, and then try and sit up."

I could still feel the electric undercurrent of panic under my skin, but it was less urgent now. Andrew rubbed my arm, trying to comfort himself as much as me. I struggled to get comfortable in the cramped space.

I'd lived with anxiety for as long as I could remember. The panic attacks in the last couple of years had become a frustratingly prevalent part of my life. It was one of the reasons Andrew left active duty military service. He wouldn't admit it, assuring me it had all been part of the original plan, but we both knew he was lying through his teeth to assuage my guilt.

When the other passengers climbed off, the basket shifted and swayed. I was deeply grateful that I couldn't see their curiosity and excitement from my position. Still, the embarrassment of sitting in the cramped basket made my cheeks flush against the cold sweat on my face.

"Ugh, can I just hide out here the rest of the day?" I moaned up toward him.

He smiled. "Don't worry. They'll forget all about it before too long. That crazy cameraman from the beginning of the trip is interviewing them all about their experience. The pilot motioned for us to wait, so we'll be able to get off without an audience. You good?"

I nodded and slowly slumped against the basket, closing my eyes. Pulling my damp hair off my neck, I wound it up into a messy bun on top of my head—the sweat causing my dark curls to coil even more. I was sure I looked like a hot mess.

A few minutes passed, and the pilot peeked his head over the basket.

"She's okay, no?" he asked. His skin was weathered and dark, and his eyes were filled with more annoyance than concern. I imagined paperwork would be involved if something untoward happened to a tourist on a float.

"I'm fine, *shukran*," I said, getting to my feet.

Andrew climbed out of the basket first, then making sure I could handle myself, helped to ease me to the ground. I mumbled an apology under my breath that Andrew pretended not to hear. Deep down, I knew it wasn't my fault—I couldn't control a panic attack, but guilt sat heavily in my gut. We'd looked forward to the balloon ride for a long time, and it wasn't cheap. Andrew squeezed my hand three times—our little code for *I love you*. I squeezed back half-heartedly, trying hard not to be too bummed out. It had been magical leading up to the blackout.

We walked over and sat on some large rocks to wait, and before long, our tour van was rumbling up the dirt path toward us. The driver, Nasir, barely had time to slow down before our guide, Hanan, climbed out and marched straight for us. Her brow was knitted together, and her mouth pursed. Her hijab was a gorgeous pink fuchsia that matched the flowers on her flowy top like they were made to go together. Though we'd just met her the day before when we arrived in Luxor, she struck me as meticulous in everything—I was sure that extended to her outfits.

"Julia! Andrew! Is she okay? What happened?"

Before we could answer, she spun on her heel. She started rapid-fire interrogating the pilot and crew leader in Arabic. The shocked look on their faces was my only clue to what she was saying. I stood up and put my hand on her arm.

"It was just a panic attack. I'm fine now, really." I tried to sound convincing, but a panic attack that bad had taken the wind out of my sails. I was utterly spent.

"Panic attack? Are you sure? We can take you to the hospital." Her amber eyes were intent on mine, a look I couldn't place in them.

"No, no. No hospital. I promise I'm fine. I just need something cold to drink."

Hanan conceded, and we all headed to the van. As I climbed in and sank into the soft leather seat, Hanan pressed a cold glass bottle of coke into my hands. "Here. Drink up and get some sugar in you. We'll take you back to get some rest today."

I protested, and Hanan pointedly sent a look of doubt at Andrew that said *force some sense into her*. He shrugged and looked me over. Nasir started the van, and the cold air pumping through the vents helped as much as the cold soda. After arguing a bit—I was insistent that I was fine with continuing our day as planned—they finally talked me into returning to the hotel and getting some rest.

It wasn't a long ride back to the hotel, and we chatted back and forth the whole time. Hanan was curious about the panic attack and asked many questions, her stern tour guide's face surrendering to one of thoughtful concern and curiosity.

The closer we got to the hotel, the more grateful I was that we were doing the tour later. A bone-deep tiredness was tugging on the recesses of my mind and limbs. While anxiety had been a part of my life for as long as I could remember, a panic attack to the point of passing out was a first for me, and it had zapped me of all energy. Between the promise of a nap and a special evening tour of the temples, where they'd be less crowded and might even involve something special, I was relieved to face-plant into the pillows, fully clothed.

Hours later, when I finally emerged, I felt human again. I felt even better when Andrew ordered room service lunch, and I had a stomach full of falafel and French fries.

2

Baptism by Moonlight

ater that afternoon, we headed back to the Valley of the
Kings. We arrived at the temple of Hatshepsut and found
it almost deserted. Hanan gave us space to explore on our own,
and we took off, searching the nooks and crannies of the great
female Pharaoh's temple.

The temperature was dropping as the sun conceded to the
moon already hanging full in the sky, and I wrapped my cardigan
tighter around me to ward off the chill. Hatshepsut's temple
felt more vibrant than the other temples and tombs we had
visited—like the air contained tiny threads filled with power—a
power I could almost reach out and touch. I'd felt something
since we'd arrived in Egypt earlier in the week. Some unnamable
and enigmatic pull from the moment we'd stepped foot in the
country, but it was different here...more formidable.

We rounded a corner and entered Anubis' chapel. I paused,
admiring the vibrant colors of the images and hieroglyphs
etched on the walls around me—the history buff in me wishing
I could read the story they told. When I turned around to say
something to Andrew, I realized he'd wandered into the next
room. The light dimmed like a cloud had passed over the setting
sun as I followed him. The air settled thick and heavy around

me, a musty smell taking over the crisp night air and muffling the ambient noise outside like I was listening through cotton.

The hairs on the back of my neck rose, and goosebumps pimpled the flesh of my arms in response to the change in the atmosphere.

I took a deep breath, hoping this wasn't the start of another panic attack when the sweet, fruity notes of jasmine flowers filled my nose. Then, I noticed the overwhelming presence of someone standing just behind me. My heartbeat picked up, and I squeezed my eyes shut.

"Shh. Relax, sister. You're safe here," Hanan whispered. Her breath was warm on the back of my neck.

"Oh, Hanan!" I laughed. "You startled me."

She just smiled and cocked her head at me.

"Come, let me show you something not everyone gets to see," Hanan said, looking over her shoulder to ensure we were alone. She led me to an alcove in the wall, and we squeezed through to another room. It was dark, and I held tight to Hanan's hand as she led the way, feeling all along the wall until we reached another alcove.

Her perfume was more potent now and mixed with something like Petrichor. The air around us was heavy—like the sky right before it opened. She turned to face me, but Hanan was barely visible in the dark, the whites of her eyes almost glowing with the contrast. I looked down at her hands; she was holding something that gave off a faint glow. She cocked her head to the side, curiously studying me like earlier that day. The light shone and revealed a hidden, curving set of stone steps descending further into the temple.

My heart was racing, and my mind was buzzing with the excitement of seeing something special.

"Shouldn't we get Andrew," I asked. "I don't want him to miss this."

"He and Nasir are off exploring together," Hanan said. "They'll find their way."

I grinned and hoped he was getting the same experience I was.

We started down the steps, and I couldn't help but wonder how many people got the chance to do this. The air was stale but cool as we made our way down. Notches were carved into the wall every few steps, but the walls were otherwise unadorned. Before I could ask what they meant, Hanan spoke.

"I wondered about you the moment we met," she said, her voice barely above a whisper as we walked down the steps. "It's rare, the power you have, but I felt it raging inside you when you shook my hand that first time. I wonder, do you feel it? Is it stronger here?"

"What are you talking about? What power? Hanan, what's going on?"

We reached the bottom of the staircase, and it opened to a small hallway. We walked through the dark towards a room lit by wavering light. The room opened up into a vast space that glowed with dozens of candles.

I could make out more shapes along the walls—a handful of feminine figures standing in dark robes, each holding the same mysterious, faintly glowing light as Hanan. I could feel their eyes on me, and I turned my head, noticing they were against each temple wall, blocking any exit I had.

My mouth went dry, and my hands clammy from the radiating warmth of the bodies and the tropical heat of the room. I shifted my stance and stood a little straighter, attempting to feign confidence.

"Hanan. I want to leave. Where's Andrew?"

"I told Andrew there was a special experience in a part of the chapel where men aren't authorized to go, so he's on his own tour with Nasir. I assured him it was worth seeing, so he isn't looking for you, and we have some time. You are safe, I promise."

She looked down at the glowing orb in her hands and began to hum under her breath. I opened my mouth to say something when the other women started to hum in unison. Between a chant and a funeral dirge, the sound ricocheted against the walls and through my body like a current, making my skin break out in a cold sweat.

Unable to form words, I closed my mouth, entranced by their song. A sweet, herby breeze crept into the room around us. The faint glow of the orbs grew brighter and brighter until I had to close my eyes against the light. Oddly, the glow shone through my eyelids and filled me with a comforting warmth that spread from the top of my head to my toes. It seemed to fill every inch of me with light.

As suddenly as it started, the humming stopped. The abrupt silence throbbed in my ears.

When I opened my eyes, I was surrounded by the chanting women wearing robes of rich indigo so deep they looked like they had been stolen from the darkest night sky. Their hair was uncovered and unbound, their bodies naked beneath their open robes. Their skin, a rainbow of different colors, shimmered with golden light. They began closing in around me, the herby scent getting stronger as they crossed the room. Frozen in panic, I felt the tickle of a peaceful calm trying to overpower the fear and worry inside me—trying to pacify me into acceptance and trust. It shuddered through me like a shiver, and I relaxed. There was no way to put words to what was happening, and in that moment I didn't want to.

For my whole life, a tight leash had been kept on me—either by my parents when I was young or the anxiety that had become such an intrinsic part of who I was. I so rarely let go that the thought of it now was intoxicating...to just let go and let this wild and weird thing keep happening. To be a part of something unknown and different.

Hanan reached over and gently touched my shoulder, re- minding me she was behind me. She carefully slipped off my cardigan, letting it pool on the floor at my feet. Another woman reached up and gently pulled the straw hat from my head. Someone else reached for my shirt and began lifting it when I jerked for the hand. Traumatic memories warred to the surface, sending me into a panic and breaking the spell of the moment.

"No," I insisted in a hoarse whisper.

The hand dropped away, and I could breathe again.

"You don't have to undress," Hanan said calmly. "But to bathe in the moonlit ritual pool of Hatshepsut's temple is to draw strength and transformation into ourselves. That is what we are here to do tonight."

"No, I want to leave Hanan. Now," I said, wringing my hands, trying to stop them shaking. Hanan looked at me and nodded.

"Okay, Julia." She reached her hand out for me slowly, testing how skittish I was. I let her lead me out of the room and into a smaller one just beyond filled with shelves and supplies. "Can you just give me five minutes to explain before we leave?"

I thought for a moment and then nodded. She took a few minutes to gather herself. I looked beyond her into the other room where the women were waiting. It was quiet there now, and I wondered what they were doing.

"I think I know why you have panic attacks," she began. I started, not expecting that at all. "What I'm about to tell you is fantastical and barely believable, but I assure you it is real. If you give me a chance to explain, I think you'll want to go back in there."

"Okay," I said. "I'm all ears."

"A very long story short, magic is real."

Before I could open my mouth to scoff, she flicked her hand and lit candles hanging in sconces on the wall. My mouth dropped open.

"Hatshepsut was more than just a pharaoh. She was a renowned witch and devout follower of Isis. Through time, magic has dwindled, and now only a few people are gifted with the same powers she carried. I think you are one of those special few. I believe your panic attacks are magic and power manifesting itself and trying to find a way out."

I froze. It was incredulous to even think that what she was saying was real. I'd heard so many things about the Ancient Egyptians but never anything about magic.

"When Hatshepsut walked the earth, she was charged by the goddess Isis with protecting the sanctity of magic. She brought together a group of devout followers to help her carry out Isis' charge, and her secrets have been guarded and passed down throughout time to us." She looked around the room at the other women gathered there before returning to me. My heart was in my throat as I tried to take everything in.

"We are all gathered here tonight to draw power from the full moon and bathe in a ritual pool that has been beneath this temple since before Hatshepsut's time. It is in the same waters she herself bathed in and drew power from."

My mind was racing as I took the time to contemplate what she was saying. A war between wanting to run away to save myself from this crazy kidnapper and believing what she was saying was raging within my mind. I wanted to understand what I'd been feeling since we'd arrived in Egypt, and this felt like it held the answer. She was giving me the choice to take a chance... To make a leap of faith.

I had felt different my whole life. I'd been a loner in school and had even gone against my parents' strict beliefs and upbringing, making me an outcast in my own family. I'd been awkward, still was, to be fair, and struggled with friendships. As long as I could remember it had felt like there was some piece of the puzzle I was missing in my life. What if this was it?

I took a slow, deep breath, drawing on techniques I'd been practicing for years, and the panic receded a fraction. Slow waves of calm made their way through my body like tendrils of smoke, and my heartbeat slowed. Was I really going to do this? Believe this was real? I had seen the flames come to life with the wave of Hanan's hand. But could that have been a trick? I closed my eyes and took another deep breath. The pull to let go and see where this took me was intoxicating.

I nodded but explained in a shaky voice that I would undress myself. I needed control of that, at least. She walked back to the room beyond and left me to change alone. I stepped out of my trousers, wondering when I'd lost my sandals to this madness. I shrugged out of my bra and panties and into a matching indigo robe. I took another moment to steady myself—to breathe deep and settle my nerves—before walking out into the room.

The women were waiting, and I searched out the only familiar face. Hanan met my gaze. The strange scent of herbs around me was more pungent now, and my bones started to feel like gelatin inside my skin, making me feel untethered.

"You are safe. We are your sisters," she whispered gently as she glided over to me.

As bizarre as I knew this was in the recesses of my mind, it was starting to feel like this moment, more than any other in my life, was meant to happen.

Though it pressed against my mind, anxiety wasn't ruling my every move. My brain wasn't screaming at me and pointing out all the dangers of a situation. There was a barrier those thoughts could not penetrate—and each step grew steadier as I walked further into the room.

Their quiet hum was a mist curling around my feet and swirling up by body step after step—a caress of power, like a siren, guiding me towards the unknown.

Toward destiny.

Cool air entangled with the mist of song, like ethereal fingertips pressed against every inch of skin.

Time passed, as it does. The cool touch gave way to a warm, damp heat and new sensations that were dizzying from every direction.

Darkness and light danced together, calling forth a growing, glowing incandescence.

The shroud of night surrounded me.

The glowing radiance bathed me.

Deep in the heart of the earth, I was in her light.

Or, perhaps, I *was* the light.

The light of the moon.

Despite my instinctive resistance, when Hanan pulled me towards her, I came, entranced. My brain was still dizzy from the contrasts of sensations around me. We walked together, and our slow steps echoed through the room. The ground was cool beneath my bare feet. The tropical air clung to my skin like morning dew on fresh blades of grass.

"Thousands of years ago, the Great Mother walked this plane. Her toes dug into this very earth. Her hands cradled magic, called down from the heavens. She is reaching out to you, daughter of Hatshepsut. Her magic is calling."

Hanan's voice danced across my skin—I focused on her words, letting them weave into my bones. As she continued to chant, the heat from her breath warmed against my skin, sweet and intoxicating as she wove a tale of magic and power—of witches. Somehow, the incredulous became possible with her words. Her perfumed scent enveloped me, mingling with the smells around us. Ever so slightly, her arm reached out behind me.

The energy in the room moved as the women closed in, surrounding us. Hands pulled at my robe, its silk whispering against my skin—languid and intimate. I shivered as they unbraided my hair. My bare skin was alive with electricity, and I jolted at the touch of a stranger's hands. The trance was broken as old, raw wounds became exposed once again. Panic gurgled up through the calm, threatening to bring the moment crashing down.

Someone, or everyone, took a deep breath, and I felt myself still as they exhaled. The bubbling panic slowly receded, giving way to a sense of calm once more. I was detached, mind separate from body, but I wandered in the dark recesses of my mind.

Fragrant smoke filled my nostrils and poured into my throat as someone swayed with a golden incense burner hanging from her fingertips.

Each woman came to me, pulling me in towards them, and pulsing energy met pulsing energy again and again.

My head tilted back in ecstasy.

They began anointing me with oil as I thrummed with life...with power.

Carefully, we slipped into the steaming pool carved into the earth. I sank into the inviting warmth—weightless and rooted simultaneously—perfectly held by the clean, sweetly scented water that mingled with the oil on my skin. A shimmering beam of light poured into the water from high above, highlighting the glow of my body within the pool.

The chanting, a celebration, and an elegy vibrated across the walls and through my body until I was one with it. With them. With myself. Lost to the knowledge of where I ended, and they began. Our slick skin brushed against each other, and the water churned and bubbled.

After years of holding back, of holding tight, I let myself go. I sank beneath the water, and my hair swirled around me like reeds in the Nile as the infinite weight of the women who came to this pool before pulled at me.

The water was a return to an ancient womb, older than the earth itself. I was being reborn. My soul cleaved into a thousand pieces under the vigilant watch of the moon. At that moment, I was given a choice: to cleave together or fall apart, to become whole or remain broken. To take Hatshepsut's hand or to deny my most authentic self.

I reached for her—for myself.

I answered the call.

Magic answered back.

With a surge of life, breath, and magic, I lived a thousand lives and none at all. I was whole and emerging, awakened.

An orb glowed in my hands as if it had always been there.

Its weight was feather-light and without substance. As I gazed at it, the truths Hanan had spoken settled firmly inside me, as if they'd been buried in my mind all along and were finally unearthed. Energy coursed through my veins, not painful but not entirely comfortable. I could feel the spirits of the women surrounding me, past, present, and future, becoming familiar with my own spirit.

My heart slowed, and the adrenaline settled in my veins. I looked to Hanan, who nodded, and we slowly climbed out of the warm water, leaving the rest of the women behind. Though the air was warm, I shivered, and my skin pebbled. Hanan and I dressed quietly while the other women pulled on their robes and toweled their hair. I was lost for words, the ritual still playing in my mind. With a gentle nod and smile from each of them, they gave me the space I needed to sort through it all. Hanan led me out and away from the women, the pool, and the person I had been before, evident as the light from my palms slowly but completely disappeared.

✦

We found Andrew sitting with Nasir at the base of the temple's steps, talking quietly over cups of tea in the cool night air. He stood up when we reached them, and I stepped into his arms.

"Have fun?" he asked. "Ooh, you smell good." He leaned down and breathed in the oil that clung to my skin.

I stepped back a bit, hoping he wouldn't notice my wet hair and immediately ask questions I wasn't prepared to answer just yet.

"Yeah, it was awesome," I said, not having any other word for what I'd just experienced and wondering if it had all been a dream. "And it's nice, yeah? It's from the essential oils we used in the meditation."

We made small talk as we walked away from Hatshep-sut's temple and towards a life that would never be the same—though I could have no idea then just how different life would become.

3

Whispers in the Dark

"Wait, hold on," Andrew said, stopping in his tracks and throwing his hands up in exasperation. "You're telling me you had some forced baptism with a bunch of strangers, and you're okay with it?"

We returned to the hotel and walked around the river, where I'd told him what had happened. His reaction was much less accepting than mine and definitely unanticipated.

"It wasn't like that, Drew. It wasn't a... baptism," I said, feeling myself deflate a bit, cheeks flushing with something like shame.

"That sure as hell what it sounds like, Julia. I'm sorry, but tell me, how is that any different from the shit your parents pulled when you were younger?" he bit out.

I flinched at his words and tried to battle back the images that rose to my mind at the mention of my parents.

"What is your problem?" I asked. "I had this amazing experience and an explanation for why my brain is so fucked up, and you're berating me for being happy about it?"

"Berate you? Seriously? That's not what I'm doing here, Julia. Did they give you something? Some sort of drug?"

I balked.

"So I can't possibly have chosen this unless I was drugged?" I argued.

"Look, I'm just trying to figure out how on earth you thought that was okay?"

"Thought *what* was okay?" I scoffed.

He narrowed his eyes.

"You're joking," he said, pinching the spot between his brows. "You go into some closed-off room in a temple—with strangers—let them feed you some nonsense about magic and let it explain away a lifetime's worth of diagnosed anxiety and depression. Then walk away thinking your life has changed for the better? Do you have any idea how dangerous that was? How badly things could have gone?"

He looked at me, and I felt myself shrinking away from him. He had never made me feel unsafe before, quite the contrary, but he was taking away the peace that had filled me in the temple. I turned from him and walked away.

I was drained from the panic attack earlier in the day and exhausted from the ritual. Yet, somehow, I was also keyed up—vibrating with energy and anger. I needed the movement of a walk to clear my mind and reign in my emotions. I knew Andrew was pacing just behind me, not angry enough to leave me alone late at night, even behind the walls of our resort.

Finally, I broke the silence, unable to stand it a moment longer. I didn't even have the heart to face him but called over my shoulder.

"I'm going to bed. If you're going to stay out here and cool off some more, that's fine. Just make sure you have the extra room key."

I didn't wait for him to respond but stormed off toward our room, closing the door behind me, hoping he wasn't coming in to hash things out just yet.

I fumed and stomped around, arguing my best points to the bathroom mirror, mouth full of toothpaste and body singing with pent-up energy. I finally deflated and fell into bed. My heart was heavy when it had felt so light before.

---◆---

Andrew came to bed after I'd fallen asleep, curling his body around mine, his skin cool from the night air. He whispered into the dark, face buried in my neck.

"My love, are you okay?"

I nodded when a lump formed in my throat that kept me from speaking.

"I'm so sorry, Jules. I'm not angry with you, just...that whole scenario could have gone so differently. It scared the shit out of me to think that you were forced into making a choice you might not have wanted to again. Or that something really awful could have happened to you."

"You don't have to worry about me like that anymore, Drew," I answered sleepily. "It wasn't like that. It was...really amazing." I pressed my body back against his, needing comfort. We didn't fight often, but when we did, it always felt like the world was shaking underneath me.

"I'll always worry about you like that, J. Always." He kissed behind my ear, settled behind me, and I slipped back to sleep.

4

The Morning After

The following day, things were awkward between Drew and me. I wanted nothing more than to tell him every little detail of what happened in the temple, but I wasn't ready to fight again. Drew wasn't one to shy away from a problem, and as soon as room service delivered our breakfast, he sat in front of me and started talking.

"Look," he began after a long sip of coffee. "I love you. I trust your judgment. But what happened last night could have gone a completely different way."

He held up a hand as I opened my mouth to interrupt.

"Just let me get this out," he said. "I've seen terrible things with my job—the absolute worst of humanity. And the thought of anything else happening to you makes me sick to think about, okay? I'm not angry with you. I never was. I just had all these crazy scenarios go through my mind when you were telling me what happened. The thought that you were unreachable, and I was just wandering around a temple like it was no big deal— it was a lot, alright?"

He exhaled, having purged a little of his fears to me over chocolate croissants.

"I get that, Drew, I do. But I don't know how to explain it," I said. "It was beyond belief but felt so right at the time. I kept thinking it was weird and I should be freaking out, but I just kept feeling this calm wash over me and chase away the nerves." I took a sip of tea, the malty warmth spreading through me.

Andrew nodded towards me, an encouragement to continue.

I told him everything then. I told him about the water feeling like the womb of the earth and the deep, internal peace I left with. I described the smells, sights, and everything—trying, in vain, to paint him a clear picture. Andrew reached over to catch a tear slipping down my cheek and kissed it away on his finger. I hadn't even realized I was crying.

"I know you think I'm crazy. And I'll be honest, the whole magic thing *feels* crazy. But it happened, Drew. It did."

"Show me," he said.

"Show you what?"

"Magic. I want to see what you're talking about," he said.

"I don't know how," I said quietly, cheeks reddening.

"Hey," he said, reaching across and touching my arm. "I'm not being mean or trying to make you feel bad. I just wanted to see, Jules."

"It's fine. I just don't know how to show you anything. I can just tell you I don't feel the same as before going there. I feel like something has opened up inside me— like what I've been searching for my whole life has finally been found. And you're being so closed-minded and refusing to see it."

Andrew sighed.

"I'm glad you feel like you've found what you've been searching for, Jules. I am. But you see where I'm coming from, right? Magic, ancient pharaohs, and witchcraft taking place in a secret ritual room? Are you *sure* what you experienced was real?"

I glared at him from across the table.

"I'm not crazy, Andrew," I said, crossing my arms in front of my chest. "I know what I experienced and what I saw. It was real. Believe me or not." I refused to tell him I'd wondered if it had all been a dream the night before.

"My love," he said gently, trying not to upset the apple cart more than it already was. "I am not trying to be an asshole here. But it sounds so fantastical and outlandish, and you expect me to believe it without hesitation. I just can't do that."

"I'm telling you, what I experienced didn't seem like a hallucination. It was real. I wish I had the right words to make you see," I said to him, frustrated that I couldn't just let him into my mind to see everything I'd experienced.

"I'm still reserving judgment 'til we can get more out of Hanan about all of this. I just want to know what the angle is."

"What do you mean, *the angle*?" I asked.

"Just, what's the reason for bringing you into this? What do they want?"

"Oh, I definitely want to know more about what it means. There's this whole world that has opened up to me now, and I need to know everything I can. Hopefully, she can answer some questions, and we can figure out where to go from here."

I nibbled on my breakfast, nerves in the way of hunger, but I knew I needed something in my stomach.

"Well, we go back to Bahrain at the end of the week, but I guess you can get everyone's contact information and ask questions when things come up," he offered. He took a last swig of coffee and stood up, wandering over to the dresser to get clothes for the day.

"Maybe I could stay longer and get to know them?" I said.

He spun around.

"What? Stay in Egypt?" he asked. "I have to get back to work. Taking this time was enough of a stretch. There's no way I can take more."

I shrugged, feigning nonchalance, but my heart was pounding.

"Yeah, well, *I* could stay." I sat up a little straighter, feeling defiant.

He looked at me like I had two heads. "There's no way I'm letting you stay in Egypt alone, Julia. It's too dangerous."

"I'm sorry, not *letting* me?" I asked, incredulous.

Andrew rolled his eyes. "Don't start that with me. You know what I mean. It isn't safe."

"I get that. But I'm not going to be roaming around Cairo alone or doing crazy shit by myself." I bristled, feeling more than a bit chastised.

"It doesn't matter. Luxor can still be dangerous, Jules. Seriously, given my job, you don't think I did an insane amount of research and talked to people to double-check my doubts and assumptions before we came here?" he asked. "There's a reason Egypt is on and off the travel list so frequently, and it's not just overly cautious intel guys in an office somewhere."

We argued back and forth over breakfast, never really getting anywhere other than more frustrated with each other. When it was finally time to meet up with Hanan, I was fuming and beyond ready for Andrew to return to Bahrain and leave me behind.

Hanan greeted us like old friends. The dynamic between us had shifted—although I supposed that when you go through a magical ritual where you're both naked, you're bound to be tighter than before you went into the water together. Drew was still irritated with me and was colder to Hanan than he had been.

I hoped she hadn't noticed, but I was keyed into him and knew he was upset.

With Nasir driving us to the West Bank, there was little room to talk freely. I was restless with questions and all but squirming in my seat. I did my best to let it lie while Hanan explained the histories and stories of the people who worshiped and lived in Luxor with ease and in an absolutely magnetic way. We spent an hour wandering around the giant columns of the Karnak temple, marveling at the detail of the hieroglyphs carved on them— Hanan having explained that they were basically used as giant, permanent papyrus. The more columns, the more knowledgeable a pharaoh was believed to be. I ran my fingers along one as Andrew followed behind, eyes above, in awe of the sheer size of the hall of columns. It was an incredible morning.

We broke for lunch after a morning of exploring. Through the archway of a local hotel and restaurant, Hanan directed us over to a quiet table where we finally had the privacy for me to let loose. Before I could open my mouth, she held up her hand, smiling.

"I know you have a thousand questions, Jules, and I can't answer them all in one day. When are you set to leave?"

"We're actually going back to Cairo to do some sightseeing the day after tomorrow."

"Ah, that's right," she said, remembering the schedule we'd booked. Her company came highly recommended by some friends who had been to Egypt a few months before us. I hadn't realized when Hanan had picked us up at the airport that she was the owner. She and her best friend, Salma—another sisterhood member—had started the tour company over a decade ago, fresh out of university, as a way for more female guides to get jobs. The country was on and off the State Department's watchlist so frequently that it caused pretty massive dips in tourism. The goal for Hanan's company was to give travelers, especially females traveling solo, the confidence to come and feel safe to explore such an amazing place. And it had been incredible. Not only was Hanan knowledgeable, but we'd felt really safe and taken care of.

"While we're on the subject," Andrew said. "I have to be honest here, Hanan; I'm uncomfortable with all of this. From where I'm sitting, it feels like everything was forced onto her without her consent at the temple."

In Hanan's defense, she didn't bat an eyelash at Andrew but spoke gently and calmly. On the other hand, I felt my cheeks flame, absolutely mortified.

"I could see how you would feel that, Andrew, and I'm so very sorry you see it that way." She looked at me. "Julia, if you had been overwhelmed or truly felt uncomfortable at any moment, we would have ended it and stopped the ritual. Going into it without expectations is important and the whole purpose for doing things as we did them."

I put a hand on Drew's leg to stop him from saying anything and giving me a moment.

"It was uncomfortable, but not in any way like I needed to stop. It was surreal and amazing, and every time I felt worry creeping up, a wash of calm came over me. I knew that everything was okay and was supposed to be happening. Drew is just being overprotective." I squeezed his thigh, hoping to convey enough emotions in that slight touch that he'd relax and stop acting like I was a child.

"I'm glad you felt that way, Julia. We'd never want you to feel coerced into something you didn't want to do."

We made eye contact, and I smiled.

"Tomorrow, we'd love it if you'd both come to dinner and properly meet everyone. Drew, maybe meeting everyone will give you a sense of relief? You can stay with me for the rest of your trip if you'd like. I've got a guest house you are more than welcome to use."

Before Andrew could say anything, I answered for him, knowing what his response would be. "Thank you so much, Hanan. That's so sweet, but we're fine at the hotel. But dinner sounds great." I didn't want to push it with Andrew's comfort level and, to be honest, my own. I was curious about this whole sisterhood thing but not quite curious enough to stay in a stranger's house.

"Before we talk further, I will order for us, if that's okay. They've got a brunch spread that we're not too late for, and you'll get a little taste of many different things."

"Ooh, sounds great! We love trying new stuff," I said.

Hanan nodded and made her way over to the waitstaff, giving us a few moments alone. I wasn't sure if she could sense that we needed it or if she wanted her own space to breathe.

"Before you say anything, can we just sit here and enjoy the food and the view and hear the history of all of this?" I said to Andrew. "We can fight and argue later, but right now, I'd like some sort of truce, please."

He sighed. "I don't want to fight or argue, Jules. And I don't think my worry about your safety is me being shitty, controlling, or even worth a fight. It's me being cautious. But fine, we'll call a truce for now and figure this out later."

I nodded, not wanting to say anything else to make things worse. I was far angrier with him than I realized. I smoothed my napkin over my lap and counted the moments until Hanan was back. We broke our awkward silence with small talk and the promise of lunch.

Within minutes, the waiter brought out a massive tray of food. Little bowls and plates of various things were placed in front of us. My little foodie heart skipped a beat as I took it all in.

"Okay, so this is an omelet, sun bread, salad, baba ganoush, tahini, a cheese spread, vine leaves, olives, fried eggplant, and that's a lamb tagine for the meat eaters," Hanan explained, gesturing to each item.

In a region where spices like saffron and cardamom were king, the scents we got when food was brought to the table were like magic. We ate in companionable silence for a few minutes, only the occasional "mmm" or "ooh, try this" breaking up the sounds of our eating. This loosened the tension before Hanan sat back in her seat and began to weave a story with so much richness and depth that we were transported back in time.

5

Questions & Answers

*A*fter a trying afternoon with her advisors, Hatshepsut was looking forward to the privacy of her bed chamber. She longed for peace and quiet and was met instead with the anxious face of her head priestess. She bowed deeply to her queen and then spoke with a shaky voice.

"My queen, we fear that Thutmose is furthering his search for immortality. He's threatening the priestesses and demanding they answer to him in your stead." Hatshepsut shook her head and dropped down onto the closest chair. Someone had lit her favorite incense before she'd come into her chambers, but instead of comfort, it stung her nostrils with acrid smoke, and she wrinkled her nose against it. She buried her face in her hands and tried to think of what to do with Thutmose.

Her stepson had been an eager pupil for years. He learned alongside her daughter, Neferure and had shown a great talent for magic. Men weren't usually so adept with Isis' gift, but Thutmose had always been special. He and Neferure were playfully competitive with their powers—both of them studying and practicing late into the night to try and best each other. But as he'd grown older, he'd begun looking into darker magics. Powers that she had the answers to but would never be willing to give up. Dark things like demons from the underworld that wished to feast on the flesh of humans, magic that demanded human sacrifice, and, of course, immortality. She'd never understood his obsession with the darker aspects of their power. Neferure had been fearful, and rightfully so. Thutmose had been fervently curious in the most unsettling ways.

She assured the priestess that she'd come up with something to dissuade him, and they formulated a plan for stronger wards and spells to protect the scrolls he sought. Another bow and the priestess quietly left the room, closing the door behind her. Finally, Hatshepsut had the silence she'd been looking forward to, but her mind was anything but quiet. She sighed deeply—exhaling a breath that felt like it was lodged in her chest.

Now that she was alone Hatshepsut carefully peeled off the false beard she'd taken to wearing around her advisors. Though she believed, without a doubt, that she had a divine right to rule, the men who acted as her counsel had been less supportive of that fact. They'd wanted her as regent while Thutmose grew. She'd reminded them more than once that she'd come from a long line of kings and had learned how to rule at the feet of her father—she was born for this. She could be pharaoh, and then Thutmose could have his turn when she'd finished her rule.

And she had united Upper and Lower Egypt in a way they hadn't been for a long time. Besides finishing out the asinine military campaign she'd inherited from her husband, it had been a time of peace and prosperity for Egypt. Her people loved her—in spite of the fact she was a woman. Or maybe because of it. And yet, the advisors hated bowing to a female and happily played along with her silly disguise.

The sticky resin that fixed the beard to her chin itched like fire, and she went to the basin of water on her table and cleansed her face. She didn't have to look in the glass to know how red and *angry her skin was, but it would fade in a few hours' time. She was used to her flesh being uncomfortable—she'd developed a skin condition that oftentimes left her covered in an itchy red rash that the false beard only exasperated. She unbound her breasts and took a deep breath, sighing in relief as they were released. Here, in her private space, she was allowed to be free.*

✦

Years passed, and Hatshepsut continued to rule her beloved Egypt and protect the powerful magic that would damn them all should it be loosed. Thutmose III grew restless and angry in his demand for the magic she refused him. There was a hunger inside of him that went beyond the short-lived childish phase she'd hoped it was. There had been many a mess of his that she'd had to clean up, and she worried constantly over what would happen when it was his time to rule. The ways in which he'd practiced darker magics had turned him towards a madness that terrified Hatshepsut. Magic demanded sacrifice and he was sacrificing his humanity and heart to the darkness he sought.

As he'd grown into a young man, he'd gathered a group of followers bent on the submission of women and the superiority of their beliefs. Their voices were loud and starting to be heard by the people of Egypt. Dread that they would do something irreversible was her constant companion.

She'd tried so many times to get through to him, but Thutmose remained unreachable. The close relationship they'd had when he was a young boy seemed myth-like as she looked back on their lives. She'd had visions of ruling together in the last years of her life—an easy hand-off from an aging monarch to her successor but those ideals had devolved as the anger and madness overtook him.

She shouldn't have been surprised to discover he'd poisoned her. He had been skilled with potions and herbs from a young age, and the crazed belief that she denied him out of spite only hardened his heart towards her more. Still, she was surprised at how broken-hearted she was at the knowledge that he would be the one responsible for the end of her life. She worked tirelessly until the very end, trying to find a cure for the poison. He'd exploited her skin condition, and what had seemed like a peace offering at first sent an invisible force of darkness to eat her away from the inside out.

It was too late for her, but she gathered Neferure, the priestesses of Isis, and her lover Senenmut, and created the sisterhood. She charged them with the care and protection of her diaries and the scrolls that Thutmose so desperately craved. They made contingency plans and promises to their dying queen, and when at last she slipped from this world into Duat, she knew that she'd done her best to protect the magic Isis herself had charged her with protecting. It was up to the goddess now to protect them all. Hatshepsut only hoped she could find peace in the afterlife.

———✦———

Hanan trailed off, letting us digest the information. We'd polished off our lunch and finished the story walking around the farm. We stopped at the perimeter fence, and I looked out past the desert to the Valley of the Kings. It was a decisive and surreal moment. I let out a breath.

"Okay. So, it's not all naked lady bathing rituals and magical powers. There's an actual... *bad guy*, I guess."

Hanan laughed, the sound rich and deep, a genuine laugh. "Did you just say 'naked lady bathing rituals'?"

"Oh god. I did! I'm so sorry, I didn't mean—"

She interrupted me, putting her hand on my forearm. "Julia, don't apologize! That is hilarious. And precisely what it was."

We all laughed together. The kind of laughter that slows down until you make eye contact, and then it picks back up again. Finally, bellies aching, the laughter died down, and we stood silently for a moment, minds spinning with more questions. Andrew turned to Hanan.

"So this brotherhood, how real is this threat from them? What sort of risk are we talking about?" Without realizing it, he'd stepped into work mode, assessing threats and figuring out ways to mitigate the danger.

"Oh, it's very real," Hanan answered. "But we aren't without protection. And they have only their hate and desire to do magic keeping them going. We actually *have* magic and the knowledge of their existence. We have pretty good information on who they are and have kept tabs on them since their inception. So, the threat is very real, but the danger isn't as bad as it sounds. Does that make sense?"

I looked at Andrew and could feel the tension radiating off him, his fears about my safety becoming more reality than him being overprotective.

"It does. But I can't help but still be concerned. Culpability plus intent." He looked down at me. "I mean, Jules is the most important thing in the world to me. I can't leave her behind if she isn't safe, but I just can't stay any longer."

Hanan put her hand to her heart as if she were making an oath and took a deep breath. "Andrew. I can't guarantee anything, but I can absolutely promise you that she will be protected to the best of our *and* her ability. She isn't without protection. Your wife has powers, *genuine* powers. She can learn more and harness her power to protect herself and you." She looked at me and reached out her hand, taking mine in her own.

"While we're on that—one last thing," Andrew said. "As much as I can appreciate a good story, and this is a great one, I'm having a hard time believing that magic is real. We've spent over a decade seeing doctors and treating Jules for anxiety and depression, and all of a sudden, by some serendipitous chance, we're being told its magic. I hope you can appreciate where I'm coming from on this one. I'm just struggling here to make it make sense."

"Andrew, come on," I said, cheeks flaming. Hanan shook her head.

"Of course, I understand, Andrew," she responded, smiling. "You've had a lifetime of reading about magic but never experiencing it. Why *would* you believe?"

She looked over her shoulder, making sure no one was around. Hanan bent down and picked up a dry stick from the ground, holding it between her fingers. She looked at Andrew and me and then down at the stick, and we watched as it caught fire like a match. It burned brightly for a few moments before Hanan said a word, and it winked out. She looked up at us and grinned.

"If that's not enough when we gather together, we can show you more," she told him.

We finished walking around the farm in companionable silence. I still had a thousand questions but needed time to process everything Hanan had just told us.

Before I knew it, we were back at the hotel, having made plans with Hanan for the next day.

6

Love & Sunsets

We dropped our bags off in our room and headed down to the patio area by the Nile. There were two-person hammocks set up overlooking the river. We'd missed out on grabbing one before they were all taken for sunset on the other nights and were determined to get into one at least once before we left. The air was cooling off from the warm afternoon sun. I had a light sweater on, and Drew wore what we dubbed affectionately as his 'old man cardigan'—a chunky knit, burnt-orange sweater that was so soft, I often stole it to cozy into.

We managed to get the last hammock hidden off to the side that had escaped anyone's notice. We clambered in and got settled, a feat that took more than a bit of finagling. Once comfortable, we lay side by side, Andrew's arm around me and my head resting on his shoulder. I took a deep breath in, filled with utter happiness and trepidation.

"I love you," he whispered. In front of us, the sun was starting its slow descent into evening, the colors of the sky changing to brilliant hues of oranges and yellows as the darkness of the night sky hovered on the edges. It was stunning.

"I love you too," I answered. "I can't believe this is our life. I know it's not always easy, but this? This moment? Makes it all worth it." I sighed, content, and curled in closer to him.

I breathed in his scent—earthy and woodsy and sun-kissed from the day spent outside. I closed my eyes, trying to commit this moment and this feeling to memory. We'd been through so much together—deployments when he was on active duty, trauma from my childhood, more moves across the globe than I could count— I knew we'd figure this out, too.

"Agreed. I could stay here forever. I'm dreading getting back to work."

We lay there a while longer, watching as the stars began to peek out from the night sky and listening to the far-away chatter of the resort.

There, in the dark and quiet, I gave a voice to my fears.

"I'm scared, Drew."

"Yeah? Obviously, I'm nervous too. What's got you worried?" Drew asked, running his hand along my back, sending little waves of pleasure through me.

"A lot of things, but at the top of the list is that this was all some mistake, and they're going to realize it as soon as we spend time together. I know I said that this feels right, and it does, truly, but I don't know, I just feel..." I trailed off.

"Like you'll never be good enough. I know. But Jules, you are. You *are* good enough. I wish you could see that." He sighed, this argument being one we had on the regular. I knew it had to be exhausting to constantly fight my self-doubt, but fight, he did. All the time.

"Ugh. I know, Drew, and I'm so sorry. I just never feel like it." My words caught in my throat.

"I know. And there's nothing I can say to make you realize that you've always been enough, and you'll always *be* enough. That's something you have to come to on your own." He kissed my head again and let his lips rest there. Our truce felt precariously perched on a ledge, but I tried to keep it from toppling over.

"I'm working on it, you know. I think therapy is helping. It just takes time to sort through everything and break old habits. It's almost thirty-six years of self-doubt and, you know..." I trailed off again, thinking of my parents.

"Yeah, Jules, I know. But they're gone, and you aren't ever going to get the validation you always wanted from them. They had their own shit they were dealing with and were so sucked into that church that they couldn't see past it and see anything else." Another kiss to the top of my head. "It's not an excuse, obviously, but it's a reminder, babe. And don't discount all the good your grandparents did. I know they did their best to try and make up for what your parents lacked, and Gram still does a hell of a job."

We'd had a version of this same conversation for years. After a major falling out with my parents, when Drew and I ran away together, they refused to speak to me. They were killed in a car crash before we could reconcile (if we'd even been able to). I'd spent most of my adult life in therapy, reconciling that we'd had no chance to reunite or work through some of the trauma I'd endured as a young girl. I was a work in progress.

"Oh, I know. And I know Gram is proud as hell and loves me no matter what. She and Gramps were more parents than Edwin and Colleen ever thought about being. God. What would they think of me now?" I laughed.

"I have no clue, but I imagine whatever it was, it would be a strong opinion."

"Oh, I'm sure. It definitely clinches my place in hell, though, yeah?" I chuckled; humor as a deflection from pain was my go-to.

"Well, between doing magic and, you know, not believing in the same god the same way they did? Yeah, your place in their hell is pretty much guaranteed. But I'll be joining you, so it's all good."

"We'll just burn together for eternity. There could be worse fates, yeah?"

"I can think of far worse."

"Okay. Enough about them. Let's go grab some dinner."

"You don't want to call off the truce and have it out?" I asked, trying for levity.

"Maybe later." He grinned at me and took my face in his hands before crushing his mouth to mine in a kiss that had me forgetting what we were even talking about. I melted into him even more and met his intensity. Something rippled under my skin that felt like the magic from the ritual. It was confusing and electric, and I didn't know what to do with it. There wasn't any way to show him what I was feeling, so I just kept kissing him.

After a few moments, we broke apart and left the warmth of the hammock and into the chilled night air. We ate overlooking the black water of the Nile and the shadowed Valley of the Kings, drinking wine and talking of nothing too deep or emotional, both needing light after our talk in the hammock.

We finished eating and spent some time walking along the river bank, hand in hand, stretching out the night as long as possible and falling into the same pre-separation habits from years of deployments. We returned to the room just before midnight and spent the night doing another pre-separation ritual. We made love until we were spent and curled into each other's bodies, needing the reassurance of the other's presence, especially after the argument from the night before.

Laying in each other's arms, sheets thrown over us, Andrew spoke in the dark, breaking the truce but not entirely.

"Look, Jules," he started. "I don't want to fight. I'm just going to say I love you, and it is okay for me to worry about you. I wouldn't be much of a husband if I wasn't worried, okay?"

I rolled my eyes but nodded, head resting on his chest.

"I need you to understand that I feel like I have to do this. I can't explain it. But I know I need to be here and doing this."

"Fine. But if we get to Hanan's and something is off, I don't know if I will feel comfortable leaving you."

I bristled at that but battled back the urge to argue. I took a deep breath before I responded.

"Okay. But Drew? This is *my* choice. And I'm choosing to stay. But that doesn't mean I'm not also choosing you and us. I'm not trying to be difficult here or dismissive of your concerns. At all. But I *am* doing this. I'll leave if I ever feel unsafe or like something is off. I'll get a hotel room and then buy a ticket home. Seriously. I've got this."

He deflated, and the fight went out of him at that moment.

"Seriously, Jules, if even one little thing is off, pull up and get home. No matter the cost." I nodded against his chest, and we both lay there, quiet, in the dark, before drifting off to sleep.

The next day was quiet. We'd found the respite we had come to Egypt in desperate search of, and we were both happy to have an entire day together punctuated with room service, naps, and lots of make-up and pre-goodbye sex.

My night, however, was not a respite.

It was filled with vivid dreams of long-dead kings and queens, poison, magic, and my parents, watching everything with judgment and disdain on their faces. I woke up exhausted and more than a little emotionally wrung out the following day. I stayed in bed for a few extra minutes of sleep, and Andrew went out for a run, leaving me be.

After Andrew's run, we spent the morning curled up in bed, having breakfast and dozing in and out, a happy change from our usually busy lives. Hanan arrived to pick us up in the middle of the afternoon, giving us a chance to settle in before the rest of the group arrived that evening. She picked us up in her car, an older Land Rover, looking formidable but well cared for.

7

Convocation

Hanan's house was a Nubian-style villa surrounded and almost hidden by greenery. Palm trees and other plants invaded the space where her home sat, giving the place an African *Secret Garden* vibe on the outside. The house itself was cream-colored adobe with rich, dark wood framing archways and windows on what looked like three floors—the uppermost floor open, though covered.

Hanan parked and led us through an amber-colored glass door with curving wrought iron accents and through a small archway of a stone wall surrounding the villa. She closed the door behind us, and I looked around, blown away. The wall was covered with plants, blocking a lot of the noise from the road and bringing much-needed shade to help block out the African sun. It was like Hanan's own private oasis, and I couldn't wait to explore. She led us around the side of the house, the ground switching between beautiful mosaic tiles forming flowers and shapes and patches of carefully cultivated grass before opening up into a gorgeous space designed for entertaining. There were wooden Arabic-style benches with white cushions, multicolored pillows, and two oversized wicker chairs grouped under a wooden pergola with matting to shade the seating area fully.

Across that space, in the opposite corner, was the small guest house Hanan had offered us. It was inviting, tucked away in such a beautiful garden, and I had a slight twinge of regret that we weren't staying there tonight, but I shook it off. Hanan asked if we wanted something to drink and left us to explore the garden while she went inside. There were still a few minutes before everyone arrived, and I knew that she'd brought us early so we could get a lay of the land before everyone arrived.

Andrew and I settled in on one of the benches under the pergola, and I took it all in. It really was an oasis. So much care and effort had obviously gone into the space and I hoped a little of that tranquility would rub off on Andrew and me. Things were still a bit strained between us, and I was a bundle of nerves and emotions. I wasn't sure if it was meeting everyone properly this time, things between Andrew and me, or just this discovery of magic and sisterhood that had been so restless and unsettled, but I was longing for some peace.

Hanan came out with a tray of tea, coffee, dates, and small buttery-looking shortbread cookies. I gratefully accepted my cup of tea and inhaled the rich, malty scent. I'd never been much of a coffee drinker, and a stint living in the UK in our twenties had turned me into a rabid tea lover.

I nibbled on a cookie from the small silver plate on the table. It was shaped with curves and points and etched with swirling designs, very Arabic style, and I loved it. The details on this side of the world were so different than in the West, and I loved how even the most mundane things seemed to have a flourish that made them feel special. I ate a chocolate-dipped date, and it melted in my mouth.

"Mmm," I made a happy noise of satisfaction. "This is delicious! Is that a pecan in the center?"

"It is. Those are my favorites." Hanan said. I nodded and made a mental note to find these and send some home for Gram to try. She was an adventurous eater and loved when I sent her new things to try from our travels. She wasn't really able to travel anymore and she and I both missed our adventures together. I did what I could to help her feel like she wasn't missing out entirely.

We finished up, and as Hanan put her coffee cup back on the tray, she asked if we'd like to have a tour of the house. Andrew gathered our cups and plates, insisting Hanan let him carry it all in for her. As we walked towards the French doors, she paused and turned, pointing at a large tree in the corner of the garden.

"It's not their season yet, but you can have fresh dates from that tree when it's time. They're juicy and sort of...sweet and astringent. An odd combination, but absolutely divine."

I nodded and made a mental note to try them when it was time.

We stopped at the doors, and Hanan looked at Andrew. She gently waved her hand in front of her, and the doors opened. Her mouth quirked up as she took in his surprise, but she said nothing as she led us in. I had a feeling we were in for an evening of small bits of magic.

"We're heeeeere!" Came a singsongy voice behind us. I turned around and recognized two faces from the ritual.

Hanan introduced Salma, her mother, Marwa, and her husband, Omar.

"Hi, again!" Salma exclaimed, coming over and planting a kiss on both of my cheeks. She reached out her hand and proffered Andrew's and began rapid-firing questions about how we were doing and how we found Luxor.

Where Hanan was reserved and quiet, Salma was quite the opposite, and I could see why they fitted together—opposite sides of the same coin. Instead of wearing a hijab, she had a crisp white scarf with bright flowers woven around her hair, tied off to the side, knotted fashionably, and trailing over her shoulder. Her outfit was no less bright—an ombre pink light-knit sweater hung on her petite frame, the front tucked into dark jeans with colorful floral embroidery down the sides of her legs. All the bright colors and patterns matching her personality to a tee.

"Salma, *habebty*, give them some space to breathe," Marwa chided her daughter, who just rolled her eyes and kept on rapid-firing questions. "Welcome, dear one, welcome." She squeezed my arms and leaned up to kiss both cheeks, a soft scent of rosewater and spices surrounding me. She greeted Andrew warmly and stepped back, allowing Omar to come through and shake both our hands.

Just as he finished shaking Andrew's hand, Omar's phone trilled loudly. He pulled it out and checked the screen. "I'm so sorry, I've got to take this. PhD candidate who needs a fire put out, I'm sure." He rolled his eyes and shoved his glasses up on his nose before stepping away to answer his phone.

"Sorry about that," Salma said. "It's inescapable right now—he's got a few students who need their hands held constantly." Omar looked over and shrugged by way of apology and focused on his call.

We left Omar to his call and wandered inside Hanan's house. It was gorgeous. The ceilings were domed and arched brick patterns that automatically drew your gaze upward, making the space feel large and airy. The white walls, instead of feeling boring or sterile, helped bring some neutrality to a room filled with the deep red of the bricks and the brightly colored patterns of carpets. Right in front of us was the kitchen, sectioned off with curved bricks framing the room on all sides. Directly across from the open door and past a small bar area and worktop was the stove and oven that had small nooks cut out of the brick. Herb bundles hanging high on the wall, in various states of drying, finished off the space.

"Wow," Andrew said behind me.

"I was just thinking the same thing," I laughed. "This is incredible, Hanan."

She smiled, obviously proud of her home and our reaction to it.

"Thank you. And welcome. This house has been in my family for years. It carries much history for the sisterhood."

She offered drinks to Marwa and Salma and put away our cups from earlier. We milled around, taking it all in. Salma chattered away, filling the room with her voice and personality.

Marwa was reserved and stood back and watched her daughter with a bemused smile on her face. She was older, her face soft and lightly lined. Her hair was a gorgeous mix of all shades of gray, styled in short, tight coils all over her head. I couldn't help but admire the cut of her long teal stylish abaya and the large brooch in the shape of a hamsa clasped at her throat. Her dark eyes met mine behind glasses with tortoiseshell frames, and they crinkled at the corners when she smiled—the ghosts of a lifetime of smiles and laughter, I felt sure.

After drinks were passed around Hanan brought us to the rooftop terrace, giving us a tour of the house along the way. We walked through the living room, the same domed brick ceiling looming overhead. The focus of this room, however, was the massive wall of bookshelves stuffed to the brim. Books were on the coffee table, and some were piled beside the sofa. I felt an instant kinship with Hanan. At any given moment, books were strewn around our house, both Andrew and I preferring a good book to the TV any day.

"Okay, so far, this is my favorite room," I said excitedly, running my fingers along the spines of the bookshelf we walked past.

"I do love it, as well. One of the bedrooms upstairs is my office, but more often than not, I find myself working down here. I just love being surrounded by all the books. They just feel..." she trailed off.

"Like home," I supplied.

She nodded. "Yes. Like home."

The whole place gave off a comfortable, bohemian vibe, with plush textiles, beautiful rugs, plants, and small details peppered throughout. There were bedrooms on the second floor, and a narrow, spiral staircase led us up to the top floor, nothing more than a doorway that opened up to a massive rooftop terrace. Most of it was covered with a pergola-style roof that matched the dark wood and style of the house, but there were only half walls, so the entire space was open to the elements and the air. Beautifully carved archways were cut into the roof, which I'd seen from the road when we'd first arrived, but they were stunning and detailed up close.

The sides of the walls were tall, coming up to Andrew's hips, a shelf built out on them that I could see acting as a place to put drinks or even a plate of food. I went to stand next to him and leaned over, Luxor spreading out in front of us, the Valley of the Kings off in the distance.

"Do you ever tire of this view?" I said, almost breathless.

"Never," Hanan replied, sounding as wistful as I felt.

"None of us do," Salma said. There's just something about this place that feels magical." I looked over at her, and she winked conspiratorially, and I knew she'd chosen the word on purpose.

Before long, two more women arrived. The older woman whom I'd noticed when she poured oil into Hanan's hand during the ritual was Renee. Her long, graying hair was down and softly waving past her shoulders. She was soft and small, a few inches shorter than me, but when she hugged me, there was a surprising strength in her arms and back.

She had arrived with Marina, a young, stylish Italian woman, tall and lithe-limbed, who had a thick accent playing over her words. Her chic, dark, chin-length blunt bob and thick lashes and brows accentuated her beautiful olive skin. Bangle bracelets tinkled soft and melodious whenever she moved her arms. I wondered how these two women had become part of the sisterhood and wanted to know their stories.

Next to arrive was Hasina. She was the perfect mix of masculine and feminine—her crisp, black suit highlighted her gracious curves and exuded power and her hair was covered in a turban that matched her blue tie and was decorated with a golden flower pin with pearls. Her handshake was firm and no-nonsense and if I was honest, she intimidated me a bit. She had an air of authority and intelligence about her, and when Salma called her *the brains*, it made perfect sense even though we'd just met. She just had that vibe about her. Hasina's husband, Karim, was a doctor, and running behind, she explained in a South African accent, but would be joining us soon.

Naomi, the youngest member of the group and the only one I hadn't met yet was hot on Hasina's heels. She had a generous figure and seemed happy to take up space, literally and figuratively, arriving like a whirlwind and immediately commanding the room. Hands gesturing wildly, the sleeves of her dusky pink peasant-style top waving about, and furiously talking at an unmatched pace, she launched into a tirade about the Egyptian government and street kids, switching in and out of Arabic at will. Her British accent flirted with her lilting Egyptian accent, melding together to form something entirely new. I tamped down the flicker of irritation at her less-than-warm welcome—everyone else had made me feel welcome immediately and she was almost dismissive. Internally I sighed and shook it off and made a mental note to connect with her later to see how I could support her work, hoping we could connect that way.

Reem and her husband, Simon, arrived last, bringing with them Hasina's husband, whom they'd run into on the street. Karim strode over to his wife, wrapped his arms around her, and kissed her, much to her evident dismay. He laughed and said a broad hello to the whole room, a thick Egyptian accent matching his darker skin and hair. He was jovial and another presence that took up space in the room, an odd pairing with the reserved and stoic Hasina. I wondered how on earth those two had come together. Then he strode over to Salma and Marwa, kissing them both on the cheek. I saw the resemblance— there was no mistaking he and Salma were siblings—and with personalities to match.

Reem was among the most beautiful people I'd ever seen. She was of Indian descent with a beautiful complexion, her brown skin flawless. Her large, sable eyes were rimmed with liner and thick black lashes, making them pop. Her hair was light brown and wildly curly, with lighter, honey highlights threaded throughout, the curls pulling away from her face.

"So sorry, everyone. The sitter was late!" She had a thick London accent, and I knew that had to be where she'd met her husband— the tall, gangly redhead who reminded me of a ginger 90's Hugh Grant. He was handsome, and I imagined their children had to be absolutely stunning. They interacted with each other like planets revolving around their very own sun.

And so the night carried on. The double doors from the kitchen into the garden were thrown open, and we mingled inside and out. Everyone passed us around like an orchestrated dance, leaving little downtime for Andrew or myself. At a certain point, I found the men huddled together excitedly chattering away about the book *Dune*, each of them with differing opinions on who was cast in the new film to play the characters and all of them seeming to roast Salma's husband for not having read it yet. I left them to it, grateful Andrew was making friends and hopeful that I would with as much ease. His posture was much more relaxed than at the beginning of the evening, so I hoped his nerves and worry would also settle.

I wound my way around and through everyone in the house and garden. Marwa stuck close, guiding me and asking questions to learn more about me. She also prevented any awkward moments, which felt like its own sort of magical ability.

"How long have you lived overseas?" Marina asked. We were standing just in the garden, and Marina had come up to me to refill my wine glass. She'd brought some bottles from her last trip to Italy and it was robust and delicious. And in addition to being delicious, it was helping soothe my nerves.

"A few years now," I answered her with a nod of thanks for the wine. "We've traveled a lot for Drew's work, so we've never stayed in one place for more than a few years at a time."

"What's that been like?" Salma asked, coming up behind us with a plate of food for the table. "I can't imagine not living in Egypt. It's always been home."

IN THE LIGHT OF THE MOON

"I don't mind it. Nowhere really feels like *home* so I like experiencing lots of different places to see what they have to offer."

"Perhaps you're searching for home?" Marwa asked.

I shrugged. "Maybe. Or maybe we'll just always feel at home in the world and with each other." I looked over to Drew. He was across the room from me, but he looked up and met my eyes. He winked at me, and I had a rush of feelings run through me. Yeah, he was home.

With a dramatic flourish of her hand, Salma lit the candles on the table and called everyone over. Every chance they got, someone was doing a bit of magic. It was incredible, and I hoped it was enough to convince Drew how real it all was. The other men seemed unfazed—so normal to their daily lives it must have been. But every little bit of magic performed felt fantastical to Drew and me.

We sat down to dinner, a catered affair with loads of small bites of Mediterranean and Middle Eastern favorites— everything from hummus and falafel to olives and feta with a multitude of bread for dipping, salads, and all sorts of flavors, new and familiar. Reem stood up and muttered words I couldn't quite make out over the table. She stirred each bowl of dip or sauce with their serving spoons, and I watched, transfixed. Everyone else sat patiently, waiting as if it were the most normal thing in the world.

"She's infusing the food with her magic," Marwa whispered to me. She was seated to my right and had her hand on my arm to get my attention. Andrew leaned over to hear her as well. "It's her, how you say...strength." I nodded and looked at Drew, who cocked an eyebrow up at me questioningly. This whole magic thing was going to take some getting used to.

I took a nervous bite of hummus and was surprised to find that it was just normal hummus. As the night wore on, a warm feeling spread through me—friendship, trust, and welcoming—and I knew that Reem had worked her magic to help me feel a part of the group.

Hanan ensured that plenty of wine flowed to everyone with an empty glass and a taste for it. She proposed a toast to the group and its newest member, and I smiled back at them all, feeling welcome.

The night came to an end, and everyone slowly made their goodbyes, kids and homes to return to. Drew and I tried to help Hanan clean, but she shooed us off, and Marwa stayed behind to help get things back to rights, telling us to enjoy our night.

8

Magic

"I feel like that went well, yeah? They seem nice?" I asked Drew nervously, back at the hotel. I had a bad habit of trusting new people too soon. And I wanted nothing more than to trust this group implicitly and learn all I could from them. I leaned on Drew, who was far shrewder than I was, to read the room and give me his take. So far, he'd not been wrong with a first impression. He crossed the room and pulled my hands away from each other, my nervous habit of picking at my cuticles in full swing.

"I actually really liked them, Jules. I'm not saying I haven't let go of all my reservations, but I liked them all a lot. I spoke with the guys about the area's safety, and they assured me that Luxor is pretty calm and relaxed, whereas Cairo is definitely the hotbed of activity. So if we come back, I'll still be nervous, and nothing can be done for that, but I *do* feel a little better."

I visibly relaxed. "Good," I said. "I know I'll come back, or maybe stay after Cairo... I feel like I need to do this, but I don't want to have you worried or upset the whole time I'm gone."

"Jules, I'm not in charge of you. I'm not about to start lording over you and telling you what you can and can't do." He reached for my arm, stopping my movements and making eye contact.

"But, I'm allowed to be worried. You can't do what I do at work and not be worried about a place like Egypt."

I nodded and stepped closer to him.

"I know. I just wish I could do this and guarantee safety and ease your mind, yeah?"

"And I wish that too, obviously," he said. "I *do* think this is going to be good for you." He brought my hands to his lips. "But, just remember, you're just now meeting everyone, and there's no requirement for them to be your best friends. You have Edie and Delilah for that," he advised.

"Yeah, yeah, thank you, Dr. Drew. I know. I'll do my best to hold back," I said.

"Honestly, I got pretty good vibes from everyone. They all seem pretty low-key and just like they're here to do what they've been called to do. I respect the hell out of that. Naomi might be the only wild card. But she's also the youngest, and we're all wild cards while figuring out who we are." He tipped my chin up and reached down to kiss me softly.

"I agree; she was a bit standoffish. I appreciate your bullshit radar so much, my darling." I kissed him back. Naomi seemed more annoyed with me than anything. I wondered if it had to do with her not being there for my ritual. Everyone else had been so warm and welcoming. The part of me who longed to fit in bristled at her disinterest, and I tried to shove it away. "And the magical side of things?"

He ran his fingers through his hair and blew out a breath.

"The logical side of me wants to sit in disbelief. But even it can't deny the things they showed us tonight." He sighed. "The guys and I talked about that too. Karim grew up with it, so he doesn't really get my disbelief, but Omar and Simon assured me they were in my shoes once. So, see, it's not just me being ridiculous."

"I never said you were ridiculous," I argued.

"I believe your exact words were *close-minded*." He kissed me as a distraction.

"I stand by that," I responded with a smirk, breaking the kiss.

He rolled his eyes and kissed me again, holding my face in both hands and deepening the kiss.

I wrapped my arms around his shoulders, standing on tiptoe to meet him and press myself into his body. Meeting so many new people in one go had exhausted me and filled me with nervous energy that needed an outlet. I couldn't think of a better one.

The nervous energy inside of me was still pulsing through my body, magnifying the energy I'd felt since the ritual bath in Hatshepsut's temple. My mind briefly wondered at the fact that I'd felt so insatiable in the last couple of days and if there was a correlation. Then, that thought was quickly forgotten with the exploration of Drew's tongue on my neck. A moan escaped my throat, which spurred him on.

"Um, Jules," he panted. "Not that I am complaining at all, but are you okay? You've been ravenous on this trip!" he said between kisses, his lips rasping against my throat.

"Maybe it's magic, jackass," I snarked, biting his bottom lip. "Instead of wondering about it, can you just fuck me?"

I was wild with lust and pent-up energy. I dropped to my knees and grabbed Drew far more aggressively than usual, taking him into my mouth. He was moaning in seconds, his bands tangled in my hair, gently pulling it out of the way. He let me go for a moment before grabbing me by the shoulder and lifting me up, my trembling body flush against his. He kissed me breathlessly and pulled my tank top down, releasing my breast and rolling my nipple between his fingers. He tasted sweet and spicy, the cardamom and date cake we'd had for dessert lingering on his tongue. I kissed him like a woman possessed, drinking in every detail, afraid to miss something. Desperate to touch him. My skin was on fire, hot and searing against his, and I wanted nothing more than to set alight with the friction of our touch.

We moved, stumbling together to the bed, and fumbled to remove the rest of our clothes, mouths barely separating as we crawled under the covers, the sheets cold and soft against our skin. I could smell the clean scent of detergent from the bed linen and the warm scent of Drew all around me, chasing the cold away. We lay against each other, hands roaming, mouths locked together.

Minutes or hours passed, I wasn't sure, but eventually, our hands weren't enough, and we came together slowly, deliberately, both crying out and then falling against each other, spent.

"If that's magic, then I'm a believer," Drew said, panting.

I grinned at him and pulled him closer for another kiss.

9

Cairo

We spent the next three days exploring Cairo and getting to know Hanan better. She had opted to drive us instead of having one of the tour company's drivers, which was per-fect—no having to be secretive or unable to talk in front of someone else. I sat up front with her, and our conversations went back and forth between Egypt facts and curiosities about magic and the sisterhood. The streets were tightly packed, and the architecture was a mix of old-world European and Arabic. It was like driving through the streets of Belgium or Paris with a flair unique to Egypt.

We drove over the Nile, and Hanan spent a few minutes talking about the life-giving river and its importance in Ancient Egyptian life as well as modern-day Egypt while we headed to the Egyptian Museum.

The sun was bright, not a cloud in sight, a brilliant cerulean blue that looked like a painting above the museum—a massive, pink stone behemoth with white marble details. We made our way to a set of giant, heavy wooden doors, and Hanan led us in and started the tour. She had a way of weaving history into a story-like tale that had us hanging off her every word. She read hieroglyphs, pointing out and teaching us the right direction to read them, told us stories about long-dead kings and queens, and pointed out tiny details we would have otherwise missed on artifacts and statues.

Guides weren't allowed in certain areas of the museum so Drew and I explored a little bit on our own. When we came to the room that housed the mummies of the ancient kings and queens, I was surprised to find myself emotional when I read Hatshepsut's name on one of the placards. She had been a faceless entity—a fairytale almost—until now. Standing in the dimly lit room, staring down at her body, only glass separating us, my throat clogged with emotion. There was a strange sort of intimacy in knowing her secrets and seeing her here. Andrew said something quietly, but I was so focused on the body before me that I didn't quite make it out. I turned away from her and swallowed down the lump in my throat. Mumbling an excuse, I left the room.

Andrew followed me.

"You okay?"

I nodded. "Yeah, it was just weirder than I thought it would be to see the mummies. I just..." I trailed off, not knowing how to put into words what I was feeling.

"Agreed. I thought it would be cool to see them, but I just feel kind of guilty," he said as he leaned against the wall next to me. "Regardless of if I believe the same things they did about an afterlife, everything they believed in has been disturbed. It seems kind of cruel to upset that and then put them on display."

I nodded in agreement. It was that and something else—something I couldn't put my finger on. I'd felt a pull towards Hatshepsut specifically—like I knew her or could feel her. Maybe I was reading too much into it, or maybe it was knowing more about her now, but I was glad to be out of that room.

IN THE LIGHT OF THE MOON

We carried on with the rest of our day, seeing King Tut's riches, statues depicting the elongated heads of royalty, *canopic* jars that once held organs, game boards, leather shoes that looked suspiciously like my modern ones, and so much more. Though my mind was reeling with everything we'd seen and learned when we climbed back in the van, I couldn't shake the quiet sense of sadness at seeing Hatshepsut. We had dinner together with Hanan that night and then met up after breakfast for another full day.

✦

Hanan had a cooler for us for the day and gestured to it after climbing into the van. I cracked it open and found glass-bottled sodas, water bottles, and candy bars. Next to the cooler was a basket with chips and crackers in it. Andrew popped the top off a Coke for me with his ring, a talent he'd mastered during his days in the Navy, and I took a long sip. The tiny bubbles, always more pronounced in a glass bottle, danced over my tongue, and I sighed with contentment at the hit of sugar and caffeine.

We snacked on dried fruit and sipped our cokes as we drove through the city, leaving Cairo and heading into Giza.

Before long, we started to see buildings crop up in the desert, rickety stone structures that were half-built and crumbling. Hanan explained that the Egyptian government had passed laws forbidding people from building on new land. People skirted the laws by adding on to pre-existing buildings. Still, nothing was to any sort of 'code' or standards, and many times, the cheapest materials people could find were used, so the buildings weren't terribly safe. The government had tried to clear them out. However, there were still destitute people living there with no other options. My heart sank. Poverty is always something that hits hard no matter where you are, but seeing the patchwork homes and the desperation just after being surrounded by the riches of the Egyptian Museum settled heavily.

"It's such a stark contrast between this and what we saw in the museum," I said quietly. Hanan nodded.

"It is. In many ways, the Ancient Egyptians were further evolved and more advanced than we are. That's not to say they were all incredibly wealthy, but the poverty line now is much starker than it was then--when it should be the opposite. Over a quarter of our population lives below the poverty line. That number just continues to rise year after year." She paused, her mood shifting from animated teacher to worried countryman. "Children live on the streets, begging for food or selling themselves for a pittance, just to survive."

I felt my heart drop.

"I feel like that's another big difference between other parts of the world and the US. We know that big cities have a large number of houseless people, but unless you visit and see it with your own eyes, it's easy to put it out of sight and out of mind. But here, and definitely in Bahrain, it's all around and hard to ignore. We've seen things all over Bahrain that I never expected. The workers there are treated worse than animals in many cases."

Hanan nodded somberly.

"Jules has really struggled with that," Andrew added, and I nodded in acknowledgment. My empathetic nature and slightly hippie viewpoint that not only should everyone be treated as equals but that everyone should have a safe place to go and a full belly each day kept me struggling against the reality of the world.

"I've traveled a lot with my job, and we've done some human-itarian work and seen a lot. It was the one thing I didn't really think to prepare her for," Andrew continued.

"It *is* hard," Hanan said. "It's also why tourism is so vital to Egypt. If we have more Westerners coming in with their hopeful ideals, we end up getting more help. As a whole, we've become so numb to it all. There are so many people who are fighting for change and fighting for a better, safer Egypt. Still, sometimes that fight feels impossibly large," she trailed off then, sorrow thick in the vehicle.

"Is there anything we can do to help?" I asked. "Any charities we could donate to or things we can do while we're here?"

Hanan smiled at me.

"That's kind of you, Julia. The best person to talk to is Naomi. She's part of a group of activists trying to change things and do what they can to make a difference. A lot of the government-run organizations don't have much funding or support. Or there's corruption on the inside and people spending the money on themselves instead of those in need."

"I'll do that. I know it won't fix everything, but I can't help but want to do *something*, you know?"

"What do you think the answer is, Hanan?" Andrew asked.

We talked for a few minutes more— Hanan's love for her country was even more evident as she spoke about ideas of how to improve things.

A quiet reverence settled in the car, all of us lost in thought, when a few minutes later, something peeked between buildings. I sucked in a breath, my worries momentarily swept away by what I saw.

"Oh my god! Are those the pyramids?" I exclaimed, unable to keep my excitement from bubbling over.

"Ha! They are!" Hanan laughed, the mood in the car lightening a bit.

We were still far enough away that I couldn't get a clear glimpse of them, but now and then, I'd see the top peek out between buildings. Butterflies fluttered in my stomach again, and I squeezed Drew's hand, grinning ear to ear.

After a few more minutes, we were closer to the pyramids, their size massive and impressive. Unlike what I'd expected, they were tucked just behind the city of Giza. We drove past neighborhoods and slums on our way, people out walking, riding their bikes, or sitting on their stoops, just going about their lives like one of the world's seven wonders wasn't sitting right there in their backyards.

Before I knew it, we found ourselves winding our way up inside the Great Pyramid of Giza. While it was true that there wasn't anything but an empty tomb to see, it was absolutely one of those incredible, surreal moments that took my breath away. The interior was steep and climbing—part of it so low that Andrew and I were crawling on our hands and knees. It was a bit precarious, my anxiety assuring me that, at any moment, I was going to tip over into the dark abyss below.

We spent a few moments once we'd climbed back down just standing in the low-ceilinged chamber just after the entrance, staring at each other in a bit of shock. We hurriedly snapped a forbidden photo inside, unable not to commemorate the moment, and made our way back to the entrance.

The next day, we wandered the souk and sampled loads of fantastic food. Hanan had an incredible energy about her—we'd known that in Luxor, but after three days in Cairo with her, we'd started forming a good foundation of friendship that even Andrew couldn't deny. As the days ticked by, I could feel Andrew relaxing around her. He was on high alert throughout Cairo but tucked into the safety of our tour van; he had been mostly back to his usual self. The night before we were due to leave, I made the call to stay behind in Luxor. Andrew wasn't thrilled and still had reservations about it, but at the end of the day, I was my own person and needed to stay behind and see if I could figure out this whole magic thing. Luckily, my job was remote—I was running the website and doing the books for a yoga studio. One of my friends was running in the States and teaching an online class or two whenever she needed. I could do it from Luxor just as well as from Bahrain.

Hanan was ecstatic and offered up her house again. It was unorthodox and so outside of my norm that I was equal parts terrified and excited. The worst-case scenario would be that I'd buy a plane ticket and head back to Bahrain sans understanding of magic.

10

Parts Unknown

On our way home from the airport, Hanan drove me around her neighborhood, pointing out local shops and where some of the others lived. It was filled with adobe-style homes with ornate wooden doors and wooden beamed pergola-type awnings jutting out to their sides. They were distinctly Egyptian but reminded me of Southern California homes with an Arabic flair. They were close together but surrounded by vegetation. Almost like the Nile had fed into an oasis, they had fitted homes wherever they could between plants and trees. Housed in the city's outskirts, it gave the neighborhood a decidedly wild and rural vibe.

After our neighborhood tour, Hanan had work to do. When she wasn't giving life-changing tours, she ran their company website, planned and organized tour packages, and did all sorts of admin. While she worked, I settled into the guest house, unpacking and acquainting myself to my home away from home.

It was welcoming and bright and smelled fresh, like it had just been aired out. The walls were the palest blue—like a wispy sky blue overlaid with clouds—and botanical prints in dark wooden frames decorated them. There was a carpet on the tile floor in multiple shades of blue and cream that I recognized as a *Nain* from all our rug shopping in Bahrain. We'd lived there for almost two years, and it seemed like there was a rug flop at least every other month.

I slipped off my shoes at the doorway, a custom on this side of the world that Andrew and I were happy to adopt, and walked across the soft carpet. The space was set up like a studio-style apartment. One whole wall was the kitchen space, which overlooked the garden, and I loved that that would be my view when I made my morning tea.

Across from the little kitchen was the bed and a pocket door that led to the bathroom. It was a marvel. A deep, round, blue-tiled bathtub was the room's centerpiece, with a skylight that shone light down on it like a spotlight. It was artfully filled with all the essentials and hanging green plants that gave it a spa-like vibe that I couldn't wait to take advantage of. The guest house was a small but inviting space that felt luxurious but also private and safe. It wouldn't be hard to settle into.

Before I'd come to settle in to the guest house, Hanan had given me an old book to read. It was a captivating history of the sisterhood that told of its inception, and a timeline of events since Hatshepsut's death. I made myself comfortable against the ornate Indian-style headboard and cracked open the soft leather tome.

Hanan had explained that years before, one of the sisters had been a writer and had taken it upon herself to consolidate as much information as possible to make one concise book that held their story. It was written well; facts and figures twined with flowery prose that read like a bestseller. Hatshepsut's life had been a fascinating one on its own. I read about her life and the magic that she used to help support a peaceful rule. There were multiple accounts of her being able to calm a rival and keep clear-headedness in the room or tend wounds. The possibilities within me suddenly became more tangible. For the first time since the ritual bath, I began to see what living with magic could be like.

✦

A knock on the door startled me from the book that was reading like the most intriguing novel. Hanan was finished with her work for the day and invited me over for dinner. I wasn't sure how this was all going to work—though we'd spent a lot of time together in the last week and a half, we were barely more than strangers.

We cooked together, creating an eggplant stew similar to the one we'd had in Cairo. While we cut vegetables and prepped dinner, we talked more about Hatshepsut and Thutmose.

Hatshepsut had not only known about the dark magic Thutmose was searching out but she'd been charged by Isis herself to protect the knowledge from prying eyes and impure hearts. Scrolls filled with ritual spells and information about the dark magics that Hatshepsut's ancestors had once practiced. They were hidden away, the knowledge of their very existence a closely guarded secret. Thutmose somehow gained access to the scrolls when he was just a teenager. No one knew how or what he did to steal the scrolls, as they were protected by the high priestess of Isis' temple, but he managed it. He performed a dark spell that called forth a demon from the depths of *Duat* that wreaked havoc until Hatshepsut and the priestesses could get control over it and destroy it.

Hatshepsut hadn't known how much information Thutmose had retrieved from the scrolls, so there was no destroying them. They were recovered and locked away from him, but she was always fearful that he'd copied something down, and she wanted to be sure to have the originals. Hanan explained that they also contained how to fight the darkness and restore things to rights. So, it would have been perilous not to have them.

Hatshepsut was trying to transcribe the antidotes when she died. No one could pick up where she left off for fear of missing something vital—the dark ways weren't taught anymore. She was one of the very few people who had been taught about them to heed against their use. She found out when it was too late but knew she still had time to save her kingdom. She brought together her closest advisors, including her lover and the architect of her mortuary temple, Senenmut. She explained to them what Thutmose had told her in his fit of rage and tasked them with helping her protect the scrolls at all costs.

She looked to Senenmut, and he agreed to secretly build her a safe place. He had already built the ritual space we were in the other day as a special gift to Hatshepsut. He then added a system of tunnels in and out of the temple so they could come and go away from the prying eyes of Thutmose. At this point, he had become obsessed with dark magic and his stepmother's whereabouts. He was mad at the thought that she was keeping the power all to herself and out of his hands. He couldn't see past his desires to understand she wasn't *using* the power hidden in the texts but protecting the world from its corruption.

And so, over the next few months, work began in earnest to create the tunnels to keep them safe and a space to house the scrolls away from Thutmose. And then, she died. And here the sisterhood is today, still protecting the scrolls and the world from the dangers held within them.

Satisfied with what we'd done, Hanan opened the oven and placed the dish in to bake. She wiped her hands on her dishtowel, a cheery, yellow, and white striped Turkish-style cloth with tassels, and then grabbed a bottle of white wine as she turned towards me.

"Wine?" she asked.

"Yes, please!" I said.

I grabbed two wine glasses from the open shelving above the countertops. Hanan pulled the cork out and poured us both a drink. She turned and grabbed a small bowl of olives for us to snack on while dinner was cooking. We clinked our glasses, and I sipped the crisp, fruity white wine. It was cold and smooth on my tongue. I could tell Hanan was giving me the space to work out questions, and I had learned this was her regular practice. Many people feel the need to fill every quiet moment with baseless chatter, but Hanan was happy to give space to the silence, and I truly appreciated it.

"Alright. So. Hatshepsut died, and the sisterhood was left to protect the scrolls. Didn't Thutmose just hunt them down and demand them?"

"He made every effort to," Hanan said. "They had things in place to protect them and their families, but eventually they fled Egypt."

"They fled?" I asked.

"They had no choice. He had captured one of them, a woman named Banafrit, and tortured and killed her when she refused to give up her secrets. Her death was the final straw for the group, and they scattered. There weren't many of them, only about two dozen or so. We know where almost everyone ended up. Once Thutmose died, they slowly returned to their homeland. A few stayed away, and their lines traveled the globe and ended up on almost every continent.

"Everyone who returned added their stories to a scroll—like a running diary—so we could piece together things from that time. It has remained a common practice to keep a diary. All of us now live in Egypt, or close to, so we can perform rituals together and stay protected. You'll be the first American in quite a long time." She smiled proudly at me.

"Oh. Awesome," I said. "So there were Americans in the sisterhood before?"

"There were. Some were killed in the Witch hunts in the seventeenth century, and the rest moved away, and one or two we lost touch with. We hope they were able to find peace and rest." Hanan grew quiet then, the weight of the sisters who had come before her settling on her shoulders.

"So, how many of you are there now? Everyone I met the other day?" I asked gently.

"Us?" Hanan replied. "Julia, you are one of our very small number. Throughout history, our numbers have dwindled. Though we never had a massive group, just for safety's sake, you make our ninth sister." She paused, letting me think.

"There are other, sort of outside members; older women who have handed over their mantles and are living out their lives without actively tracking the brotherhood or any of this and a few women who have chosen not to stay and have moved away, living their own life. So, nine is kind of a misleading number. But only nine members are actively working to protect the magic and scrolls." She paused, sipping her wine.

"Okay. I don't know why I was expecting some huge number," I said sheepishly. "Everything just seems larger than life, I guess?" I shrugged.

"I can see that. I know there are people worldwide who hold the power to become one of us. But obviously, we can't recruit new members." Hanan grinned. "The group comprises one steward, a role passed down throughout a family, and one *Nebet*, a sort of female vizier or second-in-command. It's odd because technically, a steward was lower ranking than a vizier, but Hatshepsut named the woman she left in charge of the scrolls Chief Steward, and the title just stuck. They are the only two who know the location of the scrolls. But everyone has a role and is vital to the sisterhood."

I finished my glass of wine, and Hanan poured us both another.

"You're the steward, aren't you?" I asked Hanan.

"I am, yes," she replied. "It is a role passed down in my family since the first *Djeserit*. And Salma is my Vizier—a role more or less earned. Typically, we grow up close, the children of members, and whoever bonds with the Steward when they're young ends up stepping into the role when it's time. Our moms were close, and our grandmothers are still the best of friends—they raised their children together, and now they're both widowed, they live together and are a riot. Salma and I were born only a few weeks apart and were raised as sisters. It was an effortless choice for me once we were older, and I took over when my mother died. And then Salma's mother stepped down and guided her to take over as Vizier."

"I'm sorry about your mother, Hanan. Were you close?" I asked.

"We were. She was a wonderful woman," Hanan said, her face softening with memories. "She was a wonderful steward, and everyone loved her, but she was just an amazing mother. She was kind and patient, understanding and forgiving. Losing her was the hardest thing I've ever gone through." She reached up and swiped at a tear.

"She loved the sisterhood and everything we stand for. She was convinced that things would finally come to a head in the next few years. We'd see the end of the brotherhood, and all finally find peace, and Hatshepsut, wherever she is, would finally be able to rest as well." She looked over my shoulder to a framed photo on the table next to me, and I followed her gaze.

I set my glass down and picked up the carved wooden frame painted a bright, springy green. The photo was of a younger Hanan, beaming directly at the camera, smile so wide her eyes were almost closed, and a woman wrapped in a brightly colored hijab matched perfectly to her floral, flowy maxi dress. She looked down at Hanan, part of her face obscured by the angle, but she looked at her with so much adoration it radiated off the photo. My fingertips grazed their faces, and a deep longing for a mother who should look at me like that wound into my heart. Tears welled in my eyes, threatening to slip down my cheeks, and I cleared my throat, dislodging the lump there.

"She was beautiful, Hanan. And you look so happy."

She smiled, and I placed the frame back on the table and picked my glass back up.

"Oh, I was. I had just graduated and had been accepted to university. That day was perfect. My acceptance letter had just come in— that's what I was holding in my hand."

I smiled at her.

"That's amazing! You can feel the joy and the love just seeing the photo," I told her. "Were you close to your dad too?"

"For the most part, yes. But once my mother died, a part of him died too. He moved away shortly after she died, and I moved back here. He won't come back to Egypt. It's just too painful. I know he loves and misses me, but my mother was the sun he revolved around. He just isn't the same without her."

"I'm so sorry. Where does he live now?" I asked. Do you visit him often?"

"He's moved to Morocco. They went on their honeymoon, and I think he could be there and be with those memories of them as their younger selves without feeling her ghost in their house if that makes sense?"

"Yeah, I can see that," I said.

"I don't see him often, but I try to go and visit at least once a year. Or we'll meet somewhere for a vacation together." She trailed off and took a moment to gather her thoughts.

"Okay," she said, taking a deep breath. "Enough sadness for the night. What I'd like to do over the next few weeks or so is bring in each of the sisters, and you take some one-on-one time with them to learn. While the magic we all carry is basically the same, each of us has a gift we put more time and energy into, and we will take turns teaching you about our strengths."

"That's a good idea. So everyone gets to share the thing they're really good at?"

"Exactly," Hanan said. "If you're really good or enjoy something, you're a much better teacher."

The timer on her phone beeped at us, and we headed to the kitchen to finish dinner. We ate at the dining table in a nook off the side of the kitchen, eggplant tender and delicious and rice fragrant and perfectly cooked. The conversation shifted to getting to know each other, and we tabled talk of the sisterhood and my training.

We laughed and talked, shifting back to the sofa after cleaning up from dinner, and before I knew it, it was late, and we were both yawning between travel stories. We called it a night, and I headed to the guest house. I called Andrew and assured him that I was settled in and comfortable. He wasn't thrilled with being apart, but he tried to be supportive and hide it. I let him keep up with the ruse and promised to update him on how things were going.

11

Surrender

"Every witch needs a book of shadows or grimoire," Hanan said one afternoon, handing me a wrapped parcel. "This will be your sacred space to write everything you're learning—whatever you feel is important. It'll become a sort of reference guide for your personal practice."

She handed me the heavy bundle wrapped in brown paper, tied with twine. I slowly undid the string and opened the paper, revealing a thick, leather-bound book in a rich, dark teal. Embossed on the front, in the corner, was a crescent moon surrounded by stars—the same style stars as the ceiling in the temple. I ran my fingers along the image, feeling the leather, and looked up at her.

"Oh, Hanan, it's gorgeous!" I said.

She beamed. "I'm glad you like it. I asked Andrew what your favorite color was and had it made this past week. I'm so pleased with how it turned out."

It was so beautiful, and the workmanship was incredible. I hugged it to my chest and thanked her, putting it on the bedside table as soon as I went to bed that night. Growing up, my parents hadn't been big on gifts—their focus was always on the religious meanings behind holidays like Christmas and Easter. Birthdays were hardly noted—they were all too worried that gifts and celebrations would foster a false sense of importance, and they couldn't have that. It had taken years for me to accept gifts from others graciously and not feel like I was doing something wrong. Andrew's family were joyful gift-givers, and his mom had made it her mission to get me used to it.

✦

Hanan and I had talked about ways everyone manifested their magic. Each woman had their strengths and would take turns guiding me in learning how to manifest my own power. Salma had been chosen as my first teacher, and the Saturday after I'd arrived at Hanan's was the day we'd officially start training. I'd tried and failed many times to try and do *something* magical and just couldn't grasp what to do or how to get ahold of it. I was beyond eager to get started.

I had a little time before Salma was set to be there, and since the ritual, I'd felt a bundle of energy running through my system. I rolled out my yoga mat and hoped getting some movement would settle my nerves.

I was almost finished with my practice when my phone beeped, and Salma texted to let me know she would let herself in the gate.

"Oh good, you do yoga. That helps," she said when she came around the corner and saw me on the mat. She was dressed similarly to me in leggings and a long-sleeved olive tunic, and today's headscarf was donned in a turban style and deep purple to match the marbled buttons down her top.

"What will yoga help with?" I asked, curious, standing up and meeting her with a quick hug. She smelled clean, like spring, and I hoped my deodorant had held strong through my practice.

"Oh, lots of things. But it helps sort of direct any excess energy you feel. Other things help too...running, meditation, rituals, sex, although the right sex can *be* a ritual. Do you feel any different than you did before the ritual? Like busy or unable to sit still? Or just full of energy?"

Salma's excitable energy wasn't reserved only for dinner parties, then. She rapid-fired questions at me, not waiting for my answer, and I realized I just needed to jump in.

"Um, yeah," I said, trying to figure out how to describe it. "It's weird. Like an undercurrent flowing under my skin. But I've had that for a really long time. It's like how I feel before a nasty panic attack, but I'm not panicky. There's just all this extra energy trying to get out."

Salma nodded.

"Yeah. That. When your husband was here, you had a lot of sex after the ritual, right?" she asked without pretense or judgment.

I decided it best to match her honesty, no matter how weird it was to discuss my sex life with a virtual stranger.

"Er...yes. A lot." I felt my face go red, and I blurted out. "And, um. It was really good. Like, better than normal." Even the tips of my ears went red.

"Good. That's how it's supposed to be," Salma said, grinning like a cat who'd got into the cream.

"All that pent-up energy has to go somewhere, and what better place than the bedroom...or the kitchen counters?" She laughed, and I blushed more but felt a little better that there was an explanation for my insatiability. "Though I'm happy to dish about sex all day long, I'm here to talk to you about harnessing your energy. That's the current you can feel under your skin. Have you ever had acupuncture?" I nodded. "Okay. Did you feel anything when they stuck all those needles in you?"

"Yeah. I did. I've only had it done a handful of times, but I remember feeling a direct electric current pulsing through me. It was connecting the needles, running between them, and pinging off them."

Salma smiled, looking satisfied.

"Perfect! *That* is what we're looking for, and that's what you want to take control of. It is straightforward. And it should be easy for you since you know what I'm talking about." She paused for a second, letting her thoughts catch up.

"Think about it like this: everyone is made of energy. We can take that energy, the very thing that animates our bodies, and *use* it to our benefit. We have to respect it, but we can bend it to our will by being intentional with our thoughts. Now, that can mean intentionally speaking a phrase or word to perform a spell and physically pushing that energy out, or intentionally concentrating our energy into a ritual or tincture or even with plants."

I knitted my eyebrows together and frowned.

"So...like, actual physical energy can manifest, and we can shoot wiggly woos from our fingers?" I asked, more than a little confused.

"Well, we're not all superheroes, and yes, I got that reference." She pointed to her chest. "Huge comic book nerd here." We both laughed.

"But...kind of?" she said. "We're not mutants. Well, for the most part, we're not." She stopped again. "Actually. No. We sort of are in a manner of speaking. I mean, we're human and not indestructible. But something happens in the ritual bath that sort of unlocks special abilities in all of us that we couldn't reach before we went in."

Her brain was working at a far faster clip than mine, and I let her roll with it, knowing she was eventually coming to a point. She continued rambling about power and energy, finally stopping and looking at me, eyes narrowed and focused. Her sudden stillness was jarring and more than a little disarming. I shifted, not sure what to do with myself.

"Um...Salma?" I said. "You okay?" She blinked and started moving again like someone had paused her and pressed play.

"Sorry about that. Sometimes, I have to just stop and focus when my mind gets going." She laughed. "It's hard to explain. It was worse when I was younger, trying to sit still in school and pay attention. Sorry." She apologized again and seemed to get herself under control.

"Okay. So, we're human but kind of like special-not-quite-mutants-human, then?" I said, semi-joking.

"Basically, yes. I've never looked at it that way, but I like that."

"Why us? What makes us so special?" I asked.

"Well, everyone has a different theory on that. Mine is that genetically, there's just something about us... It calls us to Egypt and somehow to the sisterhood— like calling to like and all that. But that feels a bit too serendipitous. Hanan believes that we're all traceable back to Hatshepsut by blood, no matter how diluted. I just don't see, logistically, how that could be possible. Especially because the first sisters weren't related to her, save her daughter, Nefurer."

I sat with that momentarily, my thoughts colliding and trying to fit everything together in a way that made sense.

After that, we got down to work; Salma directed me to focus and led me through some movements to help give my mind something physical to try and direct the magic towards. Again and again, I tried. And again and again, the current flowed under my skin, electric, and begging to be let out, but I just couldn't wrap my mental fingers around it and get a hold of it.

Mentally, it felt like trying to grab hold of an eel, slippery and darting out of the way just as I grazed against it. After what felt like hours, I gave up and begged Salma for a break. Even though it hadn't been difficult or particularly strenuous movements that we'd been doing, I was dripping sweat from exertion, and my arms ached like I'd been lifting weights. I laid on the yoga mat, flat on my back, and threw an arm over my eyes to shade them from the sun, which had made its way across the sky and was currently beating down on top of us.

"Why can't I get this?" I groaned, frustrated and exhausted.

"I don't know," Salma said simply. "I really thought this would be pretty straightforward. Marina had no clue what I was talking about when we first discussed about energy and feeling her magic. So that took a while, but the hardest part is usually just getting the concept."

Though I appreciated her honesty, it rubbed a bit and didn't help the sting of failure.

"Ugh," I groaned again.

"It's fine. We'll get you there, eventually," Salma said. She didn't have quite the same comforting presence as Hanan, but I could tell she was trying. "Let's leave it for the afternoon, and we'll focus on something else. But first, we need food. Let me see what Hanan's got in the fridge." She left me to my misery and went to search for something to eat.

12

Souk

"**N**othing. She's got nothing decent to eat," Salma complained after a few minutes of rummaging around Hanan's kitchen. I still hadn't moved from my spot on the mat. "You want to come with me to the shop, or would you rather stay here and wallow, and I'll bring food back to you?"

I cracked an eyelid open at her, shielding my eyes with my hand. She grinned at me playfully.

"I guess I'll go." I rolled my eyes and groaned again, overly dramatic, as I got to my feet.

We headed out, Salma locking the gate behind her.

"It's Saturday, which means market day. You want to try some proper street food?" My stomach audibly growled in response, and we both laughed. "I'll take that as a 'yes'."

"Ha, definitely a yes!" I said. We got into her tiny car, a plume of papers and wrappers shuffled from the front to the back seat, and a noncommittal grunt of apology sped off towards the market.

Where Hanan was content with the occasional stretch of silence, Salma was not. She filled the car with her presence and constant commentary, pointing out the most off-the-wall details of places as we sped by them, my eyes barely registering something before we passed it. Before I knew it, we were parking and walking towards the *souk*. Andrew and I had seen the market set up on our way to the hotel but hadn't had the chance to stop. It had a similar feel to the *souk* in Bahrain: stalls set up tightly together and the proprietors hawking their wares and fighting for everyone's attention.

"You've been to a *souk*, yeah?" She glanced sidelong at me.

"Oh yes. One of my favorite things to do when we travel." I smirked at her. "I know— don't make eye contact and just keep moving."

She laughed and nodded, pleased I knew how to keep us moving.

"So, this first part is mainly for the tourists, so just plow through, and we'll get to the good stuff."

We wove in and out of the crowd, the scents and sounds of the market vibrant and loud. Spices were piled high and shaped like pyramids, colors as bright as their smells. Bolts and bolts of Egyptian cotton spilled out of one stall. We walked past another with burning frankincense, the cloud of smoke thick and potent, fighting to overwhelm the smells of spices and too many bodies packed into such a small space.

There were stalls with replicas of every Egyptian relic imaginable and stalls with cheap junk made on another side of the world that every market I'd been to tried to advertise as one-of-a-kind. And still, we carried on.

The shouts of the stall owners and the haggling of tourists surrounded us, interspersed with bouts of loud laughter or random shouts of excitement. It was vibrant and clamorous in every direction as we wound through a few alleys that finally opened up to another quieter section of the market. I was ravenous, and way overstimulated. We eventually stopped at a juice stall, and Salma handed a few notes to the gruff-looking man who exchanged them for two cups of bright orange juice. I took a sip and closed my eyes in ecstasy. There was nothing quite like fresh, cold mango juice. I moaned in delight.

"That is what I needed. Thank you!"

Salma sucked down some of her juice and nodded at me.

"That's just to get us through. There will be a queue where we're headed, and I'm far too hungry to be civilized while we wait."

I laughed, understanding the fine line between hungry and hangry all too well.

We wove through more of the market. On this side, the sellers were more reserved and did not jump at everyone who walked past them. There were more fruit and vegetable stalls and sections with everyday items like stationery and toilet paper. This was definitely the place for the locals. People greeted Salma by name as we walked past, calling out what I assumed were the Arabic equivalents of *'How's the family? The kids are getting so big! Are you having any more?'* judging by the plentiful eye rolls that Salma doled out and her clipped but polite responses, lips quirking up in a smile every so often. More than once, I saw a shopper or stall owner open their mouth to say something and then close it again when something tipped over or grabbed their attention. From the look on her face, I knew Salma had to be using magic.

After a few minutes, we arrived at a little cafe. A line of people had gathered out the door and wrapped around the building.

"It moves fast, I promise," she said. "And totally worth the wait, besides. Absolutely the best *koshari* in town."

"It better be," I threatened, smiling at her.

Surprisingly, the long line of people moved quickly, which was a good thing because as more and more people came out, food in hand, the smell was mouthwatering. Finally, it was our turn. I'd given some money to Salma while we waited and told her just to order me whatever she was having, and when she handed me a wide, deep cup, I knew I'd made the right call. Crispy fried shallots covered the top of the rice/pasta/lentil mixture, and I smelled the tang of the vinegary tomato sauce and dug in. The hotel *koshari* had been fine when Andrew and I tried it. It was certainly edible and reasonably enjoyable. But proper, locally made *koshari* was a whole different beast. It was the perfect food to fill our hungry bellies and meander around the market.

Salma stopped at a handful of places, buying things here and there, and I bought some produce to make dinner. When Salma asked what I was making, and I promised veggie tacos, a personal best in my repertoire, she told me she'd be staying for dinner, so I ensured I had plenty.

We walked around the *souk* more, Salma pointing out the best places to get actual Egyptian-made goods. I made sure to buy a couple of thick towels, much like the ones in the guest house, made of the softest Egyptian cotton that I was assured by the shop owner, a tiny wisp of an old man with a bald head and thick, bushy gray eyebrows framing rheumy eyes, would only get softer with use.

That night, I cooked dinner for Salma and Hanan while they taught me about magic. They explained how we drew power from the moon—all phases of it—and how each phase served a different purpose. Though I was learning during a waning crescent (a time of rest and recuperation), they hoped the New Moon (a time of new beginnings) would be when I would really be able to come into an understanding of my powers. The two of them took turns showing me some of the things they could do.

Hanan leaned forward and blew on the candlesticks on the dining table, and the tapers flickered to life, and my arms pimpled with gooseflesh. Salma opened and closed the doors to the garden with nothing more than a thought. She lifted my hair up with a breeze she sent through the room. Hanan pulled Salma towards her and waved a hand in the air. I waited for something to happen. I could almost see a shimmer in the air if I looked closely enough, but everyone was quiet, waiting. I looked up at Hanan and could see her and Salma's mouths moving, but I couldn't hear anything. Hanan waved her hand again, and I could hear them once more.

"Okay, that was amazing!"

I knew that magic was real. I had felt it in the ritual and had seen them perform little bits of it here and there but watching them play with magic and have fun together made it that much more real.

Being around the self-proclaimed soul-mate friends had me missing my own something fierce. Before bed that night, I FaceTimed Edie and Dell, and spent an hour catching up. The timing was serendipitous—Edie had taken a pregnancy test just a few minutes before I called, so she could tell us both about their new addition. She had three little girls, nieces of my heart and we all wondered who would be joining them next.

I fell asleep that night, wistful but feeling better having talked to them. I promised myself I'd do better to talk to them more often—no matter how wonderful everyone in Luxor was, they were no match for Delilah and Edie and the comfort of long-loved friends.

13

Gifts

*G*ood luck tonight, Jules. I am in awe of you and love you more than words can say.

I inhaled the heady scent of flowers delivered from Andrew. Roses—creamy white and a mauve, dusky pink color—interspersed with greenery of all different shapes and sizes marked my first New Moon Ceremony with the group. I placed them on the bedside table and walked to the door, smoothing down my dress and smiling as nerves and excitement fluttered through me in equal measure.

As soon as the sun began to set, we all gathered on the rooftop. We'd spent the day transforming the space. All along the ledges of the walls were dozens of unlit white candles. Standing tall in each corner were candelabras that held even more. Thick, soft cushions, almost as large as a single bed, sat atop a rug that occupied most of the area. Pillows and blankets were piled up on the cushions around a small iron pit in the middle of the space.

We circled the fire pit, with stars and moons laser cut towards the top, a decorative way to feed oxygen into the fire. Along with the physical preparations in the day, Hanan had laid protective and privacy spells along the walls and rooftop so no one would be privy to the ritual. It felt like being inside a bubble, but it was reassuring that no onlookers would witness our magic.

Hanan said something in Arabic; her voice rang out clearly, filling the space. She turned slowly in a circle, gazing over to the edges of the walls. One by one, the candles lit, and gradually, the rooftop glowed with light as the sun went down. After the candles were alight, she focused on the fire pit, willing it to come to life. A chill went down my spine, and I shivered in anticipation. The crackle of the fire, spitting to life, filled the night air with heat, sound, and light.

"Before we get started, Julia, we have gifts for you to welcome you to the Sisterhood."

"Gifts?" I asked, cheeks reddening in surprise. She hadn't told me about this part of the evening when we discussed what to expect tonight.

Renee reached over and squeezed my knee. "Look at them as sort of a magical starter kit and early birthday gifts," she said, smiling.

"Exactly," Hanan said. "We've all brought something that helps our individual crafts or something we've made for you. You can use them to help as your magic takes shape."

She looked to Marwa, who approached me with a small box. I unwrapped it and found a beautiful cut glass perfume bottle. The dark green glass caught the light as I unstopped the gold top and inhaled the familiar scent.

"Myrrh. We anointed you with myrrh from the trees Hatshepsut had planted in front of her temple, and this is a little piece of the ritual to take with you," Marwa explained. She kissed my cheek, walked back, and again took her place in the circle.

Hanan nodded to Salma, who already had a wooden box in her lap, having reached for it while Marwa and I talked.

"Every witch needs crystals. They help harness and direct energy and are good protectors when placed around your house. Or on your person, should you desire."

The box was a wooden puzzle box like those I'd seen countless times in *souks* and markets. The carvings around the edges and sides were flowers and swirls, and a moon was carved on the top in the center. Kneeling just behind me, she reached around and showed me how to slide the catch to release the lid, and I opened it to find a handful of different crystals.

"Each crystal holds different properties or serves a different purpose. There are many specifics, but I'll just give you a vague outline."

Salma pointed each one out to me, her warm breath, sweet from the mango juice she'd been drinking earlier, tickling the back of my neck as she spoke.

Reem came over to me next.

"When I was a little girl, my papa taught me how to carve and whittle wood. I carved this spoon and bowl for you to use in your kitchen. It will help you direct your energy into your food or potions, whatever you cook in the kitchen."

She hugged me gently and went back to her seat. The wooden spoon was well-balanced and solid but not heavy, and the bowl and spoon were smooth. I marveled at how well they had been carved.

Naomi came next, passing by Reem on her way back. She handed me a small, black silk pouch. I undid the strings and tipped the contents out into my hand. A silver ring with two raw stones fell into my palm. One stone was long and thin and dark black. The stone next to it was larger, a smoky gray, and it came to a point at the top and was almost hexagonal in shape.

"A shielding ring of protective stones," Naomi explained as I slipped it on, finding the perfect fit on the middle finger of my right hand. "Black tourmaline for protection, like Salma explained. Smoky quartz is highly protective and also for grounding. It fits, yes?" I nodded. "I had Hanan ask Andrew for help with sizing."

"It's perfect, Naomi. Thank you so much," I said.

She nodded at me but didn't hug me as the others had. She'd been out of town most of the time I'd been in Luxor, so she was still a stranger to me.

Marina waited until Naomi took her seat next to her, and she got up and came over to me, holding a coffee mug in her hand.

"As promised, a mug. I've slipped a piece of paper inside the cup, which has the spell I use every morning when I stir my coffee. It's a little thing that helps me start the day and bring positive energy. It's important to remember that everything can be a ritual for us. Even the mundane making of our morning coffee. It's all about intent."

She touched my shoulder lightly, and I looked up at her in time for her to kiss both my cheeks and then turn to head back toward her seat.

I glanced down at the mug, a beautiful hand-thrown, curvy shape with a perfectly fitted handle. The glaze was a shimmery blue that caught the light of the fire and almost sparkled. There were carved and hand-painted gold stars all over it—reminiscent of the ceiling in Hatshepsut's temple. I pulled the slip of paper out of the mug, opened it up, and read Marina's spell.

Whilst stirring your tea or coffee clockwise, simply say:
'Give me the strength to face the day
no matter what comes my way.
I am open to the magic that fills me

and honor the light which guides me.'

I smiled and nodded my thanks to Marina. Having waited until I finished reading the spell, Renee handed me a velvet pouch. Inside was a deck of cards I recognized as Tarot cards. A little shudder went through me, old habits and ingrained beliefs from my childhood battling their way to the surface. I could remember the lectures about devil worship and fortune telling, and I knew it all to be stuff and nonsense now, but old habits die hard, as they say.

"Tarot is an art. The cards don't tell fortunes and can't predict the future, but they *can* help guide you or help you see things more clearly. Learning and getting used to them takes time, but I'll help you if you wish. I was gifted my first cards when I was twelve and had my first moon cycle." Renee smiled wistfully as her memories floated through her mind. "My mother was raised Pagan, and she and my aunties all celebrated my first moon cycle and the transition that comes with womanhood, and this was part of it. You'll need to get to know your deck, but it's the Rider-Waite—fairly universal and easy to begin with."

"Thank you, Renee. I'll definitely take all the help I can get. One of my best friends reads Tarot, so she can also help." Renee nodded.

Hasina turned toward me and handed me a book, a bundle of herbs, and a large and beautiful shell the size of my hand. The shell's inside was bowl-like and incandescent with purples and blues, glistening as I moved it in the light of the fire.

"A herbiary—a guide to plants, herbs, their magical uses, and lore. A bundle of sage I've grown for cleansing and clearing negative energy. It's one of the most useful tools you can keep in your home. The smoke will cleanse your home, can cleanse your crystals, and even yourself. The abalone shell can withstand the burning bundle if you want to rest it there, but it carries healing properties in it as well. Be blessed, sister."

I quietly thanked her and placed her gifts in the growing pile.

Hanan was last, and she stood up and approached me, holding a brown paper box in her hand. I slipped the lid off the box and found a large, glimmering white stone pillowed on soft cotton. It was oval-shaped and set in dark gold, the raw edges coming up around the sides of the stone. It was strung on a matching satellite chain with tiny beads every couple of inches in the links. Hanan reached over, lifted it out of the box, and stood up, motioning for me to do the same. I'd been sitting cross-legged for long enough that the blood rushed towards my feet, pins and needles shooting down my legs. I shifted uncomfortably from foot to foot as discreetly as possible with eight pairs of eyes on me.

"When we undergo our ritual in the temple, we are all gifted with an orb of light that shines within us. It is said that the orb is a piece of the moon taken from Hatshepsut herself and gifted to each of us, a reminder of our power and purpose." She slipped the necklace over my head, and the heavy stone rested just under my breasts. "This is a reminder of that inner light, so you can wear it or hang it in your house as a reminder of your power and the moment you became one of us."

I reached up and held the stone in my hand. It was warm to the touch and shimmered in the blaze of the fire—flecks of every color iridescent in the light. Hanan embraced me, her face warm from the fire against my cheek and her flowery scent around me.

She whispered in my ear just for me to hear. "I am so glad to have you as my sister."

The emotions that had been threatening all night spilled down onto my cheeks. I was overwhelmed with gratitude, joy, and even hope that this night would be what I needed to unlock the magic inside of me.

"Thank you so much, everyone," I said, my body pleasantly warm and suffused with the fire and my budding friendship with them.

Hanan let go of me, pausing to hold my arms and look directly at me. She smiled before walking back to her place in the circle.

14

In the Dark of the New Moon

"Sisters, we gather here tonight to bless the New Moon. It is the time we set our intentions for the coming month, to renew ourselves and to bless Julia's new beginning with her magic."

Her eyes shimmered in the glowing candlelight as she looked across the group at me. She reached out to either side, and Salma reached out to grasp one hand and Reem's on the other. One by one, each sister reached out and clasped hands. Renee was to my right, her hand firm but warm, and Hasina was to my left, her hand cooler than Renee's but solid.

Once we were all connected in a circle, I felt a rush of energy so intense that I startled myself with an audible gasp. Renee squeezed my hand in reassurance. My eyes fluttered closed, and I sucked in a deep breath, trying to surrender myself to the sensation. My skin felt like it was pulled tight, not uncomfortable, just tight with the magic current under my skin, flowing and rippling so much that I was sure I could see it if I looked.

Hanan guided us all to breathe deeply, in through our noses and out through our mouths. The smoke from the fire danced around us, the burning wood laced with something herby that Hanan had told me would put us in a trance-like state to loosen inhibitions just enough to calm nerves and open everyone up to the energy of the circle.

They began to hum, the same chanting they'd done in the temple. I found myself joining in, on some visceral and impossible level, knowing the way of it. It could have been hours or minutes; I wasn't sure. Time wasn't important then, but we slowed and came to stillness, still joined.

Hearts beating together.

Energy pulsing as one.

Hanan tilted her face, and her voice rang out in the sudden, throbbing quiet.

My mind was light and heavy all at once, the scent of herbs filling me as the fire burned brightly. Tendrils of smoke wafted through the night air as Hanan's lyrical voice wove through, intertwining and becoming one with the smoke.

"She's calling down the power of the new moon," Renee whispered in my ear. "She is asking for the moon, in her restful stage, to bless you and call forth your magic as she makes herself seen again in the coming days." Renee continued to quietly translate Hanan's incantation, speaking of rebirth, renewal, and the setting of intentions.

Slowly, Hanan's voice trailed off, as did Renee's, voices vibrating out into the darkness.

Quietly, we sank to the ground, listening. To ourselves. To the night sky, empty and void of the moon's presence.

I heard silence. Not even our breath stirred a response.

Eyes closed, I saw a kaleidoscope of shapes and colors. They danced like the flames behind my eyes.

The shapes became forms. Became female, lush breasts and generous hips sensuous in the moonlight. Dancing beneath its ripe fullness. Calling to her. Calling to me.

I danced with them behind my eyes, in the smoke, in the fire.

Magic crackled in the air, electricity sending pulses down my spine, tingling across every inch of my body. Or the bodies behind my eyes. Or both. Called down like lightning, shards of the moon alive within us.

Within me.

The fire crackled and spit and slowly calmed. The smoke receded, tendrils flitting into the night air in search of new lungs. The visions behind my eyes slowly faded away, chasing after the smoke.

More moments passed. My mind slowly and gently began to clear, and I tried to make sense of the night. My body was alive, humming in response to the night. The air was cool, but my skin felt hot. Hasina shifted and passed me a jug of cold water. I filled my glass, suddenly grateful and unable to pour quickly enough, before passing the pitcher to my other side. I drank greedily, throat throbbing and suddenly parched. The water was blissfully cold and sweet and sent a shock of awareness through me, fully pulling me out of the trance.

I looked around at everyone else in varying states of thirst, one jug replaced by another. Passed through the circle, each of my sisters gratefully and greedily drinking.

Thirst-slaked, we set our intentions for the coming month. Hanan and I had spent a lot of time talking about intent and what it meant. She had helped me think about what I was going to write. I took a breath to focus and began...

I am thankful for starting this new journey with magic.

It allows me to feel powerful and like a part of something bigger than myself.

I am thankful for stepping into my power, grabbing ahold of my energy, and taking control.

It allows me to feel joy, be in control, and feel like a contributing member of the group.

I am thankful for being humble and open to learning.

It allows me to feel like a student of magic and a part of the group.

I am thankful for letting go of self-doubt.

It allows me to feel worthy, secure, and love for myself.

We also had bay leaves upon which we were to write a word or phrase to burn on the fire, sending our intentions out into the universe. On my leaves, I wrote the words *new journey, let go of self-doubt* and *magic.* I placed the paper and the leaves under my bed roll, following the direction of Hasina, who had finished first and turned back towards the center of the circle. Slowly, everyone stopped and turned their attention back to Hanan.

"Tonight, we'll sleep under the clear night sky, letting our bodies and energy rest and renew themselves in the dark of the hidden moon."

She spoke slowly and clearly, letting her words fill the space. I wondered if there was something more in her words tonight, some extra oomph of power, or if it was just the ceremonial feel to everything mixed with whatever herb was burning and responsible for the headiness and floating of my mind. The last few hours felt almost like a fever dream.

"Tonight, we'll meditate fully reclined, and I ask that each of you take a turn sitting with our new sister. Lie together, sending your energy and channeling it to Julia, letting your magic get to know her, allowing us to connect and integrate fully." She paused, looking around the circle of women. "Remember, when we are together, we are our strongest. We are nine now, and nine is a significant number. Let us remember as we connect tonight."

Slowly and purposefully, we let go of each other's hands. We took our seats, each woman finding a comfortable spot on their bedrolls, further from the fire, before lying back, closing their eyes, and breathing deeply. I stared at the flames in front of me for a few moments, entranced by the movement, before laying down in the yogic pose of *savasana*—arms by my side, palm supplicant. I closed my eyes and slowly started to count my breaths. There was a quiet breeze in the night air, cool against my skin, though it was welcome with the heat of the fire just a few feet in front of me. The sounds of the flames and the deep breaths slowly becoming in sync filled my ears.

The energy shifted, and someone lay down next to me. They lightly place their hand in my upturned palm. It took everything in me not to open my eyes and peek at who lay beside me, but I refrained, letting the moment of connection be enough.

Within a few moments of breathing together, a warm rush washed through my body, almost like an internal breeze. It wasn't as strong as the rush from the whole circle, but it was no less flustering, and I struggled to stay still and let it wash through me. When I settled my thoughts, a clear image crossed my mind: a picture of Reem in her kitchen. I somehow knew that it was her beside me.

And so it went. Each sister took a turn with me, and I managed enough self-control each time not to sneak a look. The shock of shared energy, now that I could anticipate it, became less unsettling and more intriguing. My trepidation fell away more and more each time. And each time, I got a sense of who I was with. It was odd and a bit disconcerting, but mainly in the way that new things so often are. After everyone had taken a turn meditating with me, Hanan closed the night out, guiding us to put our bay leaves on the fire and see our intentions off into the universe, the leaves popping and hissing as they caught.

Quietly, we slipped into our makeshift beds to sleep under the night sky. As I drifted off, I felt someone lay next to me. I smiled, thinking someone wanted to lend comfort or give a little extra magic boost. I fought back the urge to look until I couldn't take it anymore. I opened my eyes and found the space beside me empty.

I stayed awake for a long time and watched the candles and fire burn low before they eventually winked out when Hanan fell into a deep sleep. Once more, I felt the presence of someone else next to me, not as familiar as the first time. But, when I looked again, no one was there.

15

Lessons & Connections

Mastering magic was a struggle. Everyone was patient with me, and we slowly started to become friends. They all took turns coming to Hanan's house or inviting me into their homes, encouraging me and showing me how they manifested magic in their daily lives. It wasn't long before I could manage a few basic spells, but the magic seemed faint and weak compared to everyone else. They all promised me that it was hard initially and to just keep practicing. Seeing and learning from each of them was incredible, but I couldn't help but wonder if they were just being kind and were also frustrated with my progress.

Our magic was light-based—both our innate inner light and the light from the moon that imbued the ritual waters, so light and heat were at the heart of everything they did. Everyone had the same sort of basic abilities—they could manipulate the energy around them to push or pull like the tides of the moon. From lighting candles to manipulating a person's internal light or energy to brewing potions for all sorts of things, there was magic everywhere in their lives.

Reem's magical abilities felt the most familiar to me. She was the resident 'mom' of the group, well, she and Marwa both, but Reem took it upon herself to keep everyone fed and plied with treats. She saturated her food with magic—encouraging good health and strength in everything that left her kitchen. She was meditative in her food prep and joyful in her incantations over frying pans and simmering pots. I was comfortable stirring ingredients and watching her work in her large, airy kitchen. If anything was going to be my *thing*, I felt like the kitchen witchery was it. Her grimoire read like a cookbook—recipes and notes splattered with food stains and turmeric-stained fingerprints.

And I was decent at it. But only just. I loved cooking, and its familiarity made everything more accessible. Adding a touch of magic felt like nothing more than adding an extra dash of flavor. It took a small success in the form of a plate of cookies infused with nostalgia that had Hanan happily reminiscing about one of her aunties for me to finally feel like I was getting somewhere and at least had something to offer that was more than beginner tricks like lighting candles.

✦

Marina's approach to magic was slightly different than everyone else's. She was the most adept at meditation and harnessing her focus. She and I spent hours on meditation cushions doing everything from chanting mantras to breathing exercises that pushed me past my breath control limits.

Originally from Italy, Marina came to Egypt with a former girlfriend and found her way to Hatshepsut's temple with Salma as her tour guide. With a ritual similar to mine under her belt, she decided to stay in Egypt. When her girlfriend refused to stay and didn't even try to keep things going long distance, Marina broke it off with her and never looked back. She split her time between Italy and Luxor. As the social media and website manager for a few companies, she could travel and do her job anywhere.

Off the meditation cushion, Marina was a bit scatterbrained and artistic, and she explained that she had always felt an excess amount of energy flowing through her. Where my power manifested itself into anxiety and panic attacks, Marina's seemed to have just craved an artistic outlet. She painted and sketched, but pottery was the medium that called to her the most.

She'd found pottery when she was eighteen and loved the meditative aspect of throwing clay on the wheel and letting her hands and the clay figure out how to communicate and create something beautiful. It was an easy transition for the magic to entwine with her art. My favorite mug in Hanan's pantry was one of Marina's, which explained why I'd loved it so much—she'd imbued it with her magic, just as she'd done with the one she had made for me.

Her grimoire was filled with sketches, clay and paint smears, mantras, sigils, and runes she had dreamed up.

"I like to let the clay tell me what to do," she said in her studio. I was bent over the pottery wheel, hands and arms covered in wet clay while I did my best to manipulate the lump in front of me into something vaguely resembling a bowl.

"The clay is telling me that it's slippery and doesn't want to cooperate," I joked.

"It takes time to learn," she said, chuckling. "My first bowls have corners if it makes you feel any better."

I laughed. "It does, a little bit."

"So, just feel it. Let it run through your fingertips and the palms of your hands. Surrender to the natural shapes instead of forcing what you think you want.," she said in her thick Tuscan accent. She shoved an errant hair out of her face and swiped clay on her cheek, like blush. "As far as the magic—I just pour energy into it. I go into a sort of meditation and let whatever comes up be my focus. Sometimes it's health or protection or sweet dreams. I sort of zero in on whatever comes up first and create a mantra around it, and it comes out in the clay."

I nodded. "Okay, that makes sense."

"I also scratch a sigil on the bottom that I make from whatever word encompasses the magical...vibe, I guess, so I know what each is for. Then I paint sigils or spells into the glaze, and it really digs in with the firing."

We worked for a little while longer. I had to start from scratch a couple of times, but I finally got something that resembled a bowl-like shape that I imbued with a feeling of home. I planned to make it a catch-all bowl for our entryway to welcome us home each day. Marina had thrown three mug bodies and would add handles later. I was amazed by her and excited to come back and try to learn more again.

"Do you want to go see some of the Egyptian potters?" Marina asked as I was scrubbing the clay from my hands after we'd finished.

"Yeah, that sounds cool; I'm starting to get a little stir-crazy if I'm honest," I said sheepishly. I didn't want to sound ungrateful, but I'd been spending so much time learning or trying to learn magic that I was feeling a little like the walls were closing in. I was a bit of a homebody when in my *own* home, but the magic and mystery of Egypt was still calling to me, and I knew there was so much more to see.

"I wondered about that," she said. "I know you've been focused on learning all this, but you can't forget that you're in a land filled with history and magic. You need to get out and see it!"

And so we did. We hailed a cab and sped through Luxor to get to a pottery school on the West Bank run by two brothers Marina had befriended. They were incredibly patient and kind and lit up, talking all about the history of pottery in the region. They were so excited to show off their designs, which I recognized from our hotel stay.

We toured their studio, and I watched, mesmerized, as they manipulated the clay to form figures as quickly as Marina had done with her own.

All of their pieces were hand-painted and had the look and feel of vintage art. There was nothing modern about them—but in the best way. The colors they used—rich indigo and earthy tones—echoed those in the temples at their feet, and it felt like they were honoring their ancestors in everything they produced. I bought a few pieces to keep and some to send to people as gifts.

✦

Marwa was everything you could possibly want in a mom, or at least everything *I* longed for. My own mother had left me to my own devices for a multitude of reasons. Our relationship broke down—a gap as wide as a canyon separating us, and anger and bitterness became the emotions I associated with her. Marwa was the opposite—she was patient, kind, understanding, and warm. I looked forward to our time together. She was organized and my greatest asset when working on my grimoire. I had been afraid to write anything in it for fear of messing it up, but Marwa encouraged mess-ups and mishaps as part of the process.

About a month into my stay, I was at Marwa's house, perched on a barstool at her kitchen counter as she fixed a bite of lunch for the both of us, and when she found out that I still hadn't marked up my book. She left the kitchen momentarily and brought in an old, thick tome, brown leather cover worn with use, the color lighter on the edges from her fingers. She sat it on the counter and gestured at me to open it. I cracked the spine open and flipped through the pages. I could see the multiple crossings and scribbles she'd spent a lifetime cultivating.

"You must learn that there is no... I'm trying to think of what to say in English. In Arabic, we say something like *I have my ink pen and pot til the grave,*" she explained, waving her hand, searching through the air for the right words. "It is nicer in Arabic, I think. It rhymes, at least. I am meaning to say maybe that you will not command, but that's not right."

"Um, maybe expert?"

She shook her head and tilted her face up, thinking. I wracked my brain, trying to follow her train of thought.

"No. Is different than that. It is... when you are in control. Have a firm grip, and it answers you always as expected?"

"Oh, like to master something? I think that's probably what we'd say." Marwa clapped her hands.

"Yes! Master. You will never be the *master* of the magic. It is not your slave. So you will write. And mark it out. And write again. Your lifetime will be full of learning, and the book will be a record of sorts, showing you how far you've come and how far you have left to go. *The ink pot and pen with you to the grave.*"

I smiled at her, still nervous to mess something up but excited to begin.

"Okay. So what all do you include?"

"Anything. Any spells you have learned or are working on. Anything related to your magic—from the moon to herbs or crystals. It is a way to make notes. To ask yourself questions and then answer them later." she smiled, encouraging me. "Everyone's books are different. Whatever you find yourself drawn to is what you need to write down. Your intuition is a powerful thing and will guide you."

My face betrayed my doubts, and Marwa took a deep breath and looked at me, cognac-colored eyes glittering with emotion.

"Julia, you *must* learn to trust yourself."

I looked away, cheeks aflame with embarrassment. Marwa moved closer to me, food forgotten, and wrapped her arms around me. My throat tightened, and my eyes threatened to release the tears that were just there at the surface.

"I'm so sorry." I fretted. "I just... It's a lot. I feel like I'm such a mess right now. I cry at the drop of a hat lately." I swiped at my cheek, a rogue tear slipping down of its own accord. My throat was still tight with emotion, but I carried on. "I didn't have a great relationship with my mom. She was strict and... cold in many ways. And I was a difficult teenager."

Marwa clucked her tongue at me. "No child is difficult. Only difficult situations arise. I'm sorry you were made to feel like it was you who was the problem."

"Oh, I was challenging, make no mistake," I responded, but Marwa gently shook her head. "But my mother was more concerned with 'serving' my father and letting him take charge of raising me. She took a more apathetic stance. Her answer was always to fall in line and stop asking questions."

Marwa looked at me with surprise and disgust, mingling on her features.

"How can a mother do that?" she asked. "I'm sorry, Julia. I don't mean to speak ill of your mother, but I can't imagine *not* encouraging my children, and especially my daughter, to challenge the status quo. Was she like that with your siblings as well?"

"Oh, I'm an only child," I said. "She was diagnosed with cervical cancer after she had me and had to have a hysterectomy. I always sort of felt like she blamed me for not being able to have more children."

"Oh *habebty*, I am so sorry. Surely that can't be," Marwa sputtered.

"Maybe not, but it always felt that way. And I was never her perfect image of a child. I struggled in school and had some... things happen in high school that really drove that wedge between us, and there was just no coming back from it." I trailed off but straightened, resigned.

"Well, it's never too late," Marwa said, trying to comfort me, and I sagged against her.

"It is now. My parents died in a car crash a few years ago," I said.

Marwa didn't respond; she just held me, gently kissing me on top of the head and suffusing me with love and peace. It struck me then that I'd shared more with a woman I barely knew than I had with my own mother in the years I knew her. At that moment, something broke open inside of me, finally beginning to knit together the edges of the old wound that never seemed to heal. I had always known that family was who you chose, not necessarily who you were born into. Sitting in Marwa's bright kitchen, her arms around me, trying her best to build me up and shower me in friendship, that knowing clicked into place. I felt a wave of gratitude for the women who were slowly becoming my family. I leaned back into Marwa and reached up, my hand on her arms.

"Thank you," I whispered.

She gave me one last squeeze and slowly let me go, glancing at me to ensure I was okay before walking around and finishing our lunch.

We ate together quietly after that, making small talk but skirting carefully around my earlier revelations, which I was fine with. After cleaning up from our salads, Marwa and I worked on my grimoire together. She explained that everyone used different words in different languages to help them direct their spells and, after a time and with plenty of practice, incantations would only be partially necessary.

"We Egyptians use Arabic now, but sometimes Hanan uses English. It depends on the spell. Some believe that wherever your ancestry is from is the type of magic and language that's best suited." She looked me over for a moment. "That seems a little arcane, I know. But look at it like this: our DNA carries our ancestors' knowledge. Everything from memory to trauma to a penchant for spicy foods or disease. It's written into our bones. To go back as far as we can—to the time when magic was alive—those ancestors used whatever language they spoke, and the magic answered."

I nodded, following where she was going.

"So, when magic was strongest and most easily accessed, it answered their call however they called it. If we can figure out what that means for each of us, maybe we'll have a better handle?" I asked.

Marwa nodded, smiling at my understanding.

"Exactly. It is no science. Just the educated guess of an old woman."

I smiled and shook my head at the old woman's comment. She *was* old enough to be my mother, but she had a vitality about her that made her seem so young.

"Drew and I did DNA tests last year, and I know I'm mostly Western European- concentrated in the British Isles and Scandinavia—split equally there."

"Okay, perfect. That's where we begin. We can research mythology and religious beliefs in those areas, and you can find what feels the most...I think, nature, I would say?"

"Natural?" I supplied.

Marwa nodded. Her English was perfect—far better than my Arabic—but occasionally, we had to sort out a word if she couldn't think of it. I had learned quite quickly that many Arabic phrases or words just didn't translate to English, but we did our best to muddle through when we had to.

"Yes. Natural. You find that and learn. It is not wholly the language. The intent matters most, but the language seems to lend a little extra strength."

"I'll call my grandma tonight and see if she knows anything. My grandfather was an amateur historian and did loads of research into our family tree."

16

The Gift of Gram

We spent the rest of the afternoon going through Marwa's grimoire, her pointing out the things she used most often and encouraging me to take notes and keep track of things I thought I'd use. Hanan swung by to pick me up on her way home from work, and we ended up staying at Marwa's for dinner. By the time we got back to Hanan's, I was exhausted from a long day, but I called my Gram, hopeful she could shed some light on what I needed to know. She answered on the first ring like she'd been waiting for my call, and I smiled, happy to hear her voice.

"Hi, Gram!" I said, plopping down on the bed.

"Hello, my sweet Jules." Her voice was warm like honey and as comforting as the sweaters she used to knit me when I was younger.

"What are you up to today?" I asked, making small talk before diving straight in.

We spent a few minutes catching up, and I talked around the fact that I was still in Egypt, telling a white lie that Andrew was already in bed for the night.

"So, Gram," I said. "I have a weird question about our ancestry," I said.

"Go on," she said.

"I know my DNA traced back to the British Isles and Scandinavia."

She made a slight sound of agreement on the line.

"But, I'm curious about some of their beliefs. Like...religion and that sort of stuff."

"Okay. Well, you know Gramps went through that phase, after the orchids, I think, and before the clocks." She paused, mentally going through the random obsessive phases my grandfather had gone through once he'd retired and had more time on his hands than he knew what to do with.

"It doesn't matter." I had a clear picture of her in my head, waving off her thoughts, her hands always moving when she talked. "Anyway, he went through that phase where he tracked down as much as he could about our ancestry. He did both sides of your tree so you'd have a clear picture. Well, that, and he hit dead ends with ours, but he was still on that train for quite a while." She chuckled quietly.

I knew the pain of missing him was still fresh, even after four years, but I was happy to hear her laugh at the memories instead of just feeling sorrow, which had been the case for a long time.

"Okay. I thought so. He sent me a hard copy and an email copy of the whole thing so I can do some digging on the Davis side. But what about your side? Do you remember how far back Gramps could trace for you?"

Gram was quiet for a moment, thinking.

"I don't recall the exact date, but I know it was pretty far. Into the 1600s, and at that point, most everyone was Scandinavian, with the odd Prussian thrown in here and there until my grandparents immigrated to the States in the 1900s. We'd always been told that the family was traceable to the Vikings, but we never found evidence. Just old family stories."

"Let's assume Vikings. That would be Norse Mythology, right?"

"Right, dear. The Norse gods before Christianity came into play. I've always read that the Vikings never had a name for their religion. I mean, it very well wouldn't have been called *mythology* while they were practicing it, would it?"

"No, that's true." I paused, weighing out what I would say to get the information I needed from her. "So, do you think they would have believed in magic?" I asked, nerves rattling and fingers crossed that she wouldn't ask too many questions.

"Ooh, that's a curious question." She tittered. "I would imagine so. Paganism was rampant before Christianity took over and all but stamped it out. I could never figure out why people felt it impossible to include both ways of believing and have them work together. I know we've talked about it before, but it was always what was so off-putting about the way your mother and father were trying to raise you—that close-minded 'this is the only way' nonsense just doesn't work for me." She sighed, an exasperated sigh that she still let out even after my parents were gone. She couldn't quite forgive them for things they said and did when I was younger. And she was right; we'd talked about it before, *a lot*. But, as painful as it could be to talk about them and everything that had happened, it was also reassuring to be reminded that Gram was always there on my side, fighting for me even now.

"Well, it obviously didn't work for me either, Gram." I laughed, trying to lighten her mood. Talking about my parents always took her down a dark path I didn't want to go down.

"And thank goodness for that, Julia," she replied, relieved. "I will never forget the day you swore Gramps and me to secrecy and told us about Andrew. I have never been so proud in all my life. I know it wasn't easy to keep it from your parents and take the leap, but I am so grateful you did. I know the universe was at work there, bringing him into your life when you needed a friend most and then letting that friendship evolve into something more."

I smiled, remembering that day, my heart racing and palms sweating as I took the chance and told them that Andrew and I were seeing each other. It went against everything my parents wanted. My grandparents were so supportive and happy to cover for me, cook for him, and give us another safe place beside his parents' house. It helped that they were a couple of towns over from where we lived, so it felt far enough removed from their house to be a safe haven. She and my grandfather had been our witnesses when we got married, along with Andrew's parents, the only people I truly cared about being at our wedding. She had cried at our courthouse nuptials, relieved that I had taken charge of my life and chosen love and happiness.

"I know, Gram. I think that, too." I smiled. "I know it hurt Mom and Dad something fierce for me to run away like I did. But I just couldn't live the life they had planned out for me. I was so miserable trying to be the good little girl they expected me to be... I just couldn't do it anymore." I trailed off, not wanting to get any more profound than that.

"Jules. Your parents were so blinded by their own goals and their own wishes that they couldn't see that they were making you sick with unhappiness. You had all but disappeared inside of yourself for the longest time. That other boy was rotten to the core, stealing you from us. It wasn't until Drew came along and helped you pull yourself out that I recognized you again. I won't ever be sorry that you chose to live your own life, sweet girl. I won't. And you shouldn't either." We didn't often talk about my childhood anymore. For the most part, everything had been said many times, but every now and then, the ghosts wanted attention, and we had no choice but to give it to them.

We talked for a few more minutes before ending our call on a lighter note, the conversation with her lifting me like it always did. I went to bed with my mind racing with questions about Norse mythology and whatever old pagan rituals might have been performed so long ago in my ancestral line. I spent the next few days engrossed in research—scratching Norse runes into my grimoire—finally cracking it open and putting it to good use.

17

The Devils We Know

Two weeks after the New Moon, Hasina came over to talk to Hanan about the Brotherhood. I had planned to bow out and spend the late afternoon taking a nap or catching up with Drew, but they both encouraged me to stay, another lesson to tuck away, building the bigger picture of the Sisterhood.

After Thutmose III became pharaoh and brought his supporters into the fold, people looking for power and prestige, that desire for power continued to spread and make its way across the globe. Secrets of the Brotherhood made their way across time. From state advisors whispering in their leaders' ears to infiltrating Rome and influencing the leaders there who spread it further as they spread God's word and exerted force onto the societies they took over, throughout empire takeovers and falls, and even to an exclusive gentlemen's club in Victorian London where the foundation for a secret society in North America was born, to the far reaches of Asia, and everywhere in between; the Brotherhood was there.

As time passed, the truth of things was watered down, and the magical aspects of the story became nonexistent. The Brotherhood, so intent on stamping out magic in women and taking their power for their own, had morphed into something like a good old boys' club. Powerful men sequestered in groups—the kind of men and the kind of power that feeds itself and grows bigger and bigger; each arm of the Brotherhood looking out for themselves, searching out money and influence. The type of power that corrupts.

They explained that the Brotherhood's influence was behind big moments in history when witchcraft was rooted out, or powerful women were stamped out of existence. Names like Boudicca, Hypatia, Tituba, and Bridget Bishop stopped me in my tracks. Women who had been nothing more than words in books I'd read, or stories I'd heard suddenly took up space in my heart. How many women had succumbed to the whims of men who wanted to stamp out their existence just because their power and strength threatened them?

I thought about the women I was learning to call sisters now and all the women who had come before us and had lost their lives to ignorance and lies perpetuated by a power-hungry, long-dead king who made sure to sow seeds of hatred before he left the Earth.

The job now was to keep tabs on the known groups that were extensions of the Brotherhood, no matter how indirect. While there had been no active threat against the Sisterhood directly in a long time, ensuring they knew where any attack was coming from to stay ahead of it was the name of the game.

Hasina flipped open her laptop, quickly typing in an obscene-ly long password with little effort, and pulled open a file that expanded into a world map. All around the digital map were red circles peppered across various parts of the world. My eye was drawn to the US, where there was a large circle on both the East and West Coasts. Before I could open my mouth to ask, Hasina hovered over the circle in Europe, and a vast spider web of data pulled up. Hanan shook her head.

"Uh uh. Not the techie way. You know I can't follow along this crazy analytical super nerd map," Hanan said, and I snorted.

Hasina rolled her eyes but finagled her tech in a way that consolidated it into expandable files labeled by city. Europe didn't have many factions of the Brotherhood—London, Rome, and Moscow were the only cities listed.

"We covered Moscow and Rome last; let's peek at London."

Hasina clicked on one of my favorite cities in the world, and a file opened up that said *The Hellfire Club* in large, bold letters. She clicked, and it expanded into a list of names. Another bit of tech woo, and the list shifted into individual pages. I settled back in my seat, letting Hasina and Hanan talk about the club and its members, nothing too worrisome or exciting. I let my mind wander as they scrolled through each page. It was fascinating to think that these old groups were together only because of something that happened a few thousand years ago, and yet they had no clue why they were formed.

"So, why continue to have such a huge number? I don't get it," I said, interrupting Hasina's scrolling. Each page was a sort of information sheet on the members, with a small passport-style photo in the corner of the screen.

"We don't really know. It's all conjecture at this point," Hasina said, pushing her glasses further up her nose and breaking eye contact with the computer screen. "We assume that Thutmose and those first followers wanted to keep another Hatshepsut from coming into power. He tried to erase her from history and spread rumors about what a horrible ruler she'd been to try and discourage anyone from supporting anyone but himself as pharaoh. He wanted to keep power in his direct line and to be able to shift it only to those he felt 'worthy' of holding power and who were loyal to him."

"Okay. Sort of a *women are inferior to men*, thing?"

"For them, yes. We've actually had male members in our history—men who have an affinity for magic and want the same things we do—equality, decency, et cetera. Our small group now just happens to be all female," Hanan answered.

"The Brotherhood is all male. They demand subservience and want to hoard as much power and influence as possible, taking it away from women. So there aren't female members, but these men have women standing behind them supporting them," Hasina paused and rolled her eyes, unable to fathom that sort of relationship, I guessed, and Hanan picked up where she left off.

"We're talking groups of men who come from old money. Politicians, community leaders, business owners...the extremely wealthy who cultivate connections within their groups that allow them to get away with all manner of corruption."

A shudder went through me, reality settling in that this wasn't all just a game of sorts. It was easy to think of things in the abstract until we were sitting here, looking through actual groups with real people's names attached.

"We *do* think that there is a smaller faction who truly knows the brotherhood's history and who wants to find the scrolls and delve into dark magic for a whole host of reasons," Hasina said. "But that's a separate sort of meeting. This is just double-checking that no one's stepped out of line right now, and there's nothing crazy going on."

"So what do we look out for with these spread-out groups?" I asked.

"We just keep an eye on things," Hasina responded, returning to her scrolling. "We ensure that if anyone is taking on a more influential role in society, we just watch it. We perform spells a few times a year just to tamp down any negative energy flowing around and send positive energy into the world. Keeping an eye on these guys helps give us some direction if needed. Obviously, it doesn't fix everything, but it's the best we can do."

She closed the European file; she and Hanan were satisfied with what they'd gone over.

"Next up, your home country," she said, with my full attention now as she clicked open a folder labeled *North America*.

"I can make some guesses as to some famous assholes from the states whose names are probably on that list." I joked, and we all chuckled.

"You'd be surprised," Hanan said. "Not all of them are obvious. And some people are just assholes and not part of a secret brotherhood."

Hasina had scrolled down, and I recognized a face or name here and there—newsworthy politicians with loud mouths and low morals. And then my heart stopped as a truly familiar face scrolled by.

"Wait! Stop! Scroll back up," I exclaimed, startling Hasina.

She looked at me and slowly moved the mouse up, landing on a face I'd spent years trying to forget. I stared at the photo before me, and my skin flushed, sweat breaking out all down my spine. The blood drained from my face, and I opened my mouth to formulate one of the many questions swirling around in my mind, but I just gaped like a fish out of water. Panic bubbled up to the surface, and I made a strangled noise in my throat.

"Julia! Are you okay? You look like you've seen a ghost," Hanan asked.

I managed to hold up my hand and motioned for them to give me just a moment. I closed my eyes and tried to settle myself, heart racing, fluttering against my ribs like a bird trying to escape its cage.

The walls started pressing in on me and my tongue tasted like electricity. I stood up and stumbled outside, sucking in the fragrant, clean air in great gulps. I don't know how long I stood outside in the fading light, trying to get a handle on my raging emotions, but soon I heard quiet footsteps behind me, and someone stood at my side. I knew without looking over that it was Hanan. Besides the clean smell of jasmine giving her away, there was just something steadying about her presence, and we'd grown close over the last few weeks that I'd been living there.

"Julia?" Hanan asked, her voice gentle, carrying over the quiet hum of the garden, alive with bees and birdsong. I scrubbed my hands over my face, hoping that what I saw was wrong. I took a steadying breath, but it stuck in my throat, and I felt like a scared sixteen-year-old girl again.

"I recognized that man. The one I had Hasina scroll back to," I said, eyes downcast, embarrassed because I knew what was coming.

"You know one of them? Are you sure?"

I nodded solemnly.

"Actually, a family. I think they were all listed. The Mitchell's in North Carolina. In the States. I..." I trailed off, really dreading tearing this wound open again. "There's...um...history... there with them." The last part was barely above a whisper. I felt myself slipping away—an old defense mechanism adopted by my teenage self to try and protect myself.

Hanan paused, treading carefully, realizing I was about to spook far too easily.

"Hey, Julia. You're safe here. And you don't have to tell us your history with them. I'll need to review them with Hasina, but we aren't terribly concerned with the factions in the States. They're more of a fraternity instead of seeking out the scrolls. I doubt any of them know about all of this, in truth."

I nodded, swallowing down the panic that threatened to overwhelm me.

"I'm fine." I took another steadying breath, which got deep into my lungs and shored up my defenses. "I can talk about it. It just... it just took me by surprise, is all." I met Hanan's eyes and read the concern on her face as plain as if it were typed across her forehead.

"Let me just take a minute to get myself together, and then I'll tell you and Hasina everything."

"You're sure?" Hanan asked. "You don't have to do this now if you don't want to."

I hugged Hanan, needing a kind touch as much as wanting to offer something in the way of thanks for not pressuring me.

"I'm sure. If I don't get it out, it'll just haunt me later, and they've haunted me plenty."

I let Hanan go and turned towards the guest house, needing a moment to splash some water on my face and get it together.

I barely made it through the doors before tears spilled down my cheeks. My throat was tight, and I sobbed and dropped to my knees, head falling against the bed. I let myself cry for a few moments, wringing myself out while I tried to steady my racing heart.

I stood up, smoothed down my shirt, and went into the bathroom to splash cold water on my face. My eyes looked haunted in the mirror, and a wave of anger flushed over me. Good. I could work with anger. Anger was better than terror any day.

I reached for my phone to call Andrew but knew he was at work and didn't want to burden and upset him; he could do nothing from Bahrain anyway. I tossed my phone down on the bed and changed into a comfortable t-shirt, tossing my wrinkled button-up on the bed before leaving the guest house.

18

Revelation

Hanan and Hasina were waiting for me, with hot cups of tea and a plate of butter cookies. Hasina looked up as she stirred her tea.

"In times of distress, my mother always made me tea with cream and extra sugar. I took the liberty of doing the same for you." She nodded towards the coffee table. "Those biscuits, too; something about them always comforts me."

Hanan shifted to a chair, making room for me between them on the sofa. I looked at the cookies, but the thought of eating anything had my stomach churning.

"My grandmother always made these for the same reason, Hasina," Hanan said, face going soft with memories. "I always try to have some dough in the freezer so I can make them whenever I need. They taste like home." She smiled at me, encouraging and gentle.

Hasina, more logical than emotional, was very straightforward and would look for facts within my story to help them glean as much information about who they were up against, not to my distress, but just as an information seeker. But Hanan would see the human side of it, and I knew I was safe with her there.

The weight she carried as steward was heavy, but I could think of no one better equipped. I picked up my cup, my favorite one in Hanan's collection, and one of Marina's pieces. It was a hand-thrown mug, curvy in shape and fitted perfectly to my hand—it was glazed a bright, sunny yellow that dripped down over white speckled clay. I let the warmth and cheery brightness of the cup steady me, and I took a sip, the sweet, milky tea fortifying my resolve. I closed my eyes, being selfish for a moment before I started.

"Okay." I sighed. "Growing up, my parents were part of a very strict church. Looking back, it was definitely more a cult than a church. Women and girls were expected to be subservient to the men. We weren't allowed to wear trousers on Sundays, I was only allowed to hang out with other church members, and my only extracurricular activities were those sanctioned by the church. And until middle school, somewhere around age thirteen or so, I went to a very strict, very conservative Christian academy that was eventually discredited by the state. It was then I entered public school." I paused, taking another sip of tea.

Hasina opened her mouth but closed it before she said anything, after a look from Hanan to let me just keep talking.

"Middle school is where I met Andrew, but he comes into play later. Though, that was when we first became friends." I smiled; not all the memories of that time were terrible. "Anyway, my parents were extremely close to the church pastor—Warren Mitchell. He and my dad had gone to university together and were fraternity brothers, and my mom was close friends with the pastor's wife, Gayle. They had a son, Gordon, who was a little older than me. And it became clear that we were expected to date." I paused again for another sip of tea, dreading the next part of my story. "They were all grooming me to step in as pastor's wife because Warren was grooming Gordon to take up his mantle.

"I was allowed to date when I turned fifteen, and my first date was with Gordon. He was the perfect gentleman. Dinner, a movie, and a chaste kiss on the cheek when he promptly dropped me off at home five minutes before my curfew. And things went on like that for a few months. He was respectful and kind but slowly started to become possessive. He always wanted to know where I was and who I was with.

"After about six months, he found out that I was friends with another boy— Andrew, actually; we had bonded over fantasy novels that I snuck after bedtime and passed back and forth in class. And Gordon went on a rampage. He drove me home from school that afternoon, screaming and raging at me, racing down the road as I pleaded for him to slow down. I remember him ripping his sunglasses off his face, throwing them at me, and then screaming at me for breaking them." I took a breath.

Hanan leaned over and put her hand on my knee.

"When we got to my house, my parents weren't home, but he dragged me in, anyway, still screaming at me, calling me a whore and telling me that I wasn't worthy of him and I needed to beg God for forgiveness...to *repent or burn*.

"Now, nothing had happened with Andrew. We really were just friends. Just two nerdy bookworms who loved to share stories. But it was enough to threaten Gordon. His whole existence in life was that of an entitled jackass with more money than sense and a powerful and connected daddy who could get him out of trouble. Which he did, and quite often.

"So, anyway. We got home that day, and like I said, he came into my house—a vice-grip on my arm tight enough to leave bruises. He shoved me down on my knees in front of this enormous cross my parents had hanging on our living room wall and forced me to pray for my sins. Sins that he said he couldn't forgive until I begged God to forgive me first." I exhaled, deep and ragged.

Hasina looked at me, meeting my eyes, and I saw understanding in them and wondered if someone had hurt her, too. There's a strange sort of kinship you feel with someone else who has been hurt.

"You don't have to keep going," she said. "Not if you don't want to."

"I know. But I need to. It's a lot. But I'll try to keep it as short as possible," I replied.

They both nodded for me to keep going, and their support buoyed me. Besides Andrew, they were the first to hear the entire story. I was equal parts terrified and comforted.

"After that, things shifted. There were still moments of decency, but something split open inside of him, and he seemed to realize that I couldn't go anywhere, so he could do with me what he pleased. There was an inherent darkness and sort of...madness inside of him.

"When we were kids, we'd all heard rumors now and then of him bullying someone or beating a kid up for some sort of offense, but I always just figured it was kids being kids. But it wasn't. He was, is, a sociopath and a sadist. Gordon was also convinced that he would become almost god-like if he believed hard enough."

Hasina and Hanan exchanged glances at that, but I kept going.

"He would kill small animals and try to bring them back to life just by prayer alone. He was convinced that God would give him power if he believed enough. After he snapped with me, he delighted in showing me his little experiments. I pleaded for him to stop. Tried to convince him that no God would give a mortal those powers." I laughed, realizing what I'd just said. "Kind of ironic now, isn't it?"

Hanan and Hasina both quietly laughed, humoring me. I felt almost lost in memories, their edges becoming sharper. I braced my hands against the cup again, the warmth fading but anchoring me to the present.

"I don't know, maybe a year into our relationship, if you will, he um, well, he raped me. I won't go into detail. But basically, it was known that we would be married after university and before he started seminary, and he told me that I owed him that part of myself. And, since we were promised to each other and our fathers had worked it all out, we were as good as married, and he would take what was his. And so he did. I had just turned sixteen. Young. Small and underdeveloped for my age, which grosses me out so much now since he was almost two years older than me.

"Apparently, he felt guilty and went to his father to repent. Or be absolved? I don't know. Either way, I was called into Warren Mitchell's office one night before dinner. He explained to me that Gordon was special. He had needs and desires, and it was my duty as his future wife to tend to those needs and desires and do so without a fight."

I looked up at them and continued, willing my voice to remain steady, though it wanted to tremble.

"I had fought and clawed at his face, raking my nails down his cheek and leaving marks on his perfect face. Neither father nor son liked that very much."

Hasina sucked in a breath; that was all I needed to know that someone had also hurt her. I trod carefully, then. Understanding my pain was unearthing her own.

"Warren explained to me that God had called me to protect and support the next leader of our church. And that it was up to me to play my part. Then he came over and sat down next to me on his sofa. I'm sure he'd been standing above me until that point, sort of lording over me, trying to intimidate me. He put his hand on my leg, gently at first, as he explained that it is up to men to interpret God's will and up to women to obey it and to serve without question. He slowly moved his hand up my leg and squeezed my thigh hard enough to bruise; I would find out later. I remember squeaking out a noise of protest, but he only squeezed harder."

I stopped then, finishing my cup of tea and taking a moment, not wanting to go on but needing to purge it. Memories clawed their way to the surface, not needing much encouragement from me to dig their way out of the layers I had buried them under for so long.

"He leaned close to me and whispered, his lips against my neck—I could smell the whisky on his breath. *You are as good as our property. And one day you will be. You will allow us to do with you what we please as it is deemed by God, or I will call you up in front of the entire congregation and let them know what a tawdry little whore you really are. I will tell them how you seduced Gordon, took away his innocence, and led him astray. And then, we will cast you out.* He released his grip on my thigh, trailed his hands between my legs, making his point, and asked if I understood.

"I remember one single tear sliding down my cheek as I nodded. And then he pressed his lips to the skin under my ear and whispered *Good*. And then, that was it. We left the room, his hand guiding me out, resting lower on my back than it ever had. And when Gordon's mom, Gayle, served us all dinner that night, she wouldn't meet my eyes. And I knew that she knew. And that I wouldn't have an ally in her.

"That kind of stuff continued. I tried to tell my mom, but she told me to listen to Pastor Warren. He knew the true will of God, and I needed to obey him. I needed to understand my role as a woman: to serve my future husband and father-in-law and to be grateful I had such important men to serve."

Hanan quietly interrupted me by handing me a tissue, and I realized I had been crying, tears silently making their way down my cheeks while the words spilled out of my mouth.

"I think that's enough for now, Julia," she said.

"I'm almost finished. I'm okay." I blew my nose and wiped my eyes, determined to finish it. Hasina reached over and held my hand.

"It was a little better once Gordon was away at university. I had two years at school without him. But I had strict rules to follow, and the only non-church thing I was allowed to do was play in the band. But, even then, I wasn't allowed to play at football games or anything like that. But it did give Andrew and me some time together since he was also in the band. Our friendship grew and eventually changed into more. And then we graduated, and both went away to college—mine was a conservative Christian college, of course, the same campus that my mom and future mother-in-law had attended.

"I started volunteering at a hospital and realized I had some freedom. Andrew and I started dating secretly, and for the first time in my life, I realized I could be safe. And happy. I decided I couldn't marry Gordon, give up freedom and safety, and spend the rest of my life being hurt. And I certainly couldn't bring children into the same sort of life.

"Andrew and I made a plan. And he gave up a promising musical career to join the military. It was the quickest and easiest way to get us out. One day, I left everything I owned in my dorm room and walked away without a word to anyone. Andrew and I got married, and I changed my full name, and we moved to California. And I haven't seen them since." I looked up, cheeks warm with shame and wet with tears.

"So, yeah, I know Warren and Gordon Mitchell. And I can't say that it surprises me that they'd want any power they could get their hands on." I exhaled deeply and leaned back into the sofa, utterly drained, letting the cushions hold me up. Hanan and Hasina were quiet for a few moments.

"Well, that explains why we weren't tracking you as connected to them if you changed your name," Hasina said.

"Yeah, I changed it. I refused to hold on to any part of that life anymore once we were out and I was safe. It was a long time before I even called my parents. I was so terrified that they would tell the Mitchells, and they'd track me down somehow and do something awful. Their pockets are deep, and it always felt like there was no end to what they could do and get away with. My mom sobbed on the phone, and before she could say much, my dad had the phone out of her hand and told me they no longer had a daughter. And that I wasn't to ever call them again." I bit my lip, letting the physical pain combat for attention over the emotional wounds flayed open.

"Have you spoken to them since?" Hanan asked. "Surely they would want to know you're safe and happy now?"

"They died a few years ago," I responded. "Car accident. At some point, I found a letter my mother had penned to tell me what a disappointment I was and how I had failed God..." I trailed off—nothing left to say. My heartbeat had finally slowed, and I felt empty, but empty in the way of release.

"Oh, Jules." Hanan approached the sofa and squished beside me, wrapping her arms around me.

I let go, sobbing into her shoulder, Hasina rubbing my back and lending her support in quiet solidarity.

✦

Hasina left shortly after that, quieter than usual, and Hanan confirmed what I'd already worked out.

"It isn't my story to tell, Jules, but Hasina could relate to more than a small amount of your story. I know she needed just to get home and find comfort with Karim."

"I figured. There was something about how she looked at me while I was talking. Like she knew exactly what I was saying. I hate that we have that in common; no one should endure being hurt by people they're supposed to trust."

"No, they shouldn't. And I know they've passed, and it won't change anything but your parents, Jules. I, I... I just don't have the words. They failed you. They should have protected you at all costs."

I put my hand on Hanan's arm. "I know they did, Hanan. It's taken years of therapy to realize that they were both hurting and broken people who put their faith in someone who had no business holding anyone's faith in their hands. They were weak, and yeah, they failed me. But I am safe. And I am happy. So, so happy with Andrew."

I smiled the first smile that had crossed my lips since earlier. "I hate that they died before we got a chance to reconcile. Or they woke up out of their thrall with that church, but I'm also relieved, in a way, because I think it would have hurt more if they never wanted to speak to me again. Now, I can pretend we'd eventually come to a peaceful place. I mean, I never expected a deep relationship with them. But. I never wanted to lose them without finding some peace."

Hanan nodded, understanding what I meant, and thankfully, changed the subject.

The rest of the night was quiet. We ordered food, and Hanan refused to let me skip dinner and had me choose comfort food over anything new and exciting. Luckily, she knew of a place that delivered phenomenal veggie burgers, and we spent the evening on her sofa, watching old sitcom reruns and devouring our burgers and fries, washing them down with cokes. Finally, feeling somewhat calm, my belly full of my favorite foods and laughter from my favorite show had helped. I called it an early night and left Hanan for the rest of her evening.

19

Love

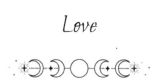

My phone was ringing as I shut the door to the guest house behind me. I kicked off my sandals and hurried over to the bed, digging around in the bedclothes to try and find them where I'd discarded my cell earlier that afternoon, forgotten in my upset state.

"Hello?" I said a little breathlessly.

"Hey babe, everything okay?" asked Andrew.

"Yeah, I'm fine. I just couldn't find my phone. Why on earth are you still at work?" I asked, mentally calculating the time difference in my head and knowing it was well past his usual, even late night, time to be home.

"Just one of those days. I'm wrapping up in a few minutes. I just wanted to catch you before you fell asleep. I hadn't heard from you today and just wanted to hear your voice." He sounded exhausted, and I knew he'd been pulling later days since I wasn't at home.

Before he could say anything else, I cut him off. "Why don't you wrap up and call me when you get home? I'm going to take a bath, but I miss you and want to talk if you can, tonight."

I desperately wanted to just unload everything on him right then, but I knew he needed the space to worry and fuss over me, and work wasn't conducive to that at all.

"Okay. Sounds good. I'll just be another few minutes. You could always stay in that bath, and we could FaceTime," he teased.

I could hear him smiling and felt such a longing for him it was damn near physical.

"Mm, I'll think about it." I tried to purr, hoping I sounded convincing, but I wanted nothing more than to crawl into the bath and wash away the emotions and memories of the day.

"Talk in a few. Love you, Jules."

"Love you too."

I hung up and stripped off my clothes, tossing them onto the ever-growing heap next to the wardrobe, and made a mental note to do a load of laundry the next day. I went to the bathroom, found a playlist of yoga music to fill the background, and perched on the tub's edge while the water began to pour in earnest. I sat, staring off at nothing in particular, just mentally checking out.

Before long, the small bathroom was filled with steam and warmth, but it wasn't enough to chase away the chill of fear that had a fist around my heart. I uncorked a jar of bath salts, the scent of roses, lavender, and sandalwood filling the space, mingling with the steam as I poured some into the water. A dark brown glass vial labeled bath oil was next to the salts. I unstopped it and was immediately taken back to the ritual pool. The death grip of fear loosened its hold ever so slightly as I poured a healthy glug into the water.

I took a deep breath and slowly lowered myself into the hot water. Enveloped with heat and the scent of the ritual oil, I was swathed in love and safety that chased the edges of darkness back. I leaned my head against the edge of the tub and closed my eyes. The quiet, steady beats of electronic, chill yoga music helping me to steady my breaths. The water was hot on my skin but comforting, and finally, I felt warm.

It had been a long time since I'd unpacked everything from my childhood. I'd seen multiple therapists over the years but always held a little back, not comfortable or ready to bear it all. Until tonight. I felt safe with Hanan and Hasina, but I was still emotionally raw and untethered. Like the top layer of skin had been scraped off, and I was exposed to the elements, everything rubbing against me, causing sensations I couldn't or didn't want to name.

Andrew was my saving grace. The person who saw all the darkness and loved me anyway but loved me enough to support me while I learned how to put all those broken pieces back together instead of just trying to put a Band-Aid on everything and wish it away.

When we'd gotten married, I'd worried that we'd been hasty and too panicked to get me out and safe and that, without the urgency, we'd realize that we weren't really suited for each other. But the opposite had happened. Not having to be secretive and being able to be together as much as the Navy allowed drew us closer than I'd ever thought possible. It was still work, and we made the choice to show up every day, but I couldn't imagine life without him. I missed him like I would miss a limb and suddenly wished I was back in Bahrain and not in Egypt. Longing and regret mingling in the water with the other emotions swirling around, churning through the water and my heart.

I sucked in a breath and dipped underneath the water's surface, water clogging my ears and creating a vacuum of sound. I could hear my pulse inside my head, slow and steady, and feel the bubbles slowly escaping from my nostrils to keep the water at bay. I stayed under until the desire for breath was greater than the desire to block everything else out. I forced myself to emerge slowly, letting the water sluice off my face as I inhaled, filling my burning lungs. And then I did it again. And again. After the third time, I came up and felt like I had a handle on my emotions. I rested my head against the side of the tub again and let myself relax for the first time in hours. Tension pinched my shoulders, building up knots at the base of my skull, and I sank a little further down to soak the places in my body that always held the most stress.

The scent from the ritual bath was all around me, and I made a mental note to ask Hanan about it. I could detect rose and sweet almond oil, but the rest I couldn't pick out. Regardless, soaking in the water with the scent of memories tied to the oil, that safe and womb-like feeling slowly made its way inside me, comfort outweighing frayed nerves.

I stayed in the water until it was too cool to be considered a decent bath by my standards and climbed out. I wrapped myself in one of the thick towels, hugging it close. I set about my evening ritual—massaging my nighttime face oil into my skin, brushing my teeth, and then digging out one of Andrew's t-shirts I'd grabbed from his bag before he'd left to go home. It was a ratty old band t-shirt, some obscure indie group he'd seen years ago. Still, it had sort of become our travel talisman. We never went anywhere without it—both of us vying for its threadbare softness and comfort. I was so grateful to have it, silly as it was. I breathed him in, the ghost of him still lingering, though barely, in the fabric. His woodsy, clean scent was as much a comfort as the sound of his voice.

I crawled into bed, lamps casting a warm glow over me. I settled in to read for a few minutes, forgoing the historical fiction I'd been so lost in the night before in favor of something lighter. The bath had calmed and softened the rawer edges of memories, but I longed for Andrew. I hadn't read for long when my phone chirped. I smiled as I read his message.

Took longer than I thought... (don't say it—I know you knew it would take longer...lol). Walking home now. Still awake? Still naked in that bath? Wink?

I hit the FaceTime icon, settling into the pillow, making sure the lighting was on my face well enough for him to see.

"Aw man, not in the bath still," he said as soon as he answered and saw me curled up in bed, mock dismay on his face.

"Sorry, babe. I soaked as long as I could. It finally reached your temperature when I gave up and got out." I laughed.

"Damn, you okay? You have frostbite?" He teased.

"Ha! Almost!" I shifted, pulling the covers to my chin and pretending to shiver.

"Sorry, that took so long. The Captain wanted the last bit of a brief for tomorrow shored up. I figured I'd just knock it out instead of waking up at three to go in and get it done."

He unlocked our door, and immediately, I heard the pitiful meeping yowl of a weirdly social cat left to her own devices the whole day.

"I hear that crazy girl. Lumeeeeeee," I sang into the phone.

Andrew dropped his bag by the door and turned the lights on. He laid out on the thick carpet in our living room—his routine with the cat every night since she'd sauntered into our house our first year on the island, a tiny, underfed stray we couldn't say no to. True to expectation, I saw her come on the screen, head butting Andrew, purr buzzing through the phone, loud enough for me to hear with clarity. I laughed.

"Good grief. That cat is so rotten."

"Ha—she is, for sure." Andrew laughed as she rubbed against him, swirling her butt across the camera view in true cat fashion.

"So," he said, talking over the cat who was settling herself onto his chest. "What did you do today?" The buzz of her purring persisted, and Andrew leaned the phone against the base of the sofa, trying to angle in a way we could actually see each other.

"Um. Well. I think Hasina had more planned for me today, but we hit a bit of a...snag, I guess?" I said, suddenly nervous.

"A snag? Like what?" Andrew asked, a little distracted.

I picked at a stray thread on the duvet, dreading telling him. I knew he'd had a long day, and a part of me wanted to just let it go, but selfishly, I needed him.

"Um. Well... It's weird. Like, disturbing and not good, weird." I continued to worry over the thread. He stopped being distracted and looked at the camera.

"Okay. What happened? Are you okay?"

I took a breath.

"I'm fine. A little shaken up, emotionally, but physically, I'm fine." I took another breath. "So, apparently, they have an idea of almost everyone involved in the brotherhood. There are... factions, I guess, all over the world. They think that the main head of the group decided to spread out arms and legs worldwide to have larger numbers to call in should they ever need reinforcements. So, all these small pockets of groups are connected to the brotherhood, but they don't think they know anything about the magic side of things. They're in the form of fraternities and secret societies. All over."

I was drawing this out, and I knew it; it was just getting harder and harder to form the words that I knew would dredge everything up and worry Andrew.

"Whoa. Like the Freemasons?" he asked.

"No. Not like that. This isn't a Dan Brown novel," I said, chuckling, grateful for even a small laugh. "Nothing huge like the masons. I'm talking about darker, more sinister small groups. Super rich men who use their connections with each other to fuck around and get away with doing whatever they want, whenever they want. And you know, being leaders in their communities while being shit human beings behind closed doors, confident their 'brothers' will protect them when needed."

Andrew's attention was unwavering now.

"And I sort of recognized a name or two on the list."

His eyes widened.

"Oh my god. Who?" He sat up, dislodging the cat from his chest, the look on his face landing somewhere between amusement and curiosity.

"Um...the Mitchells. Warren. And Gordon, both."

"Fuck," Andrew said. "God Damnit!" he exclaimed once it really registered. "Are you okay? Jules, I know that brought so much shit back up to the surface today. Are you okay? Do you need to come home?"

Even through the screen, I could see the blood drain from his face. The amusement was gone, his smile wiped clean, and his lips parted slightly in shock when I said the names. I nodded at him, tears springing to my eyes.

"I'm okay," I said.""I told Hanan and Hasina both. Everything."

His eyes widened again. "Everything, everything?"

"Yeah. All of it. It was weird but also cathartic. Maybe not in the moment, but I do feel lighter now. Like, I purged something that needed to come out."

"They're the first to know it all, right? I mean, besides me?" he asked.

"Yeah. Delilah and Edie know that things were bad, but they don't know the darker stuff," I said, eyes downcast. "I just never wanted their pity, you know? Everyone has their shit they've been through. Mine isn't special...just really shitty." I trailed off.

"Hey, look at me," Andrew said.

I looked up, making eye contact.

"Yeah, everyone has shit, but yours isn't normal shit, and it's okay to reach out to the people you trust. Edie and Dell have been there long enough. You know they aren't going anywhere." He paused. "I'm shocked you told Hasina. You don't know her well at all. I can see telling Hanan: I swear I'd spill *my* secrets to her...she's just got that presence." He smiled, but the concern was as plain as day on his face.

"Honestly, I'm surprised too. But Hasina has been through something, too. I don't know what yet, and I don't know if I'll ever know. Not that it's my business, but I just got that vibe. And I just felt safe to tell them. It was weird, but in a good way. After Hasina left, Hanan and I ordered burgers and fries and watched old sitcoms," I said, trying to lighten up.

"Good. I'm glad you ate and took care of yourself after that."

"Yeah, I needed to just zone out and laugh. I called it an early night and came for a bath."

He nodded. "Good. I know you needed just to wash it all away. Seriously, Jules. Are you going to be okay?"

"I am. I'm still shocked in a way, and not fucking surprised, in another, that they're somehow a part of this, however far-reaching."

"I feel the same. God., I can't help but be grateful we got you out when we did. I can't imagine what life would be like for you now if we hadn't taken the chance."

"I don't want to imagine that. I don't think..." I trailed off, terrified to finish the thought.

"Let's not," He finished for me. "Let's just...let's not."

His face softened, but his eyes hardened, and I knew he was searching my face for clues that I wasn't okay. He could read me like an open book, which drove me crazy some days, but endeared him to me when I needed him to see me without my having to say anything.

"Seriously. I'm fine." I assured him. "I feel absolutely wrung out, but I'm okay. I will be okay. I'm glad I can see your face right now." I smiled at him.

"I'm so glad I can see yours, love." He smiled back, making more of an effort to get the smile to his eyes.

"You need to get some sleep. I know you'll have an early morning and another long day ahead of you." His eyes were so tired, the bags underneath them bruised purple. "I'm going to turn in and get some sleep. I love you so much and miss you more than words can say."

I didn't want to hang up the phone, but I knew he desperately needed sleep. He was forever working himself ragged and not getting enough rest.

"Yeah, I'm exhausted. I will make it a point to leave early tomorrow, though, and we'll FaceTime for longer. And I'll call you while I'm at work. Just shoot me an email when you're up so I don't wake you," he said. "You need sleep after today, I know. I love you so much, J."

I smiled. He only called me "J" when he wanted me to know that he truly saw me, harkening back to the name we left behind when we started our lives over.

I hadn't told Hanan and Hasina that Andrew had also changed his name, and we'd adopted the last name Wheelright, his grandmother's maiden name, as an extra layer of protection. I'd made sure he kept Andrew Dylan; neither one of us could come up with anything else that fit as well as the name his parents had given him. The last name was the most important to change since any paper trail would be through it. It had worked, and we'd stayed safe and hidden all these years. There were moments it had felt extreme to have taken those steps, but knowing now the kind of power behind the Mitchells, I was grateful we'd done it.

"Goodnight, love."

"Goodnight. Sweet dreams, I love you." We ended the call, and I held the phone to my chest. My heart swelled with a wave of love for my husband and the life we'd created. I fell asleep at peace...though it didn't last long.

20

Nightmares

*F*ragments of dreams flashed like someone was hitting fast-forward on an old tape. The scenes were blurred at the edges before each one slammed to a stop, playing out the most brutal moments of my memories.

Abruptly, the playback stopped for good, and I was in the woods just behind the Mitchell's house. Gordon had just choked the life out of his neighbor's cat; the poor animal's eyes had almost bulged out of its head as it made the most horrific and panicked sounds and finally went limp. I had learned that if I screamed and begged for him to stop, it only spurred Gordon on and made things worse for whatever animal he was torturing. He had brought me to this place in the woods a few months before to show me how he experimented on squirrels and rabbits he trapped. Now, he forced me to the woods regularly, craving an audience for his sadistic games.

I was numb. Being in his presence no longer terrified me; I had retreated so deep into myself that I barely had the resolve to shuffle mechanically through my day. I stopped wearing makeup and wore my hair in a messy bun, washing it only when my mom forced my hand. On some level, I knew that I was trying to make myself as unattractive as possible, hoping that Gordon's attention would wander elsewhere. But my wounded depression seemed just to spur him on. He took pleasure in drawing any noise of protest out of me and spent hours every time we were together, which had become far more frequent, hurting me just for a response. I had become so versed in pain that it had become almost meditative. My subconscious, unwilling to participate, I just went to a calm place inside of myself where Gordon couldn't reach me.

"What the fuck is wrong with you, whore." He sneered at me when he saw me, dead eyes glazed over, looking above him at nothing in particular during his little experiment. I didn't respond or register the footsteps crackling on the dead leaves of the forest floor.

Crack!

White hot pain seared across my cheek.

"I said, what the fuck is wrong with you? Aren't you excited? One day I will hold the power to bring this fucker back to life. Doesn't that get you excited?"

I lifted my face and looked towards him, unwilling to meet his eyes.

"Yes," I croaked out, sounding like I hadn't spoken in a while.

"Yes, what?" he asked, raising his hand again and running the back of his hand gently across the welt on my cheek, skin cool against the hot mark already throbbing.

"Sir. Yes, sir." I dropped my gaze, and he tilted my chin, forcing me to look at him. His blue eyes were blazing, and I knew what was coming. He tossed the cat's limp body to the side and grabbed at his crotch.

"One day, I'll be strong enough to kill you and bring you back to life. And that gets me more than excited. It gets me hard," he crooned in a husky voice meant to earn attention *and admiration. "Until then," he whispered. "We'll just have to practice my strength of will not to take it that far yet, won't we?"*

He slowly moved his hand down my neck, wrapped his fingers around my throat, and squeezed. At eighteen, he was large for his age, and I knew he'd only grow bigger. I had lost weight in the last few months, and it felt like his hand was larger than life against my slim throat. I tried not to whimper or make a sound; defiance was my only weapon.

The next few moments could have lasted for hours or minutes; I had no awareness of time. All I felt was the cool autumn air on my naked skin, the crush of dead leaves and branches scratching under my back, and the pain of a sharp rock digging into my left hip, anchoring me to the spot. I could smell the loamy earth beneath me, mingled with the sharp tang of male sweat.

I heard a plane fly overhead, one of the small ones from the little airport a short distance away. I wondered who was out enjoying the perfect, clear skies and if they could see through the trees and witness my shame. Gordon was talking through the whole thing, but I had blocked out his voice, so he sounded like garbled words underwater. Another sharp crack against my face brought tears to my eyes, and both his hands gripped my neck. The light filtering between the trees began to fade around the edges, and I hoped this would be the time he would just be done with it and end it all so I could find some peace.

I came to, body dripping with sweat, clawing at my neck to free it from the phantasmic fingers of my dream. Heart pounding painfully in my chest, I took great gulps of air and tried, in vain, to calm myself down. Fumbling in the dark for the switch, I turned on the lamp above me. Only when the bulb came on and chased the shadows away was I finally awake enough to let go of the last dregs of the dream. My stomach roiled with nausea and I fought it back.

The nightmares had been so frequent when Drew and I first got married. I would wake to him violently shaking me, trying to rescue me again and again. It had been years since I'd had one, and though I'd expected it after the revelations of the day before, I was not prepared for one that bad. I had spent my entire adulthood trying to forget and escape the trauma I'd endured, and it seemed like it would do everything in its power to track me down again and again.

This time, I took another deep inhale from my nose and smelled the sharpness of my sweat, the kind of scent humans only release when gripped by terror. I got out of bed, padded to the small sink in the kitchenette, and filled a glass with water before draining it in four gulps. I set the glass back on the counter and padded over to the bathroom, stripping off my t-shirt and underwear and tossing them on the floor, upset that I'd have to wash Andrew's shirt and lose the last little bit of his scent now that I'd soured it with fear.

I turned the rain shower on and stepped under the stream once the water was hot, letting it wash away the fear instead of soaking in it. I tilted my face to the water and let the scalding heat cleanse the feeling of cold fingers against my throat. I turned and let the water warm my back, driving out the chill.

I stood there for a few more minutes, the hot steam and clean scent of soap replacing the stink of fear. Turning off the water, I climbed out, wrapping a towel around me. I walked over to the sink and looked at my face in the mirror. One side of my face was angry red across my jawline, with finger shapes along my neck. A cold chill ran down my spine, and when I blinked, the marks were gone, and all that was there was my very tired-looking and pink-tinged face and neck.

I shook my head, trying to clear it, and returned to the bedroom. I checked my phone and found it was just two. I knew I had to get more sleep, but I was terrified of another nightmare flashback. I crawled into bed, found a lighthearted comedy to stream on my phone, and fell asleep, the lamp keeping the darkness at bay and the show filling the small space with enough noise from the laugh track to drown out the memories.

21

Wounds

I gave up on sleep before the sun was up. Though I wanted nothing more than to curl up in Hanan's garden and hide away, I knew I needed to get out to stretch my legs and distract myself. I headed back to the *souk*, hoping that the crowds and sensory overload would drown out the noise in my head leftover from the nightmares.

When I arrived, the morning was dewy and cool, and I wrapped my arms around myself, trying to hold in the warmth while I watched the market come to life. It was as if some great sleeping beast awoke one limb at a time all the way down the line as each seller rolled up their doors and shook off the night. I sampled *karak* from a couple of different stalls and earmarked my favorite—one heavy on cardamom—to return to another day.

When I returned to Hanan's, I found Hasina waiting in the garden. When I turned the corner, she was standing on tiptoes to smell a huge white flower that had bloomed overnight. She looked over her shoulder at me, and I could tell she wasn't at ease with the emotions that had come up the day before yesterday, but she wanted to say something to cut the tension.

"Julia," Hasina started. "I..." I could tell she was struggling to find the words. "We have a saying in Arabic. *Gat a'la elgarh.* The literal translation is 'that came on my wound,' but it means that it resounds with me; it made my wound ache, and I got a taste of that. I don't want to get into it; it is too painful. But I want you to know that my wound aches for your wound, and I see your pain."

I put my arms around Hasina, the other woman stiffening before relaxing in my arms.

"Hasina. I see your pain. And my wound aches with your wound."

A tear slipped down my cheek. Empathy skirted around the jagged edges of memories far too close to the surface, softening in the name of unfortunate camaraderie.

"Come. Let us give our wounds a rest, and let us talk of happier things." Hasina smiled, leading me to the Arabic bench outside in the garden. The shade from the reed matting was a welcome respite from the mid-day sun beating overhead.

"Everyone calls me 'the brains,' but I am more than just the computer nerd. I have a powerful connection to herbs and herb lore."

I nodded. It all made sense since she constantly had green fingertips, and different herbal smells followed her around like perfume.

"That's awesome. So, you're a gardener then?"

"Yes, I am," she said. "Everything about the garden brings me peace, and using my magic here feels like the most natural thing in the world. Part of the magic in herbs comes from the very beginning—the planting and cultivating of life. All things carry energy, and when we plant a garden, we put our own energy into the soil. Gifting the plants with little bits of it. Harnessing and using that energy with purpose calls forth magic and makes those plants more than just sweet-smelling herbs for sachets."

"Whoa...that's amazing," I said. "So, anyone has the power to call forth the magic of plants?"

"Mm, there are people who study herb lore and understand how plants and energy works, and, of course, you have modern witches and pagans who absolutely use herbs in the right way and eke out as much from them as they can. But what we do is a bit different, though the same idea in theory. When we plant herbs to use in ritual or spells, we plant with intention." She studied me for a moment. "You've been working with the others to harness your energy, right?"

I groaned. "Ugh. Yes. And, while it's getting better, I'm still not terribly good at it." I shook my head, embarrassed.

Though I'd gotten the hang of some elementary spells and the Norse runes I scribbled over and over again had become second nature, I still felt the struggle of not quite having a full grasp of my magic. It came so easily for everyone else. Every time I meditated, I could focus on the energy coursing through my body, but I just couldn't get a tight hold of it. It was like standing on a ladder and being so close to touching what I was reaching for that my fingertips could brush against it but not grasp it fully every time. Occasionally, I got a hold of it and had some control, but it was random, few and far between.

"Everyone struggles in the beginning. Don't be too hard on yourself," she said. "Every person is different. Every way that we use our energies is different. And trying to mimic any one person will not get you the result you're looking for. You must just feel it out for yourself and do what feels right. I know that sounds esoteric, but it's the truth." She smiled and handed me a thick, grubby book with jagged-edged pages that were warped with use.

"This is my grimoire. Again, everyone's is different, and I know you've been working on yours with Marwa. Mine is almost entirely plants. I'm loaning it to you to read through and get a feel for what *I* do. This scratches the surface, but it covers what I use most often. You should be covered for plants between this and the book I gave you at the New Moon ceremony."

I pulled the thick tome on my lap and ran my hands along the surface. The cover was a deep, forest-green fabric stamped with dark leaves etched into the surface. The edges were worn with use and slightly dirty. I suddenly had a clear vision of Hasina, working in the garden and searching for an answer, hands filthy from planting, flipping through the pages, determined to find a solution but with purpose and calm and no trace of annoyance or frustration. I smiled, knowing what it meant for her to share her grimoire and this piece of herself.

"Thank you so much, Hasina. I promise I'll take good care of it."

She nodded towards me. "I know you will."

We spent the next few hours companionably. Hasina lit up while she taught me about planting seasons, her favorite herbs and plants, and how to harness a plant's energy, making sure not to waste anything. The always reserved and perfectly suited tech guru gave way to a light and relaxed woman who was almost unrecognizable with her face dirt-smudged and her sleeves rolled up to her elbows. She had me thumb through her grimoire often to get a feel for how she organized everything and laid out the book. It was the most organic way to use it, and I felt things click into place with what I wanted out of my own spell book.

We finished our lesson by wrapping bundles of herbs for hanging and drying. Hasina showed me how to bind them tight enough that the bundle wouldn't fall apart as the moisture left the plant and it shrank in size. We hung some of them in Hanan's kitchen on a wire attached to the brick above the stove, and Hasina took some to dry in her kitchen. Hasina wrapped up herbs for peace and clarity, which I took to hang in the guest house.

I fell asleep that night with fingers smelling of herbs and the verdant smell that lingers from freshly cut plants, and I didn't dream a single thing.

22

Rituals & Dreams

After a whole night of uninterrupted sleep, I felt somewhat human again the following day. Despite this, Hanan took one look at me and sent me back to the guest house with strict orders to stay in and rest as much as I could before the full moon ritual that night, so I knew one night of sleep wasn't enough to make up for a nightmare that had rattled me to my core. I wondered if I'd ever be done being haunted by the past and everything that had happened to me.

It was apparent when I glanced at my face in the bathroom mirror. My usually light skin was almost an unearthly pale, a pallid, sickly color. My eyes were red-rimmed and deeply purpled underneath—I looked terrible and in dire need of rest. I was tired. Tired of being tired and of feeling like a victim. Closing my eyes, I exhaled, tilting my face to the skylight. I wasn't ready to crawl back into bed, so I splashed cold water on my face and did my morning routine.

I was restless—torn between exhaustion, frustration that magic wasn't as easy as books made it out to be, and missing my own house with my own things. I shook myself out of my pity party, walked into the kitchenette, and started the kettle.

As my tea steeped, I gathered the handful of candles from around the guest house and rummaged around the drawers for the lighter I'd seen. I planned on doing a little work before taking a nap, heeding Marina's advice, and making the mundane a ritual. I placed them on the bedside tables and cracked the window above the bed for some fresh air.

I'd lit two candles before I stopped myself.

"Idiot. You don't need a lighter," I muttered, rolling my eyes. It would take time to get used to the fact that I had the power to make things happen with intent and carefully spoken words.

I was still learning what worked for me and playing with different words or phrases to guide my magic. Arabic proved impossible, which made sense, given what Marwa had explained. I tried some Latin words, and *ignis* worked about half the time. Old Norse words never worked, no matter how I strained and willed them to— they just felt wrong on my tongue. So I stuck to English or Latin, figuring the language it was rooted in might help. At least it hadn't hurt anything. Assuming it was due to my love of reading, I felt like using my everyday words to make magical things happen felt wrong, so I spent lots of time online, scouring the internet and taking notes on words that felt *right*.

"*Luminate,*" I whispered to the wicks of the three candles that were left. Two flamed to life instantly, and the third sat unlit. I took a breath and focused on the candle. It was hand-poured in a squat jar, the light green wax studded with leaves and flower petals with a wooden wick. I took in the details of the candle, clearing my mind of everything else but my intention to light the wick.

"*Luminate,*" I said again, louder this time, and the candle sputtered to life, wood crackling as it caught. Satisfied with myself, I walked back to the kitchen to get my tea, taking a moment to do the daytime spell Marina had given me as I stirred the dark liquid in my mug. I inhaled deeply, the rich and malty steam tinged with a bit of sweetness from the sugar filling my nose.

I settled in and spent a couple of hours in work mode before shutting my laptop and curling up under the covers for a nap.

At first, my nap was dreamless. I slept with the pleasant drowsiness of someone with all day to rest and nowhere to be, drifting in and out of consciousness and thought. And then the dream overtook me and chased away the pleasantness.

I was standing in Gram's kitchen, going through the mugs for some reason, having just set aside her and Gramps' two favorites, when I got a cold chill all over my body. I had the distinct and discomforting feeling of being watched. I slowly turned around, expecting someone to be standing behind me, but the room was empty. I closed my eyes, pinching the bridge of my nose and trying to shake myself out of the weird feeling. Turning back towards the cabinet, I felt a chill go down my spine again. I tried to ignore the feeling, but it persisted.

I finally gave up and walked through the house. Gram was nowhere to be found. I went through each room, making sure the windows and doors were all locked, which they were. I stopped in the living room and looked outside the bay window. There was a silver sports car parked in front of the house that I didn't recognize. The windows were tinted, and I couldn't see inside, but the chill went through me again, and I knew this was where it was coming from. I backed away, further into the room so I couldn't be seen and stood there. I pulled my phone out and kept it in my hand in case I needed it. Five minutes went by. Then ten. Finally, after twenty minutes, the car pulled away. I never saw the driver, but I knew who it had been. I didn't have to see his face to feel the crazed dangerousness of Gordon Mitchell radiating towards the house.

The insistent vibrating of a call finally shook the dream from my mind. I fumbled around, hand searching for my phone to answer.

"Huh—" My scratchy, sleep-heavy voice caught. I cleared my throat. "Hello?" I said, clearer.

"Sorry, babe, did I wake you?" Andrew's voice filled my ear.

"You did, but it was needed. Bad dream," I said, yawning. He groaned.

"Ugh. I'm so sorry. I wish I could do something to help," he answered.

"It's fine. They'll pass, eventually. This one wasn't even that bad nor a memory...it was just unsettling."

And they would pass...hopefully. I mentally shook my head to clear away the lingering vestiges of the dream. The heavy, panicked feeling stuck to me like an oily residue.

"Other than that, are you feeling okay? It's lunchtime there, J."

"Oh, I'm fine. I'm under strict orders to rest up today. Full moon thing tonight, and apparently, I looked like hell earlier when I saw Hanan, and she shooed me back here to take it easy all day. I caught up on work, curled up in bed, and passed out." I groaned a bit as I stretched out cat-like under the duvet. "What are you up to today?"

"I actually took the afternoon off," Andrew said, snapping me out of my languid succor.

"What? Are you sick?" I asked, a bit concerned since he rarely took time off.

"No. Not sick. Just worn out. I'm playing catch-up from the trip, and work stuff is going down; it's been a bit manic. I worked almost a full day yesterday, and I went in early today and just couldn't do it, so I left. I'm almost home now and plan on passing out on the rug with the cat." I laughed, eyes rolling towards the ceiling.

"Fool, go sleep in the bed," I said.

"You know I never sleep well if you're not beside me."

"Have you been sleeping on the sofa this whole time?" I asked. The silence on the other end of the line was admission enough for me.

"Drew! It's been almost a month! No wonder you're exhausted," I chastised him. "You can't get decent enough sleep on the sofa— I don't care how comfortable it is. Go get in our bed." I heard him chuckle on the other line.

"Okay, okay," he said. "Lumee and I will sleep in bed today. It's just not the same when you're not here."

His voice sounded heavy, and I could hear the exhaustion in it. I was grateful he was finally taking time to catch up on sleep, but it worried me that he'd worn himself thin.

"I know, love. I'm so sorry." The stirring of guilt in my belly, mixed with missing sleeping next to him.

"Don't be sorry, Jules. I'm so excited for you and happy you're there and learning. Plus, work has just been crazy, so we wouldn't be seeing much of each other as it is. I'll get a nap and cook a decent dinner, and I'll be fine." I heard the door to our house open and then close. "Are you excited for tonight?" he asked, voice faintly echoing through our home—the high ceilings and marble floors sending his tired voice reverberating.

"I am. A little anxious with not knowing how tonight will differ from the new moon thing, but nothing terrible." I paused. "Well, I guess more curious than anxious."

I heard the telltale sound of the cat's yowl, loud and echoing over the phone, and Andrew's quiet platitudes as he greeted her. I could see him squatting down, the cat swishing in and around his legs, rubbing her face all over him as he petted and scratched her. He hadn't really wanted a cat at first, but she'd taken one look at him and decided he was hers, and that was it.

"Everything still good with everyone? Still happy to be there?" he asked.

"Yeah. Definitely. I still haven't spent any time with Naomi. She's out of town right now—back and forth from Cairo to somewhere else."

"Well, she was sort of the odd man out a bit, wasn't she?" he asked. "I mean, as far as, like, a warm welcome is concerned."

I thought for a moment, not wanting to jump to conclusions about Naomi and her lack of friendliness. There was something about her that just rubbed me the wrong way, and I couldn't put my finger on it.

"Um. Sort of?" I said. "I mean...she is a lot younger than me, and I don't think she was thrilled that she wasn't there for my ritual in the temple. Maybe that's it. Maybe she'll be more friendly once she knows me a little better?" I toyed with the ring she'd given me the night of the New Moon. Surely a gift like that was an omen of friendship?

"Hopefully so. I can't imagine anyone not liking you once they spend time with you, J," Andrew said. "But, I suppose I *am* just a little biased."

I chuckled. "Just a bit, darling," I teased. "Have you made it to bed yet? Or are you still downstairs?"

I heard him groan and get up. "I'm going, I'm going." He made little noises of disagreement, but I heard him shuffling up the stairs. "You know I'm fine on the sofa."

"Well, maybe, but it makes *me* feel better to know you're in our bed with plenty of space. Just trying to take care of you from afar," I sighed. "I miss you, Drew."

"I miss you too, Jules. Not too too much longer, yeah?"

"I know. I wish teleportation were a part of this whole gig."

Andrew laughed, tiredness pulling on the edges of his words stronger now that he was home and relaxed.

"Same," he said. "Listen, I hate to do it, but now that I'm horizontal, I'm done for. I love you so much, J. I hope tonight is amazing." I heard him yawn.

"Get some rest. I love you too, Andrew. Sweet Dreams."

A muffled sound on the other end of the phone sounded in response, and, smiling, I ended the call. I lay in bed, warm and cozy, and let myself miss Drew for a moment. My time in Luxor had been amazing in so many ways, and I was grateful that I stayed to learn and get to know all the women, but it was challenging. Being away from Andrew was the hardest part.

My childhood had been traumatic but sheltered, and even university was a wake-up call to the realities of responsibility and adulthood. When Andrew and I married and landed in California for his first duty station, I had no idea what I was doing. I'd never paid a bill or signed a lease in my life—my father had done everything. Once they'd realized that I had zero life skills to take with me into adulthood, Gram and Gramps did their best to try and teach me what they could. However, balancing a checkbook was almost obsolete by then with online banking, and they had owned their house for well over forty years and hadn't signed a lease since they were young.

As we figured things out, I learned to lean heavily on Andrew, which resulted in a dependency that I both loved and hated. We worked well as a team; having someone I trusted implicitly was incredible. However, he definitely pulled a lot of the weight, and I had become very happy to have him carry it.

This meant that this time apart was just as challenging as learning magic.

23

In the Light of the Full Moon

H anan came to get me just before dark, and we headed to the temple.

We parked the car, and after a short walk, Hanan led me over to a group of trees and shrubs across the road from the temple on the verdant side of the Valley of the Kings. As we ducked in a bit to conceal ourselves, she reached up and pulled the pin holding her hijab in place, unsheathing a small blade. She winked at my surprised face. I watched as she neatly sliced the palm of her hand and squeezed it into a fist, closing her eyes as the blood welled to the surface.

She bent down, pressed her hand into the earth, and whispered words I couldn't quite make out. The spell broke as her blood beaded in the dirt, sand falling away and revealing a large round door set into the ground under the shrubbery. Hanan lifted the latch and pulled the heavy door open. She explained that powerful wards were at the entrance, tunnels, and caves to keep even the most advanced technology from finding them. Part of what we were doing tonight was strengthening the wards and adding my energy and magical signature to everything.

We descended a steep staircase and into a long tunnel. Our flashlights lit the way, but once we were underground, Hanan cast a spell to light the torches lining the walls, which would light the way for everyone else coming along soon.

We came to the end of the tunnel, where Hanan spoke quietly, her bloody palm on the wall before us.

"*Yakshif.*"

Slowly, the sand shifted and almost melted away, and a door emerged. Hanan inserted a large brass key into the lock and placed her palm against a scanner that had also emerged. The scan read her hand, and another opened up, and she leaned her face towards it, letting it scan her eye. The shock was apparent when she turned towards me, door open and beckoning.

"It's a little much, I know. But once Hasina gets something in her mind, there's very little we can do about it." She laughed. "You'd think a magical warding I seal with my blood would be enough to satisfy even the staunchest security checks, but apparently not."

"It's impressive," I said as I followed her inside, beside myself with awe. Between the tight security and the small blade tucked into her hijab, I was floored.

We entered a small chamber, and Hanan lit torches all along the wall. It wasn't a large space, and shelves and counters were carved into the walls that held all sorts of things— jars, boxes, candles, and unidentifiable things in the low light. The walls were undecorated, and I got a distinct feeling that this was a room for preparations and nothing more. Hanan set her bag down and turned towards me.

"After you change into your robe, go on through and walk around in there. I'm going to get cleaned up and ready." She pointed to an arched doorway and a darkened room beyond. "I imagine you didn't get a chance to take much in last month."

I nodded, setting my things down next to hers, and undressed quickly, slipping on the dark robe. I heard her whispering as I walked into the ritual room beyond.

The pendant from Hanan around my neck glowed softly as I walked over the threshold. I whispered the words I'd been working on perfecting, and the soft glow of candles spread across the room. I smiled, pleased with myself, and looked around.

During my ritual, I had seen the ceiling— painted to depict the night sky and the golden walls that shimmered in the flickering light. However, I hadn't noticed how detailed everything was. The walls weren't just gilded; they were hand-painted masterpieces with designs etched with gold leaf everywhere. The figures I'd seen were stunning— knowing what I knew now, I could read the pictures as a story—a history of the sisterhood and the magic that coursed through my veins. Time had been kind to the temple, though I supposed an entire group of people continuing to come and care for the space meant that any chipped paint was repaired and no one was trying to pilfer any pieces for a museum somewhere.

It was peaceful in the ritual space. I was by myself, though I didn't feel alone in a comforting sort of way. I went to the pool and looked down into the dark water. There was a bit of steam rising and the gentlest movement, and I wondered what fed the pool and how far below the surface we were. I sat on the edge and dipped my feet into the warm water, mind wandering.

I felt a strange kinship with the long-dead Pharaoh and longed to know her and know more about this formidable woman whose mantle I was helping to take up and carry. I closed my eyes and let the warmth fill my lungs. There was a quiet rustle of fabric, and I felt someone sitting beside me. I smiled, happy that one of my sisters was sitting with me but in reverence. I took another breath, a long, deep inhale, tasting the air on my tongue. Fragrant, wet earth and the cloying scent of incense, suffused within the walls from years of use, wound through my senses. I turned, opening my eyes to see who was with me, and found an empty space. Confused, I looked around. The ritual room was empty.

Before I could dwell too long on the unsettling feeling that I hadn't been alone, everyone had arrived, and it was time to begin. Hanan had explained what to expect, but my stomach was full of butterflies once everyone was together again in this space that had changed my life.

We had fasted throughout the day in preparation for the evening, and I thought I would be famished by this point, but nerves had replaced food in my belly. Everyone made their way to the center of the ritual room, and we gathered together in a circle, the gentle sound of the flames flickering and the rustling of our robes the only sounds in the room. We sat together, knees close but not quite touching, everyone on a meditation cushion. Before taking her place in the circle, Hanan walked over to the ritual pool and lifted her arms. She moved her hands above her and spoke out loud, her voice reverberating and filling the room. Overhead, I heard the shifting and moving of stone on stone, and slowly, light shone onto the pool. A clear, bright shaft of light shone down from the ceiling, moonlight shimmering onto the water.

Hanan began to hum, the sound vibrating off the walls. She held a large goblet in her hand. Earlier that day, Hanan explained that the Ancient Egyptians had ceremonial and ritual drinks like the South Americans' *ayahuasca*. They called it the *Tree of Life* and, similar to *ayahuasca*, the Acacia root and bark, when prepared correctly, could produce a psychoactive experience. I wasn't sure exactly how I felt about the herbs, but I felt confident that the unease was old, ingrained notions, and I did my best to shake them off and keep an open mind.

"Sisters, come. Let us drink in *the Tree of Life* and connect our spirits," her voice was commanding and enigmatic. I would have been drawn to it in a crowd of people.

Hanan spoke words over the goblet, blessing the ritual and imbuing it with protection.

"Blessed mother, beloved goddess, stand vigil this night over your faithful servants. Lay your protection over us, help us to see the way forward, guide us with your power and light."

She lifted the chalice to her lips and drank, her throat working as she drank it. She passed it over to me, and I followed suit, hands shaking slightly. As I tilted it to my face, I smelled the honey, tea, and other herbs steeped with the Acacia. I took a breath and opened my mouth, sipping tentatively. It was an odd flavor—green and earthy, sweet from the honey, but it was no match to mask the bitterness of the brew. I swallowed and fought the urge to shudder, passing the goblet to Reem.

After everyone had drunk from the cup, Hanan led us in a meditation to give the acacia time to work and help focus our energies. Everyone had a role to play— predetermined by their strengths and the things they'd chosen to be responsible for. Each of us would take a turn, calling out to the circle and the moon high above us, the spells needed to ward their lives, guide them on their journeys, and protect different facets of life. We would all lend our energies and support to each other, stronger together.

We breathed deeply for a few minutes, our breath echoing off the walls, creating a constant hum of life. My mind reviewed the words I had spent all week preparing and grappled with my focus or lack thereof. My body was keyed up with anticipation, worrying over getting something wrong. I fought hard to tamp down the nervousness I was bringing to the circle.

My body began to relax. It was as if someone poured warm oil on the crown of my head; the slow pour and drip eased down every inch of my body, leaving tranquility in its wake.

My mind followed suit and quieted.

The tips of my fingers and toes tingled, little shockwaves of pleasure lazily dancing through my veins.

I was weightless...floating...my sisters were the only thing anchoring me to the earth.

Voices called out. One by one, they cast their spells.

Magic swirled around me, and colors and shapes poured forth from my sisters. Each was different, but they connected to one another, creating a wispy rainbow of power.

Hanan touched me, sending electrical pulses through my skin, ripples like a stone thrown into water, waking my senses even more and urging me to take my turn. To call on the power of the moon and my sisters. My mouth moved, and the words, called up from the depths of my soul, reverberated through me and into the room. My magic was like dark teal smoke flecked with gold, joining the others in a cloud of energy.

Hanan spoke.

Guttural and ethereal sounds vibrated through me, and our magic sailed through the open moon door and out into the night. We held the chalice again one by one, drinking down the last dregs of tea. No longer bitter, it was saccharine and alive in my mouth. It snaked its way through my bones, liquefying them.

We floated to the pool. The water beckoned, and the moon enticed. The burning light within me answered.

The pulsing beam of moonlight churned the water. It bubbled and spit, heat flushing my anointed skin.

Beads of sweat washed away as I sank into the earth's wet warmth. Jolts of power rushed through me as I submerged deeper and deeper, each wave of energy a wave of pleasure.

Of pain.

My skin stretched tight, filled to the brim with magic. The push and pull of build-up and release were as constant as the movement of the water.

The light and the water fought beneath my skin. A warring triumph of magic nestled into every shadowed part of me. The water was a frothing mass of light and ecstasy. Cries rang out into the night. Power rippled through me. Through my sisters. Binding us together.

Slowly, so slowly, the frenzy of magic quieted. Power placated, the water calmed. It carried me to the edge, a shivering mass of energy. Full and empty. Floating and sinking. I was wholly myself and entirely someone new. I closed my eyes, visions swam before them, and I lay there, breathing shallow. Tingling with power. Exhausted with bliss.

Sometime later, I fully came to, thoroughly wrung out, but my mind and soul were rejuvenated. Hanan closed out the night, sending blessings and love to the moon and all those who had come before us. Quietly, we slipped on our clothes and returned to the house. When we came out of the tunnel entrance, the early morning sky was pink with the sun's arrival.

24

Literal Magic

I had hoped the full moon ritual would lend a reprieve from my nightmare flashbacks, but that hope was dashed immediately. The nightmares came in pieces, memories surfacing when I was most vulnerable and not distracted. After a third, damn near sleepless night, it was well after breakfast by the time I woke. I felt hungover, my mind foggy, my eyes burning with exhaustion, and my neck and back muscles so tight and tense I couldn't move without terrible stiffness. After getting dressed, I stumbled over to the kettle and made a cup of sweet and creamy tea. Hasina had been right about it being a comfort drink. After particularly rough nights, I'd drank my morning cup that way.

In the light of day, the mug Marina created for me was stunning. The blue was a rich color that melded into purple and even black in spots, mimicking the night sky. The hand-painted stars and flecks were a deep, rich gold, and all down the handle were tiny replicas of the moon's phases, the full globe in the center. I had been reciting the spell she'd given me each morning and loved making a daily habit into a ritual. Whether it was the magic Marina had formed within the clay or my magic at work, I felt a difference.

Armed with caffeine, I wandered outside and found Hanan in the garden, quietly reading a book and sipping her tea.

"Morning," I said quietly, lowering myself onto one of the chairs. Sinking into the lush cushions, I was grateful that the Egyptian weather allowed for such luxuries outside.

The garden was the most fragrant in the morning; the scent of flowers and greenery and the smell of water on the bricks and concrete from Hanan's early morning watering surrounded us.

"Another bad night?" she asked, taking in my sallow complexion and the deep purple under my eyes.

"That's an understatement," I said, yawning so wide my jaw cracked. "Bad dreams. Flashbacks." I sipped my tea. "It used to happen a lot when I was younger, but it's been a while since I've had anything that bad or as vivid as they've been in the last few days."

"Do you want to talk about it?" she asked.

"Honestly, I don't know," I said. "I've spent my entire adult life running from my past, just trying to escape everything, but it always finds a way back."

"Maybe running from it isn't the answer, then?" Hanan said gently.

I nodded. "Maybe not. It's just so hard to dredge it back up." I hated how my voice was cracking with emotion. "Even just the other day, seeing their names threw me so completely that I felt like that young girl all over, and I never wanted to be her again."

Hanan studied me quietly. I could tell she was taking her time to think about what to say to me. I worried at a loose thread on the cushion next to me, not wanting to meet her gaze. It was like she could see right through me some days. She leaned forward, set her cup on the table before us, and leaned back in her seat, steepling her hands under her chin, contemplative. I continued to pick at the cushion, trying my best to give my shredded cuticles a break from my nervous attentions.

"Let me think on this, Julia," she said after a few moments. I think we might be able to help you. But it won't be easy. You will have to lean into the hurt a bit longer and..." She trailed off, ruminating. "Yes, I think we can help. I'll just need some time. Are you okay?"

I nodded softly.

"I am. It was a long time ago, and all these memories will settle back down soon. I'll be fine. Thank you, Hanan." I rolled my head along my neck, trying to work out the tension. "What do we have planned today? I am so stiff from last night. Is there any time to go have acupuncture or a massage or something?"

Hanan smiled. "Now, *that* I can help with."

She reached for her phone, scrolled, and typed quickly. She waited, and I heard her phone vibrate with a message.

"All set," she said, setting her phone back down and looking pleased with herself. I have a massage therapist coming this afternoon, and we'll get you sorted out."

I balked. "Coming here? Hanan, I can find somewhere to go—you don't have to have someone come to your home."

"Oh, it's fine—it's Renee. She's happy to come and get some one-on-one time with you. I would joke and say she has magic hands, but...she actually does. No spa will be as good as her; I can promise you that."

We both laughed at her joke, and I felt a little tension ease from my shoulders.

"Oh man, I didn't even think about asking Renee."

She smiled as if to say, *that's what I'm here for*, and we settled into companionable silence after that, both of us lost in our thoughts. The rest of the day was quiet. I spent some of the morning reading and relaxing in the garden while Hanan busied herself in the house. She hadn't said anything else about what she was thinking to help me, and I wondered what she had in mind.

Shortly after lunch, Renee arrived with a massage table, cupping tools, and her yoga mat. This was our first opportunity to get to know each other one-on-one. We started with some gentle yoga in the garden, Hanan joining in, and it was nice to be led by someone else. I'd gotten my yoga teacher training certification a few years before. I loved teaching, but that always took precedence over taking classes with anyone else. I practiced at home, but being guided by someone else was always a treat, and Renee, with her quiet, steadfast voice, was a soothing presence on the mat.

I was already feeling looser, but Renee worked some literal magic while massaging me. Between whatever oil she used, the words I didn't understand but that she kept quietly murmuring under her breath, and her sheer talent, it was like being an entirely new person after ninety minutes on her table. When she was finished, she used the cups on my back and shoulders and left me alone for a few minutes, quiet music playing softly in the background while she stepped into the house.

It was the first time I'd had an outdoor massage, and with the birdsong and fresh air, it felt far more decadent than any room at a spa I'd been to. I lay there for a few moments, cups slightly uncomfortable but not painful, and breathed slowly and deeply, grateful for the situation I was in.

Renee returned just before I could doze off and removed the cups, quietly humming and working on all the areas she had just cupped. I'm not sure how much longer she worked, but finally, she had the knots and kinks worked out. She slid the crisp white sheet up to my shoulders and whispered, "Okay, Jules, I'm all finished here, I think. How do you feel?"

I groaned a satisfied noise of pleasure.

"Amazing." I managed to croak out. "I really can't thank you enough. Where on earth did you learn how to do that?"

She laughed softly, a quiet sound that fit her stoic and calm personality.

"I've been doing *that* for years. I started working in a doctor's office when I was younger, certain I wanted to be a nurse or a doctor, but eventually changed the path to a healer of a different sort. Especially when the sisterhood found me, and I learned who I truly was. Doing this just made more sense then."

I smiled and turned my head to look at her. "How long have you been a part of the sisterhood?"

She thought for a moment, pausing to pack away her things. "Going on twenty years now, I think," she said. "It's a bit of a long story."

"Wow. That's incredible...all that time. I'm a little jealous."

She smiled at me, wistful.

"I know it's overwhelming now. But one day, you'll have been a part of this for twenty years and will be guiding someone new, and it will feel like yesterday and always at the same time." She put her hand on my arm, still covered with the sheet. "Now, you rest here a while longer. Breathe in the air and take a few moments just to be still, and when we're finished, I'll tell you more about how I came to be a part of all this."

I nodded and rested my cheek against the table again, closing my eyes. I heard her move away and into Hanan's house.

25

Arcana

The next thing I knew, I woke up, having slept enough that the sun had moved across the sky and the air was cooler. I scrubbed at my face and slowly sat up, wrapping the sheet around myself and swinging my legs around the side of the table. Swaying a bit, dizzy from relaxation and sleep, I gave myself a minute to fully wake up before slipping off the table and back into the guest house to get dressed. Somehow, four and a half hours had passed. I wasn't sure how much of that she'd spent working on me and how much of that had been sleep, but I was grateful for her attention. My mind felt clearer, and my body certainly felt better. I rolled my head around my neck and shrugged my shoulders, amazed at how loose and fluid I was compared to how stiff I'd been that morning.

When I returned to the garden, Renee was there folding her table.

"Before you get settled out here, grab your tarot cards, and we can do a reading together if you like."

I nodded and turned back towards the guest house, popping in to grab the cards I'd yet to do much with since she'd gifted them to me.

"You look like you feel a lot better, Jules," she said when I joined her again.

"I feel like a new woman!" I exclaimed. "I can't believe the difference! You are absolutely magic with your hands." She laughed.

"Ha-well, yeah... I mean... I did *use* magic." I must have looked surprised. She laughed again, not making fun of me but just finding joy in coming to terms with the ease of magic around me. "Don't worry; you'll get used to it," she said.

"I just...I mean, I just thought you were really good at that!" I laughed now, and any last remaining darkness from the day and night before fell away. "So, is that your strength then?" I asked.

"It is," she said. "I've always had an affinity for healing and helping people. Even as a young girl, I would bring injured animals home and nurse them back to health, and I spent a lot of time with ailing family members. I was blessed to know all of my grandparents, but along with the blessing of knowing them came the pain of having to lose them when I was younger. I learned that I could bring peace and comfort just by being there and holding a hand or massaging a painful leg or whatever they needed. When I went into the ritual pool all those years ago, those things were just heightened. Now I understand I was unknowingly using magic with each person I sat with and comforted."

"That's beautiful." I looked down at the ground, a niggle of embarrassment creeping up. "I have no idea what my strength is. I feel like I've spent my whole life figuring out what I want to be when I grow up. I'm jealous that you've known what you were called to do for so long."

"It will come," Renee said. "When the time is right, it will come. There's no age limit to figuring yourself out."

I smiled, hoping she was right, but a part of me wondered if all of this was a mistake and there was nothing special about me at all, and they'd all figure that out eventually.

"I know that look," she said sternly, the firmness and seriousness of her voice snapping me to attention. "That self-doubt. There's no room for it here. You were chosen by Hatshepsut. Not Hanan. Not myself. But the spirit of our queen chose *you*. And she doesn't make the choice lightly or often, and she certainly doesn't make mistakes."

"I hear you. It's hard not to doubt when this all seems unreal, and I don't feel I truly have my place just yet." The lightheartedness that had filled me after my massage slowly slipped through my fingertips like grains of sand.

"We were all there, Julia—all of us. Everything is still new. Most of us have been learning our craft for at least a decade, some even longer. Be gentle with yourself. It *will* come."

All the stern bravado gave way to understanding and compassion, and I knew why that was her strength. She radiated a sense of calm and a deep sense of...something else. Something almost akin to what the ritual waters lent. And then, it hit me.

I put my hand to my chest and nodded at her, smiling softly, trying to tamp down the discomfort bubbling up from the realization that Renee had used her magic on me before. In the ritual, there were moments when my anxiety and fear were in full swing, and I'd felt that wave of comfort and peace wash over me and chase away the negative feelings. I remembered noting it, confused but distracted and focused on the ritual.

"I have to ask," I said, interrupting Renee's search through her bag. "Did you use your magic in the ritual to sort of...calm me down?" I tried not to let my voice shake.

Renee quirked her head at me curiously.

"Of course I did," she said as she pulled out a dark blue pouch that held her tarot cards. She took them out and shuffled them as we talked, effortlessly moving the cards in her hands.

"So, every time I started to freak out or panic, you sent a wave of calm through me?" I asked, stomach souring at the realization of being so profoundly manipulated. I was confused and unsure of what to say. Sitting here with Renee, I knew her intentions weren't nefarious, but I couldn't help the simmering anger.

"Basically, yes," she said, nonplussed, still shuffling her cards. I had a flash in my mind of a street magician trying to hold my attention in one place while they performed some sleight of hand elsewhere. "It seems the kindest thing to do with people too worried to let go and let the ritual occur. Fear taints the room and taints the magic. I can take that fear and soothe it and tuck it away."

She spoke so blasé about it all I had to wonder if I was overreacting and should just be grateful that she'd divested me of my crippling anxiety for one perfect night. I shook it off and changed the subject, tucking it away to deal with later.

"So, obviously, you're not a native Egyptian. How did you find yourself here?" I tried my best to sound light-hearted. I slipped my deck out of its pouch and began to shuffle the cards; their size and feel awkward in my hands.

"What gave it away? This?" she asked, laughing and jokingly twirling her hand through her long, straight graying hair. "Or this pasty complexion?"

I laughed. "Ha— both, I suppose. And I cannot place your accent. It's almost American, but not quite."

"Technically, it *is* Northern American... I was born and raised in Canada. I met my husband, Amon, at university. He was from here, and after we married, he got a job offer in Alexandria, and we moved. We had come to Luxor to see his family when I met Hanan's mom, who was friends with my mother-in-law. A very long story short, she felt whatever it is that we all carry inside of us, and they brought me into the folds."

"That's awesome. So. Was your mother-in-law part of the sisterhood?" I asked.

"No. She isn't. But she and Hanan's mom were close friends."

"What happened to Hanan's mom? Her grandmother is still alive, right?"

"She is, yes. She and Salma's grandmother live together. Like Salma and Hanan, they grew up together and are thick as thieves," she paused. "Hanan's mom just passed away a few years ago...cancer. Just after my Amon, actually. It was a hard year for all of us."

I put my hand on the older woman's arm. "I'm so sorry, Renee. I can't imagine how hard it was to lose Amon and then for the group to suffer such a loss."

My earlier annoyance fizzled out, and my heart ached for them, knowing a loss like that of the old Steward would have been impossibly hard on top of just losing her husband.

"It was terribly difficult. I was there at the end of Mariam's life, softening her pain and easing her transition. It was one of the hardest I've ever been through. Amon's death was still so fresh in my heart. Luckily, Mariam was ready and didn't linger and suffer long once she reached the end." Her face was drawn, her voice sad and heavy, lost in painful memories. She shook her head gently, clearing her mind. I couldn't help but think that the power to ease someone's suffering like that was a gift beyond anything I could imagine.

"Okay. So, have you ever had your cards read before?"

I shook my head. "Um, no. I have a friend who does tarot cards, but I always told her no when she asked if she could do a reading."

Renee cocked her head to the side inquisitively.

"Super religious upbringing," I said, by way of explanation.

She nodded. "Ah, so lots of hellfire and damnation when it came to anything not found in the 'good book' then, I assume?"

I laughed then, grateful I didn't have to explain too far in depth.

"Exactly. I feel weird even holding these, even though, rationally, I know they're nothing more than tools. This whole process has been a lesson in more things than just magic."

Renee smiled gently at me, understanding.

"So let's just learn some history first, then, nothing too wild and out there."

Renee explained the history of Tarot and its uses throughout history and in her daily life. There were many different thoughts on the origins of the cards, and that part of learning the art of reading the cards was knowing where that art came from.

"Some believe the cards were first created in Italy and used in a card game in the 15th century. But others believe their history goes further back. It's all a little muddled, and there are references to the Romani who utilized the cards for arcane purposes, which is the most widely accepted belief regarding card readers.

Some even believe that the Romani brought Tarot up from Africa and that the cards and their use for divination originated here in Egypt by the god Thoth."

I raised my eyebrows at that, all the connections to Egypt adding up here and there to create a picture of a magically advanced society.

"All of that to say, there are a lot of different beliefs around it, but none of those beliefs include devil worship or anything scary or dangerous."

I nodded, discomfort lightening up just a bit.

"So, why do people think it's so bad or scary?" I asked.

"Honestly, it's the same old reasons. Control by the church over the narrative and the people. It was easier to keep people in line by explaining horrible or amazing things as God's will. It took the power away from the people and directed them to answer to a higher power that called for their obedience to the church."

"That makes sense, I guess," I said. "So much shit was done in the name of the church."

"It was. And still is. But that's a longer conversation for a different day. Back to the cards." She shuffled them deftly in her hands once more. "Just like magic, reading the cards is all about intention. So, when you come to the deck with a question or a problem, focus on it while you shuffle the cards. If you're alone, you can even speak it out loud. Whatever feels right."

I watched her hands move and tried to mimic what she was doing, though I lacked the finesse of someone who had been practicing for a long time.

We went through the cards, taking our time with the deck, and Renee showed me how to spot little hints within the art and about the major and minor arcana. I had my grimoire close by, making notes, and by the time it was time to do my first spread, the discomfort I'd been feeling around the cards had all but vanished. The designs and depictions were beautiful. It was a bit esoteric and more than a little overwhelming, but Renee had brought a couple of books for me to hold on to and learn from. She assured me that Tarot reading wasn't about memorizing each card and that it was perfectly fine to draw cards and then crack open a book to check their meaning if I couldn't divine one on my own.

"Okay. So, pulling with intention, I got it. But how do I know how many to draw?"

"There are many different methods and spreads—each pull is called a spread. It all depends on the question. Today, we'll just do a three-card spread, and let's do *past, present, and future*. Simple, effective, and great to begin with. I'll pull for you, too, and you can compare the two spreads."

Renee shuffled the cards and got quiet for a moment, focused.

"When you draw cards, it's important to focus your intent on whatever you seek. If it's just a broad spread like what we're doing now, just focus on the words. Right now, I'm focused on you—clearing my mind and thinking your name, studying your face, and thinking the words, *past, present, and future*." As she said the last three words, she drew a card and laid them face down next to each other. She looked up and smiled. "Now we flip them over and see what we've got."

She flipped each card one by one, and I bent closer to see. The first card was a heart with three swords stabbed into it, the second had three women holding golden cups above their heads, and the last was disturbing—a bound and blindfolded woman surrounded by swords stuck in the ground. Renee was contemplative for a moment, focused on the cards. Finally, she sat back and spoke.

"The Three of Swords for your past tells me you experienced deep sorrow, hurt, and pain. The Three of Cups is an easy one for your present, and I'm so glad it showed up!" she said. "It's a celebration of sisterhood and friendship, perfect for now. And lastly, the Eight of Swords for your future. The woman is bound and blindfolded, but if you look closely, you will see that if she takes her blindfold off, she can free herself of the bindings. That tells me that you'll have to let go of things holding you back, and only then will you be able to step into who you really are."

She looked across the table at me, and I had no clue what she had read on my face, but I was a little shaken. It seemed bizarre that a deck of cards could be *that* intuitive.

"Alright, dear, your turn."

My palms became slightly clammy; the first spread felt like it carried some weight. I reshuffled the cards, clearing my mind of chatter and thought of the words *past*, *present*, and *future* as I drew a card for each word and laid them in front of me. Renee gave me a few moments to take them in.

"Okay. Past. Upside down...nine of swords. Present, the Fool, Future, the High Priestess.

"Alright. Take a look in the book and read through what they could mean. It's all about interpretation, so don't look at it as a concrete, black-and-white thing. And an upside-down card is called a reverse card."

I nodded and opened the book next to me. There were pages for each card but a section at the beginning with words associated with each one. I'd go back and read deeper later, on my own, but The Reverse Nine of Swords meant deep inner turmoil. But what stood out to me most was the imagery—a man sitting up in bed with his hands in his head and nine swords above him.

"Do you want my help interpreting?" Renee asked, sensing my unease.

"Um. I think I'm good with the first one. I...it makes sense. And I just...I just don't want to delve into it." Renee nodded in understanding and leaned back in her seat, giving me physical and emotional space to mull things over.

"What about the Fool, though? And the High Priestess?"

"The Fool is nothing more than a symbol of a new journey; you are definitely on that. It's actually a wonderful card to get in a reading! The name is a little off-putting to some people, but it's a sign of opportunity and potential." Renee smiled, eyes twinkling. "The High Priestess is interesting. She symbolizes the divine feminine and sacred knowledge. She sits in front of a thin veil representing the conscious and subconscious realms and can travel between the two. This says to me that you're going to experience some spiritual enlightenment and that you're going to connect with the divine feminine. I think, given the journey you're on, that's an auspicious card."

We finished with the cards, my mind wandering—surprised, confused, and weirdly at peace with the reading. I was anxious to pull again and divine some direction and understanding in my life.

"Now, Hanan has a night tour scheduled." She looked at me pointedly. "Not the same kind of night tour *you* had, mind you. Do you want to have dinner together, or would you like some space to yourself?"

"I hate to do it, but I'm pretty beat. I think I'll just stay here and go to bed early," I said.

"I totally understand. Make sure you drink plenty of water and try to get some rest." Renee packed up her things and left me to the quiet garden.

Now that I was alone, my mind spun in a thousand different directions. I knew, deep down, that she'd meant well, but I couldn't shake the feeling of being forced into feeling a certain way about the ritual. I was left feeling more than a little violated.

I wondered if I would have even gone through with it had I not been forcibly calmed down. I picked up my phone to call Drew, but after his original trepidation at my staying, I thought better of it and let it be. He already harbored reservations. I'd have to sort out how I felt about it on my own.

26

All's Fair in Love & War

·　∗ ·☽·☽·○·☾·☾· ∗ ·

Naomi remained the anomaly of the group. Where the other women were warm, and their energies and magic seemed to want to meld *with* mine in an encouraging and comforting way, Naomi's was more aggressive. Something about her personality rubbed against me. Whenever she was at the house, I felt defensive and intimidated, making me increasingly irritable as time passed. Being around her was like rubbing a fine grit of sandpaper on my skin. Not enough to cause pain, but enough to cause an irritation that I couldn't ignore. And I couldn't help but get the sense she felt the same way.

It was the day before my birthday, and I'd been with the sisterhood for about six weeks, though some days it felt like I'd just arrived. This afternoon, under Naomi's tutelage, it felt like I'd been here forever.

"Do it again," she practically growled, annoyance rippling off her in waves.

"I know you're frustrated, but believe me, you aren't anywhere near as frustrated as I am with myself," I assured her, gritting my teeth and planting my feet for another magical assault.

"Somehow, I doubt that," she replied drolly.

I rolled my eyes as I turned away from her.

We'd spent the better part of the afternoon trying out offensive spells, and all I'd managed so far was a light tap of energy against her roaring aggression. Defensive spell-work was much more straightforward. In fact, learning how to protect myself had been the one thing I'd excelled at since I'd started learning magic. It had almost become second nature to throw up a physical shield of energy—the magic actually listening to my direction when I needed it to protect me. However, she'd knocked me off my feet more than once, and sore spots and bruises peppered my body.

"You can't just expect everyone to stand around throwing out spells to protect themselves and you too, you know." Naomi's words were sharp and cut to the bone.

I turned and looked at her, willing myself not to cry as anger welled up and threatened to spill down my cheeks. Cheeks that I knew were furiously red.

"Have you ever thought that maybe changing tactics when you teach me might help?" I snapped. "I don't see how even the most powerful witch could manage to even light a candle with you berating them," I huffed, hands shaking with anxiety and heart pounding in my ears. I'd never liked confrontation, but I had had enough of Naomi.

"Maybe if you were good enough to *deserve* these powers, I wouldn't have to bully you into using them." The words were clipped and dripping with venom, hitting me in the gut--her intended target. She had pulled out my darkest thoughts and laid them bare for me.

"Fuck you," I managed to choke out as I turned towards the guest house, stomping towards it, fuming. Angry tears coursed down my cheeks.

"We're not finished here," she called after me.

I stopped in my tracks and spun around, hair whipping into my face. She stood there, feet planted and hands on her hips, annoyance and disdain written as plainly across her face as if she had the words tattooed there.

"I said fuck you, and I meant it. We're done here."

I threw my hands up, fists clenched, and groaned in frustration. Magic shot out and sent her flying against the side of the house. I watched her flick her palm down and slow her impact. Judging by the force she'd moved, it was the only thing that kept her upright. She stood there, chest heaving, glaring at me as a sardonic smile spread across her lips. She raised her hands and pointed them towards me dramatically, slowly clapping like a smartass. I spun on my heels and stormed into the guest house, slamming the door behind me with nothing but the force of my will, but I was far too angry to be proud of myself. I forced my hands to relax and saw half-moons from my nails marking my skin. I worked at the indentions, rubbing out the tension in my hands and my mind all over the place.

✦

I fell asleep soon after lying down, exasperated, exhausted, and confused. The exhaustion won out over everything else—even a shower to wash off the sticky sweat and rage.

When I woke up, the room was cast in shadows and golden light from the setting sun. I checked my phone and answered messages from Hanan, assuring her I was fine but that I was taking the night for myself and I'd see her the next day. I sent the message and didn't wait for a response before calling Andrew, just wanting to hear his voice. When he didn't answer, I groaned and tossed the phone to the other side of the bed.

I laid there, trying to find the motivation to get up and wash off the day but finding it impossible. My mind oscillated between downright fury at Naomi and sheer joy that I'd managed to grab ahold of my magic without thinking. I just hoped I'd be able to do it without having to be so pissed every time. A quiet knock on the door shook me out of my thoughts. I groused a bit, not wanting to face Hanan and certainly not wanting to come face-to-face with Naomi.

I pushed myself off the bed and padded over to the door, taking note of my very stiff and sore arms. I smoothed my hair back away from my face and opened the door. Neither Hanan nor Naomi was standing there. Instead, a bouquet of flowers with legs greeted me. A face peeked around the bouquet, and I squealed, thrilled to see Andrew's beaming face on the doorstep.

"What? How? When?" I laughed as he stepped in, wrapping me in his arms and lifting me off the ground in a bear hug. He kissed me, and I breathed him in. Tears sprang to my eyes, emotions so close to the surface after the day I'd had.

"Hey—don't cry. I can leave if you really don't want to see me that badly," he said, trying to make me laugh. He kissed the tip of my nose, and I squirmed enough that he put me down. I stepped back, swiping my hand across my cheek.

"Oh, stop," I said, reaching for my flowers. I stuck my nose in the bouquet and inhaled deeply, the intoxicating scent filling me. "It's just been a shit day. But seeing you make it a hell of a lot better." I looked up at him and smiled. "What are you doing here?"

"You seriously didn't think I would miss your birthday, did you? It's a big one this year... last one before double digits!"

He laughed, and the sound did more to soothe my frayed nerves than anything I could have done on my own. He dug in his bag, producing an oversized rose gold number nine candle. I couldn't help but laugh then; my leap-year birthday was always a target of his teasing and adoration. He loved any sort of hullabaloo. Each year, we celebrated on the 28th of February and the 1st of March, but on leap years, when we celebrated my proper birthday, Andrew always went all out. It shouldn't come as a shock that he'd surprised me. I turned and set the flowers on the counter, and when I turned back, Andrew had closed the space between us.

"I missed you so much, Jules," he said, tenderly kissing me. I closed my eyes, relaxing against him, my body melting against his. He slowly ran his fingers down my arms, tracing lines up and down, his touch featherlight.

"I missed you too," I whispered against his lips. "I needed this today. I need you." He leaned his forehead against my own, and I kept my eyes closed, breathing him in and letting his presence steady me.

"How long will you be here? And did Hanan know?" I asked, finally working out the logistics in my head.

"Just a long weekend, I'm afraid. It's all I could swing. I leave late Monday night. I wanted to get here earlier, but this was the best I could do."

I smiled, joy filling me up and bubbling over.

"It's perfect! I can't believe you're here. I know it hasn't been that long, but I feel like so much has happened—it feels like forever." I wrapped my arms around him and laid my head on his chest, feeling the rise and fall of his breath and listening for the calming beat of his heart. His voice rumbled against my cheek as he answered.

"I can't believe you thought I'd let you celebrate an actual birthday without me. And yes, Hanan knew. I'd talked to her about it before I left the last time and hoped I could make it work."

He stroked my back, and I reveled in his touch, happy to be near him. You don't realize how much you miss physical affection from another human until you've been without it for some time and suddenly get it back. None of the sisters were cold, by any stretch of the imagination, save for Naomi. Still, a buss on each cheek from Marina, a quick hug from the others, or even Marwa's mothering affections was no replacement for a genuine connection like this. Weeks of tension slowly started to drain out of me.

"Have you eaten?" he asked.

"No. I actually just woke up from a nap," I said sheepishly.

"That bad of a day, huh?" he said. I released him, and he walked over to the bed and set his bag down before sitting on the edge. "Want to talk about it over some food?" he asked.

"I can eat. But there's nothing much to tell past the fact that Naomi is a wretched bitch, and I refuse to learn anything else from her."

I crossed the room, grabbed my phone, opened up the food delivery app, and sat next to him, resting my head on his shoulder and holding the phone where we could see the screen.

"What are you in the mood for?" I said, trying to shake the bitterness out of my voice.

"Whatever you want, babe. It's the night before your birthday...you choose."

After ensuring Hanan didn't want anything, I settled on pizza and placed the order. I added an extra dessert, wanting something sweet to soothe my frayed feelings from earlier in the day.

Drew headed to the shower to wash off the airplane germs. After he was finished, I hopped in and took a blistering hot shower. I was disappointed we had to wait on our food delivery and couldn't just shower together, but I was also grateful that I could turn the temperature up higher than he'd ever tolerate.

Being a leap baby always felt unique and magical on its own, but Drew and his family celebrated birthdays in a big way every year and had no problem incorporating my special birthday into their family traditions. They spent the day pampering their birthday celebrator, starting with birthday pancakes and continuing to spoil them rotten. I loved every minute of it.

I turned the water off and stepped out of the tub, toweling my hair off and standing in front of the mirror, taking in my almost thirty-six-year-old face. Besides bestowing me her cast iron skillet and love of food, my grandmother had taught me the importance of a good skincare routine, which had paid off. My skin was smooth and supple, just the faintest lines crinkling at the corners of my eyes when I smiled. I slathered oil and moisturizer on my face, sending a mental thank you out in the ether that I'd been blessed with decent skin.

I came out of the bathroom, towel wrapped around me, and found Andrew doling our food onto plates.

"Just in time," he said.

After toweling off, I slipped on some comfy sweats and a tank top, not bothering with anything else, knowing we'd be staying in the rest of the night.

We ate our dinner, laughing and catching up, our conversation light. There was so much I'd told him over the phone but still so much I wanted to tell Andrew about, but I didn't want to ruin the moment with my troubles.

After clearing away the food and getting ready for bed, we slipped under the covers, sheets cool against our skin. As always, I curled up against Andrew, his skin running hot and warming me through. I stretched out against the length of his body, pressing tight against him, his arms wrapping around me. I nuzzled into the crook of his neck, his scent clean from the shower but still him. He'd grown up hiking and camping in the mountains as a kid, and I joked that he'd spent so much time outside there that the mountain air had embedded itself in his skin.

"Mm...this is exactly where I've missed being." I sighed, an air of solace settling over us.

"Same," Andrew agreed as he slowly scratched my arm, running his fingers along it, sending tingles of pleasure through my body. "I'm glad I don't ever have to deploy again if I don't want to. I don't think we'd make it being apart that long anymore."

I laughed softly. "I don't think so either. Remember that one deployment that got extended to twelve months after you guys had done all those workups beforehand? We didn't see each other for what felt like two years. I know I couldn't do it again."

I shuddered, remembering how lonely that time had been, and cuddled closer to him.

"God, that was awful," he said, remembering. "I didn't think they'd ever stop putting out extensions." He kissed the top of my head. "I'm glad to not have to do that anymore. The job was fun, and I miss port calls and some of the people, but the uncertainty and length of deployments just got to be too much. I'm glad we made the call to get out."

I nodded. "Homecomings were pretty fun, though," I said, smiling.

He grunted in agreement, lips still pressed against my hair. He slipped the hand running along my arm underneath my shirt, and I angled my face towards him. Our mouths met, lips soft and tentative at first. His hand slowly crept up along my skin, gently caressing the skin on my ribs. I shifted more, and our kiss went from soft to urgent.

Andrew rucked my shirt up and kissed his way down the length of my torso, stopping at the apex of my thighs where he looked at me and then busied himself, teasing me first before shimmying my panties down and then settling in and focusing on my pleasure.

It didn't take long before I was panting and shaking, heart pounding and blood coursing through my veins, every sensation electrified. That hot flush of desire shot back up my body, leaving me feeling animalistic as I grabbed his face and brought him back towards mine. Andrew settled in between my legs, and I guided him inside me, gasping at the sheer pleasure of our skin coming together. He moved slowly at first, ever one to take his time and draw out pleasure. I was restless and hungry for more bliss, sensation, and everything.

I wrapped my legs around his waist and pulled him closer, tighter. Squeezing around him, desire took over, and I chased down the feeling. He breathed into my ear.

"Ha, you better slow down and quit squeezing unless you're ready for this to be over."

I smiled against his skin and licked his collarbone, tasting a hint of salt and soliciting a moan. I loosened my grip on him and gently pushed him to the side, rolling over and climbing on top of him. He pulled my shirt over my head and tossed it on the floor. I settled down on his length and rocked back and forth, finding a rhythm, my hand on his chest. He reached up and held on to my hip with one hand and reached between my legs with the other, helping me chase down more pleasure as I took charge.

Pleasure built up deep in my belly, and I worked against him, zeroing in on that feeling. I leaned over, bracing against the bed, hands on either side of him, breasts in his face. He reached up and sucked a nipple into his mouth, laving and sucking, adding more sensation. Soon, I was there, cresting the wave of a powerful orgasm, my body filling up and spilling over with dizzying gratification. In the next moment, Andrew tensed up and rode his own wave of pleasure with me, bodies moving together and slowly going still. I draped myself on top of him, utterly spent, both of us breathing heavily, skin damp against one another.

Afterward, we lay there curled against each other, content just to be pressed together, and fell asleep. Andrew's quiet snoring was an odd comfort after sleeping in the quiet for weeks.

27

Lucky Number Nine

"Happy birthday to you, happy birthday to you, happy birthday to you, dear Jules."

Andrew's crooning voice and birthday tradition woke me in the happiest way, making me grin ear to ear before my eyes were even open.

I sat up in bed, fluffing the pillows behind my back, and readily accepted the tray of birthday pancakes he'd made.

"Did you make these here?" I asked, confused. I hadn't heard him up rustling around at all.

"Nah, Hanan, let me take over her kitchen as long as I promised to make her some," he said, grinning. "Happy Birthday, gorgeous."

He leaned over to kiss me, walked over to the other side of the bed, and crawled in next to me.

"Is there anything you want to do today?" he asked.

"Hmm...I don't think so," I said around a mouthful of pancakes, raising my hand to cover my mouth—ever mindful of Andrew's pet peeve. He grinned.

"Good." He grinned wider when I looked at him, face screwed up, confused. "I hoped you wouldn't have anything specific—I have the day planned out, and you're going to love it!" he gloated.

We finished breakfast, and Andrew handed me a few small packages to open.

"This one is from Gram," he said, handing me a package wrapped in brightly colored paper. I unwrapped it and found a handwritten cookbook filled with recipes.

"Oh!" I said, tears spilling down my cheeks. I was touched by the work she put into the book and the love she threaded throughout. I held it up to show Andrew, and he smiled and wiped a tear off my cheek.

"She has been so excited about that cookbook, Jules!" he said. "She called me months ago to tell me about it."

I grinned, flipping through the pages and running my fingers along the lines of her handwriting, neat cursive written in blue ink. There were little notes at the end of each recipe, anecdotes, or memories attached to our favorite foods. She'd even left blank pages for me to fill in my recipes, knowing how much I loved experimenting in the kitchen.

I set the gifts aside and shifted down the bed, curling up against Andrew, finding that perfect spot against him, and sighed.

"Honestly, we could spend all day here, and I'd have the best birthday ever."

"No, ma'am," he scolded jokingly. "It's not every day you turn nine...or thirty-four, but still. We'll get dressed and head out in just a few minutes. You want to be surprised or know everything?" I thought for a moment.

"Maybe a little of both?" I asked. He kissed my head, running his hand up and down my side.

"I can work with that," he said. "First, you and I are going to the spa. I talked to Hanan and got us booked into a nice place with the full treatment—including a private lunch hand-picked by the chef at this restaurant, which is supposed to be really amazing. Then we'll come back here a little before dinner. Does that work?"

I playfully smacked his side.

"Um, that work? Yeah, I should hope so!" I joked. "How expensive is all that going to be, Drew?"

"Stop, Jules." He cut me off with a kiss. "Don't worry about it. If it makes you feel better, we're not paying for all of it—my mom kept harassing me about what to get you. When she asked what my plans were and I told her, she happily put money towards it, and so did Gram."

We spent the day being pampered and cared for more than any place I'd ever been. There was nowhere on earth quite like this part of the world regarding the hospitality industry. Andrew and I started splurging on spa treatments a few years before at the suggestion of some friends post-deployment as a way to reconnect and celebrate homecoming. We'd balked at the prices initially but truly had left after that first one feeling refreshed and connected. We started making it a part of our lives every few months—factoring in the extravagance and making it work in our travel budgets for almost every trip we took.

Lunch was a gourmet affair of little bites of the most decadent foods, decorated with swirls of punchy sauces, edible flowers, and wild additions like cloches trapping smoke over an eggplant dish. It was lavish and fanciful, and I enjoyed every bite.

After lunch, we found ourselves whisked away to a private spa room. An oversized soaking tub took up most of the space, and it was filled with mineral water and flower petals, the fragrant steam as intoxicating as it was inviting. I sank gratefully into the hot water, groaning in pleasure as I lowered myself onto one of the deep-set benches built into the tub. I laid my head back, resting on the lip, the water feeling like pure bliss. We soaked for a few minutes in silence, relishing the peace. I cracked an eye open to say something to Andrew. His posture mirrored my own, and he looked so beautiful sitting there, arms stretched out beside him, tattoos shining with water and body oil, shimmering in the room's low light.

I shifted and closed the space between us, floating between his legs. Oil-slick skin glided against each other like liquid silk and sent shivers down my spine. I kissed him, body flushed with heat—from the water and the fact that we were soaking together—and fanned the simmering burn of desire into flame. I answered the hunger with lips and teeth and exploring hands, coaxing Andrew's desire to roar up and meet mine.

We were too lost in each other to hear the knock on the door from the spa attendants. When we heard the startled "I'm so sorry, sir! Ma'am!" We jumped apart like two teenagers caught by their parents.

We stammered our apologies to the attendant, who quickly stepped back out. Andrew climbed out of the tub and lent a hand, helping me out, our bodies shaking with laughter we were trying to quell. I pulled him close and kissed him deeply, one last shot of heat and a promise for later. Dignified once more, we left the room, robes pulled tight and high on our chests just to be sure and followed to the next room for the final treatment of the day.

After manicures and a quick snack of tea and dates, we returned to Hanan's house, my body feeling pliant and soft. Since it was morning in the States, I took a few minutes to answer texts and video chats from Gram, Edie and her family, Delilah, and Andrew's parents. All of whom were surprised to hear we'd come back to Luxor for my birthday since we didn't typically travel back-to-back like that.

After catching up with everyone, we got ready. I knew the sisterhood was coming over to celebrate—that much we'd all planned out together once they found out my birthday was coming up. I slipped on a maxi dress, a flowy, light floral thing I'd found in a thrift shop years before that had become one of my favorite travel pieces. The crepe material, already wrinkly, made it perfect to throw in my bag and go. My hair hung loose in big, soft curls past my shoulders. I flipped my part to the opposite side, giving a boost of volume to my roots, and swiped on some mascara and a light smokey eye and felt like a million bucks.

Andrew, in snug jeans and a well-fitted button-up shirt he'd had tailor-made in Bahrain, the tiny flower pattern delicate and detailed up close, came up behind me in the bathroom as I finished my makeup. He looked in the mirror, over my shoulder, and ran his fingers through his curls, taming them a bit but leaving them loose. He moved my hair over my shoulder and kissed the back of my neck, lips soft and gentle.

"Happy Birthday, my love," he whispered against my skin. I finished what I was doing and turned towards him, twining my arms around his neck and looking up at him.

"Thank you. Today has been damn near perfect."

"Not over yet, love."

We met everyone on the rooftop, drinks in hand and big bulbs of soft lights strung all around the perimeter for when the sun went down. There were small bouquets of flowers and a handful of balloons with a giant number nine hovering above the rest. I looked at Andrew, who was grinning ear to ear as everyone shouted, "Happy Birthday," and met his grin with one of my own.

We spent the evening nibbling on food everyone had brought and devouring a decadent rose and pistachio cake that Reem had baked. The rooftop was filled with laughter, stories, and friendship.

We fell into bed that night, exhausted, stomachs sore from laughing so hard, but undeniably happy. We came together in the dark and the quiet. Our movements were lazy with the late hour but no less enjoyable.

"That might be one of the best birthdays on record," I said, curled against Andrew, just before drifting off to sleep, limbs pleasantly languorous.

✦

The next day, I took Andrew to all my newfound gems in the city. We sipped mango juice as we walked around the more local part of the souk, devoured the best vine leaves and hummus, and watched the sunset over the Nile.

The following day before his flight, we stayed home, spending the morning in Hanan's garden, showing off the things I'd been working on and learning while I'd been in Luxor. I'd already shown him the tarot cards. Ever an artist, he went through them, intrigued by the imagery and pointing out little things here and there that caught his attention. I'd done a couple of spreads for him, my initial nerves about the cards all but gone.

I lit candles for him and shut the door with only a thought. After she got off work, Hanan and I worked together, pushing and pulling against each other, similar to what Naomi and I had been trying to do, though with far less turmoil. Andrew volunteered to be the practice dummy, and I sent a wave of magic at him that didn't do more than ripple his faded denim shirt, which was rolled to the elbows.

"Wow! I felt that! That was crazy, babe!" he exclaimed, making me feel better about the tiny bit of magic I'd just performed.

Hanan looked at me as if to say, *let him be excited; don't tell him you don't think it's enough*. And so, I did. When we drove him to the airport, he was impressed, if not a little jealous. His excitement and awe helped give me a little boost, and seeing him go was hard.

28

Farewell

O ver the next year, I traveled back and forth to Luxor every couple of months to spend more time with the group. My magical abilities were...mediocre, at best. I was convinced I was destined to have no innate talent. Everyone assured me I was just being too hard on myself, but it was hard *not* to think that or compare myself to everyone else.

Our time in Bahrain was drawing to a close, and we had yet to decide on our next place to land. The choices were finally narrowed down to Singapore and Washington State; both locales came with a hefty price tag for travel to Egypt, so I had no idea when I'd see everyone again.

Andrew had some administrative things to do before a decision *had* to be made, so we were headed to Washington, D.C., and some time in the States with Gram and Drew's family for a bit. While I was excited to go "home" for the first time in years, my frequent trips to Luxor and the sisterhood were coming to a close, and I was already feeling the loss of it deeply.

———◆———

Before the big move, we held a special full moon ritual on my last trip to Luxor. This time, everyone convened— even the older members, the grandmas, and aunties who had stepped down from being active with the group. Some I had met over the year, and others were new faces. Together, we totaled twenty, which felt huge and tiny all at once.

While all evidence pointed to not ever having to confront the brotherhood or the tight-knit group of men who still searched for the scrolls to try and bring Thutmose back, I couldn't help but worry over such a small group making a stand against one much larger and more sinister. Everyone assured me that they'd all felt the same way in the beginning, and now and then, little moments of worry sprang up, but that the scrolls were safe and we had magic on our side. In some ways, the sisterhood felt like not much more than a witchy book club, our ultimate purpose being so esoteric and our magic more of a unique hobby than the deep calling I'd expected it to be.

The energy in the temple was excited, and when it was time to begin, it was reverent.

We came together, interlacing our fingers and forming a circle in the temple's main room. At the moment of connection, the jolt of power was far greater than I or anyone else had anticipated. Gasps sounded off the walls. Energy pulsed through us, a thing more tangible and alive than ever before. My eyes squeezed shut with the force of it, and I gripped the hands I held hard. They met my grip, startled by the intensity of our joining.

Lines of power ran through our hands and bodies. Connecting us. Binding us together.

I opened my eyes and saw the magic current rippling through the air. Shimmering like heat from a fire. Pouring off us in waves.

Hanan spoke, but her voice was muffled as if she were calling from another room. Slowly, her words drew strength from the magic, and her voice rang out into the room, calling us to join her and sing out, calling to the moon for power.

Our voices sang out one by one, chanting above the waves of power. Incantations older than the ground beneath our feet rang out from the depths of our souls.

We moved with the music of our spirits. Bodies swaying. Hands gripped tight. Hair unbound, heads thrown back in supplication. In ecstasy. Bliss rippled through my skin, my bones like jelly.

And, still, we sang.

She was there. In the room.

Everywhere and nowhere all at once.

Hatshepsut. Our sister. Our mother. Our divine.

She called us to her pool. To her power.

I found myself sinking into her womb once more.

Ritual oil, water, and bodies sluiced against my skin, heady with ripples of power and pleasure. I was hedonistic at that moment, searching out sensation. It was all too much and not enough.

She flowed through the water and the moonlight.

She was palpable and impossible to hold.

She was life. And power. And magic.

She was pleasure and pain.

She was the woman next to me. In front of me. Behind me.

She was me. I was her.

There was no beginning and no end to Her.

To power.

To magic.

The water was a tempest. The violent waters of birth. The raging storm of youth. The calm seduction of death.

The maiden. The mother. The crone. Together, we were all of them.

Together, we were divine.

————————————✦————————————

Time passed. Eventually, we returned to our bodies after we'd collectively spent ourselves, drawing down more power than ever before. We'd begrudgingly returned to Hanan's, no one ready to break the spell of the night. Earlier in the day, we'd set up the rooftop with the same pallets and bedrolls we used when we performed rituals and slept under the stars. The energy from the ceremony and the full moon vibrated through us all night, swirling through my mind as I slept.

The next morning, as the sun began to rise, my now tighter-knit group of nine who had slept out in the full light of the moon woke together, a quiet rustling of quilts and sleepy movements. The clear morning air greeted us as we all wordlessly stood together watching the sunrise.

The scent of food shook us out of our sunrise trance, and we headed down the stairs in search of breakfast. We found Hanan and Salma's grandmothers in the kitchen, leading the charge for breakfast. Pots and pans bubbling, amazing scents making my mouth water, and the yeasty, warm smell of bread excited me for what was to come. They shooed us out of the kitchen, and we spilled out into the garden to find steaming carafes of tea and coffee on a side table by the door, waiting for early risers. We all greedily took cups of warm drinks and found seats throughout the garden, greeting the sisters who had slept in the house and already awoken. We fell into a comfortable and reverent silence as the day began around us.

We all broke our fast together, and there was excited chatter amongst us all, the older members I'd met just the day before asking questions to get to know me better and my doing the same in turn. Hanan's grandmother, whom I'd met a couple of times earlier in the year and connected with instantly, was seated to my right. She was warm and friendly and told me tales of her wild travels when she was younger. She had been to places I'd only dreamt of. She had an insatiable curiosity about the world, driving her to search out ruins and temples of long-forgotten tribes and peoples. I could have talked to her for ages—each of her stories is grander than the next.

Eventually, the day wore on, and everyone returned to their homes, but we all took the strength of the night and the energy from the moon, feeling recharged and vivacious.

29

Home

I had an odd feeling as I boarded the plane to Bahrain. I had woken up feeling a heavy sense of unease, the lightness of the full moon ceremony long gone. I chalked it up to the melancholy of an ending, but it was still a much harder morning than anticipated, and the feeling lingered through the day.

The flight from Luxor to Cairo had been barely an hour, and then I'd had to hotfoot it to a separate terminal to catch my second flight. At that point, the unease grew stronger—weighing me down like I carried bricks in my backpack. I attributed it to the short layover time and the confusing nature of getting from one terminal to the next, but now that I was seated on my last flight of the day, I still couldn't shake the disquiet.

The flight wasn't crowded, and I was grateful to have an empty seat next to me, not one for small talk on a good day. I was feeling more and more on edge and needed the space. I dug through my bag for my AirPods and shoved them in my ears, scrolling my phone for something to help settle my nerves.

The telltale energy spike that preceded a panic attack rolled under my skin. Though they'd become fewer and further between, I still had panic attacks occasionally. They were easier to manage now that I understood the energy was magic, looking for an outlet. There wasn't much I could do on an airplane about that, so I settled back in my seat, closed my eyes, and let the music distract me enough to drop into a meditation.

Eventually, I drifted off and was roused by an abrupt landing, the plane skipping back up and touching down again, jarring me awake. I looked out the window to the dusty sunset, a big orange ball in the sky making its way down for the night, and sighed. We only had a few more weeks until we left the Middle East, and now that I was back and faced with saying goodbye and settling out our life here, I didn't know if I was ready.

After a few minutes on the tarmac, the plane parked at the terminal, and we all disembarked. I walked down the hall, heading toward Passport Control, and still felt off. For whatever reason, the weight of disquiet and dread was still there. The line for Customs was unusually long, and the wait did nothing for my mood. I was edgy and downright irritable—still on the verge of a panic attack—when I finally made it to baggage claim.

I sent a message to Drew telling him the luggage from the flight still wasn't there and that I'd be out as soon as I could manage. If he'd arrived on time for my flight's arrival, he'd already been waiting in the terminal for two hours or so. I knew he had to be tired of waiting. The Bahrain airport was many things, but comfortable was not one of them.

The shrill alert sounded at the carousel slated for my flight, and I watched as bag after bag made its way around. Finally, I caught sight of my suitcase. I hauled off the heavy black case, noticing a huge scrape down the side and a wonky wheel. A wave of annoyance joined the myriad of odd emotions I'd apparently packed on this trip. I headed out the door to the arrivals area and, hopefully, a much better mood once I saw Drew.

The whoosh of the automatic door past security opened up, and I saw Drew standing on the other side of the barrier. He was looking down at his phone, but he glanced up when he heard the door and caught sight of me. He offered a small smile, but we'd been together long enough for me to notice the telltale wrinkle of concern around his eyes. I wondered what sort of work drama he was dealing with.

"Hey, you," I said when I reached him.

"Hi gorgeous," he replied, hugging me and lifting my pack off my back to carry it. It was always odd to arrive back home and not kiss each other at the airport—the social norms in a Muslim country were so different from our own. We headed for the doors, and I was met with the warm night air.

"You okay, Jules?" Andrew asked, sensing my mood.

"Meh. I'm fine. I've been in a weird mood all day. I think I'm just tired," I answered.

"I'm sorry, babe. I know you're worried about when you'll see everyone again."

"No. It's not that. I've just felt...off all day. I don't know how to describe it. It's just weird."

Andrew was quiet as we walked to the car. He opened my door and loaded the bags before getting in the driver's seat. Instead of putting it in gear and setting off, he turned to me in his seat. I was looking at my phone, sending a message to the group to let them know I was home. He cleared his throat and put his hand on my arm. I looked up.

"I don't know how to tell you this," he started.

My stomach dropped, and I knew that something terrible was coming and the feelings I'd carried around all day had been there for a reason. A lump formed in my throat, and I knew.

"Don't say it. Don't tell me." I shook my head, tears falling.

But I knew.

"Jules-"

"It's Gram, isn't it?"

Andrew looked gobsmacked. "What? How do you know that?" he asked.

"I don't know. I've had a terrible feeling all day...a sense of dread. You started to say it, and it just came to me, clear as day. God, Andrew. I just—I'm supposed to see her in less than a month!" I broke off in a sob, body wracking, tears flowing down my cheeks.

Andrew leaned over and tried to wrap his arms around me, but the car made it awkward. He murmured platitudes in my hair that I couldn't hear over the pounding in my head and the ocean of grief that had opened inside me.

"What happened?" I asked, calming down after a few moments.

"She suffered a catastrophic stroke," he said, and I could tell by his voice that he was trying his best not to lose it. "She was at her mahjong game with her friends, and they noticed her speech changed, and then her face drooped. By the time the ambulance came...she was unresponsive." He paused, gathering himself, swiping tears away from his cheeks. "They made it to the hospital, but she had another stroke before they could do anything and that...that was it. They said she didn't suffer or feel any pain. She was unconscious for the second one..." he trailed off.

He waited a moment, letting it all sink in before I finally asked him to take us home. I was numb and overwhelmed with grief. We drove in silence from the airport to the house, Andrew's hand gripping mine, our hands growing clammy as tears poured down my cheeks without my even noticing. I dropped my bag at the door, muttering a quick hello to the cat, who was overjoyed that both of her people were home. I headed straight up the stairs, stripping off my clothes and letting them fall wherever they would.

I turned the water on, a quiet part of my mind hoping that the water heater hadn't been turned off for the summer months just yet. I needed blistering heat, not lukewarm water warmed by the sun. Much to my blessed relief, steam billowed over the top of the shower curtain, a cheery floral pattern that made me irrationally angry that it didn't match the darkness storming through me.

I stood under the hot spray until I couldn't stand anymore. I dropped to my knees, sobbing. Andrew found me and wordlessly turned the water off. He wrapped a towel around me and helped me to the bed. He climbed beside me, our bodies curling against each other, heavy with grief.

30

Grief

I slept. It was not the sleep of the tired but the sleep of someone who needed oblivion. I surfaced several times the next day to gulp water and nibble enough food that Andrew wouldn't force it. Each time I woke up, the stark reality that my Gram was gone hit, and I sought out the quiet darkness of sleep. The nightmares that plagued me in Luxor were kept at bay by the yawning maw of grief— there was finally something stronger than my demons, but I was too broken to care.

I don't know what it was about Gram's death that had cracked me wide open, but it felt like an impossible chasm of grief that I could not close. Perhaps it was because she had sounded so alive...so vibrant the last time I'd talked to her. It seemed impossible for that life to be snuffed out so immediately by a stroke. Maybe it was the loss of the plans we'd made. Plans to travel once Drew and I were stateside. Meals we'd talked about having together. Holidays we'd planned to celebrate. It all felt so abrupt. My Gramps' death hadn't been sudden. We'd all had time to say our goodbyes, and we knew what was coming and had time...there just hadn't been enough time with Gram.

Two days later, I dreamt of Gram.

She stood by my bed, watching over me. She said nothing but looked at me as if she truly saw me—all of me. The trauma, the hurt, the ugly, the beautiful. She saw the magic, power, love, and fear. A deep sense of peace settled over me. It wrapped me in warmth and smelled like my Gram- Elizabeth Taylor's Passion perfume and her scent—a mix of earth and rain and a hint of sugar from her baking. She came and sat, perched on the edge of my bed, before laying down and pulling me close to her. My head was pillowed on her breast, and her hands stroked my hair. And then she spoke, her voice barely above a whisper but commanding the room nonetheless, her soft, Southern lilt comforting after so long without hearing it regularly.

"My darling girl. I know that you grieve for me. I can feel your pain so deeply that it's almost my own. But you mustn't give up like this. There is work to do. Andrew needs you. They need you...the sisterhood. You were chosen for a purpose that will become clearer with time. You must lift the veil to see the truth. I see it within you. You have to see it, too."

I began to weep in my dream, tears creating wet splotches on Gram's soft cotton shirt, worn thin by so many years of use. She shushed me and made comforting noises in my ear, bringing me comfort and making me ache all over.

"Darling girl. I must go. But know that I will always be with you. I love you with all that I am. Do not be afraid to live your life, Julia. To live your life and live your truth. To lift the veil. You are so strong, lovely girl. So strong. Always..."

She began to fade, her body going translucent before disappearing altogether. I sat up in bed, awake, and could smell the faintest hint of her perfume. I shook my head, confused, and it vanished.

The next few days were a whirlwind. Not only did I have to try and logistically figure out funeral and legal things for Gram from half a world away, but we had a pack-out scheduled for the next week. The house was so far from being ready to be packed up and shipped off. We still hadn't decided where to go for our next posting. Andrew needed to prep for two interviews, and I needed to get to North Carolina sooner rather than later. I spent my days organizing the house and calling or going into the personnel office to show documents from the Red Cross that would placate them enough to authorize changing my flight from D.C. to North Carolina ahead of Drew.

I supposed I was lucky to have so many things to juggle because, after those first two days of all-consuming grief and the vivid dream, I didn't have much time to sit with my sorrow. I missed Gram every day, but her permission to let go, even in my subconscious, was enough to knock loose a little of the grief and help me move forward.

Andrew was beside himself with stress. He would have to handle the movers alone when we received the altered flight itinerary for me and realized they'd moved it back a little too far. But there was no changing it at that point, and we had to make do. We did our best to get as organized as possible, going through our things and deciding what to keep versus what to get rid of—the typical 'PCS purge' timeline having been shortened.

Saying goodbye to a place we've called home for the last couple of years was an odd feeling. All of my good friends, not that there had been many, had long left the island. The turnover rate of a place like Bahrain meant a steady stream of hails and farewells and more than a bit of loneliness. I drove to my favorite places on the island—restaurants that served huge spreads of Bahraini breakfast, *karak* chai places with the richest tea imaginable, and a small walkway next to the mall with the perfect view of the big orange sunset over the gulf that I had loved since the moment I first saw it hanging in the sky. I made my peace with leaving, quietly and reverently, and alone, as Andrew did turnover with his replacement and couldn't beg off work to say the same farewells.

The day before I left, Andrew was home from work, taking the time to spend the day together, making sure I had everything I needed. I was the executor of Gram's will, and while her best friend, Barb, was the interim, I knew that I had a lot of work cut out for me. It was my first time going to North Carolina since my Gramps' funeral. Every time we'd been to visit, she'd met us at Andrew's parent's house, or we'd meet somewhere fun for a little vacation—not wanting me to have to face the past.

"I've got everything," I said for the hundredth time. "I promise, Drew. It's sorted. The cat's export paperwork was signed yesterday, so she's good to go. I have a copy of your orders and all our legal documentation in the travel folder in the bag. I'm good."

He was pacing our bedroom, running his hands through his hair, making it frizzy and unruly.

"I know. I just wish I was going with you. I hate that you're doing this alone." He frowned at me.

"Drew. I will be fine. And I won't be alone. Delilah and Edie will be there. They're both staying at least that first week to help me start getting things sorted in the house. And your mom has said she'll come after they leave until you can get there if I need her to."

"I know. And I'm beyond grateful. I just wish it were me going. I know it's going to be hell to be back there again. Are you sure you're going to be okay?"

We'd had a version of this conversation over the last week as we'd prepped like mad to ready ourselves for this goodbye.

"I will be fine," I assured him. "Dr. VanHorn prescribed Xanax as an emergency if I start to panic. The girls will be there, and I will just come clean about everything so they get it. It's time for them to know, and it will help if I have a rough time. Honestly, I think it's going to be fine. I'll be cleaning out the house and getting it ready to put on the market. And the house is far enough away that I won't be revisiting old memories with every trip to the store I have to take." Andrew looked at me.

"Are you absolutely sure you want to put the house on the market? It is one of the few places in that god-forsaken town where we had some happiness?"

I shook my head, swallowing the lump in my throat.

"Gram and I talked a lot about it. It's what she wanted. I love that house, but that area carries too many shitty memories, and I know we'd never move back. She wanted us to sell and take the money to buy our own home, travel, or whatever we wanted to do with it. I'm good with that."

I stood up from the bed and walked over to him, wrapping my arms around his waist and resting my head on his back.

"Besides. I don't need little moments of happy memories from when we were younger. I have you now and all these new memories we're making, and there's nothing better than that."

He squeezed my arms and turned so that we were facing. He kissed an errant tear that slipped down my cheek and tilted my face to his.

"I love you, Jules. I really do." He took a deep breath. "I wish we weren't leaving here like this, but I have had the most amazing time in Bahrain with you." He kissed the tip of my nose.

"Same. I'm so glad we came."

I kissed him on the mouth, lips tentative. Between the grief and the utter exhaustion at the end of every night after dealing with the stresses of everything, every kiss had been chaste and, in a way, timid. The only thing resembling sex we'd had was when I accidentally rubbed against him when scooting around him in our closet a few days before.

The apprehensive kiss gave way to urgency, our bodies suddenly remembering what they'd been starved of since I'd been away this last trip.

Desire shot up my spine and then pooled in my belly, awakening a yearning inside of me that had laid dormant in my grief. Our mouths were hungry now—lips and tongues searching and soothing, reacquainting. Drew unbuckled his pants and shoved them to the floor, stepping out of them as he cupped my face, insistent and meeting my hunger with his own.

He walked me backward, pushing me against the wall. Rucking the thin cotton dress I was wearing up over my hips, he found me bare and growled with pleasure and lust. I wrapped my legs around his waist when he lifted me off the ground, and I cried out in pleasure when he seated himself inside me.

"Jul- I—"

I cut him off with my mouth, greedy kisses assuring him that I was okay. The wall was cold against my back, but Andrew was a fever inside of me. The contrast was dizzying.

"This time won't be long, love," he said against my lips, but I had no response but to meet his urgency. He sped up, hips roughly slamming me into the wall, but the pain was an anchor for that moment, and I was wild with wanting. Andrew cried out as he emptied himself inside of me and slowed down.

He shifted his grip on my hips and eased himself out before slowly setting me down.

"God, Jules. I'm so sorry. Is your back okay?" he asked after the heat of the moment had cooled.

I put my hand on his chest and pushed him away. "My back is fine, but I'm not done with you yet."

I moved away from the wall and pulled us both to the bed, collapsing against the soft mattress and upsetting the sleeping cat, who screeched and made her displeasure known by jumping off the bed and sauntering off in search of a less volatile sleeping situation.

We spent the rest of the afternoon in bed, making up for lost time and gearing up to say our goodbyes the next day. We ordered food, ever grateful that anything could be delivered in the land of sand. We ate in bed, sheets wrapped around our naked bodies to protect us from the drip of soy sauce from our sushi, cat pawing at the door we'd closed in her face.

We fell asleep that night, my head on his chest and his arm around me, and I felt at peace for the first time since landing in Bahrain. We came together once more, sometime in the night, bodies needing the connection just one more time before we separated again. Afterward, we lay there in the quiet dark, listening to each other breathe, not saying a word and not needing to.

31

Friendship

The flights from Bahrain to the States were long. By the time we made it to Norfolk, Virginia, I was exhausted, sore from sitting in a cramped airline seat that didn't recline all the way, and I was in possession of one very pissed-off cat.

After a quick line through Customs, Lumee and I waited for the bags for ages. I had all but wilted when I saw the bags on the carousel, and I was worried about the cat's poor bladder exploding. She'd done well on the trip to take advantage of the travel litter box I'd paid far too much money for, but it had been a long time since our last stop in Spain.

As we left the baggage claim area, I juggled a giant backpack, the cat carrier, and two huge rolling suitcases.

Standing there with giant grins on their faces were Edie and her girls. The oldest, Elise, was holding a sign that said *Welcome Home Auntie Julia*, and the two youngest, twins Enid and Emory, were holding a smaller sign that said *And Lumee* with looping, curly letters and sketches of cats all over it. They were all vibrating with excitement. They rushed me the moment they laid eyes on me, barreling into my legs and throwing their little arms around me while I tried very hard not to upset the cat carrier and drop poor Lumee, who was making her displeasure known in great yowling cries.

I managed to navigate us out of traffic and set everything down, including the cat, and the girls all crouched down to coo at her and beg to let her out. I stood up, finally free of baggage, and looked at Edie. She had a tiny bundle strapped to her chest with a soft, long piece of fabric wound around her in a complicated way I couldn't begin to understand. I stepped over to her and the newest bundle of joy, and she moved the floral fabric to the side, and I caught my first glimpse of my newest goddaughter.

"Hi, Elliot," I whispered, wrapping an arm around Edie's side. She was a few inches taller than me, which put me at boob height, but I rested my head there looking down at the perfect rosebud mouth, open in a sleeping 'o' and the dark thatch of curly hair.

"Elliot Jules," Edie said, and I just looked at her. They hadn't decided on a middle name for Elliot yet—hell, they hadn't decided on *Elliot* until a few days after she was born. Edie moaned about having to stick to an E name when they'd never planned for four kids when she and Eric named Elise a dozen years before. Tears sprang to my eyes as joy bubbled in my chest.

"Oh, Edie. Seriously?" I said, choking up.

"Absolutely. Should have done it with the first, but we had some grandma names for their middles to get through," she laughed and squeezed me. "Let's get you out of here and settled at the house. I love you, but you smell like an airplane."

I laughed and grabbed my bags; Elise, ever the helper, rolled one of my bags for me.

We made it to their house, the ride there filled with excited chatter from all the girls. I got Lumee settled in our room, Edie's pride and joy—the only room where the kids weren't allowed. It was a guest bedroom like something out of a magazine and a harken back to her days as an interior designer—before motherhood had put her very lucrative career on hold. I knew from many a visit to the house that high thread count sheets and an obscenely comfortable mattress awaited me. As tempting as it was to face plant directly onto the bed, I felt like my clothes could probably get up and walk away all by themselves, so I headed straight for the shower.

I hadn't been in the water long when I heard the door open and a little voice.

"Auntie?" I poked my head out of the shower curtain to find Enid's big brown eyes and wild, coiled curls staring back at me. She held a box of fruit snacks in her arms as she looked up at me. "Mom is feeding the baby again, and I can't find Elise. Can you open these for me, please?"

I laughed and tucked the shower curtain under my armpit. "Sure, toots, bring it over here."

I opened the box for her, which she took with a word of thanks. Then, unceremoniously, she dumped it all out on the bathroom floor and started rummaging through until she found the package she wanted. Then, surrounded by small packages of fruit snacks, she ripped her prize open with her teeth and started chowing down. I shook my head and went back to my shower, chatting back and forth with her as she snacked.

Edie and I met in San Diego, both new Navy spouses trying to navigate life in the military. Her husband, Eric, and Andrew met on the boat. They got along well—both being young and married and uninterested in port calls' more colorful aspects. After a short exercise in Hawaii, where some of their mutual friends had spent all their free time inside smoky and sketchy strip clubs, they teamed up and became good friends. They introduced Edie and me when they returned.

Our friendship was built on the mutual experience of not knowing what to expect from the Navy. Initially, we clung to each other, spending duty nights together and becoming each other's family. Where I'd left home in secret and to escape, Edie left behind a warm family that she struggled to be without. When she and Eric had the chance to move back to the East Coast, they jumped at it, and she'd been much happier being closer to their families.

Delilah had come in a few months after Edie and I met; her husband at the time was new to the ship. Dell had been on active duty herself for a few years. She and her husband Corey had met when they were young and on their first deployment. They'd tried to make it work for a few years but, ultimately, realized that they were better off friends and split amicably. They still vacationed together yearly, Delilah meeting him if he was deployed and exploring the world together. In truth, I think they both loved each other but loved their freedoms a little bit more, and neither one had found anyone worth giving that up for yet.

Delilah had taken one look at Edie and me, taken us under her wing, and shown us the ropes of military life. It helped to have someone who'd been on deployments and knew what it was like to navigate how to support our husbands and just what to expect. After the divorce, Dell had become sort of the Samantha of the group, regaling us with wild tales of her sexual escapades that made Edie and I cringe, drop our jaws, and cling to our husbands with gratefulness.

I finished my shower and wrapped myself in a towel before fully opening the curtain to find Enid still eating fruit snacks.

"Child. Your mother is going to kill me. How many of those have you eaten?" I said in mock horror. She grinned her smile gummy where her top teeth were missing.

"Shh. We just won't tell her." I winked at her and then motioned around the bathroom. "Well, if you don't want her to know, you've got to clean it all up. Hurry and return that box to the pantry—I'll get the empty wrappers."

Together, we cleaned her mess, me silently groaning at the five empty packets. I hoped Enid wouldn't barf up fruit goo any time soon and give us away, but I couldn't be sure.

After getting rid of Enid's snack evidence and getting myself dressed, I braided back my hair so I didn't have to dry it. I headed in search of Edie. I found her and Elliot in the nursery, both sound asleep in the glider, the shape of the baby's head matching the curve of Edie's swollen breast. I turned to leave quietly, and Edie's voice stopped me.

"I'm not asleep. Just rest my eyes and pretend Enid hasn't eaten half a box of fruit snacks in the bathroom or Emory isn't glued to the Nintendo. Elise is the only one I'm not worried about, and I wish she'd get into mischief sometimes. That child is such a little grown up." She smiled with her eyes still closed.

"They're all great kids. And you're not supposed to know about the fruit snacks," I said, chuckling quietly to not disturb the sleeping baby.

"I know everything," Edie replied. "It's mama magic."

I had a weird jolt go through me at the use of the m-word, but we both laughed, and she cracked open her eyes.

"Come sit before they come looking for us or burn down the house."

I did as I was told. Edie was formidable in any room—even a sweet pink nursery. I sat cross-legged on the floor and then decided to stretch a bit, muscles stiff from so long on an airplane.

"Okay. I know you're not okay. But...how are you?" Edie asked, concerned.

"Um. I don't know. Exhausted. Anxious. Terribly sad. Just...a lot," I said.

"I know. I am so sorry, Jules. I really am. Gram was amazing, and I know you've got to be devastated."

"I am. It was just so unexpected. I think that's the worst bit. Watching her waste away would have been awful, too," I said, quietly thinking of my Gramps. "But I just never expected it. Obviously, she was older, but after the hip replacement, she bounced back. She was in her garden all the time, she traveled, she was just so vibrant. It seems impossible to think that something could take her so suddenly." While the overwhelming grief had subsided, a deep sadness had taken its place.

"I know. I can't imagine. I remember how hard it was to lose my Nan. If you need anything, just say the word."

"Just being here is helping. Seeing you, the girls? It's the best thing to soothe a broken heart."

We heard a crash and shouting from downstairs. I looked at Edie, and she looked at me, eyebrow quirked and mouth pursed.

"Yeah, that sounds like the perfect remedy for grief if I ever heard one," she said sardonically. She shifted the baby in her arms, who gave a mild noise of protest. I stopped her.

"I'll go see what the damage is. Just stay here and relax."

I got up and headed down the stairs to find the twins arguing over who had dropped their Nintendo Switch, but neither one moving to pick it up. I walked over to them, their shouts and snarls reminding me of the feral cats in our compound.

"Girls. Chill. Stop yelling at each other and tell me what happened."

I gingerly picked up the Nintendo. It was warm in my hands. My fingertips tingled with knowing, and I dreaded flipping it over to find a spiderweb crack across the glass front. I took a breath, narrowing my eyes at the girls, and flipped it over, surprised to see it whole and intact.

"Dude. Nothing is wrong with it—why are you screaming?" I asked, shutting them up.

"Auntie, it is broken. We heard it shatter when *she* knocked it out of my hand," Emory said, pale face flushed with rage at her sister. Luckily for everyone, because they absolutely would have used being identical to their advantage, the hellcats had been born total opposites and, therefore, easy to tell apart. We had all joked at how much harder life would have been had they looked alike. Emory had come out with her mother's coloring—fair skin and red hair, though it was the same texture as her sisters. Enid had come out with Eric's darker skin and features but with Edie's blue eyes, which were striking on her face. Both girls were equally stunning but equally wild and precocious.

"Well, I don't know what you could have possibly heard over your screeching at each other, but look, it's fine," I said, presenting them with the handheld console, not a scratch. Both girls looked at the Nintendo and then back up at me.

"What?" I asked.

"Uh. What did you do, Auntie? Is that a new one?" Enid asked.

"Yeah, the chip in the corner is gone from where I dropped it outside."

I looked back down at the Nintendo in my hand. It looked brand new, not even typical signs of wear and tear on it, and I knew they'd had it for a little over a year—it had been a Christmas gift from Andrew and me the year before last. A knowing shudder rocked down my spine.

"Um. Maybe it was just some plastic left on the screen, and it came off?" I said, trying to hide the fact that I had just randomly and unexpectedly manifested magic to fix something.

I left them playing video games, confusion forgotten in favor of battling each other in Mario, and went in search of Elise. I found her in the kitchen, flour on her cheek and all down the front of her apron, a sweet vanilla smell hitting me as soon as I walked in.

"And what are you up to, kiddo?" I asked.

I heard a telltale meow and looked down to find Lumee winding around Elise's long, gangly legs. The twelve-year-old hit a growth spurt recently and looked like an awkward stork— all long limbs she hadn't grown into yet.

"Looks like you made a friend."

"I did. And I made cupcakes," she said.

I grabbed the dishtowel on the counter in front of her and swiped at her cheek.

"Oh really? All by yourself?" I asked. I had no frame of reference for the right age for kids to do things, but twelve seemed awfully young to have that ability.

"Yeah. Mom used to stay here and supervise," she said with air quotes around supervise, rolling her eyes. "But she finally realized I am not one of the hellcats, and I can do it on my own."

I smiled despite myself. "Are you supposed to call them *hellcats*?" I asked, trying to suppress my amusement.

She turned back towards me and narrowed her big green eyes at me.

"Auntie. Everyone calls them *the hellcats*. It's who they are."

I laughed, throwing my head back and belly laughing. A deep sound filled the room and made me realize how long it had been since I'd laughed like that. Swiping at tears in the corner of my face, I walked over to Elise, surprised to find her almost my height, and hugged her.

"I've missed you, Elise." I kissed the top of her head and breathed her in. Her hair smelled fruity and almost cloyingly sweet, and I remembered my preteen days of too much body spray.

We stayed like that for a moment and were interrupted by the oven alarm, which alerted Elise to take her cupcakes out. She skillfully slipped on oven mitts and took out two tins of cupcakes, perfectly rounded and with golden brown tops. I was beyond impressed and told her as much.

"Well, I love all the baking shows, and Mom likes having help in the kitchen, so it works out. I'm going to have my own bakery when I grow up," she told me.

"Elise, honey, if these cupcakes taste half as good as they look and smell, I don't doubt you'll have a roaring success on your hands." And I meant it. They looked damn near perfect as she tipped them out onto a cooling rack and then got to work on her frosting.

I perched on one of the barstools around the kitchen island. I watched her work, catching up with what she'd been doing and hearing about her friends— we fell back into easy patterns with each other. Eric had been deployed when she was born, and I'd been in the room with Edie. The midwife asked if I wanted to help deliver the baby, and an exasperated nod from Edie permitted me. I moved from her side to the foot of the bed and welcomed the slippery, goo-coated, and beautiful baby into the world, marking one of the best moments of my life. Since then, we'd had a strong bond, and I loved her like my own.

Edie came into the kitchen, hair a bit of a mess and a wet spot on her shirt where one of her boobs had leaked. I stood up and hugged her, just happy to be around my people and able to dole out hugs again. She assessed the goings-on in her kitchen and asked if I wanted a glass of wine, which I declined. Jet lag and twenty-four hours had exhaustion pulling on me in every direction, and I knew if I drank even half a glass of wine, I'd be done for.

Eric arrived home shortly after that. We cooked dinner and spent time catching up while spaghetti sauce bubbled on the stove and garlic bread baked in the oven, filling the kitchen with homey and comforting smells. Dinner was a loud affair with laughter and noise, and I sat back in my chair, happy to be a part of it.

It wasn't long after that I trudged up the stairs to the guest room, unable to stay awake any longer. My eyes were heavy, and everything down to my bones was tired. I brushed my teeth as fast as possible and crawled into bed, scooping Lumee up as I went, exhausted and falling asleep before I could even plug my phone up to charge.

32

Memory Lane

I woke in a dark room, unsure where I was or what was happening. My heart was racing, and my skin was dewy with sweat. I sat up in bed, trying to get a grip on reality to pull me out of the last vestiges of a dream. Finally, I woke up enough to remember where I was and that I was safe. I flopped back onto the pillows, exhausted but wide awake. I reached for my phone on the bedside table and checked the time. Three a.m. Too early to be up for the day.

I checked my messages from Drew and sent him a note wishing him luck for the pack out. We chatted back and forth, him updating me on the mover's progress and asking after the girls. After an hour, I forced myself to put the phone down and try to get back to sleep. I tossed and turned for a while, tired but unable to just drop back to sleep.

By the time sunlight filtered through the curtains in the room, I was still wide awake, cranky, and needing vats of caffeine to temper the throbbing in my head. My entrance to the kitchen was met with yelps of excitement and hugs from three very energetic girls whom I envied very much at that moment.

"Morning, Jules," Eric said, Elliot strapped to his chest in the same fabric wrap Edie had worn the day before. He was moving around the kitchen at a bounce, patting the baby and making breakfast for the big girls. "Pick your poison—tea or coffee?"

"It's going to have to be coffee this morning. Jet lag sucks." I yawned deeply as if to prove my point. "Got it. Do you need milk and sugar to make it resemble anything other than coffee?" he asked.

"Oh. I definitely need it to taste like anything other than coffee, please."

He shook his head. Like Andrew and most military people I knew, Eric couldn't understand anyone who drank coffee anything but thick and dark with a strength that would knock your socks off. While I needed the strength, I had never acquired a taste for the bitter brew all on its own. I accepted my very doctored cup of coffee and took a sip. Milky sweetness with a hint of caramel and cinnamon did a great job at masking the coffee taste and giving me hope that I'd get rid of my headache and lose the fatigue fog quickly.

"Mm...perfect, Eric. Thank you," I said gratefully.

"I aim to please," he said, grinning. And he did. He was such a chill man; he and Edie were opposites in many ways, but they made it work and were the perfect example of opposites attract. "Would you mind sneaking Edie's coffee to her? She's in the shower, trying to find five minutes of peace. This one was up quite a bit last night, and a certain set of twins were up before the sun this morning."

I nodded and headed to the main bathroom, knocking before hearing an exasperated Edie.

"Whaaaaaat? Mama needs five minutes, please!"

I laughed. "I think Mama also needs coffee."

That was greeted with a whoop and an excited invitation to come in. I closed the door behind me, trapping the steam that had filled the bathroom, and walked over to the shower, where an arm shot out and grabbed the mug. A few seconds went by, and Edie groaned.

"God, that's good. Nothing like shower coffee," she said, mood markedly improved by a quick jolt of caffeine and sugar to the system.

"Enjoy your shower; I'll meet you downstairs," I said as I walked towards the door.

"Don't you dare leave me. We can have an uninterrupted conversation, and you can ward off any little trespassers so I don't have to. They have a teacher work day today, so, for once, I get a shower to start my day, and I don't have to rush around like crazy to get everyone out of the door on time."

"Happy to oblige, madame."

I leaned against the counter, a cup of coffee cradled in my hands, warmth seeping through. I sipped as we chatted, catching up about nothing in particular, just the conversation of two long-time friends with time on their hands.

After Eric made pancakes and scrambled eggs for breakfast, Edie and I packed the van. With a flurry of hugs, kisses, shouts, and waves from the big girls, we pulled out of the driveway, baby in tow, and headed to North Carolina and Delilah.

When they both offered to help with Gram's house, I jumped at the chance—not only for help but to have us all together again. It had been far too long, and a part of me was so excited to be together, no matter the circumstances.

The drive was surprisingly calm, and our little stowaway was a happy traveler who only woke up to eat and have her diaper changed. The feline stowaway made more noise than the baby, though I couldn't blame her after having been stuck in the carrier for so long. We spent the five-and-a-half-hour drive switching between driving duties, eating too many fast-food French fries, drinking too much soda, and talking nonstop.

Crossing the border into North Carolina made my heart skip a beat, but the turn into the neighborhood sobered the mood of the car. The weight of grief settled back on my shoulders as I turned down the cul-de-sac. I steadied myself, knowing that walking into Gram's house without her to greet us would be impossibly hard.

I pulled into the driveway and parked behind her Subaru. Edie gave me a minute to gather my nerve and got out of the car to get Elliot and the diaper bag. I closed my eyes, hands still on the steering wheel, and took a deep breath. It was now or never, and it was better to just get it over with.

Finally, I got out of the car, grabbing the set of keys Andrew and I had made sure multiple times I had with me. I grabbed Lumee's cat carrier, and we walked up the steps to the front porch, me not daring to stop and take in the little house that held some of my happiest childhood memories. I shifted the carrier to my other shoulder and opened the screen door, letting it rest against my hip as I unlocked the cheery yellow front door. I did my level best to ignore the handmade wreath on the door, a reminder of Gram's artistic side stinging.

I opened the door to a wave of scent-tinged memories. Gram and Gramps' house had always had a distinct smell, as everyone's does, but I hadn't been back for years and been faced with it directly. I choked back a sob and let us in, lowering the cat carrier to the floor and unzipping it. Lumee sniffed apprehensively and took her time coming out. Eventually, curiosity won out over trepidation, and she took off to explore. Edie walked over to the oversized lazy boy that still held the imprint of Gramps' butt and plopped right down, releasing a breast and attaching Elliot to it in the practiced way of a mom four times over. I mumbled something incoherent about the litter box and returned to the van for some air.

I grabbed Lumee's things and headed back inside, a little more prepared for the familiarity and sadness to hit. I sorted the cat out and walked the house, ensuring everything looked okay and just taking time to say hello and goodbye all at once.

The house was a bit musty from the stillness of being empty for three weeks, so I opened a few windows, grateful that it was a clear, warm day—the first little taste of spring in the air. I finally sat down on the sofa, an oversized floral monstrosity that I had teased Gram mercilessly about upgrading, but she refused, claiming it had finally worn in just right. She wasn't wrong. It was perfect, and I sank back into the cushions. Edie looked at me, tears in her eyes.

"You okay?" she asked.

I nodded, not trusting myself to speak just yet. I sat back, closed my eyes, and breathed it all in.

"How long til we have to get Delilah? The airport's an hour away, right?"

I nodded again, swallowing the lump in my throat. "Yeah. It's an hour or so. You and Elliot can stay here if you want. I know she's been in the car for so long already today."

Edie looked relieved. "You sure? It's no bother- she doesn't mind riding."

I shook my head at her. "No, it's fine. You guys can rest, and Dell and I will pick up dinner on the way home. In the mood for anything in particular?" I asked.

"Nah, whatever you guys want is fine. I'm easy."

Elliot was awake and looking up at her mom, making little sounds and squeals of happiness.

"Okay. We'll figure something out." I took a breath. "I guess I need to check the pantry and fridge. There's no telling what's been here for weeks going bad."

We headed into the kitchen and found it spotless. The counters were clean and empty of fruit, the fridge had been cleaned out, and the trash can was empty. I found a note beside the kitchen sink and picked it up, reading the perfect looping cursive of Gram's best friend, Barb.

Julia,

I knew you wouldn't mind if I let myself in and made sure the house was ready for company. Alice wouldn't have wanted you to come home and clean. I made sure the trash was taken out and to the curb and all the food that would spoil was taken care of. I also did her laundry so you and your friends have clean sheets on the beds and clean towels in the bathrooms.

I know it will be overwhelming at first, but honey, please call me and let me come and help you. There's a lifetime of things here, and you'll need help sorting through them.

I put some meals in the freezer—just a lasagna and a couple of casseroles. Say the word, and the cavalry will come and bring you girls some food. No arguments, dear; it's what we grandmas do.

Love to you and Andrew-
Barb

"I like Barb," Edie said, reading over my shoulder. "She can bring all the food she wants over here if it means we get a break from cooking and enjoy some real southern grandma food." I laughed at that and agreed.

"You actually *will* like Barb. She's very no-nonsense and likes to take charge. She and Gram butted heads now and then, but only over silly things. They loved each other deeply and have been friends as long as I can remember."

I smiled, thinking about them bickering over who made the best chicken salad or whose tea was too sweet or not sweet enough. Good-natured jibing was as much a part of their friendship as the constant companionship that widowhood within six months of each other had pulled them towards. Barb had been there with Gram at the end of Gramps' life and vice versa. As bereaved as I was, I knew Barb was feeling it, too, and I hoped their other friends were rallying around her.

I took a moment and phoned Barb, letting her know that we'd arrived, making plans to see her the next day, and riding together to the meeting with the estate lawyer. Edie and I unloaded the car and plopped Elliot on her playmat in the living room. We turned on the TV and scrolled Netflix to find something mindless to put on, both of us wanting a bit of quiet and a distraction.

✦

I made it to the Charlotte airport in record time and with no traffic to speak of, talking to Drew almost the entire trip. The pack-out was finished, and the moving company had come that day to load the boxes onto the truck. Drew was exhausted from cleaning the house and making sure everything was handled. I hung up the phone just as I pulled into a parking space at the airport, right on time for Dell's flight.

Less than five minutes of standing there, I saw Delilah heading down the escalator at a clip, a small bouquet of roses in her hand, picked up from god knows where. She smashed them between us when she slammed into me. I cried then—great, wracking, embarrassing sobs right there at baggage claim. Dell tut-tutted and shot nasty looks at passersby till I calmed down. I still sniffled and rubbed my red eyes as we walked to the car.

We grabbed food on the way home—Mexican food complete with to-go margaritas that Dell had somehow sweet-talked them into packaging up for us. We spent the night cooing over baby Elliot, who was thrilled to have the undivided attention of three adults, gorging ourselves on chips and salsa and, in mine and Dell's case, drinking too many margaritas since we didn't have to breastfeed a baby all night.

We poured ourselves, giggling, into bed after settling Edie and Elliot into one of the guest rooms and ensuring she had everything she needed. Dell climbed in next to me and fell asleep almost as soon as she was horizontal. Soft snores filled the room and helped me fall asleep, and I was thankful not to be alone.

33

Shock & Candor

Barb came over the next day bearing coffee cake, groceries, and an iron will to help me do what needed to be done. She took one look at me and declared that I'd lost too much weight and that she'd see to it while she could. She wasn't wrong; between all the traveling and the grief, my clothes were loose.

We left Edie and Elliot at the house. Edie planned to go through Gram's clothes and organize them into piles for donation or the bin, should anything be too worn. I'd kept aside her old cotton cardigan, one that had lived on the back of her rocking chair on the screened-in back porch for as long as I'd been alive— probably longer. It was a faded peach color with deep pockets that always held tissues or candy wrappers, and I couldn't bear to get rid of it. Dell had claimed a tacky Christmas sweater, and I was happy to find new homes for the rest.

Delilah, Barb, and I drove to the lawyer's office armed with every piece of documentation I could think of that I might need. I had legally changed my full name, and Gram and Gramps had been aware. Still, I worried they hadn't changed their wills to reflect it, so I was armed with old documents bearing the name I'd left behind all those years ago.

Dell and Barb got on like a house on fire and talked nonstop the entire way there, which was fine by me. I was contemplative and somber—the finality of the will reading staring me in the face.

We arrived at the Main Street of town and found parking in front of a little shop filled with multiple stalls of local artisans that Barb gushed over and made us promise to stop in before we left. It had been years since I'd been back. The once run-down main street had been gentrified— quirky eateries and shops using the vintage-style storefronts and turning what was once almost a ghost town into something out of an off-the-beat-en-path travel article.

The office for Abernathy, Johnson, and Coombs was above the local drugstore—one complete with an old-fashioned soda fountain and the best grilled cheese sandwiches on the planet. It was one of the few things that seemed left from my childhood.

A friendly, older secretary seated us in a conference room with a large table and office chairs and assured us that Mr. Willis would be with us shortly and that she was sorry for our loss. We took our seats, the faux leather swivel chairs squeaky and uncomfortable, and waited less than five minutes before a man about my age walked through the door.

He was of average height and had a build that had gone paunchy around the middle. His receding hair was slicked back with too much gel. He looked familiar, but I couldn't quite place him. His eyes were beady, cheeks flushed, standing out against his pale face, but his charcoal suit was well-fitted, and he had an air of authority (and a musk of expensive cologne) around him. I stood up and shook his hand, his grip clammy but firm.

"Mrs. Wheelright, I'm so sorry for your loss. Mrs. Lane was a fine woman. I'm Mr. Willis. Mr. Abernathy is in court today and asked me to meet with y'all and get things sorted," he said, drawl thick and syrupy. He held my hand a bit longer than customary and looked hard into my face, thin lips pursing. "I know you, don't I?" he asked, sending my hackles right up.

"Um. I don't think so, Mr. Willis," I replied, trying not to sound too ruffled.

"Yeah," he said, sure of himself. "You went to East Mountain, right? A couple of years younger than me." He rifled through his paperwork, trying to find my name. "Julia Wheelright..." He looked at me for confirmation.

Recognition punched me in the guts so hard I almost doubled over. He'd been in Gordon's class in school. They hadn't exactly been friends, but everyone had known Gordon. Which meant everyone knew his girlfriend. I was hot and cold all over, my pulse racing. I shifted in my seat, the faux leather squeaking.

"Yes. That's correct. Julia Wheelright."

Dell felt my discomfort and put her hand on my back, assuming, I was sure, that it was just grief making me uncomfortable.

"And I'm Mrs. Barbara Coker. Alice's best friend and the other person listed there in her will. Julia travels and lives away, you see, and Alice knew she'd need someone local just in case she wasn't home." I mentally kissed Barb full on the mouth for distracting Luke Willis. "Mr. Abernathy has already started a few things for us at my request, wanting to get ahead for Julia here. Now, we don't want to take up too much of your time, Mr. Willis, so what needs doing today?"

The lawyer looked slightly flustered at being redirected, but he recovered quickly and drew out the paperwork, eyes scanning.

"Yes, I can see that here, Ma'am," he said to Barb. "Well, I just need some identification and a few signatures, and then we can get down to it. It's all fairly straightforward. Mrs. Lane didn't want anything too convoluted. She didn't want to make a fuss."

I reached into my purse and pulled out my driver's license. We'd changed our residency to California when we'd moved there after we first got married, and I hoped that would throw him off a bit.

"Oh, I definitely recognize you in this photo. We went to school together." He looked at my ID and back up at me, seemingly proud of himself for guessing correctly.

I inwardly groaned, not even thinking about the fact that a new photo hadn't been taken since I was twenty.

"Um. Yeah, maybe. I was a bit of a loner through school, though, so I doubt we would have crossed paths," I stammered. "So, what do I need to sign?"

It was taking everything in me not to have an absolute meltdown around the conference table, frayed nerves splitting wide open. Dell's hand was still steady on my back, and I knew I'd have to explain why I was so jumpy when we were finished. I knew that she had to be able to feel the heat and dampness of my shirt—my entire spine having broken out in a sweat as soon as he'd recognized me.

"So, I've got a copy of the death certificate and sent that through, so it's all been verified. As Mrs. Coker said, darlin', we got started on some of the basics; everything has been left to you, and it looks like your grandma made sure your name was on everything so it will be straightforward."

Delilah stiffened next to me at his use of *darlin'*, her West Coast upbringing not understanding the sticky, sweet, and condescending terms of endearment thrown around as often as *Sir* and *Ma'am*. Luke Willis flipped the page and read something else.

"Looks like I've got one other person listed. An Andrew Wheelright...that'll be your husband then?" He asked.

"Yes," I answered. "I have a Power of Attorney and copies of his IDs if you need them. He's overseas right now."

"I do, so copies of those would be great. It looks like this is a later addition to the will, and it's for the contents of her safety deposit box over at the Community Bank."

I slid the papers over to him, and he looked them over.

"Oh, I know him too!" He slapped his hand on his knee. "High school sweethearts, then, you two?" He asked in the nosy way of southerners who think they have a claim on your story.

"Not exactly," I said noncommittally.

He studied me for a moment, making me shift in my seat. My heart had stopped pounding in my chest, but it was beating erratically. The walls felt like they were closing in, and the miasma of smells in the office was stifling: stale coffee, industrial cleaner, and the lawyer's strong cologne all but choked me. The tell-tell swell of panic was bubbling up. I wished there was a spell I could do to magic the recognition right out of him and end this, but I just shifted again in my seat. I cleared my throat, making it clear I was ready to be finished—tamping down the panic and thoughts of magic.

"Well, all the particulars are sorted, so the only thing left is to tell you what's coming your way. Mrs. Coker, I'll start with you." He straightened his already straight tie, a punchy red paisley, and read directly off the paper.

"To Mrs. Barbara Coker, I leave fifty thousand dollars, a cookbook handwritten with all the best recipes she needs to know, and anything she and Julia agree on from the house that she might want."

I looked at Barb, who had gone stark white and was frozen.

"I'm sorry, Mr. Willis. What was that figure you said?" Barb asked, obviously flustered as she fanned her face with a folded handout Luke had brought about the firm. The stern photos of the three lawyers on the front waved back and forth as she fanned herself. For some reason, it reminded me of those huge, wacky, waving men from used car lots, and I stifled a hysterical laugh.

"Ma'am. I said fifty thousand dollars."

Barb sagged in her chair. "Why on earth would that confounded woman leave me so much money?" she said, shocked.

"Actually, Ma'am, she answered that very question right here—*tell her I want her to do all the things she's put off. To travel and go shopping and, for God's sake, re-do the damn kitchen*, begging your pardon, ma'am, that's verbatim."

Barb laughed then, and then the laughter turned to tears, and she sniffled quietly in her seat. She dug through her handbag resting on her lap and came out with a pressed white handkerchief, tiny flowers embroidered along the edges, dabbing her face. After she'd settled, I reached my hand out to hold hers. Her warm hand squeezed mine, and I felt a wave of solidarity and love with Barb, grateful for her presence.

"She's also leaving a big donation to a charity, which looks like the local Women's shelter, but we can take care of all of that for you," he continued scanning the paper. "*To Julia Nell Wheelright, I leave the house at 2 Pollardswood Drive, the Subaru Outback registered in my name, the total sum of my banking and investment accounts, and the entirety of my life insurance policy save the fifty thousand dollars for Barbara Coker and the fifty thousand designated for charity.*"

Luke Willis shuffled through his papers some more, pausing to read them.

"So, after the hospital bill is paid, which we have copies of, and the sum she had set aside for Mrs. Coker and charity, that leaves you with one point five million dollars from her life insurance policy and about the same in assets—her bank accounts and investments." He looked at another piece of paper. "The only debt she has, it looks like, is an outstanding balance on a store charge card of ninety-seven dollars and thirty-four cents."

He looked up to find three absolutely stunned women, mouths hanging open, staring at him. My panic momentarily paused in favor of utter shock. Unfazed, he continued.

"Mrs. Lane left a note, Mrs. Wheelright. She said she knew she'd have some explaining to do." He passed over a thick envelope that was sealed with wax.

Just like Gram to be so extra, even in the end. I ran my fingers along the hard blob of green wax. Gramps had his post-retirement obsessions, but he hadn't been alone in that. Gram had undergone a handwritten letter phase, everything sealed with wax and various seals. All of a sudden, he clapped his hands together, startling us.

"You dated Gordon Mitchell in high school!" he exclaimed. "I knew I knew you from somewhere! I don't know that we ever actually met; I was sort of on the edges of Gordon's group back then. Good man, Pastor Mitchell," he said, full of conviction. "He's taken over for his dad, you'll know, as head Pastor of their church now that he's a big to-do in Washington. I always thought you two would end up married with a whole brood of little 'un's runnin' around. He never let you go far from his sight, did he, honey?" he said, accent thick and rich, dripping with southern sweetness and memories from a time I had tried to run from for years.

"Well, we didn't," I said abruptly and coldly. "So, Mr. Willis, what must I do to get the house sold and the assets transferred to my name? The less time I spend here, the better," I said.

Barb shifted uncomfortably next to me and knew I'd have some explaining to do for how callous I must have sounded. I didn't care. I needed out of his office and into the fresh air, or I would crack.

"Well, everything has to go into probate, sweetheart, so you have a bit. We put something in the paper after Mrs. Coker here got things started right after the death, and no one's come forward to collect any debts. It's all pretty straightforward and shouldn't take too long. Maybe a few months," he said, demeanor shifting with mine. "We're pretty much done here. I will need a forwarding address if you plan on selling the house since that's the one listed.

As for the bank, all you need to do is contact them directly and see what they need, but more likely, it'll be a copy of the death certificate and your ID. Your name is already on the accounts; it will just be a matter of closing out the joint account and transferring the money into your account."

He shuffled all the paperwork, slipping it back into a file folder. I pushed my seat back away from the table and stood up, Delilah following my lead. She had a quiet look of concern on her face when I didn't meet her eyes.

"And the house?" I asked, voice clipped. My body was flushed, sweat pooling under my arms and dripping down my spine. "Do I deal with the bank there, as well?"

"Oh. No, ma'am," he responded quickly. "I have the deed here, and you're already on it. Again, it will just be a matter of having a copy of the death certificate and paperwork to put it on the market." He looked at me, leaning back in his chair, hands steepled under his chin. "We usually recommend that the family wait a while before making rash decisions. Maybe you should talk with your husband and see what he says, honey. See what he wants to do with everything."

My teeth were set on edge, and my temper went even colder. I opened my mouth to say something, but Delilah was quicker on the draw.

"Um. I don't think she'll need to ask her *husband* for permission to do anything about all of this. It is in *her* name, after all, not his. And I don't think that's really any of your business, is it?" she said. "Now, if we're finished here, we have other things we need to see to. Thank you for your help, Mr. Willis."

Delilah steered me by the elbow, past Barb, and then stopped to help her out of her seat. I hurried out the door and headed down the stairwell, bypassing the tiny elevator, file clutched against my chest, tears burning in my eyes, and desperate for fresh air.

34

Truth Be Told

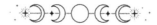

I was already in the car, head on my arms, leaning on the steering wheel when Barb and Dell found me a few minutes later. Barb slid in the passenger seat wordlessly, and Dell got in behind her and then leaned up between the front seats.

"Hey. Jules. You aren't okay. What happened up there?" she asked, rubbing my back. "I mean, he was a bit of a douchebag—oh, sorry Barb. He was a bit condescending, but you went next level cold on him."

Barb chuckled and made noncommittal noises, giving us space. I sat up, flipping the visor down and looking at my face. My mascara had run, and my skin was splotchy from crying. I didn't even try to right my face but turned to them.

"I'm so sorry. I can't get into everything, but high school was just not a good time for me. And the guy he was talking about—Gordon—my old boyfriend. Um..." I trailed off.

Barb reached her hand out and put it on my arm.

"Honey, we've all been there," she said quietly. "I was married before Herb. He was a terrible man who thought it was his right to lay his hands on me. It took him pushing me down the stairs when I was pregnant with our first for me to snap out of it and leave him. And it wasn't easy back then, girls. Not like it is now. It was a shameful thing to be divorced. Though it *should* have been shameful for a man to put his hands on his wife, it was just a different time back then."

"Not so different, Barb. That's why I left. Why I changed my name."

Dell froze, hand still on my shoulder.

"Why Andrew and I didn't have a big wedding. And why my parents stopped speaking to me. Seeing that lawyer and hearing his name and what a 'good man' he is, it, it j-just brought it all back," I stammered. "I just needed to get out of there. I should go back and apologize."

Dell and Barb started talking at the same time. Then, Dell quieted down to let the elder speak.

"Oh no, you won't, honey. That bit about talking to your husband? I may be old, but even I know that doesn't fly anymore. And that's specifically why Alice left everything directly to *you* in your name. She wanted you to have your own money and your own means, just in case. Women need an escape plan, no matter what. She knew that. Also, that Luke Willis was, what was it you said, Delilah? A *douchebag*." Barb smiled, looking pleased with herself, and we all laughed.

"Barb, I like you," Delilah said, laughing still. "Plus, Jules, you gotta remember, you're grieving, and the lawyer deals with far worse outbursts than that, I'm sure. At least there's no one to contest anything and drag it out. I'm sure he's seen worse than an old classmate giving him the cold shoulder."

It was Barb's turn to laugh.

"Oh, honey. You are absolutely right. Do you know the Smiths--that old codger who lived a few houses down from Alice's house?"

I nodded, and her voice took on the practiced strength of a storyteller, as all Southerners are wont to do.

"Well, he had some old skeletons in his closet that came calling, and they were stuck trying to sort it out for years. Apparently, he'd had an entirely separate family living in another state that no one knew about, not even his poor wife. I think three other children he'd kept secreted away that he'd visit on 'business trips.' Well, every few weeks, all those grown kids of his, the public and the private ones, would storm into the lawyer's office, all yelling and creating the awfullest ruckus everyone could hear in town." She patted me on the leg. "I really wouldn't worry about it, dear. It will be fine."

After that, we headed back to Grams, and Barb left me with a kiss on the cheek and a promise to return the next day. Delilah and I walked into the house to find Edie and catch her up on everything that had happened at the lawyer's office.

"Okay. So, you're set for life with the right investments, Jules," Edie said matter-of-factly after hearing how much Gram had left me. The numbers hadn't quite sunken in yet, but the whole experience of being recognized overshadowed anything else.

"I guess so," I said cautiously. "It's just so crazy to think they had so much money all this time. Gramps had a great job, and so did Grams, and I know they got in early with some big-name stocks when they were just starting out, but I never expected this."

"What did Andrew say?" Edie asked.

"Fuck," I blurted, throwing my hands up. "I haven't even called him yet. Damnit." I looked at the baby, wide awake in Dell's arms. "Sorry, Elliot."

"Honey, she's the only one who can't talk yet; she hears all the words," Edie assured me. "Go call Andrew, and then we'll figure out food. I know you must be starving; I've snacked all morning, but you guys haven't."

I turned and walked out to the screened-in back porch. The air was pleasant but not hot, what we liked to call fake spring in the South. I knew one last cold snap would be coming soon, but this little tease of warmth was nice.

Andrew picked up on the first ring, obviously awaiting my call. I laid it all out for him, and he was quiet for a long time.

"So, uh, I guess we can take our time deciding on your next posting, huh?" I joked.

"Um. Yeah, I guess so, Jules," he said, shock making his voice breathy. "I'm just. I don't know what to say. I mean, your Gramps told me that they were financially set, and he really pushed for us to make investments from the beginning. I just never would have guessed they were this well off. I just...I mean. I don't know what to say." He was as flustered as I was. I couldn't believe we'd had no idea how well off they were.

"I feel like now that I've said it out loud, I realize just how much freaking money it is," I said, realization dawning on me that we really had some control over our lives at this point. Between what we could get for the house and everything else, we could do anything and go anywhere. "What should we do?" I asked.

"I don't know," Andrew replied. "I guess we just move forward with cleaning the house and getting it ready to put on the market. And I do the interviews in D.C., and then we make a call-Singapore or Washington State," he trailed off, and I could practically hear his brain whirling.

"Okay. Or...maybe you quit. And we do something else?" I muttered.

"What?" he exclaimed. "I can't just quit, Jules. This is my job. You won't have access to that money for months; we can't just live off what's in our bank account right now."

"Um, actually, I have access to the bank accounts. Gram had me put on their account after Gramps died, remember? I never accessed it, but the money is mine. And the assets through the bank. Plus, whatever is in the bank box that's yours. So, we've got plenty to keep us afloat while we think of something else," I replied. "I mean...if you want to keep your job, keep it. You know I support you no matter what. But Bahrain was rough. I've never seen you more stressed out. Is this really your passion? Do you want to keep doing it?"

I heard his sharp intake of breath on the other end, and I stayed quiet, letting him mull over what I'd just said.

We'd talked for years about what we'd do if he didn't have to keep taking contracts. We'd never been fantastic with money. Moving so much prevented me from holding a job and turning it into a career. Government contracts were great money and a little bit of freedom as far as being able to choose where you went next. But I knew he didn't want to do it forever. And I didn't either.

"Jules, I can't make a decision right now. We just found all of this out, and it's overwhelming and crazy. I need some time to think, and so do you. Let's wait to make any decisions. Take a minute to breathe, yeah?"

"Yeah. I agree. It's a lot to process right now."

We talked a few minutes more, ignoring the elephant in the room and hanging up, both still slightly shocked.

———✦———

That night, over dinner, I came clean to Edie and Delilah about my past and what had happened with Gordon. They'd known I had a shitty high school boyfriend and strict, religious parents, but they had no clue about the depths of the trauma. We all cried—a lot. I cried mainly for the young girl who hadn't had two strong and amazing friends to confide in when she needed it most. I hugged them tightly and thanked them for being those friends I so desperately wished for when I was young.

That night, we all slept piled into Gram and Gramps' king-sized bed, baby Elliot in her travel cot on Edie's side, like a proper, grown-up sleepover. Surrounded by their love and protection, I slept and didn't dream a thing.

35

Deja vu

The following week was a flurry of activity. Barb came every day and helped us go through Gram's house, helping me to box up things to donate and things I wanted to keep. Each time, she brought another covered dish or baked goods with her. The only things that were truly important to me were Gram's rolling pin, cast iron skillets that had been passed down through the family, a Santa and Mrs. Claus salt and pepper shaker set and a bottle-green glass candy dish that had held hard candies for as long as I could remember and still housed little flecks of sugar from years of use.

Barb wanted very little in the way of trinkets. She kept the cookbook we'd found that Gram had written specifically for her, a sad smile on her face and tears running down her cheeks as she read through the little notes Gram had written with each recipe—a time capsule of their friendship and the meals they'd loved together. I was grateful Gram had taken the time to do one for her.

Saying goodbye to Edie was harder than I anticipated. She had to get back to her family. Eric had taken leave for the week so she could be with me, but he had an underway the next week, so there was no extending her stay. I promised to keep her posted on where we were going next and to talk Andrew into taking some leave to visit them before leaving for wherever we'd be going.

We still hadn't decided. He was somewhere over the Atlantic and out of contact until the following day, so I hoped he had spent some time figuring out what he wanted to do. I was at a loss and just ready for him to make the call.

I struggled to keep up with everyone in Egypt. I missed them and the routine we'd all fallen into when I was there learning. But the time difference made it impossible.

Being around Edie and Dell had kept me from using my powers as much as I would have liked to. I took any opportunity I could when they weren't around to do little things to practice. It was silly, but I worried I'd somehow forget and 'lose' the magic. As separated from them as I'd felt in Egypt, I felt the same now that I was away from the sisterhood—so closed off from them. I wondered if there would ever be a time when I felt whole and not pulled into different directions—parts of me closed off from the people I loved.

Dell extended her stay by an extra week. I was deeply grateful not to be alone while waiting for Andrew to get everything sorted in D.C. We had busted our asses over the week with Edie and Barb and had the house almost cleared out. The local women's shelter and the Salvation Army both knew us by name.

I found a multitude of treasures in Gram's house that I kept back for my new magical lifestyle. Herb bundles, plant books, crystals, and even a journal similar to my grimoire—proving that Gram had been a bit more witchy than I'd ever known—were in a box next to the bed marked with the Norse rune for knowledge.

Hiding my excitement from Dell had been impossible, and I told her that I was interested in Paganism, and she jumped at the chance to teach me some things. We spent our days cleaning and organizing, readying the house for eventual sale, and our evenings drinking wine and smoking some truly amazing weed she had brought from Colorado, giggling and having deep, esoteric conversations about all things witchy.

Whether it was the weed, which always calmed my nerves, or the distraction of Dell, or the comfort of being surrounded by memories of Gram and the love she and Gramps had shared in the house, I relaxed bit by bit and felt the grip of grief loosen its hold.

I finally read my note from Gram. She explained how seriously they had taken saving their money. Still, she assured me they'd spent plenty and had lots of fun traveling and doing what they wanted with it and urged me and Andrew to do the same. She also told me about another note she'd written, a more personal one, and where to find it in the house, but I hadn't quite gotten up the gumption to tear into it just yet. I was content for it to sit on the bedside table next to me, a thick creamy white envelope, also wax sealed, filled with Gram's last words. Once I read it, that would be it. I'd never hear anything new from her again. I was holding out as long as possible to save it for when I really needed it.

"I can't believe you still haven't read it," Andrew said a couple of days after arriving in the States. Having been lucky enough to score a commercial flight from Bahrain to D.C., he sounded far more put together and rested than I had after landing in Virginia after my Military flight.

"I'm just waiting for the right moment," I said, absently stroking Lumee, curled around my legs and purring loudly. "And it just isn't now."

I didn't know *when* that would be, but I knew I'd know when the time was right.

"Jules, I think I have an idea if you're on board," Andrew said.

"Okay." I waited, sitting up straighter in my seat, finally ready for him to just make the call. I was exhausted from making decisions— even small ones.

"What if I took a leave of absence? Not quit outright and close that door, but a leave of absence to give us a chance to travel and do what we want to do for a little bit? And a chance to talk it out and figure out what we want out of life," he blurted it all out. His usual calm demeanor sounded frazzled.

"Um, babe. I think that's perfect!" I beamed. It was the perfect answer and gave us the freedom to figure out what we wanted from life.

"I figured that would make you happy," he said, sounding relieved. "I know you wanted me just to quit, but I don't want to shut the door completely, just in case. I will let them know to-morrow, and they'll probably schedule some exit interview-type stuff in the next couple of days, so it'll probably be the weekend before I can get down there. Is that okay?"

"Love, that's fine. I'm doing okay here. Much better than I thought I would," I assured him.

And I was, truly. I'd only had a handful of nightmares the whole week I'd been in North Carolina, and they were more disjointed flashes and things that weren't even memories, which made them slightly more bearable.

Andrew and I hung up, and I found Delilah, who had started work on the kitchen—the last room left and the one I knew would take me the longest. She reached over and turned her phone down, taking her earphones out and setting them down on the counter.

"You guys don't need plates or anything, right?" she asked, cabinets wide open.

"No. We've got all that stuff. I'll keep an eye out for anything kind of unique. Definitely any vintage Pyrex—I love that stuff."

Dell rolled her eyes. Her aesthetic was far more modern than mine.

I moved to the cups and mugs cabinet and wrapped the myriad of glassware collected over the years. When I got to the mugs, I had the oddest feeling of déjà vu wash over me. I reached for another mug and stopped, skin prickling with awareness. I turned to see if Dell was looking at me, but her back was turned, wrapping plates and boxing them up. I turned back towards my cabinet and wrapped the mug I was holding— a faded floral pattern that matched the plates in Dell's hands. When I reached up again, the discomfort persisted. I looked back at Dell, earphones back in place, her head gently bopping to music. I walked out of the kitchen, slowly wandering around the house. I checked the doors and windows to assure myself of what I already knew—everything was locked up tight.

I was standing in the living room facing the bay window when I looked out and saw a car at the curb. I walked closer, careful to stay out of sight. The feeling that I was being watched crept over me again. It was a silver sports car with windows tinted so dark that I couldn't see into it to tell if someone was there or if it was empty. With a jolt, I remembered the recurring dreams I'd had a few times over the last year.

I made a strangled noise in my throat, panic rising to the surface as I backed away from the window and towards the kitchen. I tried to make a sound, but nothing would come out. I turned my back on the front of the house—skin alive with awareness and electric with energy. I finally reached Dell and grabbed her arm. She jumped and spun around towards me with a shout.

"Shit! Jules! You scared me. Oh my god! What's wrong?" she asked, jerking her earphones out.

"I. He—I—dream. He—" I stammered, making no sense but unable to control my panic and formulate words.

"Jules, you're scaring me. What is it?"

I could hear the alarm rising in her voice. I tried to take a breath but couldn't get more than a sip of air into my lungs. The panic clamped down on me like a vice, clouding my vision and turning dark teal around the edges—like the color of my magic in the ritual.

"Jules. Jules!" Dell shouted, but her voice sounded far away, like I was underwater.

Magic and energy were coursing under my skin. I was certain Dell could see it rippling underneath the surface with how violent and angry it stormed inside me. My skin was flushed with fever, and a bright light was seeping out of my hands. I squeezed my fist to try and tamp it down and hide it, but it was no use. I opened my mouth to say something, and the overwhelming panic exploded in a shimmering wave of heat and light that I shut my eyes.

Glass shattered as I dropped to my knees, and Dell's panicked scream rang through the air.

I wrapped my hands over my head, rocking back and forth on the floor, the cold tile biting into my knees. The weight lifted, and a sense of relief flooded through me. I could hear an animalistic keening sound from somewhere, and I realized it was me.

Realizing that shook me out of my panicked trance, I stopped rocking and looked up. Dell was backed against the cupboards, knees drawn up to her chest, face white as a sheet, and body heaving with deep breaths. There was a cut above her forehead and a small drip of blood running down the side of her face.

The ground was littered with shattered plates and bowls and fragments of glass.

"Oh god, Dell," I croaked. "I'm so sorry. Fuck. Are you okay?" I asked her, slowly sitting up and crawling towards her.

She skittered away from me like a wounded animal.

"What the fuck, Jules! What the fuck was that? What happened?" Her panicked voice rose an octave with each question.

I shifted away, shoving my back against the cupboard, glass cutting into my hands. The pain anchored me and kept the panic at bay; I pushed into it, needing something to steady me. I took a deep, shuddering breath, knowing that I would have to explain as I took in the destruction of the room.

"Dell, it's a long story, and I don't know that you will believe me. Just first, are you okay?" I asked, pleading with her to answer.

"Fucking terrified. But I'm not really hurt if that's what you mean," she answered, eyes still wide and face drained of color.

I took another breath, this one steadier, and told her everything, staring at the floor and the shattered ceramic and glass around us instead of looking her in the face while everything poured out of me.

"Hold up. You're serious?" Dell said when I was finished and finally looked up at her.

"Look, you don't have to believe me, but I promise you, I'm telling you the truth," I said. I knew what I was asking her to believe was a lot. Hell, I barely believed it most days, especially since leaving Luxor. I felt disjointed and separated from that part of me, and my time there felt more and more like a dream the longer I was away. However, if today taught me anything, it was that I was not finished learning by any means and needed help.

"I just...I don't know what to believe. I know you're not a liar. But this is a lot, Jules."

I looked down, cheeks flaming.

"I guess that's why you're into all the pagan stuff now, huh?" she said, voice a touch lighter.

"Yeah, I know," I said softly. "It's a lot. I don't have control yet, obviously. And I don't know what happened just now other than a nasty panic attack that set it off. I didn't do this on purpose," I assured her, looking around us. I just...ugh! This sounds so stupid!" I said, dropping my face to my drawn-up knees.

"Um, nothing will sound stupid after everything you've just told me. Out with it," she said, regaining a bit of herself as she calmed down. Hearing her settle gave me a little boost of strength.

"It's just...I've had this recurring dream a few times in the last year that I was in Gram's house sorting through mugs, and I felt like I was being watched. And when I looked outside, there was a car parked at the curb, and I couldn't see who was in it, but I knew, deep down, it was Gordon—my ex. And I swear to you that the exact thing happened just now. While I had my hands on her mugs, I felt a chill all over, like I was being watched. And there was a sports car parked at the curb." I looked towards the living room, and a cold chill raced down my spine again.

Delilah got to her feet and tiptoed around the glass, brushing her sweats off. Little tinkling sounds of glass filled the otherwise silent room. I watched her walk to the window and didn't know what to hope for—a car or no car.

"Holy fuck Jules," she breathed. "There's a car out there. Silver sports car. Tinted windows. Oh my god."

She backed away from the living room and squatted by the kitchen doorway, looking at me.

"I don't know who it is out there, but even I get the distinct feeling it's no one that means you any good." She stood up and reached a hand towards me.

"Come on, let's get you cleaned up, and then you can answer the million questions I have for you." She thumbed towards the yard. "We're just going to ignore that for now, and I'll call the cops if it's not gone by the time I get this glass out of your hands."

I nodded and stood up, glass shifting and moving as I got up. We headed towards the bathroom when Dell stopped.

"I'm going to snap a picture and get his license plate. I'm fairly sure I've seen that car in the neighborhood this week, and I want some proof just in case we need it. Go on, I'll be right there." She sounded more like herself, and the color had returned to her cheeks, but there was a space between us now that hadn't been there before, and I had no idea how to broach it. A few moments later, she entered the bathroom, looking down at her phone.

"Well, whoever it is, we know he's an asshole because only assholes have vanity plates," she laughed, but it was a hollow sound. She was still shaken up. "What do you think RPNTRBRN means besides card-carrying asshole?"

"What is it?" I asked.

Dell brought the phone over and zoomed in on the license plate. "RPNTRBRN," she answered and then looked up at me.

What little blood was left drained from my face.

"It means *repent or burn*, and it's definitely him."

I squeezed my eyes shut, hoping I was wrong but knowing deep down that I wasn't.

"You think it's him, really?" she asked, worry knitting her forehead together.

I closed my eyes and took a deep breath to settle the rising panic. I couldn't afford to lose control again. Not now.

"Yeah. It's him. That's been his catchphrase since high school—I don't know how many times he said it to me, and that's been his license plate since he got his first car. Fuck. He's found me," I said, resigned more than in shock. It had always just felt like a matter of time.

"How?"

"Probably that douchebag Luke. You have to remember this is a small town, even though we're a couple of towns over from where I grew up— the *good old boys club* runs rampant here. I'm sure he was chomping at the bit to call Gordon and tell him he'd seen his old girlfriend. Not knowing..." I trailed off.

Dell crossed the room, closing the physical distance between us. She paused before she touched me, hand hovering over my upturned palm. I looked up at her.

"I am so sorry, Dell. So, so sorry. I never meant for you to get hurt. I just—"

She cut me off.

"Jules, I know you'd never purposefully hurt me. I just...I need some time to come around to this, you know? It's a lot."

I sagged a bit. "Yeah, I know."

Dell took her time with tweezers, pulling out shards of glass from my hands, pieces lined up on a paper towel on the counter in varying sizes. Luckily, all the cuts were shallow, and none needed stitches. She poured hydrogen peroxide over my hands, the liquid foaming white all over my cuts, making me wince. Gently, she patted it dry and wrapped some gauze we'd found in a first aid kit under the bathroom sink. We'd talked quietly, her questions distracting me from the sting in my palms, and by the time we were finished, the distance between us closed just a bit.

I wasn't sure if she truly believed me, but she was less scared of me, which was all that mattered.

"So how dangerous is this guy now, you think?" she asked while she worked.

"I don't know," I answered. "I mean, I would hope not danger-ous at all, but there was something deeply wrong with him, and obviously he was out there just...whatever he was doing."

Dell looked at me, worry still written across her face.

"So how did your parents not see him for what he was?"

"Because of what they believed. That church was a cult, Dell. You could walk in and visit on a Sunday, no problem, but to become a member or work on a committee? A whole vetting process had to be done, and if someone didn't line up with what they wanted as part of the church, they didn't become a part of it." I narrowed my gaze at her. "Think, wealthy, connected, and prominent in the community—no *riff-raff*, as they would say. Whatever Pastor Mitchell said was law; my dad was one of his chief enforcers. He was unwilling to give up that power, and my mom obeyed his every word. What I wanted was no match for what they believed to be God's will," I trailed off, lost in memories.

When we returned to the living room, the car was gone, and we both breathed a sigh of relief. I went to the bay window and shut the gauze-y curtains before collapsing on the sofa across from Dell in Gramps' chair, exhausted as the shock drained out of our systems.

36

Acceptance

Dell had slept in the guest room, needing space, but the loss of our giggling nightly sleepovers left me feeling very alone. I hadn't the heart to tell Andrew what had happened—I knew he was overwhelmingly busy in DC wrapping up that part of our lives. I didn't want to worry him more than he already was. Our nighttime conversation was quick and even a bit shallow, only adding to the feeling of isolation.

It was late in the afternoon when Delilah came to find me. She'd gone out for a run early in the morning and had busied herself catching up on work while I finished going through the kitchen. The job was much faster since everything in the open cabinets the day before had been shattered beyond repair. I had done some yoga on the back porch and was sitting on my mat, nursing a cup of tea, when she plopped down in front of me.

"Okay. So I've decided that you aren't crazy," she said matter-of-factly.

"Um. Okay?" I replied.

"I mean, we're all a little crazy, and some grade-A crazy shit has happened to you, but I don't think you are need-to-be-hospitalized crazy."

I laughed, the heaviness in my chest loosening a little bit.

"Well, that's good to hear, I guess."

She grinned. "Seriously, though, I'm willing to entertain the possibility that you have some wild, magical powers. There's literally no other explanation for what happened in the kitchen yesterday, and I've never seen you behave like that." She paused. "Not to mention, I've spent my whole life learning about Paganism, wearing crystals in my bra, and changing out a seasonal altar. Who am I to challenge magic when, in some ways, it's been a part of my entire life?"

I visibly relaxed, releasing a proverbial breath I had held since the day before.

"Dell, I can't even begin—"

She held up her hand and stopped me.

"I was up all night sitting with this. Trying to reconcile everything I knew or thought I knew. And the only thing I kept coming back to was how would I want you to respond if it were me? And Jules, you've always accepted my quirks and never made a big deal about them. If I can't do the same for you, what kind of friend would I be? I'm so sorry you've been carrying this around alone on top of everything else. You've got to be one of the strongest people I have ever met."

She leaned forward and put her arms around me, drawing me closer to her. We stayed like that for a few moments, holding each other up and feeling the gap created the day before slowly closing back up.

"Just one question," she said earnestly, pulling away and looking at me. I nodded. "Does Edie know?"

I burst out laughing, the sound true and deep.

"Oh God, no! Can you imagine?" I asked between wheezing laughter. "I love her dearly, but there's no way she would just accept magic; it's too literal."

"I mean, I agree, and I didn't think so. I just wanted to be sure," Dell said, laughing. "I love her, but her staunch agnosticism doesn't allow much wiggle room for the unexplainable."

"No, it doesn't," I agreed. The tiniest bit of weight lifted off my shoulders. I loved Edie, but Dell was right—I couldn't imagine a time when she'd accept magic or some fantastical explanation about dead pharaohs and saving the world. It just wasn't who she was. Though, deep down, I knew she'd try...for me. I just hoped I'd never have to test that theory and could get myself under control before I saw her again. I thought about the Nintendo Switch I'd somehow managed to salvage and was grateful she'd been feeding the baby when it had happened.

"So...I guess one other question," Delilah said, corners of her mouth quirked up in a mischievous grin. "Can you do something magical without exploding glass all over me?"

I pursed my lips, trying to hide my smile.

"You *would* ask for proof after yesterday's display," I sighed dramatically. "Yeah, I can do something."

I got up and walked into the house, not waiting for her to follow me. I walked to the kitchen where the clean, scented candle we'd kept to freshen the space still sat. I brought it outside and set it between us as I plopped back on my mat. Delilah looked at me questioningly but didn't say anything.

"*Luminate*," I whispered, and the candle sprang to light.

"Holy shit!" Dell exclaimed. "That's awesome!"

"*Deflammo*," I said, and the candle blew out, scented smoke wafting above us, tickling my nose. "There are other things, but those are the first two I mastered," I said.

We spent the rest of the night with me showing off, further explaining to Dell what I could do and receiving her excited support in return, encouraging me to dust off the skills I'd been so focused on in Luxor. It felt like stretching a muscle after sitting for so long, and I was grateful to have the freedom to practice in front of her.

I knew I'd have to tell Hanan eventually that someone else was in the loop, but I hadn't mentioned the scrolls or Thutmose and hoped I wouldn't have to get too deep into the purpose of the sisterhood. Dell, being a practicing Pagan and part of a coven in Colorado, helped with that, for sure.

37

A Change of Plans

"I really don't like that weaselly little jackass," I said to Delilah, hanging up my phone.

"The lawyer?" she asked, looking up from her computer. The kitchen counter was currently serving as a makeshift standing desk while she caught up on work.

I nodded. "Miz Wheelright," I said, mocking Luke Willis's syrupy accent. "I was just checking to see if you needed anything from us, sweetheart. Ugh. It grosses me out!" I shuddered.

"Dude. If anyone ever *thought* about calling me *honey* or *sweetheart* and they weren't a super old grandma or grandpa type, I'd be livid."

"I am. I mean, I totally get that it's a *thing* in the South and seen as a term of endearment, but it's just condescending and shitty to me."

"It is," Dell agreed. "It doesn't help that you're not that southern anymore." She laughed. "You'd probably be better with it if you guys had never left and you didn't have a break in it, you know?"

I nodded. That was true.

It hadn't bothered me when I was younger; it was so commonplace to be *honey'd* or *sweetheart*-ed that it was just as much a part of the vernacular as *y'all* or *ain't* or any other myriad of southern-isms. My phone rang in my hand, the vibration startling me a bit. I looked down and groaned, facing my phone towards Dell so she could see the caller.

"Shit— you don't think he heard anything, did he?" Dell shook her head.

"No, but put it on speaker just in case!" I answered the call, doing as she asked.

"Hello?" I said as sweetly as possible.

Delilah covered her mouth to stifle a laugh, and I glared at her, trying to keep my own laugh from escaping.

"Miz Wheelright, I'm so sorry to be botherin' you again, dar-lin', but I meant to offer when I called earlier. We at the office just loved Mrs. Lane so much; she was always so caring and warm, you'll know. And we'd like to be doing something to help you out in this tryin' time."

"Okay. I'm not sure what more you can do, Mr. Willis," I replied, confused.

Dell shrugged her shoulders.

"*Weel*, we'd like to go and get Mr. Wheelright from the airport for you, honey. It's just one small thing, but I know I'd have sure liked the help when my own Grannie passed, and we had all manner of out-of-towners flyin' in. That Charlotte traffic can just be such a mess most days."

"Oh. No, it's fine. You don't have to do that," I assured him, making a face at Dell to convey how weird I thought this was. Another noncommittal shrug from Dell, and I rolled my eyes.

"Oh, I know we don't *have* to," he said. "But it's the good Christian thing to do, as I'm sure you'll know."

Delilah snorted then and coughed to cover it. I cleared my throat, unsure what to say. When a Southerner brought their religion into the mix, which was more often than not, there was very little arguing with them.

"Um, I'm just not sure how Andrew would feel about that, Mr. Willis."

He interrupted me. "Please, call me Luke, honey. After all, we're all just old classmates. It's the least I can do for an old Rebel."

Delilah looked at me, shocked at our ridiculous class mascot. I just shook my head and pinched the bridge of my nose between my fingers, squeezing my eyes shut.

"Okay, Luke. It's just, it's been—"

"Now look, I know you're going to make excuses, but I can assure you that it's not so far out of our normal procedures," he interrupted again. "We like to do things like this for all our long-term clients, and your grandma has been with the firm since old Mr. Abernathy started it. That would be the younger Mr. Abernathy's daddy."

If I remembered correctly, the *younger* Mr. Abernathy was about 100 years old, so I couldn't imagine how old the *old* one was. Dell just nodded at me, encouraging me to accept.

"Can you hold for just one moment, Luke?" I asked, hitting mute before he'd had a chance to respond. "This is fucking weird, right?"

"Yeah, it is to us. But it sounds fairly normal for this area. And besides, if someone else goes to get Andrew, you don't have to deal with driving down there and traffic and all that. Weren't you just saying that his arrival time was one of the worst times for traffic?" I nodded and opened my mouth to say something else, but she continued. "Plus, we are supposed to be meeting with the director of the Women's Shelter that day to tell her about the insurance money, and it was cutting it close anyway to having to get him. Just let the little weasel do something nice."

I groaned, knowing she was right.

"Fine," I said, resigned. I unmuted the phone and confirmed Andrew's flight information with the lawyer, having to grit my teeth through another round of *darlin'* and more well-intentioned but no less obnoxious advice about not selling the house. When we finally hung up, I set my phone down on the counter and walked away from it, unwilling to talk anymore should he call again. I didn't want to seem ungrateful, but so many things had happened here, and it was hard to put my trust in anyone I didn't know well or choose to be in my life—no matter how kind they were trying to be.

———— ✦ ————

Andrew was happier to accept the help— ever the more laid back of the two of us.

"Need I remind you how things are in the south, little lady?" he joked when I told him about the lawyer's office picking him up.

I huffed dramatically at his 'little lady.' "You'll pay for that, sir," I said mockingly.

"Happy to, darlin'," he drawled, laying it on thick.

I rolled my eyes and quirked a smile.

His meetings had gone well in D.C., and the contracting company was happy to oblige him with a leave of absence and assure him they'd take him back as soon as he was ready. Even though we weren't sure what we would do and where we'd end up next, having the fallback of a steady job was obviously a comfort. He'd even managed to reroute our household goods to a storage facility just outside of D.C., giving us plenty of time to figure things out.

The day of Andrew's arrival was a whirlwind. We had brunch with Gram's MahJong gang. We spent the morning and early afternoon laughing until our sides hurt and tears poured down our cheeks, listening to stories about Gram and her friends. Gram had forbidden a funeral— making strict notes in her will that we were to scatter her ashes in her garden, tilling the soil with them and helping her to become a part of the earth again and celebrate her life, not wallow in grief. I hadn't done that yet, but I would before we left. But Barb and her friends needed at least a little something to say goodbye.

Dell and I left brunch and headed straight for the women's shelter, making the day of a very tired-looking woman when we told her she'd be receiving fifty thousand dollars at some point once the insurance money was paid out. Looking at the stacks of papers on her desk and the lines etched deeply around her eyes, it felt amazing to see some stress lift just a bit. I made a mental note to add a donation of my own to Gram's.

Delilah and I were leaving the shelter when Andrew's text that he'd landed came in. I looked at her sideways.

"Well, I guess it was a good thing we aren't the ones picking Andrew up from the airport," I said. "He's landed."

She laughed. "Ha! Told you! I wouldn't have wanted to leave right after telling them about the money, anyway. It was important to stay and let her show us around and explain what the money would go."

I nodded, still a little shaken up by the experience at the shelter. It had been amazing to see her excitement and to know that Gram's money was going to a good cause and that it was dearly needed, but also touring the common rooms and class-rooms that were filled with women and children with a rainbow of bruises shadowing their faces and arms was gut-wrenching.

"Oh shit," I said, opening Andrew's text and reading further. "Wouldn't have mattered. He landed in D.C. They had to reroute and go back. He won't be on a flight till the same time tomor-row."

"Oh man—that sucks!" she said, "I hate that for him."

"Yeah, same. He sounds super annoyed. But he's let the lawyer's office know, so at least I don't have to deal with the weasel again."

I responded quickly, pausing to text before we kept walking.

"And yeah, I know what you mean about the shelter. I'm glad we stayed, but it was hard to see," I said quietly.

Dell looped her arm through mine as we walked around the corner to the car. The haunted look on some of the women's faces reminded me so much of my own face when I was younger. I knew, without a doubt, that I would have one day ended up there had my life not taken the turn it had. Or rather, the turn I had chosen to take.

38

A Homecoming Surprise

Since Andrew wouldn't be in until later in the afternoon, Delilah and I had spent the next day shopping and getting our nails done. We both wanted some carefree fun to cap off her trip since our time together had revolved around cleaning out Gram's house and dealing with the logistics of closing out someone's life. We had a wonderful day together, and it was the first time in a long time that I felt like myself. We even video-chatted Edie over lunch so we could all be together.

Delilah had gone to get some dinner while I waited for Andrew to get to the house. I still hadn't heard from him past his initial text that he'd landed, and one shortly after that said "traffic." It had been two hours since I'd gotten that one. I was getting a little nervous that something had happened on the way. Traffic in Charlotte could be bad, but this seemed a little much, even for the busiest time of day.

I sent another text and poured myself a glass of wine when I heard Delilah pull into the driveway. My stomach lurched, and I didn't think I'd be able to wait much longer for Andrew to show before I ate at least a little something. We'd had an early lunch, and I was damn near starving. I poured a glass for Dell and turned to the living room, taking a sip of the chilled white, the crisp bubbles dancing on my tongue, when she rang the doorbell.

"Coming—sorry, Dell!" I shouted, hurrying for the door. "I must have locked it behind you—" I opened the door and stopped dead in my tracks.

"Well, well, well. If it isn't my own little whore of Babylon. Or, I guess I should say *Julia* now?"

I dropped the glass in my hand, and it shattered against the tile, wine and glass splattering my bare feet and soaking my jeans. I froze, mouth formed in a shocked 'o'. I tried to slam the door in his face, but Gordon palmed it, banging it open against the wall behind me as he stepped over the threshold. The glass crunching under his feet was as loud as gunshots.

"No, I don't really like that. You'll always just be little Jolene to me. Temptress, plaything..." He trailed off as he looked me up and down.

His voice was the same—charismatic and warm. It was the kind of voice that a congregation flocked to. The kind of voice that had tricked me into thinking I was safe before I associated it with pain.

And it was the voice that had haunted my nightmares for almost twenty years.

I had backed up, but he closed the space between us, pushing me further into the room as he reached behind him, not even taking his eyes off me. He slammed the door shut with a force that rattled the walls. I jumped at the sound, unable to help myself.

The wall pressed against my back and my heart and mind raced, trying hard to catch up with the insanity of Gordon Mitchell standing in my Gram's living room. My nightmares, alive and in the flesh, crippled me with terror. I opened my mouth to speak, and he slapped me hard across the face, knocking my head to the side. Face burning, I tasted warm, coppery blood from my split lip.

"No, no." He clicked his tongue like I was an insolent child. "You're not going to speak for a few minutes, *Jolene*. You're going to listen." He ran his finger down the hot slap of my cheek, always balancing the hurt with the gentle—all a part of his twisted games.

My chest hurt with how furiously my heart was pounding, and a small part of me was screaming inside to do something—anything. But that part wasn't anywhere near as big or as loud as the wounded animal I was quickly retreating into. I could smell the sharp stink of my fear mingling with his smell—rich and citrusy cologne that had been his signature scent even in high school. I'd always thought of it as the scent that masked the decay inside of him.

He leaned down, ice blue eyes bright with excitement, and I felt my gorge rise.

"You're going to come with me, Jolene," he whispered, breath hot against my face. It smelled sweet and sickly, like the chewing tobacco he'd often stuffed in his cheek. I shook my head, unable to form words. Each *Jolene* he bit out, tore into me, a painful undoing of the person I'd fought so hard to become. Little pieces of Julia began to slip away as terrorized Jolene emerged from the shadows I'd put her in.

A yowl from across the room distracted me from his attention. I cut my eyes to the hall doorway and saw Lumee coming to investigate the newcomer. I squirmed, terrified at what he would do if he caught the cat. He looked down, the bully inside of him too desperate for a punching bag to ignore something smaller than him coming into his periphery.

"Oh. What do we have here? A little pussy to play with," he said menacingly, eyes boring into mine with promise. He aimed a kick at her that barely missed as I made the hissing noise that Lumee hated, the one I used to get her away from the kitchen when I was cooking. Between that and her feral instincts kicking in as she scented a predator, she bolted. I sagged in relief, grateful she was safe for the moment.

I opened my mouth to speak, finally finding the words.

"Oh, I don't think so," he said, turning back to me and pushing his finger roughly against my lips to silence me, my teeth biting into my lip as he pressed harder. "You're going to want to come with me, Jo. I've got something of yours that you'd be mighty interested to see— I can assure you of that."

He bared his teeth at me in a nasty grin. Despite the tobacco use, they were pearly and white, straight after extensive dental work as a kid. It was the perfect mouth to preach the word of his God.

"I don't care what you have, I'm not coming. You need to leave, or I'll call the cops," I said. My voice cracked but finally found its way out. I mentally pleaded with Luke Willis to drive faster and get here with Andrew.

Gordon's pale cheeks flared red, and he reached up and gripped my neck in his hand. He squeezed just enough to begin to strangle me and cut the words off from my lips. I scrabbled at his hand, scratching at his fingers, which only gripped tighter, making spots dance in front of my eyes. He was a large, thickly built, and strong man, and he hadn't let his body go soft with age. The muscles in his arms rippled as I tried to push him away.

"You listen here, you little bitch. You *will* come with me. You *will* do as I say like you should have been doing all these years. And I will not tolerate any argument from you," he growled and stepped back, arm extended from my throat, running his free hand through his perfectly coiffed blonde hair, mussing it and visibly trying to calm himself. He seemed to notice my face, which I was sure had gone some shade of purple, as he squeezed pinpricks of black at the edges of my vision and finally loosened the grip. I gratefully gulped down the air, the sound wheezing through my sore throat.

"And I know you'll care for what I've got." He looked down at me, blue eyes bright and crazed as he toyed with me. He reached into his pocket and pulled something out, making me flinch as he opened his palm. He let go of my neck so I could look down. I let out a strangled cry from my bruised throat.

In the center of his palm was Andrew's wedding ring—the distinct and delicate whorls and designs we'd drawn for the jeweler all those years ago; our rings were our one big splurge as newlyweds. I looked at him, panic-stricken.

"Where did you get that?" I squeaked, my voice scared and raw, and any pretense of defiance was gone.

"Where do you think? Slipped it off his finger myself. Let's go, and you can join him."

He shoved me forward and steered me towards the door by the back of my neck. "Jolene, you will go quietly and without a fuss, or you will regret it," he threatened, his breath hot behind me. I knew by the tone of his voice that he was serious.

"I like hurting him," he whispered, and the blood turned to ice in my veins at the thought of Andrew being in his grasp.

I went quietly then, stepping over the broken wine glass but feeling a sharp prick as a shard cut into the bottom of my foot. I shut the door behind me and walked to the drive, the grip on my neck relaxing around my shoulder in what neighbors would read as friendly. I robotically climbed into the car— the same silver sports car that Delilah and I had seen a handful of times in the neighborhood and parked in front of the house.

A hot stab of panic went down my spine as I thought about Dell and how close to home she must be with our dinner. I wished there had been some way to leave her a note, but I didn't even have my phone. It was sitting, face down, on the kitchen counter next to the glass of wine I'd poured for her.

With just the push of a button, the engine roared to life, a wave of exhaust mingling with the scent of expensive leather. I gulped, trying to swallow the threatening panic at the edges of my mind. I needed to take the time to think clearly. I wasn't the same little girl I had been all those years ago. I could find a way to handle this; I just needed her to go back to the recesses of my mind. We raced out of the driveway, careening backward in the cul-de-sac before he shoved it into gear and gunned it. The car roared like overpriced and souped-up muscle cars do to get everyone's attention.

As we were pulling up to the stop sign at the front of the neighborhood, I saw Gram's Subaru that Dell had taken to get dinner, slowing down and turning to pull in. Gordon had to wait for the car and wasn't paying attention, so he turned the other way. Somehow, by sheer force of will or a miracle, Delilah looked through the windshield and saw me, recognition lighting over her face as she mouthed words I couldn't hear. I sat as still as I could so I didn't attract Gordon's attention, but stared at her—screaming in my mind at her to do something, *anything*. As soon as she turned in, Gordon hit the gas, tires squealing as he sped out of my safe haven and down the open road.

39

Nightmares

G ordon drove like a maniac, swerving in and out of traffic at speeds that had me squeezing my eyes shut to try and remain calm. He didn't yell. In the time that we'd been apart, he had cultivated that nasty rage into something more controlled and sinister, which was, in a way, more terrifying than if he'd been exactly the same as before. Despite this, I kept having flashes of nightmarish drives with him speeding and screaming at me, terrorizing me for the sheer pleasure of it.

"I wondered who you'd conned into taking you away from me," he said, voice restrained but definitely on edge. He fought to gain control over himself. "I should have guessed it was the little fag who was sniffing around you when you belonged to me." His words were clipped and filled with venom. I stayed quiet, willing myself to be invisible.

"I looked for you, you know. I never dreamed you would be smart enough to change your name."

Out of my peripheral vision, I saw him turn towards me. I stiffened but looked straight ahead, breathing deep and trying to calm the raging storm inside me.

"I am thrilled to have finally found you. If I had known that all it would take to get you back home was your grannie dying, I'd have killed that bitch years ago. I'd have enjoyed it too." He sighed in a way that sounded like contentment, sending a chill down my spine.

"What about your wife?" I asked, unable to stop myself. "Won't she be upset that you've brought an old girlfriend home to play with?" I said the words carefully but quickly, unable to stop them from spilling from my lips.

"Don't worry about her," he said. "Once I learned from that little shit, Luke Willis, that you were in town again, I sent her away to stay with her family for the week, so we've got plenty of time. They live in Georgia, and she's probably happy to have a break from my special attention. I've been very excitable since that sniveling lawyer called to gossip. Sometimes I take things too far with her...she's more—" He paused, thinking of the word. "*Delicate* than you. This isn't her true calling like it is yours."

It didn't matter how far I'd run or how many hours I'd put in with therapists; all it took to bring the visceral fear back to the surface was to breathe the same air as my tormentor. I was crippled with fear, thoughts swirling in my mind, flashes of memory fighting for purchase against the rational side of me trying to stay calm long enough to formulate a plan.

"Why did you leave me, Jolene? We were creating something special together, and you just left. You ignored your calling from God," he said softly, almost childlike. The constant back and forth between maniac, polished preacher, and whatever this play innocence was was dizzying. I didn't answer him, and he was quiet for a moment before he shook his head and found his anger again.

"Maybe I'll call Dad in a bit. He always liked to share, if you'll recall."

He let me sit with that idea. Visions and memories of Pastor Mitchell and his cold, probing fingers...his hurried grunts and dirty words spit into my face as he punished me for being a 'temptress.' His attentions were less painful, physically, but felt dirtier and far more shameful than Gordon's. My mouth went dry at the thought of facing them both again.

Gordon continued, speeding down the road and spewing hate at me, but the skill I'd once learned to retreat into myself and away from his voice blissfully returned, and I blocked him out. My heart pounded in my chest like it was trying to escape and my skin was on fire with the panic running through me. I had no doubt that he eventually meant to kill Andrew and me. But first—*first*—he would make us pay.

40

House of Horrors

The sun was setting when we pulled into the tree-lined driveway of Gordon's massive house. The drive was long and winding and led up to a well-lit and impressive plantation-style mansion surrounded by beautiful and carefully cultivated landscaping. The overall impression was lush and gorgeous, but I knew the kind of ugly that hid inside the walls. Every semblance of calm vanished as we pulled into the garage, and Gordon shut the engine off, the silence throbbing around me.

"I can't wait for you to see what I've built," he said, like a child who's brought a piece of artwork home to show to his parents. The edges of rage were tamped down with excitement—his mask of calm back into place.

I swallowed thickly, struggling to keep the fear-induced nausea at bay. Though maybe, I thought offhandedly, vomiting all over him would keep him from doing anything.

He approached my side of the car and opened the door, pretending to be a gentleman. I was frozen with terror at the thought of going into the house and enduring any more abuse at his hands, shaking in my seat.

"Fucking come on," he growled, rage back, mask slipping. "Now!" He shouted the last word, the outburst startling me into movement.

I reached over and unbuckled my seat belt. I moved to get out of the car, and he grabbed a wad of my hair and jerked me up, my head cracking against the frame, rattling my teeth, roots of my hair pulling. Hot pricks of pain I could sense almost individually rippled across my scalp.

The calm facade began falling away from Gordon's demeanor as he tugged me to the door. He hit the glowing button on the wall, closing the garage door behind us. I flinched when his hand had smacked in front of my face to close the door, and that was all it took to spur him on. He pushed me violently up against the wall and shoved his tongue into my mouth, probing. His face was rough against mine, prickly mustache and goatee, nothing like Andrew's soft facial hair I loved so much. The taste was sweet and sour from tobacco, and I felt the nausea rise in my gut. He ground himself against me, and he was hard against my hip. Flashbacks and memories collided, fighting for space in my mind. He grunted a guttural sound that disgusted me.

"Let's find a better place to continue catching up, shall we?"

He opened the door, the hinges silent, and motioned for me to walk in. I stepped into his house; it was warm and smelled of fresh citrus. The mudroom was neat, nothing out of place, and I noticed little hooks and cubbies with three backpacks hanging up, and my heart broke for the kids he'd brought into this world. Sports equipment was in the corner, but the set of pom-poms on a shelf above one cubby had my stomach in knots. I wondered if he abused his daughter as well as his wife.

There was a doorway leading to a large kitchen on our left, but Gordon steered me to the right, hand pinching the back of my arm to move me. He dug out his keys, unlocking another door that opened to a set of steps. He flipped a light switch and pushed me to the edge, forcing me down the stairs. The citrusy scent was gone, and I smelled the raw odor of unfinished wood and dust. I tried to fight down the panic that threatened to overwhelm me. I stumbled halfway down, caught up in a flash of memory of another set of stairs that led to his parents' basement. A basement that housed years' worth of memories and pain.

"I can't tell you how happy I am that you are visiting my home office," he said behind me. "You were there in the beginning with my special calling in the woods, Jolene. This place is far more advanced and allows me to continue God's calling. I think you'll like it. And I really think tonight is the night I will finally reach my full power. I've been so close for so long."

My blood ran cold as I stepped off the last step into an unfinished basement serving as a storage area. Boxes, plastic tubs, and sports equipment lined the walls on built-in shelves that were floor-to-ceiling height. Gordon vibrated with excitement behind me. I couldn't hear anything but his breathing, almost panting, in my ear. The light was dim, but I saw no signs of Andrew. I didn't know whether to be relieved or terrified.

"This way, Jolene," Gordon said, his voice raw and hungry.

He shoved me towards a set of shelves in the corner. He came around me and reached up, doing something I couldn't make out. The shelves swung open on a hidden door, revealing a short hallway with two doors—one to the right and one straight ahead. A naked bulb was hanging from the ceiling, and the light was low but cast shadows around us as we stepped in. Gordon closed the hidden door, the click sounding like a shot in the small space.

I could smell my fear, sharp, acidic, and more pungent now than Gordon's cologne. He had a hold of my arm, grip tight and bruising, encircling my bicep as he pulled me to the door at the end of the hall. Another key was in the lock, and he opened the door to a small room. A bed was pushed against one wall, made up of decorative pillows, a falsely welcoming addition to the stark concrete walls and floors. There was a large bolt fastened above the headboard, and chains with cuffs at the end hung down, resting on a cheery yellow pillow. My throat constricted. He'd never restrained me before, and I could all but feel the heavy metal that would bite into my skin.

"What do you want with me? Where is Andrew?" I stammered as he closed the door behind us, terror clouding every thought, all hope of rational thought gone.

"Oh, I want many things, little Jolene. Many things." He smiled— the kind of twisted look on his face that he got when he was torturing something, the kind of look that was once so familiar to me. "But first, you're going to clean yourself up. I can't touch you, dirty as you are."

He motioned towards a doorway where a sterile-looking bathroom lay. Concrete floors continued with a toilet, a small cabinet, a counter with a sink, and an overhead shower faucet in the corner.

"You will clean and prepare yourself for me," he said. "I am a man of God and deserve cleanliness." He narrowed his eyes. "You will shave yourself clean—every inch. I won't have filthy hair anywhere except your head. You can leave those pretty curls for me."

He stepped back and leaned against the doorway. I didn't move. "I said, you will clean yourself. Now," he said. I stood, still frozen. "I won't ask again. I'll do it myself," he warned.

I forced myself with sheer will to move, turning from him, humiliated and terrified, and slowly pulled the edge of my shirt over my head. I reached for the button on my jeans and shim-

IN THE LIGHT OF THE MOON

mied out of them, letting them pool at my feet before kicking them off. I stepped over to the faucet set into the wall by the shower and turned it on. The spray was cold, and I turned the knob, hoping and praying to whatever God would listen that this would all just be over quickly.

"What have you done?" he bit out, words choked. "You marred that perfect skin. The skin God gave you."

I clamped a hand down over my shoulder, hiding what he'd already zeroed in on—a tattoo across my shoulder and collarbone, an open book with flowers bursting off the pages. I'd had it for years and loved it dearly—an homage to my love of stories.

"That won't do," he tutted behind me. "You are full of sin. I'll have to scrub you myself."

He grabbed a long-handled brush from the counter and walked towards me as I pleaded.

"Please, I can do it," I said, my voice barely above a whisper. "I promise I'll do a good job."

He shook his head.

"I don't think you will. You've forgotten how to follow directions like a good girl." His eyes were dark in the low light, and the darkness scared me. "Look what you've done. Your body should be a temple to God. Not a cheap coloring book." His slap rang out and echoed in the room. He hit the same cheek as before, and the pain was so sharp I saw stars.

"I will be good. I promise. See?" I stepped into the spray, the water cold and hard as it poured down on me, the cold soothing my hot cheek but making my teeth chatter. I grabbed a bar of cheap soap and a Bic razor from a small shelf on the wall. I lathered the soap over my body, bra, and panties. I could feel tears, hot on my face, warming tracks through the cold cut of the water rushing down over me. I grabbed the razor and swiped it on my arms, ignoring the random nicks from the cheap razor that burned as water sluiced over the fresh cuts. I raised my underarms, cleaning them of the hair I'd let grow there after years of razor burn issues. As I lathered my legs again, shaving them in a hurry, I thought, in a detached way, about how badly my skin would hurt later, and then Gordon spoke, cutting off thoughts.

"Now do your dirty bits," he said, voice straining. "Then I'll scrub you of your sins." I balked at the thought of the rough bristles scrubbing freshly shaven flesh. "Now. Take those panties off and do it now." Silently sobbing, I slipped my sodden underwear off, thinking absently about how I'd worn a nice set of matching black lace for Andrew's arrival.

"Bra, too. You look like a whore," he spat out, on edge. All facade of calm was gone. Whatever control he'd wrangled over the years had slipped, and I could see his face alight with madness.

I unhooked my bra and slid it off my arms, breasts hanging heavy as I tossed it to the corner. I lathered with the bar of soap as best as possible and pulled the blade across my skin. The tug and pull hurt, each little bite of pain and irritation flaying my insides open with shame. The wound on my foot had finally seemed to go numb as I stood there. The bite of the water had reopened it when I'd stepped under the spray, and I hoped I had washed any remaining glass out of it.

I finished shaving, skin stinging, and Gordon stepped closer to me. He ignored the fact that he was fully dressed, polo shirt darkening as the water hit it. He began to scrub at my skin, the bristles of the brush rough and painful, and he scoured my skin of the invisible dirt that drove him mad. He muttered under his breath, saying prayers and speaking in tongues— the sounds throaty and grating. He ran his free hand across my skin, and the simultaneous mix of pain and softness was maddening. I couldn't hold it anymore and bent over to vomit all over the floor, the sour stink acrid in the room and more pungent than the scent of soap.

"You disgusting bitch!" he cried, punching me hard in the stomach as I stood back up, knocking the air from my lungs. He hit me again, a hit that knocked me into the wall hard, my shoulder slamming against the shower knobs, a sharp crack loud above the water, white-hot pain searing through me.

"I'm—s—sorry," I wheezed, trying to force air back into my lungs, wiping the back of my hand across my mouth. He scrubbed harder. Free hand no longer being gentle. His unintelligible words grew louder and more fervent when he scrubbed between my legs. I fought down another wave of vomit, the pain sharp and awful in its intensity. He finally deemed me clean, making me rinse my vomit-soured mouth with a small bottle of mouthwash before he marched me back into the adjoining room.

He walked over to a small dresser, pulled out folded clothing, and tossed it on the bed. I toweled off with the rough towel he'd provided, the cotton coarse and harsh against my raw skin. Picking up the folded bundle, I opened it up. t was a long, soft, thin nightgown of virginal white—complete with sleeves and a drawstring neckline. It was well-made and looked like an expensive replica of an old-timey shift. My mind wandered briefly to the historical fiction romances I loved so much. The fabric was thin but soft as I slipped it over my head and shifted it down my body. I shivered in the cold room, nipples pebbling and visible. I crossed my arms in front of my chest, trying to protect what modesty I could—not that there was any point to it anymore. I shifted again, grabbing the towel and roughly drying my hair, quickly braiding it to the side, hoping it wouldn't drip down my back and freeze me. Gordon stepped back, assessing.

"I don't like that you've grown. Your breasts are too big, and your hips too wide. I liked it when you were smaller," he said thoughtfully, and I had a flash to when I'd started my period. I had been a late bloomer, and when I'd started at sixteen, he raged that I was dirty and that my hips and boobs would begin to grow. The realization that my earlier question about his daughter was probably answered had my heart beating wildly against my ribs, panic over another helpless young girl at the hands of this monster sending me spiraling.

"No bother, I'll make do."

He stepped forward and grabbed my arm again, pulling me against him, wetting the nightgown with the wet clothes he didn't seem bothered by.

"Now, let's get to the main event," he whispered sinisterly.

41

Extraordinary

We left the little bedroom and went to the other closed door. Another lock, and he swung the door open triumphantly. Next to me, Gordon was humming with excitement. I looked in, the only light from the hall barely reaching the room ahead, so it was bathed in shadows.

Then stink hit me, urine, blood, and fear. The room was stifling and humid, and the smell was a wave of awful that poured out into the frigid hallway. My skin went clammy, and my legs began to shake. Gordon flipped a switch, and the room was awash in light. I fell to my knees then, a mixture of a sob and scream escaping my lips.

Andrew was chained to the far wall. Naked. One arm hung limply above his head, and his hair was greasy and dirty-plastered to his bruised and swollen face. There were cuts and bruises littering his whole body, and there was blood everywhere. He had been asleep, but the light and my gasp had roused him. He struggled to lift his head and looked at me, one eye swollen shut.

"Jules," he croaked, and the sound split me wide open. The panic and fear I'd try to get a handle on came rushing to the surface. I heard it throbbing in my veins, noise blocking out everything else.

Gordon was talking next to me, words garbled in my ear as he pulled me back to my feet. I absently felt his hand on me, untying the neckline of the nightgown, pulling it down one shoulder, one breast exposed to Andrew. My vision clouded then with the blue-green shadow of magic. The panic surged fast within my racing heart, and as soon as I felt Gordon's bare hand on my skin, I exploded with a scream. The energy inside me clawed and pulsed, begging to find a way out. Another crack and searing pain like nothing I'd felt before as Gordon punched me in the face, pulled me out of my panic and shoved the energy back down.

"You bitch! That was right in my ear!" he shrieked. He shook his hand like the punch had hurt him too, and then he turned back towards me and leaned down, his face close, pupils huge. "You are not behaving, Jolene." Out of the corner of my eye, I saw Andrew stiffen when he heard the name. "You promised you'd be good." I nodded, my head feeling like it was hanging on by a thread. It throbbed so badly. He shoved me down to the ground, and I fell with a crack, knees bursting with pain.

"Leave her alone!" Andrew cried out. His voice was weak but angry, and tears slipped down my cheeks at hearing it.

"You shut up!" Gordon roared, cheeks red with rage, sweat dripping down his forehead, all pretense of a well-groomed man gone. He turned back to me, forcing his face to soften as he squatted before me. He swiped his hands through his hair, smoothing it back, forcing the mask back into place.

"Now, I saved something extraordinary for you, Jolene. I've gotten better over the years at extracting the maximum amount of pain in little bites to draw out the pleasure of it. Do you know how much pain the human body can endure?" he asked.

I shook my head, not trusting myself to speak.

"Well, I've discovered it really depends on the person," he said conversationally as if he were giving one of his sermons. His voice slowly changed as he stood up, taking back on the charismatic quality he used to charm everyone.

"A person of strong faith and hearty constitution can last for days, given water and small bits of food." He wandered the room, picking things up here and there and putting them down.

The room was made for his little experiments. I could see with one eye that wasn't swollen and cloudy with pain. There were stainless steel shelves and countertops all along the length of one wall, littered with tools and implements I didn't want to get a closer look at. A drain was in the center of the room, and the floors were slightly angled towards it. I risked a glance at Andrew while Gordon was focused on the counter. His long fingers, the fingers that had played the guitar since he could hold one, and the fingers that had caressed my skin and written love notes were swollen and purple, unrecognizable as fingers, and my heart broke more.

"Are you paying attention to me?" Gordon snapped, catching me looking at Andrew. I nodded and stammered a word of response. Gordon crossed the room and leaned down again, metal tools clinking in his hands as he shifted.

"Good. This is the extraordinary part, Jolene. This is what I've saved for you," he said. "You see, Andrew here is going to pay for your sins. He's already started, but the cost for yours is high. You left me. You ran away. You have to pay for that. And you must pay for all these years of sin and going against your true calling."

He turned away, ignoring my pleas. I was sobbing, tears pouring down my face, and alarm bells ringing in my ears.

Andrew said my name, and Gordon silenced him with a punch in the mouth, his head snapping down with the force.

"I told you not to speak to her!" he barked. "Now, if you move while I'm doing this and you ruin it, I will hurt her. And I will hurt her while you're watching. Do I make myself clear?" Andrew nodded, a tear running down from his one open eye. Gordon reached for the hand that wasn't chained, and I saw it was unmarked. He laid it flat in front of him, face down on the concrete, and looked at Andrew again.

"This is not only a payment for her sins but a test of your mettle. How much of a man are you? Do you have what it takes to hold still? I think you are nothing. I think you will move. But if you do, she won't like it very much," he warned again.

My heart was pounding in my chest, but I was frozen, terror holding me in place as Andrew and I locked eyes. I sent love his way, as much as I could imagine, love and friendship and every moment of joy we'd shared over the years—I mentally sent it to him with everything in me. I watched as another tear slipped down his cheek. Gordon was panting now with anticipation, and he paused to rub at his crotch, unable to contain his arousal. He reached next to him and lifted a metal spike, placing the blunt tip into the center of Andrew's hand. Happy with the placement, he picked up a heavy mallet and looked at me.

"Get ready, Jolene. This is the moment. This will make you clean again. And then, when we kill him together, I will finally be able to bring him back because you're here with me. We'll do this together. It's our calling, Jolene."

He spoke in tongues again, reverent gibberish filling the room as he lifted the mallet and brought it heavy down on the spike. I screamed, unable to bite it back. He gasped, but Andrew didn't move. Gordon lifted the mallet again, unfazed by my scream or pleading, and struck the spike again. The crack sounded through the room like a shot, echoing off the walls and boring into me.

I slipped away. The wounded girl, the healed woman, and every person in between. They were all gone at that moment, replaced by only hysteria. The sound that burst out of me was guttural and animalistic. I squeezed my eyes shut as magic and raw energy ripped itself out of me in search of destruction. It was stronger and angrier, more turbulent than it had been in the kitchen with Delilah—a wrathful urgency that couldn't be held back. My skin felt flayed open as it poured out of me, a turbulent explosion of pain and light that blinded the room.

With every throb of my heart, energy poured out of me and into the room. I could form no rational thought past Andrew's name, a chant in my mind. My eyes were squeezed shut, bright light burning behind my closed lids. A scream and other unidentifiable noises made themselves known on the edge of my consciousness as I collapsed, blackness overtaking me.

* * *

Sometime later, I came to; I looked up at Andrew, the room bathed in darkness; the light had gone out in the burst of energy, but for the eerie glow of green emergency lights around the baseboards. My chest was heaving as I gulped in deep breaths of fetid air. His face was shocked and pale despite the bruises, and his mouth was moving, but I couldn't focus enough to make out the words. There was a crushing weight on me, and I panicked. I shoved Gordon off, his heavy body falling to the side with a limp thud. He didn't move towards me. In fact, he didn't move at all. The panic rose again like a great beast.

"Oh god! Oh god! What happened? What did I do?" I said, talking over Andrew's worried voice, still not taking in a word he was saying. I heaved Gordon over to his side, his head lolling over, eyes wide in shock, mouth frozen in surprise. I skittered away from him, body slamming against the cold concrete wall, hands over my mouth, terrified of the dead stare. Finally, Andrew's voice cut through the panic.

"Jules. Julia!" he pleaded. "Come here. It's okay. He can't hurt us anymore." His cracking voice shook me out of my daze, and I hurried over to him, careening into him and throwing my arms around him.

"Oh god! Andrew! I am so sorry. Are you okay? What's hurt?" I asked, sobbing into his shoulder.

"It would be faster to answer what *isn't* hurt, love. Can you see if he has the manacle keys on him? They're on his key ring."

I let him go and hurried back to Gordon's body. It was cold and wet from the shower, and I gagged as I touched him. I fumbled in his pockets and found the keys, hurrying back to Andrew and trying them until I found the right ones. His arm sagged at his side, and he winced, pain lancing through him as the feeling rushed back. His wrist was raw and bleeding. I jumped up and ran to the corner, vomiting again, my body heaving and emptying itself until my stomach was sore.

I felt someone behind me and stiffened in terror. I spun around and saw Andrew, clutching his hand to his side, spike pulled out and discarded on the ground, but he was coming to try and comfort me.

"We can't stay here another second," he said, pale and sweaty. I heard him say the words, but I couldn't move. "Jules, come on, we have to go."

I nodded, words caught somewhere in my chest. He reached down and pulled me up, shaking me out of my stupor. I stumbled, getting up, my body weak from pain, fear, and magic. He tugged me close to him and towards the door. We hurried out, stepping around Gordon's body.

"Leave it for now," Andrew said coldly when I looked back.

We limped out of the torture room, holding each other up, and closed the door behind us. I fumbled with the keys, trying to find the right one in the dark—the hall light had burned out—and locked the door, just in case. We stepped out into the basement, feeling around, emergency lights glowing around the baseboards of the shelves, throwing eerie shadows all around us and lighting Andrew's face in a sickly glow. Andrew made a noise and pointed to a dark pile of stuff in the corner, and I helped him limp towards it and realized it was his luggage. I dug through his bag, handing him clothes to slip on. He winced at every slight movement. I grabbed an extra shirt and wrapped it around the hand that had been ripped open, hoping we could slow the bleeding.

"Do you know where your phone is? We have to call someone," I said.

"He used it to text you. And the phone call I made was him—he threatened to kill you if I didn't act like everything was fine."

I made a noise in the back of my throat—a desperate, animal-like sound. A small part of me had hoped he'd just had him for a few hours—that the flight had actually been delayed and he had been picked up this afternoon.

"How long have I been here?" he asked.

"The flight arrived yesterday, love," I said quietly. I was bent over and rummaging through his carry-on. After a minute, I triumphantly pulled out his phone. I powered it on, the bright white glow lighting his face, making the bruises stick out like morbid paint.

"It feels like a hell of a lot longer than one day," Andrew mumbled. He looked down at his phone screen. "There's only fifteen percent battery left; should we call the cops?"

"No. First, we call Delilah to get us out of this hell hole. Then we figure out what to do," I said.

I took the phone from him and opened it up; dozens of missed calls and texts from Dell. I called her, and she picked up on the first ring, her voice panicked and loud in my ear.

"Andrew! Thank God. Someone took Jules! I think it was her—"

"It's me!" I cut her off. "Dell! It's Jules. Slow down," I said.

"Oh God! Jules, are you okay? I saw you in that car, and I swear to God, I could hear you screaming in my head! Are you okay?"

"No. Well, yes. Sort of. We're safe right now. But I need you to come get us."

"I'm on it. I tried to follow him, but he was a psycho on the road, and I lost him. I called the cops, but they wouldn't do anything until you'd been gone for at least twenty-four hours. I came back to the house, and there was blood on the walkway and the porch and glass at the door. Are you sure you're okay?"

"We're not. But we will be," I said. "But I need you to hurry. Gram's place is about half an hour from here. I'll send you the location."

"Okay, Jules. I love you so much. I'll be there as quickly as I can."

We hung up, and I sent her our location. I looked up at Andrew, who was holding more of his clothes.

"I can't look at you in that any longer. Can you put these on, love?"

I quickly stepped out of the nightgown and tugged on Andrew's shirt and sweats. I felt steadier in regular clothes. We looked at each other then, and I fell into his arms, both of us sobbing and trying to make comforting noises and empty words to wash it all away.

42

Shattered

I t was the longest half hour of my life while we waited for Delilah.

I was afraid to take Gordon's car all the way to Grams' house. We toyed with the idea but the risk of someone seeing us was too great. Instead, I drove us to the next neighborhood over—far enough away that if anyone came to the house, we'd be well out of sight but close enough to drop the car back quickly. I sent Dell the updated location and slumped down in the seat to wait.

Andrew was battered and bruised from head to toe. It was difficult to look at him but I forced myself to turn in my seat and reassure myself that he was really there and breathing still. All the adrenaline had drained out of him, and he was pale as could be between the bruising. I reached out to hold his hand but pulled back when I saw the damage to it. The whole time we waited, I couldn't quite swallow the lump in my throat.

Headlights swerved around the corner and came up behind us before cutting off, and I had a moment of panic. What if it wasn't Dell? The doors were locked, and I had my hand on the ignition, just in case. My heartbeat kicked back up, and I felt another rush of adrenaline pump through me. The car door opened, and the figure that got out was recognizable even in the dark. I blew out a breath and opened my own door to get out.

Dell rushed me and threw her arms around me, whispering incoherently in my hair. She looked past me and into the car and made a choked sound in the back of her throat. I didn't know what to say. Drew looked awful. She helped me get him into the back seat of Grams' car where he could lie across it. He curled up in the fetal position and passed out. Dell threw her arms around me and choked out another sob.

"Not here, Dell. We have to go now!" I said, dislodging her and throwing Andrew's bags into the back. "We've got to get his car back to his house." She nodded and went back to Grams' car. I closed my eyes for just a moment and settled myself. Almost there. Almost free.

The terror that someone would be standing at the top of the driveway waiting for me pounded through my veins. My fear was a live wire under my skin, and I could taste the metallic bitterness of it on my tongue.

No one was there.

I pulled into the garage and parked the car, shaking the entire time. I left the keys on the seat and hurried out.

I scrambled to get into Grams' car, desperate to escape. We drove in silence, my focus on Drew's ragged breaths in the backseat. I turned back around to the front, trying to clear my mind and focus on what we needed to do.

"Jules," Delilah said softly. "Where's the asshole?"

Despite myself, I smiled. She didn't know Gordon's name and, of course, would call him that. I sobered once I had to answer her. It would be another make-or-break moment in our friendship as I chose to tell her the truth.

"I think he's dead," I said quietly. "I think I killed him." I cleared my throat as emotion threatened to spill over. I would not cry tears for my torturer. "He took Andrew yesterday. There was never a flight mishap. He's had him for twenty-four hours. He was chained to a wall in his basement. A room he'd made for torturing people," I paused, letting it sink in. The color had drained from Delilah's face as she drove, looking straight ahead, but I could see her pulse beating fast in her neck.

"Oh my god," she breathed.

"He came today while you were gone and forced me to go with him. He had Drew's wedding ring." I realized with a start that it was still in his pocket in the basement. "So I went. And he hurt me and planned to kill us both, but I just...I just sort of exploded. Like I did that day in the kitchen, only...stronger. Worse. And it...I...it...killed him."

Dell opened her mouth and then closed it again. I began to cry softly. The tears were for Andrew and me, not Gordon.

Dell cut her eyes to me, taking her focus off the road for a moment. I heard her swallow, an audible gulp of horror. The car was thick with silence while she processed my confession.

"Look, I probably shouldn't say this, but good fucking riddance," she finally said. "I was trying to come up with something better than that, but no. You protected yourself and Andrew, Jules. It was self-defense!"

"I know," I muttered. "I just—"

She cut me off. "No. It. Was. Self. Defense. A maniac abducted your husband and spent twenty-four hours torturing him. Then he attacked and abducted you and was going to do the same. Or worse. Not only is his death the best thing that could possibly happen to anyone who would come in contact with him, but it was self-defense, and you did what you had to do to protect yourself, Jules. Period."

I was quiet then, mulling over what she said and knowing it to be true, but I was also struggling with the reality of what I'd done.

"Be that as it may," I finally said. "I still killed him. And we still have to figure out what the fuck to do. He is so well-connected. That good old boys bullshit with the lawyer? It's way worse with him. When we were younger, his dad got him out of every sort of trouble you can imagine—the county commissioner, chief of police, hell, even the mayor are members of their congregation. I don't know what they would do if they found his body—even if it was obvious self-defense like this is." I took a breath. "And besides, how the fuck do you explain death by magic?" I asked.

My nerves were shot, but I still had some room for anxiety to come to the surface. Dell was quiet for a few minutes, and I looked back at Andrew. He looked awful—his face was swollen and sallow around the bruises and cuts. His breath was ragged in sleep.

"I don't know, Julia, but a man is dead, and you guys have been attacked. We *need* to call the cops!" Her voice was thready and had ratcheted up in panic. My own panic rose to meet hers.

"Dell, we can't. I'm not joking when I say that Warren Mitchell will make *us* out to be the villains here, and none of us will see the light of day again. I watched things happen again and again when I was younger that you wouldn't believe," I pleaded with her, trying to get her to understand. There would be no sense of justice if the authorities were called in. I knew what would happen. Delilah gripped the steering wheel hard and tensed her arms in frustration, a guttural noise of acceptance escaping her lips.

"Fine. If you don't call the cops, then call your Egypt people—your coven," Delilah finally said, cutting through the quiet tension of the car. "They'll know what to do."

"It's the middle of the night," I said. Delilah cut a glance at me. "Okay, okay. I'll call. Did you, by any chance, bring my phone?" I asked.

"Actually, I did," she said. "It's in my bag there." She pointed her long, freshly manicured finger towards her satchel.

I reached down, noticing blood underneath my nails, the paint from earlier in the day chipped, and one nail broken, the end jagged. A weird sadness washed over me seeing it—like it symbolized a perfectly normal day gone horribly, nightmarishly wrong. My hand was shaking as I pulled out my phone; adrenaline zapped from my body, leaving nerves raw, exposed, and exhausted.

I opened my phone, ignoring Dell's multiple texts and missed calls, and found Hanan's number. I hit call. It rang and rang, going through to voicemail. I hung up, dropping the phone in my lap.

"Call her again," Dell said. "Jules, you have to. It's late; maybe the first call will wake her up, and the second, she'll answer. But we can't handle this alone."

I nodded and called again. She picked up on the second ring, her voice breathy but concerned like anyone would be with a call ringing in the night.

"Hanan. It's Julia. I am so sorry to be calling so late," I started.

"Julia, what's wrong?" she asked, voice clear and awake.

"Everything," I said, crying. "A really, really long story short, Gordon Mitchell kidnapped and tortured Drew. Then he got ahold of me, but I...some...I...I killed him. With magic."

IN THE LIGHT OF THE MOON

I heard Hanan suck in a sharp breath and sensed Dell tense beside me. Shame burned through my body, worming its way around the cuts and bruises that should have been enough evidence for me not to feel guilty about protecting myself.

"I panicked. It just exploded out of me!" I cried. "I didn't mean to do it, but I have no idea what to do now!"

"Okay, Julia. Take a deep breath," Hanan said. "We'll figure this out. Where are you now?"

I breathed deeply, filling my lungs and willing myself to calm down. Dell reached over and put her hand on my arm, trying to comfort me as best she could.

"We're in the car with my best friend, Delilah," I said. "She had to find out; I'm so sorry, Hanan."

"Don't worry about that—as long as you're safe, that's what matters. Where's Gordon Mitchell?" she asked.

"Um. He was locked in a secret room in his basement that he built to torture people. No one is home. He sent his wife and kids out of town." Emotion bubbled up again, and I tried hard to tamp it down.

"Good. That buys some time. Give me twenty minutes. Go home. I'll call you back," she said. "And Jules, it will be okay."

She disconnected, and I let myself cry, my body emptying itself by the time we pulled into Gram's driveway, warm lights glowing from the inside, welcoming us home.

Mercifully, it was fully dark when we pulled into the drive, and no neighbors were out. We managed to rouse Drew and get him in the house before he passed out again on the bed. I sent Delilah to get some towels and hot water, and I grabbed the first aid kit from the bathroom. I cleaned his face gently, careful not to reopen a deep cut above his eye. He moaned under my

305

touch, and my heart shattered. My phone rang, startling me, and I grabbed it, quickly silencing it and answering Hanan's call.

"We'll be there tomorrow," she said as soon as I answered.

"What? No. I just need you to tell me what to do?"

"Naomi and I are coming. Her dad has a private plane, and she has already called and ordered them to prepare it. We're leaving here within the hour to fly to London to board a flight directly to you. Don't go anywhere. We'll be there as soon as we can, Julia."

I let her go and went back to cleaning Andrew up. He went wild when I lifted his shirt to clean him up further. He grabbed my hand, thrashing in the bed, groaning and shouting, voice gravelly.

"Drew! It's me!" I said. "You're safe—I'm just trying to clean you up." He relaxed back on the bed but grabbed my wrist to stop me, pain lancing through him as he moved his hand.

"Stop," he moaned. "Just—leave. I...don't touch me right now," he croaked out.

"But—" I protested. "You have blood caked and dried on you and filth all over you. Let me-"

"No," he interrupted. "Leave me be."

He went slack then, body unable to stay conscious any longer. I dropped my hand to the bed next to him, the wind taken out of my sails.

"Come on, Jules," Dell said at my side. "Give him a bit. Let's get *you* cleaned up." I shook my head but got up and followed her out of the room; one last glance at the bed and my tortured husband.

Delilah took me to the bathroom, starting the shower without a word. I slowly peeled Drew's clothes off, mind numb, body filled with aches and pains that were more than happy to make themselves known. When I raised my arms to lift the shirt over my head, I felt a sharp pain in my side, and Delilah sucked in a breath.

"God, Jules. What did he do to you?" she asked, warm fingers touching my side lightly. I flinched at her touch, and she pulled away.

"I'm sorry," I said, embarrassed. "It's not you. It's just..." I trailed off.

"I get it, Jules. But between the fingerprint necklace around your throat, the fact that your eye is swollen shut, and this massive and nasty bruise on your ribs, and, God, the one on your shoulder, I'm not entirely sure that we don't need to be heading straight for the hospital. To say nothing of Andrew's hands and whatever wounds he has that we can't see."

I sighed and stepped gingerly into the shower.

"It looks worse than it is. My ribs aren't broken, just bruised. He broke one before, two days after my sixteenth birthday," I said nonchalantly like we were talking about horrific trauma that wasn't my own.

Dell made an odd noise, and I peeked my head out of the curtain. She had closed the lid and sat on the toilet, crying quietly. I ducked back in and showered, cleaning off the blood, sweat, and horrible trauma of the day. I stayed under the spray, water as hot as I could stand, but the heat couldn't cut through the chill of Gordon's basement and everything that had happened.

Delilah had pulled herself together by the time I was finished. She handed me a clean towel and forced me to sit still while she wordlessly inspected the bruises around my throat and eye.

My throat was sore where he'd started crushing my windpipe, and my voice felt scratchy every time I spoke, but I knew he hadn't done permanent damage. I was a little more concerned about my face. My eye socket was a bright point of pain that was impossible to ignore. I slipped on underwear, and Dell stopped me, grabbing her phone and taking photos of my battered body. I knew it needed to be done, just in case, but it was awful to stand there, bared and battered, letting her document it.

She quietly slipped out of the bathroom, letting me finish getting dressed; my softest black leggings and Andrew's t-shirt were the only things I could stand against my skin. I was cold as I walked into the living room; Andrew was sleeping when I checked on him, so I grabbed Gram's cardigan that I'd kept and slipped it on. The soft cotton wrapped around me and surrounded me in Gram's scent, and I finally settled. Delilah brought me a cup of tea laced with whisky and sat with me on the sofa, close but not quite touching. I drank some of the tea, letting it scald my mouth, and felt the hot liquid travel through my body, the whisky chasing the chill away from the inside out.

"Dell. I don't know what to do," I said softly. The whirring of the heat pump was the only sound in the room.

"I know, Jules. I don't either," she said, face haunted. "But your people are coming. They'll know what to do, yeah?"

I thought about Hanan and her leadership, how much guidance she'd offered me, and of Naomi, hot-headed but so sure of herself I knew there was no way she couldn't know what to do. I nodded.

"Yeah," I said. "They'll know what to do."

I spent the night curled up against Andrew, our bodies sore and broken. At some point during the night, I woke to a cold and empty bed. I could hear the shower running in the bathroom, and when I went to check on him, I heard Andrew throwing up. When I reached for the doorknob, it was locked. I stood there a moment, hand and forehead resting on the door, wishing I could go in and comfort him before returning to the bed and crying myself to sleep.

43

Magical Cavalry

The next day dawned bright and early as pain lanced through my head like a shrill alarm. I moaned and groped gently beside me to see if Andrew had returned to bed. I relaxed in relief when I felt him there. I slowly got up, every inch of my body either aching or sharply painful as I moved. Hobbling quietly to the door, I closed it behind me, leaving Andrew to the peaceful oblivion of sleep; Lumee curled up in the bend of his knees, standing guard over him.

I found Dell on the back porch, the tell-tale musky cloud around her greeting me.

"A little early for a smoke, no?" I asked jokingly, trying to sound like everything was normal.

"I can't survive the day without something to calm my nerves. You could probably do with a little bit of pain management, Jules. You look like absolute hell."

"I feel even worse than I look. I don't think any part of me doesn't ache in some way. I don't know how Andrew is even able to sleep. The pain from my head woke me up, and he is far worse off than I am." I leaned back against the rocker I'd eased into, closing the one eye that wasn't swollen shut. My face was throbbing with every beat of my heart, the bruise hot to the touch.

"Jules, I'm serious," Dell said. "The only medicine we have here is Motrin or weed. I brought the strong stuff for my Endo—I'm supposed to start this weekend, and I can feel it coming, and I knew I'd need it if I stayed long enough. Just take it, please. We have a while before the magical cavalry arrives; get some relief."

I sighed, knowing she was right. I gave a slight nod, which made me wince, confirming even more that I needed something more potent than the eight hundred milligrams of Motrin I'd taken the night before and just before I came outside. I heard her leave for a few minutes, and she returned with a vape pen and a steaming cup of tea.

I took a few puffs from the thin pencil-shaped vape, inhaling deeply, letting the action of doing something I knew would bring relief to anchor me.

"Holy shit, Dell," I said, coughing. "That's strong!"

"I don't have much choice on the first day of my period. It's either that or narcotics, and narcotics make me barf and leave me feeling worse than just dealing with the pain." She shrugged.

I took another deep drag, and a few minutes later, the wall of pain lifted at the edges ever so slightly. It was enough to risk a sip of tea without the pain making me nauseated. We didn't speak much—the pain was too much to let me focus on a conversation. A few sips of tea later, I felt a wave of relief and peace settle over me like a warm blanket. I relaxed fully, melting into the rocker and dozing off.

I dozed on the porch, the relief from the vape allowing me to finally rest. Delilah covered me with a thick blanket at a certain point, tucking it under my legs to keep out the early morning chill. When I surfaced an hour later, the porch was warm, and the pain in my face had eased from nauseatingly sharp to a dull, albeit intense, ache. Dell was worried my occipital bone might be broken, and I wasn't sure she was wrong. The pain was unlike anything I'd felt before, and Gordon had punched me in the face plenty when we were younger. I shuddered at even the brief thought of him and slowly got up to check on Andrew.

I found Dell perched at the foot of the bed, talking in a low voice to Andrew. The floor next to the bed was littered with towels, old bandages, and wrappers from clean ones. Andrew was propped up against the headboard, pillows under both hands, bandages obscuring the damage. I felt a little pang that he'd let Dell clean him up, not me. Still, I reminded myself that she'd spent six years in the Navy bandaging up sailors, had seen it all, and could clean him up with an emotional detachment I didn't possess.

I stepped into the room, not wanting to disturb their conversation but needing to be near them. The weed had knocked the edge off, but I was still very much aware of my body and the hot spots of pain left by Gordon's fists.

"Morning, Jules," Andrew said, seeing me and cutting off Dell's argument for going to the hospital. His face was tired and his voice heavy, like the spark of life had come close to being beaten out of him.

"Morning." I walked towards him, on edge. The sight of him lying there, body broken and unfamiliar with discoloration, threatened to throw me into a panic. Tears, hot and stinging, ran down my cheeks.

"Hey, I'm okay. We're okay, Jules," he said, trying to soothe me, but the words were shallow. We both knew none of this was okay. I nodded, and Dell came over, wrapping her arm around me, making me wince with pain when she put pressure on the shoulder I'd slammed into the shower faucet.

"Shit, Jules, I'm so sorry!" she said, pulling away and opting to hold my hand instead.

Andrew flinched, his face pinched with worry, pain, or both; I couldn't tell.

"It's fine. I'm fine," I assured them, though nothing was fine at all, and I didn't know whether it ever would be again.

We spent the day waiting for Hanan and Naomi. Everyone was on edge and in pain. Dell's period started early, leaving her curled on the sofa with a heating pad, blazed out of her head, trying to rid her body of the pain that ravaged her insides. She'd tried to tough it out, but I finally forced her to smoke and get the relief she desperately needed.

Andrew and I were nervous around each other, a weird shyness that was unfamiliar and discomforting. He wasn't quite ready to talk about everything that had happened with Gordon, and frankly, I wasn't either. I was terrified of what I'd done, no matter how many times I told myself I'd had no other choice and no matter how horrified I was at how much harm Gordon had managed to inflict upon Andrew in twenty-four hours. I'd finally forced him to give me a rundown of his injuries, which were overwhelming. I cried, tears pouring down my face as he rattled them off with a cold detachment, only giving the barest details when I forced the issue.

Gordon had started on his right hand, breaking all his fingers one by one. Then he'd moved to his feet, breaking some toes, burning spots on the tender soles of his feet, cutting large gashes in between the burns and dripping alcohol on the open wounds, burning them and making Andrew howl in pain, unable to control himself. Between his hands and his feet, his body had been battered and tortured with a multitude of instruments that inflicted different levels and types of pain. I was scared to touch him— afraid of inflicting any more pain on top of what he was already feeling.

Gordon had given him drugs. Andrew wasn't sure what, but things that kept him awake and alert with every nerve ending on fire with awareness. Even when Gordon had left him alone for hours in the middle of the night, he'd been unable to calm his racing heart. He lay there, terrified and in pain, unable to escape even to the oblivion of sleep. It wasn't until the drugs had worn off late in the afternoon that he'd passed out and gotten a reprieve. I wanted nothing more than to cling to him, to wrap myself around him and hold him tight, giving us the connection and assurance that we were okay, but neither could do it. I settled for curling against him and listening to him breathe as he dozed in and out of sleep all day.

After the longest day of my life, Hanan messaged me to let me know they were ten minutes from the house, Naomi having hired a car to bring them straight to us. I ensured Andrew was settled and paced the living room, counting the minutes. Dell had surfaced and waited with me, anxiety clear on her face, mingled with pain.

Finally, they pulled into the drive, and when I saw they'd brought Marwa with them, I let her gather me into her arms, and I wept with relief.

We'd all gathered in the bedroom, huddled around Andrew, still propped up in bed, unable and unwilling to put any weight on his feet. In turns, he and I explained what happened, both of us sweating and shaking by the time they were caught up. Everyone was quiet—too shocked to do much more than open and close their mouths as they processed what we'd told them.

Delilah had known, for the most part, what had happened, but hearing it all laid out in detail left her pale. Naomi was thoughtful, a plan formulating, I could tell. I'd been nervous about how things would be between us. After the big fight on my birthday the year before, we'd not spent much time together one-on-one—but she had wrapped her arms around me when they'd arrived and whispered in my ear that she was proud of me for being so brave, surprising me with her olive branch.

Exhausted from reliving everything, Andrew passed out. Whether coming down from whatever drug Gordon had given him or just his brain needing an escape from his wounds and the trauma, he hadn't been able to stay awake for any length of time since getting to Gram's house. Dell was sure he had a nasty concussion, but he assured us that he was fine, which hadn't satisfied Dell, but he wouldn't budge. The ramifications of a hospital trip weren't worth the risk.

As soon as he began to nod off, we all headed to the living room, leaving Andrew to rest. Dell chattered, an endless stream of conversation, which she always did when nervous. Naomi headed straight for the back door and went outside for some air without a word.

Marwa went for her bag while we settled in the living room. Delilah curled up in Gramps' old chair, and the heating pad was plugged into the wall next to it and pressed against her abdomen. Hanan and I sat on the sofa, quiet as Marwa entertained Dell's chatter. She gathered an armful of pouches and jars and brought them to the coffee table, laying each out.

"Hasina and Renee send their best," she said, laying each thing out on the table before me. "Hanan called us all to let us know what was happening, and they both rushed these things over for you and Andrew. A couple of teas from Hasina—pain relief and a calming and restorative blend to help you sleep. And there's a salve here from Renee. She and Hasina worked together years ago, coming up with the right mix of herbs and things, and it's very effective for pain relief and healing. I wasn't sure if you'd brought any with you. I believe this one is stronger than the one they taught you about."

I nodded and reached for the amber-colored glass jar of healing salve. Unscrewing the lid, I was met with the strong, pungent scent of camphor overlaid with herbs. I dipped two fingers in and scooped a bit out, mentally crossing my fingers to relieve the throbbing pain in my face. Gingerly, I pressed my fingertips to my eye, the liniment slippery and cool against my skin, but a wave of warmth immediately rushed through me. The heavy weight of pain lifted off my face, making me gasp in relief. On one of my many trips to Egypt, Hasina showed me how to make it, but I had yet to try my hand at the recipe.

"Oh!" I exclaimed. "It's working!"

Hanan and Marwa both tittered.

"Magic, darling," Marwa said, smiling. Now, I'm going to make some tea for you and Andrew, and then we'll figure this out."

I nodded, amazed at how much better my face was feeling.

"Um, Hanan, would you mind putting this on my shoulder?" I asked. I pulled my shirt over my head, and she sucked in a breath.

"It's awful, isn't it?" Dell said. "I wanted them both to go to the hospital, but the stubborn asses refused."

I looked at her, face blanched white with pain, but I still shook my head at her. No hospitals.

"Julia, she's right. You both need medical attention," Hanan said, gently rubbing the ointment into my shoulder and ribs. The relief was euphoric. I took my first, truly deep breath since the day before, tears in my eyes from the sheer joy of being able to do so without my ribs screaming in pain.

"I know," I said quietly. "But how on earth would we explain these kinds of injuries? Andrew had a railroad spike hammered into his hand! What would we have said to that?"

Hanan stiffened behind me.

"*That's* the only reason I didn't fight her," Dell said. "She's right. How would we ever have explained that?"

I grabbed my t-shirt and pulled it back on just as Naomi strode into the room. She sat on the sofa beside me, almost vibrating with energy.

"Okay. First of all, I warded the house." She pointedly looked at me. "Julia—you seem to have forgotten you're a witch. That's the first thing you must do when you come to a new place you'll be staying at for any length of time." She waved a hand dismissively as I opened my mouth to protest. "It's fine. But you have to remember to do it. It's a simple spell but an effective one."

I nodded, suitably chastised and annoyed with myself.

"I didn't even think to remind you, Julia. I'm so sorry," Hanan said.

"None of us did," Marwa said, coming into the room with two cups of tea.

The mugs were plain and white, new, cheap ones we'd bought to replace the ones that had shattered with my outburst. I gratefully accepted my cup from Marwa, and she walked over to Dell and handed her the other cup. "Drink up, sweetheart, this will help."

Delilah reached for her mug, grateful. I took a cautious sip and let the earthy, odd tea warm me. The taste was palatable, though not pleasant. But I didn't care. If it worked as well as the salve, I knew I could choke down anything to feel better. I wondered to myself if there was a special tea to erase memories.

"Andrew looks a lot worse off than you," Marwa said. "I'm letting his steep a bit longer so it's quite strong, and then you can take it and the ointment to him and give him some relief."

I nodded, taking another sip. Warmth spread through me, chasing away the raw feeling of my insides.

By the time I finished my tea, forcing the last bitter dregs down, I was pleasantly warmed and not in excruciating pain. The color had returned to Dell's cheeks, and I could see the relief on her face. I got up, leaving Hanan and Naomi to continue formulating the plan, and went to the kitchen. I got Andrew's tea, taking the jar of salve with me, hoping they'd packed plenty.

Marwa followed quietly behind, and I found Andrew still asleep, his breathing uneven and face pinched in pain. The room was warm, almost stiflingly so, and I saw Marwa, out of the corner of my eye, go to open the window to let fresh air in. I hurried to Andrew, putting the mug and jar on the bedside table and gently touching his forehead. He was burning up with a fever. His skin was clammy and a sickly green tinge around the edges. My stomach dropped with worry. I whispered his name, pulling him out of unconsciousness, and told him what we had to help him. He nodded once in ascent and turned away from me as I carefully unwound the bandages on his hands.

Marwa stood beside me, hovering close in case I needed her. She placed her hand on my arm to stop me.

"Andrew, we need you to drink some tea first."

He turned his head and struggled to wake up enough to drink. He coughed and sputtered with the first sip, the liquid dark and murky—much more potent than what I'd drunk. We gave him a minute, and then he took another deep gulp, shuddering at the strong taste.

"I don't know what that is, but it better work," he said, his tone almost light but still laced with pain. He laid his head back down, and Marwa and I got to work.

We focused on his hands and feet first, going slowly and keeping our touches as featherlight as possible. In moments, his face relaxed, his body going slack as the worst of the pain receded. I wept in relief as we finished administering the ointment, taking care to go back over his hands before stepping out of the room and shutting the door behind us.

We walked back into the living room, where the others waited. They'd talked about it as best they could on the plane, wrapping themselves in a sound-silencing spell that gave them the freedom to speak. But after hearing that I had house keys and we had some time before Gordon's wife returned, they'd formulated a pretty sound plan.

We'd wait until later that night, just past midnight, hoping no neighbors would be awake to see us around the house. We'd slip in and clean up, doing our best to erase all evidence that Andrew or I had ever been there. Naomi assured me she'd handle Gordon, and I didn't push for details—I wasn't sure I wanted to know.

44

A Reckoning

We watched the minutes tick by on one of Gramps' old clocks on the mantle. It was my favorite and the only one I'd wound when I came back—though the house was peppered with loads of antique clocks from one of his many hobbies picked up along retirement. As the rhythmic ticking thundered through the quiet room, I regretted having wound it at all and felt a slight pang of half-hearted regret that it hadn't been one of the casualties of my outburst.

"That's it," Dell said. "I can't sit here a minute longer listening to that damn thing tick. Can we just go?"

"Now or never, I suppose," Naomi said and got up from her seat on the sofa.

Now that it was finally time to get up and face Gordon again, the nerves to get up and move gave way to sit and stay ones. I squeezed my eyes shut and forced myself out of Gram's chair. I peeked in on Andrew while everyone else gathered their things. When I turned around, Dell was in the hall behind me.

"I'm coming with you," she said. I shook my head. She put her hand up before I could say anything. "Before you argue with me, listen. Rescuing you guys from that house was one of the scariest things I've ever been through. I can't sit here and wait, not knowing what's happening."

I looked at her, an argument on the tip of my tongue that I bit back and swallowed down. I didn't trust myself to speak and not plead with her to stay, so I just nodded and walked to the door.

We piled into Grams' car, Naomi in the passenger seat and the others squished in the backseat. The car was empty of any sounds besides the rumble of tires on the road and the whoosh of air conditioning pumping through the vents. We were all too lost in thought to find the right thing to say to break the tension.

The closer we got to the house, the more visceral response I began to have. Little tremors of panic coursed through my system, and no amount of breathwork or trying to calm myself did anything. Marwa, seated behind me, reached up and touched me. Afraid to speak, knowing I might break down in the driver's seat if I did, I nodded my head, and Marwa lightly squeezed my shoulders. A wave of calm washed over me, tamping down the worst of the panic and taking the edge off. While I could never quite get past feeling manipulated by Renee's calming magic, Marwa always asked permission, and the comfort she gave was readily accepted.

We arrived, and I swallowed down another wave of anxiety. Marwa laid her hand on my shoulder again, and I felt another wave of calm lap over me. I parked as close to the garage as I could get, opting for a quicker getaway should we need it instead of parking and walking up the long drive. With a final look at each other, we got out and crept along the house— trying to stay out of the direct line of the floodlights that had come on when we pulled in. I fumbled with the doorknob at the side door and let us in, heart pounding in my chest and mind struggling to stay calm as the memories of the day before flooded back. Marwa did her best to steady me, but no amount of magic was enough to stop the onslaught of emotions when I walked into the house.

Silently, they followed me to the basement door, Marwa never losing contact with my shoulder and Dell squeezing my hand the whole time. Hands shaking terribly, I managed to get the door unlocked. With each step we descended the stairs, dread and fear grew heavier in my gut. Finally, we all stood in the basement. Someone reached over and found a panel of light switches, and the overhead lights blazed, eliminating the shadows and turning the space from sinister to ordinary.

There was a strong, astringent smell mingling with the odors of the basement that I hadn't noticed the day before. I took a shuddering breath and walked to the corner where the hidden door was. I wasn't sure what Gordon had done to open the door, but I fumbled around, reaching up and searching blindly along the shelf. I felt a switch and pressed it down, releasing the catch. The door opened, and my heart slammed against my ribs. Naomi pulled the door open, and the bleach scent slapped us back violently. My eyes watered, and I heard Dell cough next to me. I looked at all of them, confused. The torture rooms had been a miasma of nightmarish smells—none of which were clean.

"What the hell?" Hanan said.

"I have no clue. I don't remember it smelling like this when we were down here." Dell rubbed my arm, trying to comfort me.

I walked into the hallway, the bulb glowing brighter than it had seemed the day before. Still shaking but just wanting the night to end, I unlocked the door holding Gordon's body. I took a deep breath, trying to steady myself before opening it, but Naomi stepped by me and nodded at me to let her go in first.

I backed up against Dell, who was behind me, hand wrapped around my forearm. Her presence is solid and reassuring.

Setting her shoulders and looking at me with a quick nod, Naomi pushed the door open. I braced myself, ready to confront what had happened and what I'd done when the bright lights all but blinded us.

"Um, Julia—are you sure he was dead?" Naomi asked.

The room was empty, with nobody in sight. There was no evidence that the day before had even happened. No chains were hanging from the wall, and no tools were on the gleaming surfaces of stainless steel. The smell of disinfectant was more pungent here, stinging my nose and burning in my throat, so much so that I pulled my shirt over my nose, as did everyone else.

I opened my mouth to say something, shock punching me in the gut as hard as Gordon had.

"He was dead," I whispered with a shaky voice and even shakier resolve. "I know he was dead. I—" My stomach flipped, bile rising as I swallowed it down. My skin broke out in a cold sweat, and I began to shake uncontrollably.

I turned, shoving past everyone, running out of the room and to the end of the hall. I unlocked the door and swung it open, the room beyond empty. Even the bed was gone. The space was empty and cold, stinking of bleach. I couldn't make sense of anything—the nightmare from the day before was so clear and vivid in my mind compared to this sterile nightmare in front of me. The torture devices, the shattered light bulbs from my outburst, Gordon's body, still and haunting with its death mask. My mind was racing—trying, in vain, to make sense of everything that when I backed out of the room and turned towards the concerned faces of the women who had come with me, we were all too confused and distracted to have heard the footsteps on the stairs.

A large shadow blocked the bright light from the basement, and I jumped, shrieking and making everyone turn. There, in the light, risen from the dead, was Gordon. My vision tunneled, and I felt Naomi grab my arm to steady me, holding me in place and keeping me from passing out.

"Well, well, well. If it isn't Jolene Davis, in the flesh," he said, voice calm and relaxed. "I had no clue what sort of surprise Gordon had in store when he called me a few days ago and said he had a special gift for me."

Standing in the doorway of the hidden rooms of his son's basement wasn't Gordon but Warren Mitchell, amusement shining on his face. He looked to the room where everyone else stood, huddled together. "I'm not sure who all you people are, but this is between you and me, honey," he said. "Ah—I don't think so." He pulled out a gun and trained it on Naomi, who had moved to step in front of me.

"Nobody moves. We're going to stand here and talk like adults. I really don't want to have to call in the cleaning crew again. Between the strength of disinfectant needed and the discretion I had to pay for, this has been one hell of an expensive mess to clean up."

"Please, Pastor Mitchell," I pleaded, hating how small my voice sounded. "Just let them go. We can talk." I was shaking, adrenaline needing a way out.

He had aged well, body softening and face lined lightly, but he looked much the same as when I was young. I fought internally, forcing myself not to retreat into the girl he'd traumatized as a child.

"Not just yet," he answered calmly. He holstered his gun but ensured we could still see it—a warning should we step out of line. "And actually, it's *Congressman* Mitchell now."

He leaned against the doorway, his large body blocking our way out and cornering us like prey. He took his time, assessing, eyes taking in each woman but landing back on me. He looked me up and down slowly, and I could feel his eyes lingering on every inch of my body. I fought back panic and forced myself to stand tall with as much defiance as I could muster.

"What do you want?" I asked.

"Oh, just to thank you, really," he said sardonically. "In one fell swoop, you handled a problem that's been getting out of control for years."

I felt a shock run through me at his words. "What?" I stammered out.

"Oh. Gordon." His voice was still calm, hand gesturing nonchalantly like we were discussing the weather. "He's been getting out of hand for years. I could look the other way when he was toying with animals or even the occasional bruise left behind on Missy that couldn't be covered with a high neck or sleeves. But that's not the first body I've cleaned out of that room." He stepped forward just a bit, closing the space between us and lightly touching my swollen cheek, my body stiffening in fear, feeling every inch of his touch like a flame against my skin.

"He always took it too far. You're never supposed to lose control and leave marks this bad. People ask too many questions. Plus, it just looks hideous." He stepped back, reassuming his lean against the door frame, casual—like we weren't talking about his dead son.

"Anyway, I'd been trying to figure out what to do about him for some time now. It's a shame your father is gone," he said wistfully. "He was always so good at cleaning up messes. Luckily, I have other friends who were happy to help. To tell you the truth, I was not the only one trying to find a way to control Gordon and his more...base urges." He narrowed his eyes at me. "You know he's always been special, Jolene. But when you left, it snapped something inside of him."

I swallowed thickly, frozen in place, unsure what to do. Everyone was behind me, their attention and energy trained on Warren Mitchell, letting him speak, but I knew their defenses were ready.

"It took a few years for things to get truly bad," he continued, caught up in the telling of the story, ever an orator. "He seemed content, at first, to continue terrorizing the neighborhood cats and dogs and eventually Missy once they were married. But he was mad with trying to find you, Jolene. He was mad with obsession, driven by something even *I* couldn't reign in." He paused momentarily, letting his words sink in, always one for a dramatic pause.

"Then he found the drugs. He swore that God himself had sent them to help make him stronger, and I knew then just how weak he'd become. I'd allowed his little indulgences to go on for far too long. People had started to talk, you see," he said. "Missy wasn't so good at covering her bruises and pretending everything was okay like she should have been. His sermons were erratic, just enough to make people start talking; we couldn't have that. Not after everything it took to build this up." He absently gestured around him.

"I wasn't going to let his weakness and selfishness tear down a lifetime of work. So, Jolene, you did me a favor, darlin'. It didn't take much to finish him off when I showed up, and he was still breathin'."

Relief washed over me, tinged with something dark that I shoved down.

"What did you say?" I asked.

"Oh, well, you did me a favor but didn't quite see it through. Though I wouldn't have expected you to have it in you— you're nothing like your father. I made sure to finish the job for us both, and that's that."

I swallowed the bile that rose in my throat. The ease with which he spoke of killing his flesh and blood was too much.

"As it stands, I will repay the favor by letting you go."

I was nowhere near as proficient at schooling my face into neutrality as he was, and he laughed, the sound barking and loud in the room.

"Weren't expecting that, were you?" He laughed.

I shook my head. "Not exactly."

"I like to look out for people who do me favors. That's how life works, you see," he said, his mask of calm firmly back in place. "And you're going to return the favor. All I ask is that you leave here and never return." He narrowed his eyes at us. "And I mean that, Jolene. You'll go and never step foot in North Carolina again. I'll know if you do, and then I'll have you taken care of. You'll remember how close I am with the Mayor and chief of police, yes?" he asked pointedly. I swallowed, nodding. "Good. Then you'll know how serious this is."

The calm slipped as he gave his orders: "You have twenty-four hours to leave my state." He turned to go, and Marwa moved in front of me, gently pushing me back towards everyone else.

"Just a moment," she said, her voice bold and clear. "We'll leave, and you'll have no argument from us about that. But you need to understand something. She is ours now. *Ours*. And you won't be hurting her anymore." She put her hands on her hips and stared Warren Mitchell in the face, defying him in a way I knew no other woman had ever done.

He smiled, lips curling up nastily.

"Oh? And what do you think a bunch of women will do to me? You're obviously not from around here, so allow me to let you in on how things work in my town. I can do whatever I want here, sweetheart. I own this place. And if I wanted, I would own her too." His face was smug as he raised himself to his full height, broad shoulders and chest taking up space, menace oozing off him like an oily film.

"You really don't want to know what we could do, Mr..." she trailed off, waiting for him to offer his name.

"How rude of me," he said sarcastically. "As I said earlier, Congressman Warren Mitchell, ladies."

"Well, Mr. Mitchell," Marwa continued. "You will leave our girl alone. You won't attempt to contact or hurt her in any way again, or you will regret it."

Suddenly, he balked, eyes wide with shock as he stood frozen, face purpling as his mouth opened and closed like a fish. I spun around and saw Naomi and Hanan; both focused intently on Warren Mitchell. I turned back, and Marwa walked up to him, unafraid.

"Do we have an understanding?" she asked sweetly.

He nodded, and they released him, hands flying to his throat, loud pants as he sucked in huge gulps of air echoing off the walls. He staggered backward, still bent over and wheezing.

Dell, Marwa, and Hanan rushed past him, heading straight for the freedom of the stairs. I walked out of the hall, determined not to be afraid of him any longer.

Unable to let old habits die, he grabbed me as I walked past, jerking me roughly back.

"You're still just a weak little girl, Jolene," he growled. My heart fluttered, and I tamped down the rising panic. "But I shouldn't be surprised. Your daddy was weak in the end, too. I had to take care of him just like I'll take care of you one day. He tried to turn against me in the end. He wanted to find his precious Jolene and make amends, but I couldn't have that."

The realization of what he was saying swirled in my gut, making me sick. He smiled a sinister smile, pleased with the torment his words had landed.

"It was easy enough to make it look like an accident..."

Seeing Hanan and Naomi overpower him and Marwa stand up to him had shaken something loose inside me. I had a clear picture of what I needed to do. For so long, I'd run from my nightmares. Run from the trauma that had been inflicted on me. But I couldn't spend the rest of my life running. And I refused to allow him to hurt me any longer.

I turned behind me, meeting Naomi's face. She gave me a nod of encouragement, emboldening me. I knew I could do this. Knew that I had to. Knew that if I didn't, he would forever haunt me like his son had; he would forever hold power over me. He leaned heavily against a shelf, still wheezing and clutching his throat. His one hand was tight around my arm, bruising my bicep, a maniacal smile spreading across his face while he thought he'd regained control. I stepped closer to him, pushing against his grip, and reveled in his flinch away from me—my defiance unexpected.

"Not only will you not hurt me anymore," I said, voice strong and confident. "You will stop hurting any other woman who comes your way. Keep your hands off Gayle or any mistress you might be using."

I mentally squeezed, taking hold of the most precious and tender parts of Warren Mitchell with my mind. I sent my energy into them, squeezing and shriveling, my hands tense and talon-like by my side. He dropped to the floor, his legs unable to hold him up any longer. He curled around himself, trying to protect his testicles from the invisible hands that clawed and choked them from the magic I sent raging inside him. I only squeezed harder, energy latching on— happy to have something to take hold of; the tight reigns I'd held on it loosened.

I glared at him and felt my eyes flash in anger. I knew I had to pull back or risk killing him. A darker side to my magic was eager to take it that far. Keen to be let loose. Warren Mitchell's eyes were wild and terrified, full of fear. A small part of me reveled in being able to turn it around and inflict the same paralyzing horror that he and his son had administered to me and countless other women. I leaned over him, drawing close so he could see me clearly and not mistake my words.

"If you ever think about hurting anyone again, even the faintest, most absent thought, they'll shrivel inside your sac," I said, voice hard, one last squeeze for good measure. He emitted a squeak, high pitched and pained, and I smelled the stink of his fear, sour and musty, and it spurred me on. I was so hot with the pulsing need for revenge that my cheeks flushed and sweat dripped down my spine.

"Do you understand me?" He nodded quickly, sweat dripping down his face. "Good," I said, releasing my hold on him. I turned back towards the stairs, meeting everyone's frozen faces. I stopped then and turned one more time.

"Oh, and Warren," I said smugly, sending energy and intent into my words for assurance. "You will donate half of Gordon's life insurance and twenty percent of your annual income to all the battered women's shelters within a hundred-mile radius of here. And when you're casting your vote in Congress, it will always be to protect women and their rights."

I didn't wait for a response but spun on my heel, storming up the stairs and out into the cool night as fast as I could, sucking down great gulps of air as soon as I burst out of the garage door.

In seconds everyone else ran out behind me, sucking in their own deep breaths and rushing to the car. I knew there was no way Warren Mitchell would get off the ground any time soon, but I certainly wasn't taking any chances, and neither was anyone else. Naomi drove us back to Andrew. Adrenaline and power rushed through my veins, making it impossible for me to navigate there safely.

The car was quiet on the way back; everyone was shocked into silence and relieved that we'd made it out. I rested my head on the window, the glass cool against my skin. The fear and crushing weight of running from Gordon Mitchell my whole life had lifted.

I should have felt a sense of freedom, but something settled in its place— shackling me with a new weight. The power I held inside me that had hurt the Mitchells scared me. But the dark pleasure that had snaked through and pooled in my belly terrified me more.

Epilogue

❋ ☽ ◗ ○ ◖ ☾ ❋

*T*he golden fields of Aaru lived up to its name. As far as her eye could see, Hatshepsut was surrounded by the most beautiful, glowing countryside. Her eternal resting place was the lush and verdant jungle she'd grown up exploring, made perfect by the gods. She couldn't imagine wanting to be any-where else. The Mother Nile flowed powerfully beside her as she walked along the riverbank.

Here, in this place of peace and eternity, Hatshepsut spent her days wandering the perfect Earth. It was unencumbered by buildings or carts. There was no war or famine. No droughts or plagues. Unless she sought someone out, she had the peace of solitude as her constant companion. It wasn't long after her arrival that some of the priestesses appeared. Years passed, and more of them came. They gathered and lived at the temple Senenmut had built for her—the rooms expanding to fit their every desire.

Death in Aaru was similar to life on Earth—a sun rose and set, the moon cycled through her phases, plants grew, and Hat-shepsut ate and drank (though she never felt hunger or thirst and did it for the sheer pleasure of the food of the gods grown on this plane). She was surrounded by the people she was closest to in life, including Senenmut, who'd found her sunning herself under a sun that never burned her skin. She had known he'd come *eventually. They were fated to be together in life and eternity, and she felt no surprise to see him standing above her, only a deep sense of contentment. The difference in* Aaru *was that she was free—free from the heavy responsibility of being Pharaoh. She was free to just...be.*

Worry over Thutmose and the dark heka *he had killed her for was the only thing that held her from finding total peace in* Aaru. *Hatshepsut worried about what he would do to her people—whether he'd succeeded in finding the way to immortality or hurt anyone else. There were moments she lost herself to the disquiet of worry. Senenmut would find her wandering the river and vexed over what she'd left behind, and he would do his best to bring her back to him. She'd always assumed that the afterlife was a place of eternal rest—tranquility that life would never afford. And while she knew repose in this place of golden rushes, the darkness in which her life was taken had tainted her.*

On those days when the dark stain felt like it was spreading and taking over, she would bathe in the ritual waters—their power in this place was as strong as it was earthside. Hatshepsut would wash away the darkness that stained her and find peace in the healing water. In her darkest moments, she would swear that she could hear the murmuring voices of priestesses in the water just beyond. She hoped they remembered her and knew the strength of their power. On those days, she wouldn't leave the pool in the hope of reaching and lending her power to whoever was beyond the veil of water.

The once great Pharaoh dipped her toes in the Mother Nile—the river that gave life on Earth. It was cool against her sun-warmed skin, and she stood in the water, letting it swirl around her ankles and pull silt between her toes, feeling for all the world it gave her, if not life, vitality. She closed her eyes and tilted her face to the sun, smiling.

A cloud passed over the sun, darkening across her eyelids.

An oppressive shroud of cold—the kind of cold only death knows—draped over Hatshepsut, and with a violent tug in her navel, she was ripped out of the river and plunged into darkness.

Pronunciation and Definition Guide

Hatshepsut (Haht-SHEP-sut)—the fifth Pharaoh of the Eighteenth Dynasty of Egypt and the second documented female pharaoh. She ruled from 1479-1458 BCE. Upon the death of her husband and half-brother Thutmose II she stepped in as regent for her stepson, Thutmose III when he inherited the throne at age two. As the daughter of Thutmose I, she felt she had a divine right to rule and established herself as more than just a stand-in for Thutmose III. She wore a false beard and dressed as a male to gain more acceptance from anyone who would argue the need for a male ruler. Her reign lasted a little over twenty years and was prosperous and peaceful. She was one of the most prolific builders in Ancient Egypt and left her mark not only in the hearts of her people but in the landscape of Egypt.

Experts think she died of bone cancer from a carcinogenic skin lotion that she was probably using to soothe irritated and inflamed skin.

When she died Thutmose III took over as Pharaoh and towards the end of his reign he began to erase all evidence of her—statues were defaced and destroyed and her achievements were parceled out to other pharaohs. Even her burial was not what she planned—during Thutmose III's reign it is thought that she was moved from her father's tomb to another, unmarked tomb, with her nurse and separate from the rest of her burial things (including her canonic jars). Years of speculation and testing of teeth have led to believe that they've found her and she's currently in the Egyptian Museum in Cairo.

Shesout (sheh-soo)—nickname for Hatshepsut

Maatkare (maht-car)— A name or title shared by many different women in Ancient Egypt. The name is roughly translated as **Maat (the goddess of truth) is the life force of Re (the sun god)**

The Golden Fields of **Aaru** (ah -roo)—The name for Heavenly Paradise in Ancient Egyptian Mythology (Also called The Golden Rushes or the Fields of Aaru)

Heka (heck-ah)—Ancient Egyptian word for magic

Isis (eye-sis)—Major Goddess in Ancient Egyptian mythology. Goddess of magic and wisdom, kingship and protection of the kingdom, mothering, and mourning. She was believed to have helped usher people into the afterlife.

Senenmut (Sen-in-moot)— also rumored to be Hatshepsut's lover

Thutmose (THuwT-mows) **III**— Hatshepsut's Stepson—the first born son of Thutmose II. Next in line from the throne after his father, his stepmother stepped in as Regent when he was a young boy and reigned in his stead.

Duat (doo-aht)—Ancient Egyptian Underworld or Afterlife

Neferure (nef-er-ra)—Hatshepsut's daughter

Habebty (Hah-beeb-tee)— Arabic term of endearment meaning honey or sweetie

Souk (Sōōk) —an Arabic market or bazaar

Mashallah (mah-shah-la)—an Arabic phrase that translates to "God has willed it"

Bahrain (Bah-RAYN)—Small island in the Middle East off the coast of Saudi Arabia

Hanan (Han-ann)
Marwa (Mar-wah)
Salma (Sal-MA)
Hasina (Ha-seen-ah)
Omar (Oh-Mar)
Karim (Ka-rim)

Acknowledgements

This book wouldn't have been possible without a lot of people who cheered me on and encouraged me from the start.

I grew up surrounded by readers who fostered a love for the written word. To Mom, who never knew how late I was up reading, whose books I used to always (and will now be able to again) steal, and who will always and forever be my biggest cheerleader. To Dad, who read Terry Pratchett for my bedtime stories when I was little and always fought in my corner. To the grandparents who read to me, wrote their own stories, and taught me the sanctity of books. To the extra grandma who threatened me with bodily harm should I ever dog-ear a page and taught me that a well-placed "fuck" is always a good choice. And to the grandparents who inspired the grandparents within these pages with their love, eccentric collections post-retirement, and constant support from oceans away... I love you always and am so grateful for how you all shaped me.

To my Alpha readers... those who read this story when it was barely more than a first draft and in *rough* shape. Christopher, Mom, Denise, Charlotte— you guys championed this story when it was at its worst and encouraged me to keep going. You read typos, caught plot holes, answered a barrage of questions, and loved it anyway. My thanks can never be enough. I hope it's something you love even more now!

To my Egyptian experts—Nelly and Marwa—thank you for your suggestions and help to enrich this world, making sure every element of that amazing place found its way onto the page, and for Arabic phrases and sayings that brought my characters to life. Marwa and Hagar, our guides on our great Egyptian Adventure—you guys inspired so much of this story and made history come to life on that trip. All these years later, we're *still* talking about it and dreaming of coming back!

To my editor, Lindsey Clark, I don't know that I have the words to adequately thank you. You took care of my book baby and made her the best version possible, all while holding the hand of a very anxious fledgling author. Your grace, kindness, and support were the big pushes I needed to finish this thing and see it through!

To my sensitivity reader Garrett—thank you so much for your time and opinions and good luck on your own writing journey!

To Candice—thank you for letting me vent about nerves and failed readers, and for encouraging me to just go for it! Our "podcasts" are my favorite!

To Jasmin, thank you for helping me do the work. For teaching me to set boundaries, that my own validation is enough, that I am a carefully curated museum, and for helping me to become the best version of myself. I owe you more than words will ever be able to say.

To my bonus kids—Carley, Gavin, Avery, Ellory, Natalie, Ryan, Liam, Asher, Delanie and Lillie—Love you all so much and I'm so glad to call you my extra kiddos/nieces & nephews!

To my own Delilah & Edie—Amanda and Liz—I don't know how I could ever do life without you guys. Thank you so much for your love, friendship, unwavering support, and for being easy inspiration for Jules' besties! And to their partners—Big Sexy (because you know I'd never live it down if I didn't include you) and Tim Timothy—thank you guys for sharing them with me and for being my own besties as well!

To Stella, you might not be able to read this one yet, but I hope that when you're old enough, you enjoy it and are proud of your Mom! Thank you for being patient with my long writing sprints and days of editing squeezed in between and around teaching you and for your encouragement and praise even when you haven't read a word of this story. I hope that you are always brave enough to chase down your own dreams and that you remember how loved you are.

And finally, to my partner... my best friend, the love of my life, Christoph. I couldn't have imagined all those years ago when two kids from a small town in North Carolina got married, that they would see the world and have the most epic adventures together. It's been one hell of a ride, my love, and I am grateful beyond measure that we're doing it together. I couldn't have done this without you. Your encouragement and celebration of each milestone, your white-boarding everything with me, your ferrying cups of tea to the desk, and plying me with late night snacks to keep going held me together and pushed me through. You are in every word I wrote. Oh, and thanks for asking.

About the author

JW Kingsley has been a voracious reader since the age of four. As soon as she could hold a pencil she was scribbling stories, bad poetry (and some decent poetry), and dreaming about writing her own books.

She is currently making a new home in a small town in North Carolina after spending the last twenty years traipsing around the world with her partner, their daughter, their spoiled rotten dog, and half-feral cat. If she's not writing she's home-educating, gardening, cooking, or traveling—all while drinking ridiculous amounts of tea and reading a mix of smut, fantasy, and time-travel novels.

———————✦———————

Also by JW Kingsley

Pathfinder—Book Two in the God's Wife Trilogy (coming in Autumn/Winter 2024)

The God's Wife—Book Three in the God's Wife Trilogy (coming in Winter 2024/2025)

The Bone Cottage (TBA)

Printed in the USA
CPSIA information can be obtained
at www.ICGtesting.com
CBHW031602260624
0698CB00011B/341

9 798990 772205